SOMETHING'S BOUND TO HAPPEN

Something's Bound To Happen

Jamett & Joseph Series: Books 1 - 3

Renee Vincent

writing as
Gracie Lee Rose

SOMETHING'S BOUND TO HAPPEN
Copyright © 2017, Renee Vincent
Digital ISBN: 978-1-944484-14-9
Trade Paperback ISBN: 978-1-944484-13-2

Cover Art Design: Renee Vincent
Editors: Wendy Williams and Karen Block

For my dearest friend and author, Amy Gregory.
I'm so glad I finally found my twin after all these years.
Here's to many more days of successful brainstorming,
brilliant writing, and less rewrites and edits!

SOMETHING'S BOUND TO HAPPEN

Jamett Penelope Sutherland hates her name, but loves her new loft apartment especially after she meets her handsome next-door neighbor in nothing but a towel one fateful morning.

Joseph Scarbrough is proficient in fixing clogged sinks and leaky roofs, but he's not all that great at falling in love. Convinced he's incapable, he tries to move on from a humiliating breakup with his childhood sweetheart, and finds consolation in the company of the brunette who just moved in next door.

As Jamie and Joseph refuse to jump into another relationship doomed to fail, fate seems determined to make their worlds collide on a regular basis. Is destiny being clumsy or is something bound to happen between the two unlikely neighbors?

The Start of Something Good

Chapter One

"You're such a jerk!"

The malicious tone and volume of a woman's complaint caused my head to turn in the direction of the chaos a few doors down the hall of my apartment complex. After whipping her scarf around her neck in finality, the angered woman marched down the corridor. A man, who I assume was the jerk in question, pursued her. At this moment, I realized their argument was not meant for my eyes or ears. The guy showed up for the fight in nothing but a towel. His bare chest and arms boasted the remnants of a golden summer tan, even in late November.

I rolled my eyes. How was it possible that men still looked divine in winter, while we women have to make an occasional visit to the tanning salon so we don't appear pasty white? Sure, some of us tried rockin' the pale skin look of the Twilight vampire craze, but it never seemed to catch on with the male population. They still preferred their women toned and tanned. Realize, this was merely my conclusion given no man had yet to fall head over heels for me.

"How can I be a jerk for trying to help you forget about your horrible day?" he asked, grasping the woman's arm and tugging her back. Thankfully, he was oblivious to me standing three doors down.

"No, you're a jerk because *you* tried to forget about *my* horrible day by coming on to me," the girl corrected.

The woman then looked past the man's shoulders and suddenly took notice of my presence. The minute our eyes met, heat flushed my entire body. I quickly averted my attention and pretended not to notice their public tiff, fiddling with my keys to find the right one for locking up. I didn't know what angered her more—the fact that I had taken an interest in their argument or that I had seen her boyfriend in a state of near nakedness.

I half expected her to call me out. Instead, she went back to berating the guy. From where I stood, I had established him as a normal, sexually-active (given he came on to her), heterosexual male. It also bears mentioning that he looked very fine in his bathroom apparel.

"I came to you because I needed you, Joseph."

Ah, the jerk in the towel had a name. Not sure why I made a mental note of it, but I did.

"And I'm still here," he concluded, spreading his arms wide. "You're the one who's leaving."

Clearly, the man was not in tune with the proverbial emotional needs of modern day women. If I were keeping score, he'd have lost a point for that little sarcastic remark. However, his choice of morning attire kept the tally in his favor.

"You just don't get it, do you?" she barked back, slamming her hands upon her hips. "You think everything can be solved with a song or sex."

A song? Now this just got a little more interesting.

"You didn't like what I wrote?" he asked.

With my eyes still buried in the ring of keys clutched in my gloved hands, I couldn't help but notice the slight hint of sadness in Joseph's voice. My heart longed to sneak a peek at him, another potential point in his favor should I see a pitiful expression of pain in his face. But the girl's harsh reaction forbade me to even try a nonchalant glance his way.

"Oh, don't you dare! Don't you dare turn this around and make me the bad guy."

Okay, I was weak. I couldn't help it. I had to catch a glimpse of what was to come. I inserted the correct key into the lock of my apartment door and peered out of the corner of my eye. She poked him in the chest. Repeatedly.

"Again, this is why you are a jerk. You think the world revolves around you and that you play no part in its destruction when it's crumbling around you. You're above it all, yet so far up its ass you can't see the light of day."

He didn't budge or even stop her finger-poke punishment. He stared at her, stunned. "I can't believe you didn't like the song. I was up all night. I wrote that for *you,* Caroline."

My eyes grew wide of their own volition. A songwriter? My sexy, half-dressed, James Tudor underwear model-like neighbor was a songwriter? My heart melted as I stood there. I imagined this man—yes...he was still sporting the towel—hunkered down over a well-worn set of piano keys, pounding out words of love and emotion with each lyrical stanza, every consecutive note inspired by the last. In my mind, I stood tall and proud, holding a white square sign with a bold, black, number ten on it above my head.

Fireworks went off behind me in the distance, and a fluttering cloud of confetti fell around me.

This guy is a keeper!

I wanted to run up and give him a congratulatory hug on his big win, but the girlfriend—or soon-to-be-ex-girlfriend, if all of my assumptions were on the money—rolled her eyes and turned her back to him.

"You were never cut out to be a songwriter, Joseph. Just like you, your music lacks heart."

She left him standing in the narrow hallway, injured and bleeding. The knife in his chest remained at such a vicious angle that I began to wonder if he'd ever live through it. If it were me, I would have been crushed to the core. Then again, I wouldn't have settled for someone like her. I would have been smart enough to keep my standards raised and my heart better guarded.

Inwardly, I sighed. I supposed it was easier for me to say those things when I was outside looking in. I shouldn't have been listening in the first place. That's when my brain kicked into panic overdrive.

If he turned around right now, he'd see that I'd partaken in being a rude onlooker with a front row seat to his pathetic break-up. And I'd no longer be the cute, little neighbor who he—hypothetically speaking—might run into one day because he wasn't watching where he was going as he walked down the hall. He wouldn't suddenly feel compelled to ask me out on a date because he was a hopeless romantic and believed wholeheartedly in love at first sight. And fate. Surely fate had a part in all this.

My mind raced as I continued to stand there like a deer in headlights, freaking out over the moment when he'd give up staring down the hall and turn toward his door. If I made a break for the elevator, he'd see me do so. If I stayed where I was, he'd still see me. No matter what I decided, I was doomed to be caught eavesdropping.

Considering the perilous situation I was in, one would think I wouldn't dare take one more peek down the hall. But I did.

My terrycloth-kilted neighbor ran frustrated fingers through his dark, nigh-in-need-of-a-cut hair and, just as I feared, turned around.

I don't know who was more shocked, him or me. It was evident he hadn't expected to see anyone in the hall, much less a pale, brunette with barely a curve to her body, all of which were hidden behind a fluffy winter parka, scarf, and gloves.

I stared, frozen in my boots, my eyes bulging from their sockets. He returned the same stunned look. For a split second, I thought I saw the corners of his mouth twitch upward in a smile. So, I smiled back out of courtesy.

Short-lived as that thought was, his brow furrowed. He glanced back over his shoulder as if gathering his bearings on where he and his girlfriend had chosen to have their dispute and determining whether it were possible I witnessed it all from where I stood. I could have sworn I saw a hint of embarrassment on his face as he scratched his head. "Did you…I mean, did we disturb you? Could you actually hear us from inside?"

"Oh, no," I tried to explain at the same time I aimed to comfort him. "You didn't disturb me. I was out here the whole time." I clamped my mouth shut. I had just blatantly admitted to eavesdropping on his personal conversation.

He eyes widened, and his chin tilted upward a bit. "Really…"

"I-I mean, not the whole time, just…well…."

It was my turn to be embarrassed, and I squeezed my eyes closed. Tightly. At least now, I could proudly say I was both weak and a horrible conversationalist.

Okay, you big idiot, say goodbye, cut your losses, and consider yourself lucky that he doesn't know your name. For all he knows, you're just a friend of the person who lives in Loft B and you were just leaving.

Better yet, perhaps he'll be so distraught over this whole morning that days from now when he runs into you again, as you're visiting your friend in Loft B, he won't even recognize you.

I liked the idea. So much that I'd already started plotting out my strategy. I'd donate this coat and the rest of my winter outerwear to Goodwill and buy a whole new ensemble, just in case he had a photographic memory. I'd act like we had never met and start anew.

He came closer, his eyes zeroing in on me. They rivaled the bluest Montana sky on a summer afternoon. "You're the new girl, right? You just moved in a couple weeks ago. Sutherland, is it?"

There went that plan. Wait. Did he just reveal in a very subtle, yet sly fashion that he took enough notice of me to remember my name? And *how* did he know my name? Had he broken into my mailbox and rummaged through my mail? Or worse, the dumpster?

No. I refused to believe this beautiful creature, as bold as he was talking to me in a towel, would resort to dumpster diving for any reason. Still, the question remained.

"Yeah, that's me. I'm Sutherland. Jamie Sutherland."

I had to look away. Joseph's eyes threatened to spellbind me, and I wondered how Caroline had the strength to deflect his hypnotic powers. By the looks of her glamorous appeal, I imagined she was a regular temptress herself, with the ability to stop traffic a mile away. I, on the other hand, was a plain Jane; brown hair, brown eyes, small build without a voluptuous curve in sight—the girl next door with the body of a twelve-year old boy—which was how a grudge-nursing ex-boyfriend once described me four years ago. To this day, I still choke up over his unpleasant portrayal.

"Welcome to the building, Jamie."

I dared to sneak another peek at him, hoping I could get through this conversation without looking like a faint-hearted schoolgirl. "How did you know my name?" I finally asked.

"Your name is on the mailbox for Loft B. I just put two and two together and came up with you."

It was nice to know the man knew his math. It should come in handy when he counted the reasons why he should've steered clear of me. Granted, I was not as needy as that Caroline girl, nor was I an attention-seeking drama queen. I avoided sinking to those emotional levels at all costs. I was a strong, independent woman who had no need for a man in her life. I'd tried the "couple" thing—multiple times—and I'd failed royally each go round.

Given the copious amounts of money I'd lost and the countless tears I'd shed over those "Mr. Rights" gone horribly wrong, I swore never to get sucked into the ridiculous notion of romance and all the frilly fringe benefits that supposedly came with it. I was a pessimistic woman. What I remembered most about love was not the endearing looks, warm hugs, or the cute butterflies in the stomach. It was the sucker punch in the gut when I least expected it.

"I should go," I said in haste, trying to remind myself that even this Greek Adonis-like man with kind blue eyes was capable of throwing a TKO punch.

He grinned, glanced down at his rather inappropriate attire, and thumbed over his shoulder toward his open apartment door. "Me too. Gotta get to work."

The innocence in his smile knocked me off balance. He went from bold and witty to downright adorable. It was a good thing he had already started to take a few steps backward, else I might have reached out and pinched his cute, five-o'clock-shadowed cheeks. The longer I stood here, the more I was convinced Caroline was clinically insane for going all diva on this man.

Stepping beneath his doorframe, he nodded once, reaffirming the beauty of his boyish grin, and closed the door.

A breath I had no idea I was even holding escaped me. My arms fell limp at my sides, keys rattling in my hand. I still had no grasp of what had really happened. The only thing that registered was Joseph and how he was quite possibly the best-looking jerk I'd ever seen

Chapter Two

All the way to work, I recapped the morning.

Joseph was a healthy, heterosexual male, a songwriter, who had a steady job, or at least, I assumed he had one since he said he had to get to work—wherever that might be. He was not afraid to express his emotions, though he may have some issues with understanding and predicting the emotions of the opposite sex. A major setback as far as the female race was concerned, but I could work on that. It was fixable with the right amount of nurturing.

He was confident, bold—without the arrogance—and looked mighty fine after a shower. His eyes were blue, his lashes long, and his face chiseled. His hair hung in his face at times, but not enough to annoy me. In fact, it had taken everything I had not to thread my eager fingers through its wild softness. And the best part of all—after checking his left hand for a ring or a tell-tale tan line—Caroline was indeed just a girlfriend and not a wife.

Three hours into work, and I was still thinking of this guy. I had more pressing things to do than wonder whether I'd run into him again when I got home, like unpacking the rest of my things from my recent move. Although I wouldn't really call it a move, since I was still in the same area code as before. I'd left one apartment complex, for reasons too boring to mention, and moved into another a few blocks away.

I didn't care much for drastic changes, and I was not a

wanderer. I enjoyed knowing I'd lived in the Northern Kentucky/Southern Ohio area all my life. In the last seven years of it, I owned my own little coffee shop in downtown Cincinnati called *I Like You a Latte*. It might sound like a spin-off *Starbucks*, but my little corner café offers great tasting coffee without the hefty prices.

"Can I get you anything else?" I asked routinely, before cashing the customer out. While I ran on autopilot for most of the day, my brain continued to take detours toward Destination Joseph. The view was always great, but the amount of time I spent in this one-track automobile was getting to me.

"You okay?"

I glanced in the direction of the voice and smiled. Melissa knew me better than I sometimes knew myself. I had hired her the same day she applied, assuming she would be the perfect person to help me take this pipe dream and turn it into a successful business venture. As I'd thought, she was all that and more. Melissa was not only a great employee, but also a wonderful, loyal friend.

"I'm fine," I played off, wiping spilled cream from the counter in front of the espresso machine.

Melissa stacked more cups beside the countless flavored elixir bottles. "You seem frazzled."

I wanted to laugh. Joseph had caused me to feel a lot of emotions in such a short time today, but frazzled was not one of them. I went for slightly off-kilter. "Thanks for asking, but really, I'm fine."

"Does he have a name?"

Joseph almost left my mouth before I caught on to her sly inquiry. I held my tongue and rolled my eyes. "There is no *he*. Therefore, there is no name to speak of. Good try."

Melissa gave my hip a disco bump and continued arranging the lids. "He's *that* good looking, huh?"

"I don't know what you're talking about." I tried to sound convincing, but again, I sucked at lying. The look on Melissa's face illustrated that very point. "Look," I placated, aiming for a different approach. "I just had a rough start this morning. I was up late unpacking—"

"Still?" Melissa interrupted. "I thought you said it would only take a few days."

"Yes, it would if I were in the mood to rummage through boxes of stuff I probably don't need. I already unpacked the essentials."

"So, get rid of the extra boxes. Toss them. Don't even look inside. If you haven't needed anything from them in the past two weeks, you probably can do without them altogether."

Melissa's logic sounded perfectly rational. I'd love to be able to chuck the unpacked boxes of crap and never look back. The problem was I inherited the pack rat gene. I couldn't get rid of anything. For whatever reason, I looked at my junk, even items of fad clothing and college memorabilia from fifteen years ago, and couldn't get away from this crazy idea I'd need it someday. My inability to declutter was a curse.

"I told you I'd help you," Melissa reminded me. "We could get it finished in one night."

Somehow I doubted that. Melissa, as good a friend as she was, had never seen my 'stash,' and I'd rather keep it that way. "I appreciate the offer, but I'll get it done one of these nights."

"Well, you better do it fast before this cute guy asks you out." Melissa leaned in close and spoke softly so only I could hear. "Nothing's worse than being in the middle of a hot, toe-curling kiss at the door, and you can't invite him in because there are boxes on every flat surface in your apartment." She raised her brow, hoping I caught the subtle hint.

I slapped my wet rag at her and frowned. Her attempts to get me to admit there was a man in my life were ridiculous. Joseph was not in my life. He was in my apartment building on the same floor, but nothing more. I'd hardly call our encounter in the hallway this morning an introduction to a love affair. If that were the case, I'd be having a seriously torrid affair with the teenaged dog walker who insisted on holding the lobby door open for me each evening so I could trip over five drooling hounds on tangled leashes.

"For the last time," I said, my voice taking on a strange tone of seriousness and determination. "There is no one in my life, nor is he about to ask me out. I barely know him."

"I knew it!" Melissa fist-pumped triumphantly.

Most everyone in the joint looked in my direction. I closed my eyes and hung my head.

Ignoring the weight of our customers' stares, Melissa slid closer to me. "How did you two meet? Come on, you can tell me. Is he that construction worker who whistled at you the other day from the scaffold across from *The Red Squirrel*?"

I cringed. I remembered that guy, and I wanted to elbow Melissa hard for even bringing his foul image into my head. "Eww...no."

Another idea popped into her head. Her eyes grew wide, and she almost started jumping up and down. Melissa was always an animated chatterbox. "Is he the professor from NKU who asked for directions to the Aronoff Art Center after he bought a Pumpkin Spice Latte, light on the cream, double cinnamon?"

"No, he is not. And how in the world do you remember what the professor ordered?" If I recalled correctly, he came in almost three weeks ago and hadn't been back since.

Melissa rubbed her neck nervously as if she'd suddenly developed chickenpox. "I don't know how I remember those things. But I'm glad your man is not the professor." She bit her lip. "'Cause I was hoping to get all over that the next time he comes in."

I was not surprised. Melissa always had a thing for male teachers.

"Come on, Jamett Penelope Sutherland, tell me who he is."

I glanced around, hoping no one had heard her. I gave her a strict look. "You know you're not supposed to call me by my full name. *No one* is allowed to call me that, not even my own mother who blessed me with that horrible name."

"Tell me his name, and yours shall remain..." She made a zipping-of-the-lips gesture and baited me with challenging eyes.

I knew Melissa wouldn't share my despicable secret in this blackmailing fashion, but the look on her face had me second-guessing. "I only know his first name," I confessed.

"A first name will do," she reasoned. "I can tell a lot from a man's first name."

I cocked my brow. "Like what?"

"Like if he's upstanding and intelligent versus a dimwitted louse. You know what I mean. Never will you find a man with the name of Maxwell to be an unemployed drug addict. He'd be wealthy and well mannered, unlike

Willard or Clyde. You can just see the picket fence of rotten teeth and smell the stench of day-old cigarettes and Jack Daniels with those names."

"Oh my goodness," I feigned my best look of disgust and disappointment. I swallowed hard, hard enough that Melissa could see my throat bob. "His name is Clyde."

I loved the look on her face. It was priceless. Immediately, she began comforting me by rubbing my arms and adjusting her own explanation. "No, I didn't mean Clyde, I meant…" She struggled to come up with a believable name at the drop of a hat. I almost felt sorry for her.

I cracked a smile as she stuttered about, wishing I had a camera so I could capture this moment. It was not every day I could pull one over on Melissa. Eventually, she caught on to my ruse, and it was my turn to be slapped.

"Girl, I oughta…." she warned with a theatrical fist.

I couldn't help but laugh. "His name is Joseph," I surrendered, as I went over to wait on the next customer. From behind me, I could practically hear the gears churning in Melissa's head, turning the name over and over, though I hadn't expected to hear her say it aloud, pairing my name with his.

"Jamett and Joseph."

I flashed a glare over my shoulder, expressing my displeasure of her outspoken thought processes, but she paid it no heed. Instead she mouthed, "I like it," and sashayed her way to the crowded café tables.

Chapter Three

The day had been extra long. I tried to blame it on the fact that it was Friday and the last day of the sale of our seasonal Thanksgiving line of cappuccinos, but rationale told me it was because Joseph had made a lasting impression on my brain. I normally didn't get all hung up on pretty men. Truth be told, I didn't understand what made this guy so special that I'd obsess about him throughout my entire day.

Sure, I had the privilege of eyeing the man in a towel, ogling his tight little gluteus maximus without his knowledge. And I'd salivated over the view of his muscled chest just perfectly dusted with the right amount of hair as he soothed me with the sound of his deep, dulcet voice. But did that really make him worthy of taking root in my thoughts and refusing to leave?

It was kind of rude, if you asked me. I never wanted him there. Towel or no towel.

Okay, that didn't come out right. It was bad enough I had images of this man draped in nothing but soft, white terrycloth, much less introducing thoughts of removing said cloth. Not good.

I shook my head and locked my coffee shop for the night, eager to walk the streets of Cincinnati and breathe the brisk Midwest air without ruminating over Joseph.

I barely took three steps before the man invaded my thoughts again. Seriously? Was I this feeble and weak-minded that I couldn't go a single minute without fanaticizing about Joseph's body and eyes and smile and...

Yeah, I was pathetic.

Accepting myself for the pitiable excuse that I was, I walked the remaining blocks from Fountain Square to the local grocery store on Seventh Street, succumbing to the realization that Joseph, and his exquisite body, would accompany me.

* * * *

After picking up what I needed to fill my pitifully empty refrigerator—and by fill, I meant no more than I could carry on foot without my arms breaking off at the elbows—I entered my apartment complex. Somehow, I dodged the dog walker and made it to the elevator without bumping into a single person who suddenly felt compelled to welcome the new girl.

Upon stepping off, I noticed the hall was clear. No Joseph.

Just as I had this morning, I fumbled with my keys and reminded myself that before I did anything else, I would get rid of any unnecessary ones (yes, I hoard even my keys), so I wouldn't tarry at my door and run the risk of running into Joseph again.

Staying clear of Joseph was pertinent to my sanity. I was trying to forget him.

"Here, let me help you."

I jumped out of my skin at hearing someone's voice behind me. I jerked away so quickly that one of my grocery bags ripped at its bottom, sending a few canned goods to the floor with a thud and several oranges bouncing and rolling down the hall.

Immediately, I bent at the waist to retrieve the nearest oranges before they could get away. This person had the same idea. We hit heads, and I fell flat on my rump. I blinked several times so my eyes could focus. My assaulter had taken off down the hall and, to my surprise, he ran after the unruly fruit.

"I'm sorry. I'm sorry. I'm sorry. I was only trying to help you unlock your door since your hands were full."

I couldn't take my eyes off the man chasing my oranges. It was quite a sight to see. He was dressed in casual slacks, a button-up white shirt, dress shoes, and a tie. When he succeeded in apprehending the fleeing produce, he stood up with his hands above his head, holding the captive goods in a celebratory stance. "Got 'em!"

My eyes nearly popped out of my head. The savior of my rolling oranges was Joseph. I barely recognized him with his clothes on.

I scuffled to my feet, my head pounding, my mind scrambling. This was not supposed to happen. I was *supposed* to get into my apartment, unload my groceries, throw away the useless keys, and collapse in my nice comfy sleigh bed. I had so looked forward to it, and now the opportunity had slipped through my fingers. I felt like I was watching reruns of this morning's reality show. And I hate reality TV.

I grimaced as I gathered myself and my belongings, trying very hard not to look at Joseph. He picked up the ripped brown paper bag and handed it to me with a smile, probably hoping to smooth things other. I didn't return the gesture, hoping he'd kindly back away.

"I truly am sorry. Is your head all right?"

I wanted to push him away. Childish, I know, but he threatened to ruin the balance I'd come to enjoy in my solitary existence.

"Jamie?" He touched my hand, which had begun to insert the key into the doorknob. My hands were absent gloves this time, and I could feel the warmth of his palm on my wrist. Inwardly, I was thankful that I wore a huge parka, for I had hoped it was thick enough to mute the sound of my hammering heart from his ears.

Our eyes met again, and I swore I lost all feeling in my legs. The spectrum of color in his irises hypnotized me, and I couldn't break the spell.

"Are you all right?" he asked again.

I swallowed and shook off the trance he'd put me in. "Um, yeah." I resumed inserting the key into the lock, despite the pressing realization of his hand still on mine. I turned and pushed, and the door swung open.

Finally, he let go and stepped back.

"Yeah, I'm fine," I tried to smooth over the awkwardness. "I appreciate you chasing my fruit." I held up the one I had in my hand. "Orange you glad you came by when you did?"

He gave a chuckle, though I was certain he only meant to humor me. I was not that funny.

"Actually, I am glad I came by when I did."

I added charming to this guy's list of redeeming qualities. I could've added more if I wanted, but it wouldn't do me a bit of good. I refused to let myself fall for him.

Ignoring his statement and the intensity of his gaze, I entered my apartment and set the undamaged grocery bag and my purse on the entryway table. When I turned around to salvage the rest of my canned goods from the floor, I froze in my tracks. Joseph was standing in my doorway, holding the oranges as if they were objects of a truce offering, and he branded the most beautiful, honest smile I'd ever seen.

His eyes scanned over my darkened apartment. I wasn't sure what he was looking for, but I knew I wasn't ready for a man to peek into my personal space.

I grabbed the door and closed it enough that only my body could fit through, forcing him to step back into the hall. With my foot, I slid the canned goods past the threshold and confiscated the oranges from his hands.

"I'd love to stick around and chat some more," I fibbed, "but I'm…" I stumbled on my words. *What was I doing tonight?*

"Yeah, me too," he finished for me. "I've got to be somewhere…" He checked his watch, "in an hour. Big date."

Big date, huh? Even I could see he made that up so he didn't look like a pitiful schmuck with nothing to do on a Friday evening because his girlfriend had broken up with him less than twelve hours before.

Two can play this little game.

Before I knew what I was doing, I spilled forth my big imaginary plans for the night. "Yeah, I've got a big date too. He's a professional bodybuilder."

His face furrowed.

Clearly that career choice was not as awe-inspiring for Joseph as it was for me. I needed to do better. "And a doctor. Surgeon. He just does the bodybuilding on the side."

"Really," he nodded, pretending to be moved by my make-believe date's credentials. "Impressive."

"Yeah, he's always so busy, and this is the first night off he's had in months. I'm cooking a huge dinner. Candlelight."

"I see…sounds nice."

I nodded my head in time with his. We seemed to be measuring each other up, hoping to rouse some small amount of jealousy with our sorry stories. Or waiting for the other to give in and initiate the farewells. He broke first.

"Well, I don't want to hold you up."

"Thanks," I replied, starting to close the door. "And thanks again for—"

"No problem," he said, dismissing my gratitude with a wave of his hand. "If not for me, you wouldn't have lost your oranges in the first place."

His sudden change in tone pulled on my heartstrings. Yes, he was the reason my head hurt and my groceries had hit the floor, but deep down I knew his intentions were good. He was only trying to help me open my door since my hands were full, and I reacted like a skittish rabbit zigzagging in headlights.

If anything, I owed him an apology for the lies I told. Come to think of it, I told so many today that if I were made of wood, I'd put Pinocchio to shame.

Inch by inch, I closed the door. His wave goodbye was the last thing I saw before the lock clicked shut. I listened with my ear pressed against the wood until I heard his footsteps fade down the hall. Only it wasn't his door closing I heard, but the ding of the elevator.

I guess he did have plans. And I was the pathetic schmuck now.

Chapter Four

I could actually say I accomplished something tonight, besides running off the most handsome man in the Midwest. I'd sifted through my keys and thrown away the ones I didn't need. I know it may not sound like a big deal for the average unsentimental person, but for me...it was like parting with ancient family heirlooms.

My key ring now only had six keys on it—one for the security door of the complex, one for my apartment, one for the mailbox, one for the coffee shop, one for my safety deposit box that has nothing in it, and one for the car I used to drive. I didn't own the car anymore, but I loved that automobile. It was a 1989 Chevy Beretta, and it reminded me of the carefree part of myself that rarely came out.

Anyway, I felt good about the forward progress I made at becoming a more efficient, organized woman of the twenty-first century. I could now look around my box-strewn apartment and know that soon the mess and the things connected to me in some way that I longer wanted would all disappear. I felt uplifted and ready to tackle more of the items on my to-do-list. Melissa would be so proud. Funny how a bunch of carved metal trinkets lining the bottom of my trash can could make a person feel like a million bucks.

I was determined not to lose my gumption, so I headed straight for the closest box marked COLLEGE in bold,

Sharpie-black letters. I opened the flaps and sighed. The contents inside propelled me back in time. Images of my dorm days and wild frat parties flittered through my mind. An automatic smile creased my lips.

I missed those days when oodles of homework were my chief concern. When my current grade point average, or how to raise it, was my biggest problem. Oh, how I'd take the stresses of the past—like staying up all night trying to finish a six-page report or cramming for an anatomy test—over the stresses of my present career-world.

I reached in and pulled out a stuffed turtle with the symbols Delta Zeta on its shell. This cute little reptile was the mascot of our sorority, and, for whatever reason, I'd felt the need to purchase him from NKU's campus gift shop my freshmen year. He used to sit on my bed next to the pillow my grandmother embroidered for me. I still had that pillow too, though it was already unpacked and sitting on my bed in the next room.

I clenched my teeth together, finding the strength to say goodbye. A woman in her early thirties had no need for a Greek-alphabetized tortoise. Taking a deep breath, I walked over to the garbage can and tossed him on top of the keys.

Hands on my hips, I stared down at the poor little guy. I couldn't do it.

I grabbed the box with COLLEGE written on the side, dumped it out, and set the empty box next to the garbage can. I scratched out COLLEGE and wrote GOODWILL. I reached into the trash and switched him to his new home. While I was still getting rid of the plush reptile, I felt better that I wasn't sending him to a landfill.

With a nod of affirmation, I went back to the heaping pile of college paraphernalia and decided their fates, one by one. Within an hour, I had sifted through the mementos and had moved onto another box labeled CHILDHOOD.

At this point, I decided to open a bottle of wine. My reasons were two-fold. I had successfully eliminated an entire box from my ownership, and I knew this particular one would take more bravado than I had. From my years of co-existing with hunky jocks and cute frat boys on campus, I came to learn that wine was courage in a bottle.

No sooner had I poured and consumed the first gulp of Pinot Grigio, than I heard a loud noise from the hall. It sounded like someone had tripped and fallen. Concerned, I went to my door and peeked out the security hole. I saw nothing.

I knew I hadn't imagined the sound, and because of how loud it was, my curiosity got the better of me. I unlocked the door and peered out. Lying against the wall, in a contorted fashion, was an unconscious Joseph.

I ran to him and dropped to my knees. "Joseph," I called, giving him a little shake. "Joseph, are you okay?"

He stirred and turned his head in my direction, fanning a wisp of alcohol-infused breath in my face. Whiskey. There was no mistaking that smell. The man had not tripped and knocked himself unconscious…he was drunk. So inebriated he was content to sleep wherever his body had fallen.

"Joseph, you need to get up," I lifted his heavy, dead-weighted arms. He stirred again, but made no effort to help me. Instead, he mumbled a chain of slurred words that made no sense. "Yeah, I know, darlin'," I replied, patronizing him. "You've had a rough night."

"Lonely," he managed to say. "'ts lonely night without you."

I assumed his off-the-cuff admittances were meant for

Caroline's ears. I couldn't help but pity him. He was a heartbroken man who'd just lost someone he cared for and had no idea how to deal with it. From the looks of him, getting dumped probably wasn't something he was used to. I imagined he'd done his fair share of breaking hearts in his day, but now that the tables were turned, drinking to forget was the only therapy available to him.

Perhaps if I'd have been more compassionate and appreciative after he'd chased my fruit down the hall, he wouldn't have drank himself into an oblivion. As far as he was concerned, two women had shot him down in the same day. For a man of his caliber, I was sure that was a shocker.

Poor guy.

Although…I had to relish this moment. Even in his drunken stupor, he was beautiful. A hunk of dark, unruly hair had fallen over his brow, and nothing stopped me from brushing it back this time. I took in the strong angles of his face, the way the shadow of scruff across his jaw complimented the high rise of his cheekbones. His lips were full and soft. His nose was straight as an arrow. And he had a small dusting of salt at his temples, making him more appealing to my eyes—as if he wasn't already stunning enough.

I was grateful for this moment. I could admire Joseph fully without anyone knowing. Without *him* knowing. Heck, I could probably strip the man of his clothes and get my eye-full and he'd still be none the wiser given his present condition.

As tempting as that sounded, I worried about how I was going to get him into the safety of his apartment. I couldn't just leave him in the hallway all night. And Lord knows I wasn't going to spend the night chaperoning him as he slept in the hall. I needed my sleep too.

With a deep breath and the sudden determination of ten men, I grabbed his wrists and yanked. "Come on, Joseph. On your feet." I pulled for all I was worth, getting a small response from him.

"Wh'ya doin'?" he slurred as his eyes fluttered opened. "'M try'n to sleep."

"Not out here, you're not," I said, pulling harder. "Come on. Let's get you to your bed."

His head teetered on his shoulders, but he seemed to perk up. "Your bed?" he asked with a crooked smile.

"No, *your* bed," I corrected.

"Th-that's what I said," he stuttered, looking at me like I was an idiot.

I decided to go with it. Anything to get this man on his feet and into his apartment where he belonged, so I could get back to mine. "Yeah, Joseph, I'm taking you to your bed."

He cocked his brow, or tried to. The alcohol in his system had numbed even the muscles in his face. He lugged his heavy arm around my shoulders as if he wasn't the slightest bit intoxicated. He made every effort to be suave, but his speech lacked the smooth debonair quality it required to pull it off. "I though' abou' your bed 'll night. An' how I's gonna make y'call m' name."

Again, I assumed the dirty talk was meant for Caroline and not me. If it wasn't so slurred, the idea might have intrigued me. To a degree, my mind wandered with the notion of what Joseph could do to make me call out his name, but of course, it involved the sober version of him, an adaptation that was too far out of reach.

My mind couldn't dwell in that tantalizing picture for long. He staggered so much, even with me trying to support him, that my brain's focus remained on doing everything in my power to keep him upright.

When we finally faced his door, he leaned forward and rested his head on the wall, his legs beginning to buckle.

"Where are your keys?" I asked, jerking him back to a standing position.

I saw a huge grin slice between his lips. "Ther' in m' pocket."

I knew what he expected. But it wasn't going to happen. "Joseph, reach in your pocket and get your keys."

"You do it," he challenged, his face contorting in a weird expression. I assumed it was his best attempt at arousing me with a not-so smoldering stare.

I rolled my eyes and tried to barter with logic. "Joseph, if I get your keys, I'll have to let go of you, and you'll fall. You've got a free hand…use it."

I heard him sigh before he made a move toward his pocket. I was more thankful than ever when he pulled them out and offered them to me. Unfortunately, his key ring looked like mine, that is, the ring of keys I used to have before I discarded the extras. Struggling to hold him up with my left arm, I sifted through the keys until I found a likely candidate. I used my right hand to attempt to unlock his door. I tried many times to get the damn thing to line up in the slot, but with Joseph's body threatening to collapse at my feet, it wasn't an easy task. On the brink of giving up, I finally got the key to engage and kicked the door open.

The sound jolted his head upward, and his eyes flashed open. "Come in!" he shouted, as if awakened by someone knocking. "Door's open!"

I ignored his drunken outburst and led him into his apartment. Grateful for the large windows that ran the length of the wall in our historical building, I silently thanked God for the blessing of the moonlight pouring in so I didn't have to contend with flipping on a lamp. The evening illumination didn't seem to aid Joseph any, however. In fact, it could have been broad daylight and he still would have stumbled into everything in the room.

Needless to say, I was eager to dump his sorry butt in bed and get back to what I was doing. We wandered aimlessly through his living space, with no guidance from my co-pilot, looking for the bedroom. I did, however, find a guitar leaning against the wall. I smiled. Whether he hammered on the ivories or tickled the frets when composing his songs, I couldn't help but hold him in high regard. Drunk or not, I found this man fascinating.

Moving on, I finally located his bedroom. I ushered him into the spacious room and a waft of cologne tickled my senses as we tottered past his dresser. I couldn't name the cologne, but it certainly smelled wonderful. I imagined him coming out of the shower in his towel and splashing some over his damp neck and shoulders.

What are you doing?

Sorry, I was in a man's bedroom. What did you expect from me?

"Joseph," I said, taking a shot at gaining his attention. When he rolled his head in my direction, he looked at me with the most sincere, pleading eyes. I swallowed, trying to disregard how intense they were when his gaze fell over me. "You're safe in your bedroom now. Just lie down."

"Thanks," he mumbled, and collapsed on the mattress.

I assisted him with hoisting his legs up and removing his shoes and tie. Again, weakling that I am, I thought of taking off his shirt, but I couldn't bring myself to do it. Instead, I pulled the thick duvet over his body and smiled down at him.

One last time, I took this moment to marvel at his raw handsomeness. I doubted I would ever get this chance again. We were on different playing fields, and a guy like him would never be interested in a girl like me.

I touched his face with the back of my fingers and lightly stroked his cheek, never thinking he'd feel it. Evidently, he wasn't as numb as I thought. He opened his eyes and stared at me.

"Jamie," I heard him whisper, though his lips barely moved.

I sat on the edge of the bed and leaned closer so I could hear him. "Yeah?"

"She broke m' heart."

Caroline again. Back to Caroline. That woman didn't deserve as much reflection and consideration as she was getting from this man. I tried my best to comfort him. "I know she did. And I'm sorry you had to go through that."

"S'okay now," he mumbled. "Yer here."

His choice of words threw me. They always say drunk men are honest men, but did my simple presence actually bring Joseph comfort? I contemplated the idea a little longer and eventually came to the conclusion I was putting way too much emphasis on a plastered man's inarticulate remarks. Come morning, he'd have no recollection of this night or what he said to me.

I patted his chest—wow, it was solid—and went back to placating him. "Go to sleep, Joseph. It'll all be better in the morning."

"Stay wit' me…"

I froze. No sooner than I heard his words, I felt his hand rest at the small of my back. Through my T-shirt, I felt the heat of his palm and all five pressure points of his fingertips. His touch ignited feelings I had buried long ago. We locked eyes, and for the span of a few breaths, had I been breathing at all, we both seemed to consider the offer.

No.

I blinked rapidly, affirming I was not going to succumb to something as rash, not to mention reckless and utterly foolhardy, as accepting his proposal. The only reason he asked me to stay was because he was brokenhearted, drunk, and desperate. If he were sober and in his right mind, he would never have made such a suggestion in the first place.

No. I will not be the easy, rebound girl.

"Joseph, you don't know what you're saying. Just close your eyes. You never know…Caroline might come to her senses and call you tomorrow."

"I don' wanna see Caroline 'nymore. She doesn' love me. She doesn' look a' me like you do. I like th' way you look a' me."

Surely, I heard wrong. Perhaps it was my overactive imagination running rampant as I lingered in somewhat of a near embrace with this man. My hand remained on the solid wall of his chest, and his hand still pressed against my back. This position hardly had the makings of a lover's clinch, but considering it had been more than two years since I was this close to a man, I deemed our situation as much of an embrace as one could fathom.

It amazed me that Joseph had thought I looked at him in a manner which evoked significance. I remembered hardly making eye contact with him at all, except for those couple of times I fell entranced by his gaze. Like now.

I looked away and pushed myself from him. He caught my wrist and held me affixed to the side of his bed. The strength in his hand startled me, but the sweet, endearing look in his eyes had me melting.

"Thanks."

With one tiny word, he touched my soul. I opened my mouth to speak, but thank goodness the alcohol had begun to take effect on his attention span before I blurted out something I probably would've regretted.

His eyes fluttered, his head relaxed, and his grip released. His arm dropped and hung off the side of the bed. I reached out and placed it gently across his chest, drawing the covers over him. Within a few seconds, he began snoring.

Chapter Five

Mornings were not my favorite time of the day. I was not, nor have I ever been, a morning person. I guess that's why I owned my own coffee shop. I absolutely, positively needed my coffee in the morning to begin to see the goodness in sunlight.

This morning, in particular, was worse than most.

I'd left Joseph's apartment last night with my mind in a whirlwind. It was cluttered with questions, and 'what ifs', and emotions I would've rather not felt. I'd been a single woman, happily living my life without the complications of a man's presence for many years now, and I didn't need this man—albeit a sexy, charming, and extremely intriguing man—to waltz his way in and mess things up,.

I was not one for change. I liked things the way they were, and I didn't feel comfortable getting involved with a guy who was my neighbor. I had searched for just the right place to live near Fountain Square, with all the historical charm and architecture I could afford. When I found this place, I nearly begged on my hands and knees for the owners to approve my application. So, if it didn't work out with Mr. Towel Man, this apartment would no longer be the ideal place to live. It would be awkward and problematic because, although I normally avoided confrontation, I was still a woman with pride.

Today, I was just a grumpy woman with pride who hadn't finished her unpacking last night because a certain gorgeous man put far too many thoughts and images in her mind to work, sleep, or do anything. To make matters worse, my coffee maker was incredibly slow.

I gave it a slap, as if it would make the java juice pour out faster and checked the clock. Nine o'clock. I was determined to rid my apartment of these darn boxes today, if it killed me.

A knock at the door disrupted my internal pep talk. I grumbled and sighed, wondering who in the world it could be. Probably Mrs. Tibbs from Loft A needing another cup of sugar for her baking fetish. She probably assumed I got sugar free since I owned a coffee joint. One of these days I was going to have to break the news to her that I didn't own stock in the sugar cane market. Mentally preparing to do just that, I whipped open the door and gasped.

It was not Mrs. Tibbs, but Joseph, whom I caught trying to smooth his bed-head crop of hair. Immediately, he dropped his arms to his sides and nervously adjusted his stance a few times until he chose a pose where his thumbs jabbed in the front of his jean pockets. He leaned against the doorframe and smiled.

"Hi," he said casually.

I stood stunned. I wasn't expecting to see his face so early in the morning. He might be looking all perky and bright as he occupied my entryway, but I could tell from his bloodshot eyes and slight creases in his brow that he was nursing a serious hangover.

"Hello. And how are you feeling this morning?"

I didn't mean to sound so condescending, but I hadn't had my coffee yet.

"I was hoping you could tell me," he said with a boyish grin. "For some reason, I have a huge bump on my forehead and my shoulder kind of hurts. Why is that?"

Images of Joseph taking a face-plant in the hallway came to mind. I brought my hand up to my mouth to hide my amusement. "I can tell you exactly why that is. You passed out in the hallway, and it wasn't gracefully executed."

He hung his head and closed his eyes. His face furrowed a bit as he pondered his next words. "I don't remember much from last night, but I feel like I owe you an apology. Did you help me to my room after my swan dive?"

I crossed my arms, kind of proud of this moment. "I did."

He looked even more confused than before. "Did I ask you to?"

"I don't think so, but then again it was difficult to make out some of the things you said. I caught most of it though."

"I said things?" He swallowed. "To you?"

I nodded, knowing this was when he was about to make excuses for his drunken slips-of-the-tongue and that every bit of it was meant for Caroline. He stared at his feet with his hands now on his hips, his lips stretched to fine lines.

His next words floored me.

"I'm not going to apologize for what I said to you because I'm pretty sure whatever it was, I meant it. But *I am* going to say I'm sorry for interrupting your evening. I know you were entertaining your doctor...boxer friend, or whatever he was, and I hope I didn't ruin anything by dropping ass at your doorstep."

His choice of words cracked me up. "You didn't ruin

anything." I rolled my eyes, kicking myself for concocting this ridiculous lie in the first place. "I didn't have a dinner date, and I don't know any doctors. Or boxers or bodybuilders, for that matter. I was home alone. So, quit your worrying. I was happy to help you."

I watched him cock his head to the side, his hair falling into his right eye. "You lied to me?"

I scratched my head, feeling the ground slipping from under me. "You believed me? I mean, come on…a bodybuilder slash doctor? Does that kind of person even exist? Surely, you were smart enough to see through that translucent veil of blatant deception."

I hated to do that. To take his accusation, though completely true, and turn it around on him. But this wasn't about me. This was about him invading my personal time and dumping his problems in my lap. I didn't want to be involved with this man or his convoluted issues of the heart.

"Right," he replied, seemingly at a loss for words. There might even been a little disappointment in his tone because I'd made him sound foolish, but I had to remind myself that it was all for the best.

"Well, I hope you feel better soon," I said, closing the door.

His hand stopped it. "I wasn't finished with you."

My mind downshifted into first gear. *Not finished with me? What did he mean by that?*

He took a gander past my shoulder into my apartment and breathed in. "Is that coffee?"

Lagging behind in the conversation, I tried to catch up with reality. "W-what did you ask? I'm sorry, I missed that."

He laughed. "I asked you if that was coffee I smell."

"Oh, yeah." I looked back toward my dreaded coffee maker. Pot was full, thank goodness. "Yeah, I'm making coffee. Would you like a cup?"

What are you doing, Jamie?

"Thanks, I could really use one."

Great. I just invited the man I was supposed to avoid into my apartment. An apartment cluttered with unpacked boxes of personal mementos. Where was my head?

Actually, this might work out perfectly. He'd see all the junk and chaos in my home, which was completely the opposite of his pristine living space, and run for the hills. I wouldn't have to break the news to him that I was uninterested, and he'd never feel the need to come over again.

Bingo!

"Please, come in," I offered with a pleasant smile.

As he stepped in, I could see he harbored a slight sense of fear, as if a booby trap were about to spring open on him. He scanned the room, taking in my mess. His thumbs were back in his front pockets, and he had a swagger in his stroll.

"Nice apartment," he complimented.

Liar.

"It looks like yours, but without all the disarray."

He turned to face me, his smile beaming bright. He seemed to enjoy the idea that I had been in his home, even if he didn't remember a single moment of my visit. I began to realize my plan for scaring him away wasn't working. He was tougher than I thought.

I ditched the original plan and headed for the coffee pot, having no idea how to drive him away. I was as skilled at being cold-hearted as I was at lying, so telling him he was too pretty to be my type was out of the question.

I shot him a quick look over my shoulder. He was eerily quiet, and I wondered if my untidiness was messing with his head. I raided the refrigerator for whipped cream and French vanilla creamer as he gazed up at the high ceilings, down the oversized windows, and around the open floor plan of the area.

His lips arched downward in thought. "They're similar apartments, yours and mine, but you've enhanced the appeal of some of my favorite things—mahogany wood, wrought iron, and leather. Are you an interior decorator?"

I wanted to laugh. I was a lot of things, but not a person who could beautify the indoors with color, texture, and design. My talents went as far as pressing a button on a machine and watching it brew the world's most beloved liquid.

"I appreciate the compliment, but I'm not an interior decorator."

"What *do* you do?" he asked, meeting me in the kitchen. He leaned across the island, his biceps bulging above the right angle of his arms. I tried to keep my focus on the technique of pouring two cups of coffee. When I scooped a huge dollop of whipped cream to top them off, he came off the counter.

"Whoa, whoa," he said, raising his hands. "What are you doing? You're ruining a perfectly good cup of coffee."

"I take it you like yours black?"

"I like mine the way Juan Valdez intended."

I recalled the vintage 1980s Columbian coffee commercial. I hadn't heard that name in forever, but I could still see the early riser slipping into his boots after the crow of a rooster and heading to the fields to pick the richest coffee in Columbia.

I handed him his mug and took a quick sip of mine, the cream settling on my upper lip. My tongue, licking it off, caught his attention. His eyes lingered on my mouth, but as soon as he realized I saw his drifting gaze, he looked away.

"So, what do you do again?" he asked, clearing his throat.

"I own a coffee shop on Fountain Square." I gave a wry smile. "I ruin hundreds of cups of coffee on a daily business."

"I Like You a Latte?" he asked, almost surprised. "That's your place?"

"Yes, it is. You've been there?"

"A few times," he admitted. "Guess I'll have to go more often now."

I bit my lip and felt the blood surface beneath my skin, my cheeks warming under his comment. As great as Joseph walking through the door of my café looked in my head, I wanted to change the subject. I didn't really like when it was on me. "So, what do *you* do for a living?"

He lifted the cup to his mouth, puckered his lips in the most alluring way as he blew the steam from the top and took his first sip. He seemed to enjoy the taste, savoring the comfort of the hot brew easing his hangover. "I do a lot for a living. Jack-of-all-trades kind of guy. Whatever comes up."

My spirits plummeted. I wasn't supposed to care about any of this because I wasn't getting involved. But like a sensible woman should, I always kept my options open and considered them with a frugal mind.

At least Joseph had a job.

Be that as it may, it sounded like he hopped from

opportunity to opportunity. Was it wrong of me to deduct a couple points from his tally because he was a drifter? Maybe. But I didn't like change, and Joseph clearly rolled with the punches on a frequent basis. That was not something I could mesh with easily.

Suddenly, I pictured him strumming out a tune on his guitar, a beautiful melody with heart and soul in every chord. I remembered Caroline and her critical remark about his songwriting. Perhaps he was a musician at heart and a blue-collar worker by trade, just until he could land his big break.

"So, how's the songwriting going?" I blurted without thinking. I wanted to kick myself.

His eyes leapt to mine, and he put on a serious mask. I buried my face in the mug so I didn't have to make eye contact with him, but I could feel the heat of his stare burning through my ceramic cup.

"I'm sorry, I shouldn't have pried."

"No, it's okay," he reassured kindly. "I just didn't know it was public knowledge."

"Well, with all due respect, anything said in an open hallway of an apartment complex is considered public."

His head tilted backward as he understood where I came from. "That's right…you were eavesdropping on my dispute with Caroline yesterday morning."

Sensations of heat prickled up my neck and enflamed my cheeks. "I wasn't eavesdropping,"

Joseph's smile returned. "Oh yeah? What do you call it then?"

I took a deep breath, hoping to redeem myself. "I call it being at the wrong place at the right time."

He reached out and clicked his mug with mine. "I'll

drink to that."

I felt empowered by his simple toast and his cordial gesture. I felt I'd risen a few rungs on the caliber ladder, nearing his level of acceptance. We seemed to be genuinely enjoying each other's company, despite the awkwardness of how we first met. I was ready to relax a little in his presence.

"Do you want to sit down?" I motioned toward the dinner table. I slipped into my normal spot, and he found his across from me. Before I could get comfortable, he dropped a question into my lap.

"So, why did you lie to me?"

I wasn't prepared for this. "Excuse me?"

"You said you had dinner plans last night. A date. Why did you say that? What was the point?"

I stared into my cup for answers. Not one floated to the top. "I don't know. I guess I thought you were pretending to have a date too, so I did the same."

"But I *did* have a date. Well, plans," he reminded as he took another sip. "I was in a tie, remember."

"For all I knew, you could have been coming back from work, just as I was doing."

Joseph narrowed his eyes on me. "For future reference, I never wear a tie to work."

"Good to know. But just to reiterate, I didn't know it then. You were a stranger."

"I'm still a stranger." His flirty smile shot straight through my heart.

"Not really. Would a stranger know the color of your sheets, the size of your shoes, and a tiny tattoo on your right wrist with the initials L.M.S written in a script-like heart?"

Joseph's laughter echoed throughout the room. "Touché, Sutherland."

At the instant he spoke my surname, I realized I didn't know his. I was also curious about the initials he choose to permanently ink on his body, but figured that question would have to wait for a later date. "Since we've graduated from strangers to acquaintances, do I get the privilege of knowing your full name?"

He slouched back in his chair and stretched his legs out in front of him. "Joseph Alexander Scarbrough. Named after my grandfather."

"I like it," I said sincerely. "It's sounds regal and chivalrous."

Again he laughed. "I don't think anyone who knows me would knight me under those traits."

"What about Caroline?" I dared to mention the ex. I couldn't help it. I wanted to know how he felt about her. "A woman like her doesn't give her heart away to just anyone. Surely, she found a redeeming characteristic in your personality."

The way a man talks about his ex-girlfriend was a good indicator of what kind of person he was. If he belittled her and had nothing but bad things to say about her, then he was liable to be judgmental, insensitive, and rude. I was hoping Joseph was none of those things. I waited for his answer with baited breath.

"Caroline might have thought I hung the moon when we were younger, but I guess she's not that impressed these days."

I lifted my cup to my lips, pondering Joseph's bleak outlook. While he didn't exactly insult Caroline, he didn't offer a kind word about her either. Hmm...I was still on the fence. Teetering, but still on it.

Joseph stood up from the table. "May I?" he asked, thumbing toward the coffee pot.

"Sure," I said, staggering out of my thoughts. I glanced into my cup. "I'll need some too."

He brought the pot with him and poured my cup first. *What a gentleman.* As he filled his, he returned to the previous subject. "I suppose I can't blame her though. I tried to be there for her. I really did. But I guess she needed more than I could give." Eventually, he sat back down at the table and stared out the ten-foot windows lining the south wall. "She's better off finding someone else."

"Why do you say that?" The look he gave me sent my heart aflutter.

"Because I'd only hold her back. I can't fall in love. I've tried. I thought it would be easy with Caroline, since we were childhood friends and I knew her so well. For years, I tried to let myself fall. But it's never happened. I don't think it ever will."

If I were a woman on the prowl, I would have taken Joseph's words as a dare and set my mind to proving him wrong. Whether he meant it that way or not, any woman with a pulse would have already started plotting her next move to make this guy fall in love. Fortunately for me, I was not one of those women, and I could easily disregard the temptation of setting my sights on this handsome test subject. I had better things to do with my life than woo a man incapable of love just for the sake of saying it could be done.

All betting aside though, I had to admit for a second I flirted with the idea of trying.

Chapter Six

My day took quite a turn. I'd gone from shy and reserved to comfortable and giggling in the span of a few hours. Joseph and I had finished one pot of coffee and were halfway into the next, digging through my unpacked boxes.

I knew this stuff was supposed to be my personal stash of childhood memories and trinkets, but when Joseph asked me about them, I had no choice but to come clean. As I was spooning more whipped cream into my coffee in the kitchen, he peered inside one of the boxes and inquired about its contents. I expected him to ridicule me for the odd assortment of saved items, but *au contraire!* He pulled out my collection of cassette tapes and marveled over them, as if I'd stockpiled objects from a sunken treasure.

"Oh, my gosh, you have Hootie & The Blowfish and Radiohead? I haven't heard these guys in forever." Joseph opened the case as if he had to see it to believe it. "I used to play their songs all the time in my garage when the band would get together to practice. My mom hated it."

He smiled as if he enjoyed ticking his mother off.

"You played in a band?" I wasn't questioning him out of disbelief. He owned a guitar and wrote songs, so the organized musician thing wasn't a far fetch. But I longed to know all there was to know about Joseph.

For purely conversational reasons, of course, I reminded myself.

"Yeah," he said reminiscently. "We called ourselves 'The Best the World Has Ever Seen.'"

We both laughed at the idiosyncratic stage name. I could just picture him standing at the microphone with his guitar strapped to his body, his fist high in the air as he announced the group's alias. I wondered if he sang the songs he wrote, or if he was just lead guitar.

"That's quite a mouthful,"

"Yes it was," he concurred. "But it's a name you'd never forget. Right?"

"I'll give you that."

I sat cross-legged on the floor wearing nothing but baggy sweats and a ponytail, drinking coffee, talking and laughing with a guy I had never expected to give me the time of day. It felt amazing to hang out with someone, particularly a male, without feeling the need to impress. Was I dreaming? No way. It couldn't be a dream. My heart sang, and my face hurt from smiling so much.

A few more hours passed by, and a few more boxes had been emptied. Somehow I had Joseph carrying boxes to the dumpster and a couple to his truck to donate to Goodwill. With his help, I'd been able to go through each one, decide the fate of its contents, pack the keepers away, and trash the rest. I'd rid my apartment of the clutter, and my to-do-list had been completely checked off.

Melissa would be so surprised. Not only for unpacking the rest of the boxes, but unpacking the rest of the boxer while hanging out with Joseph. I could just hear her now. *You mean you turned me down for a hunky, songwriting neighbor with beautiful biceps and great hair?* I could see her giving me another one of her disco bumps and adding *Don't sweat it, darlin'. I would have too.* A high-pitched squeal would likely follow, along with her begging for the dirty details.

"Oh, if only I had some to offer," I muttered under my breath, as I finished the last of the dishes.

"If only you had what to offer? And to whom?"

I gasped and turned around at the sound of Joseph's voice as he re-entered the apartment. I had no idea he had returned so quickly from the garbage run. I fished for a properly evasive reply. "Um…If only I had some donuts to offer. To you. You know, coffee and donuts…they go great together."

He approached the island and sat at one of the stools. "Don't give me some lame defense, Jamie. I know what I heard. You were talking to yourself, and I don't think it had anything to do with donuts."

I sighed and unplugged the drain, drying my hands on the nearby towel. "I was just imagining what my friend, Melissa, would say on Monday morning when I tell her that I've officially unpacked everything. So, there."

"And…"

"And that the person who helped me was not her, but you."

"She was supposed to help you?"

"Not exactly," I amended. "She's offered to help me many times, but I've always declined."

"I see." He folded his hands on the counter. "So, what do you wish you had to offer her?"

I turned around, hiding my embarrassment. There was no way I could face this man while confessing the truth. "After Melissa learns I had a man in my apartment, she's the type of girl who'll want details. You know, the dirty details. More explicit the better."

I felt his presence behind me. I hadn't expected him to

ditch his place at the counter and approach me so daringly. "You mean details like, how close I stood to you when I said goodbye? Or whether or not I kissed you before I left?"

I swallowed.

Hard.

I couldn't breathe. I couldn't think about anything but Joseph behind me. He turned me around and lifted my chin with the curve on his index finger. The simple contact he made with my face rooted me to the floor. His hand felt warm against my skin, and I could smell the faint aroma of last night's cologne swirling around me.

He tested me, this I knew, but my normal brain function took a hiatus. I was left with nothing but my own addlebrained thoughts and emotions, neither of which could save me from the intensity of this moment.

I saw a glint of amusement in his eyes. The corner of his mouth twitched into a smile. "How about you let me take you out tonight, and we'll see if we can muster up some of those details your friend might ask for."

"Like a date?" I asked stupidly.

He released me and crossed his arms, leaning against the refrigerator. Satisfaction beamed from every aspect of his face. From the twinkle in his eyes, to the depth of his laugh lines, he looked very proud of himself. "Yes, like a date. Will you let me take you out, you know, since we're no longer strangers."

A thousand thoughts ran through my mind. Indeed, we were no longer strangers, per se, but I couldn't forget that he had newly separated from his girlfriend. A little over twenty-four hours was not long enough for anyone to get over a break-up. At this stage in the game, I'd be nothing but the rebound girl.

"Okay," he stated, holding up his hands. "I can see I've put you on the spot and you're worried I'm moving too quickly. I mean, Caroline just left me yesterday morning and I'm already asking you out on a date. I get that. But here's the thing. I'm not asking you out so I can pursue you."

You're not? The question echoed in my head. *Then what are you doing?*

"I'm asking a woman I really enjoy being around to spend some time with me."

I blinked in rapid succession. I had no idea if I was supposed to be happy or disappointed about his platonic objective.

"I like you, Jamie," he concluded. "I like talking with you and hanging out. I've never had someone I could be this comfortable around. It's nice. And I think you feel the same."

Again, I was dumbfounded. I could hardly catch up. I was still stuck at *I like you, Jamie.*

He checked his watch. "It's only four o'clock. You've got time to think about it, and I've got time to make some plans. If you decide you'd like to take me up on my offer, knock on my door. If not, then so be it. No hard feelings."

He winked at me and casually walked out.

Chapter Seven

I threw out my arms and braced myself between the island and the sink counter. The earth shattering invitation Joseph had challenged me with softened the bones of my legs into spaghetti noodles. I said 'challenged' because everything about his offer was just that. It was a challenge to think clearly. It was a challenge to know whether he had ulterior motives behind the date. It was a challenge to forget the way his touch felt upon my skin and the things my body felt because of it. And let's not forget, it was also a challenge to turn him down.

While I reminded myself that accepting his offer was a huge mistake, I wanted nothing more than to rip open my door, chase after him, and scream *yes* at the top of my lungs. It was not every day a woman like me would get a chance to be with a man like Joseph. He was strikingly handsome, confident, and mysterious. He had the power to look through me when he gazed into my eyes, but I'd be darned if I could read his. He held himself with as much poise as a wealthy aristocrat, but without conceit and preeminence. And he listened to me when I spoke as if he hung on my every word.

No man had ever done that.

I took a deep breath and exhaled slowly, counting the seconds until I completely expelled all the air in my lungs. I tried to force myself to relax, to convince my scarred heart that it had nothing to worry about. Oh, how I tried, but it had been broken too many times not to fret about old wounds and the pain of reopening them.

I gathered some leftover strength and walked over to the window. The sun had begun to set over the Covington skyline. Daylight savings time had ended a few weeks ago, and the last bit of sunlight struggled to illuminate the riverfront.

Dusk was the time when the city came alive. The B&B riverboats cruised up and down the Ohio, and Newport on the Levee lit up with local bands playing on the banks and people dancing on the walkways beneath the flickering Christmas lights tightly woven around the bare trees. Fountain Square would be crawling with holiday shoppers, kissing couples, and festive friends painting the town red.

I imagined being out amongst the crowds, Joseph at my side. I could see his smile and hear his laughter over the jazz band playing on the corner. I could feel the warmth of his hand around mine as he led me down the busy sidewalks toward the special place he planned to take me. I could see myself enjoying his company and having the best night of my life.

If only I said 'yes.'

What stopped me? The idea of Joseph rebounding for starters. I understood he felt unwanted and I made him feel desirable again, but that didn't make it right for him to use me to get over Caroline.

Another big reason I hesitated was because I didn't want to get hurt. I'd been in the committed relationship scene before. This wasn't my first rodeo. But with each go-round, I'd been thrown from the saddle, eaten dirt, my heart broken, my pride bruised. I had dusted myself off so many times that getting back on that temperamental horse had no appeal to me anymore. I feared one more wild ride would darn near kill me.

The last and biggest obstacle I had for steering clear of Joseph was that my life didn't have room to accommodate him. I had my routines, my rituals, the things I did each day that kept me focused and sane. Having someone like Joseph, who probably flew by the seat of his pants all the time, would throw a serious monkey wrench in my predictable existence.

I didn't adapt well to change. When things in my life were modified or altered at a moment's notice, I felt like my world was spinning out of control. I had to have my hands on the wheel at all times, at ten and two. No surprises, no compromises. It was the way I liked it.

I looked toward the door of my apartment. Beyond the wood of that two-inch barrier laid an opportunity to be someone else. To do something different. To have something new.

My heart skipped a beat. I had no way of knowing whether its rampant rhythm was coerced by the anxiety of the unknown or the excitement of the thrill. The comfort of predictability usually kept my pulse at an even pace, but right now it pounded so wildly against my ribs, I thought it might burst from my chest.

I stood up, throwing my hands above my head in surrender. "All right! I'll do it!"

I ran for the door, delighted by my impulsive decision. I gripped the handle and jerked it open. The sound of a woman's voice stopped me in my tracks.

I peeked into the hallway and saw Caroline stomping toward the elevator, Joseph on her heels.

"Caroline, wait."

I closed the door enough that no one would notice it ajar, but left it open enough so I could still hear. I knew it was wrong to eavesdrop on their private conversation—again—but I had to. I was not about to run to Joseph, ready to accept his offer with foolhardy exuberance, if he intended to jump back into a relationship with her.

My heart skidded to a halt, preparing for the usual disappointment I came to expect with men. I held my breath, waiting to hear what Joseph had to say.

"Caroline, listen to me." His voice sounded desperate, and the elevator door took the brunt of his command as I heard him forcibly slide it back open. I envisioned him holding it with a strong arm. "We've known each other since we were kids. Doesn't that count for something?"

My spirits plummeted. He wanted her back. I should have known.

Close the door and save yourself from hearing the rest.

I ignored the voice in my head. I had to be sure how he felt about her. He, at least, owed me that much.

"I can't be friends with you, Joseph," Caroline snapped. "It would be too hard for me to see you with someone else."

"There *is* no one else."

"There will be," she laughed sardonically. "There always is. You never stay unattached for long."

"Don't do this," he begged.

"Joseph, you did this."

"How? What did I do that made you feel you have to walk away from what we've always had?"

"That's just it. We have nothing because you refused to give all of yourself. Ever since your sister died, you've built these walls around your heart, and no one is strong enough to tear them down. Not even me, the girl you've known all your life."

I pressed further against the door, not wanting to miss his next words. The identity of those tattooed initials on his wrist suddenly became apparent.

"So, our life-long friendship means nothing to you?"

I couldn't see either of them or how close they were to each other, but I imagined Joseph's spellbinding eyes boring into her soul. Caroline was sure to give in now.

"It means the world to me, but I want more. I *deserve* more. Damn, Joseph, I've spent all of my childhood chasing you, crushing on you. You say you want to love me, but you won't let yourself. You won't give me any more than what everyone else gets."

"It's difficult for me, you know that. But just because I can't love you like you want me to, doesn't mean we have to throw everything away We've been the best of friends since we were kids."

"If I can't have your heart, then I refuse to waste any more of my life with you."

"So, this is it?" he asked, his voice cracking. "You're going to throw away our friendship over…" He never got to finish. Caroline said her goodbye over his plea, and I heard the elevator close with a ding.

I listened intently. I wondered if he was the type of guy to chase after her and beg for another chance. I wondered if he wanted to.

A loud bang startled me as if he'd struck his fist against the wall, and the sound of solid footsteps approached. I quietly pushed the door the rest of the way closed, holding the handle at full-twist so it wouldn't generate a click on the hinges.

In a few seconds, a slamming door echoed down the hall. I breathed a heavy respire, my heart in my throat.

What do I do now?

Chapter Eight

I stood at my door for what seemed like an eternity. Should I act like I didn't hear anything that had transpired down the hall and knock on Joseph's door anyway? Maybe he'd be too upset to go out, and he'd have to figure out how to renege on his offer without feeling like a jerk. Or maybe I should knock on his door, like a good friend would, and just be there for him.

There was no doubt he needed someone right now. Caroline had ripped his heart from his chest and left him to bleed. If anyone knew what he was going through, it was me. I had been left for dead countless times with no one to sop up the blood or stitch the gaping wounds.

I may have only known Joseph for a day, but I was the closest thing he had to a loyal friend. I would not let him suffer alone.

I swung open the door and froze. Joseph stood there, his fist suspended in the air as if he were about to knock. Our eyes met, and for once the mystery vanished. I read the emotions behind his eyes, as if they were flashing neon lights.

Sadness, the kind that was deep-seated and destructive, pervaded every inch of his persona. He stood with his back hunched, his chin lowered, and his confidence in shambles. The luster in his sapphire eyes had dulled to a gloomy shade of grey. He forced a smile, though I saw through his façade, for I'd done the same many times.

"Hey," he said, shuffling his feet. "We seem to be doing this a lot lately."

I gave my warmest smile, hoping it would dissolve some of the awkwardness between us. "Yeah, we do."

I thought he'd make up some excuse as to why he suddenly had to cancel the date. I'd be okay with that, for I'd never want a pity date anyway. What I *did* want was to take his pain away. To reach out, wrap my arms around his neck, and squeeze for all I was worth. The notion of never letting go sounded even better. I imagined Joseph had the best hugs in the world. Strong and secure.

I could give him that too. I wanted to give him that, but I stood motionless. My nerve had been shot full of holes. The way he looked at me caused my backbone to lose its resolve. The sadness I initially saw in his eyes faded away. His chin had lifted slightly and so had the corners of his lips.

He scoffed aloud and shook his head.

"What?" I asked, priming myself for the let down.

"I was going to tell you something," he said earnestly, "but I completely forgot what it was. You do that to me, you know?"

"Do what?" My curiosity spun into overdrive.

"Make me lose my head."

I apologized, though I wasn't sure why.

"Don't be sorry," he coaxed. "I don't mind. Seeing you…" He fished for the right words. "…helps."

"But you've only been gone a few moments." I decided not to let on I'd overheard their conversation in the hall. For the sake of his injured pride, I thought it best.

"I know I just left, but…"

He furrowed his brow, as if sorting through his

emotions. Men didn't typically know how to come to terms with their innermost feelings. I figured Joseph was no different. So, I helped him along.

"Did you need something?"

"What?"

I had to smile at the pure, unadulterated ditziness he suddenly had. "You came back after offering to take me out. I was supposed to knock on *your* door, if I decided to take you up on your invitation. Did you forget something?"

I allowed him enough time to catch up. Apparently, his blond moment was short lived. "No, I didn't leave anything behind. But…" he pointed at me and smiled. "You were headed out this door right before I knocked. Should I assume you were coming to knock on my door?"

He had me. I fidgeted with my hands, brushing a few strands of hair out of my eyes. "Maybe."

He hiked his arm above his head and leaned his forearm on the doorframe, crossing his ankles casually. Little by little, the Joseph I'd spent the entire day with came back. Had I brought about this change in him? Was simply being around me enough to place his heart on the mend?

I certainly gave myself a lot of credit. It made more sense to think Joseph was no stranger to such tragedies. Take losing his sister for instance. Joseph seemed like the kind of man who'd shake off his afflictions and carry on.

I eyed him carefully, uncertain of the right words. "Let's say, hypothetically, I was coming to knock on your door. And you were on the other side of that door, where you were supposed to be."

"Go on."

"Would you be happy in hearing a rap upon your door? Or would you be burdened by it? Tell me the truth."

"You want the honest-to-God's truth, Jamie?"

My heart gave out for a second. I wondered whether I could physically handle the truth, should the truth be detrimental to my self-esteem. Depending on what he said, he might find me collapsed at his feet in a fetal position, protecting myself from further psychological damage. Just thinking about it had me breaking out into a cold sweat. I suddenly felt dizzy. My hands began to shake.

"Yes," I said wearily. "I want the honest-to-God's truth."

He stepped toward me and reached for my hands. The zing of his touch jolted up my arms and ricocheted throughout my body. The energy he supplied to every axon in my central nervous system went into complete overload.

"If you knocked on my door, I'd be so happy, I might even kiss you."

That was the last thing I remembered before everything went black.

Chapter Nine

My eyes fluttered open, and Joseph's beautiful face stared at me. He looked concerned, if my frazzled brain was registering correctly, and I wondered what had happened.

I could feel something soft beneath me, as if I were lying down. But with the shock of opening my eyes to the sexiest man in the world only inches from me, I had no idea where I was. I tore my eyes from his gaze and checked my surroundings. The familiarity of my living room comforted me to some extent, but knowing Joseph had probably carried me in his arms and laid me on my couch unsettled me. I had no recollection of it, and I could kick myself. It wasn't every day that a woman found herself in the arms of a desirable man.

"Are you all right?" he asked, brushing back a strand of my hair.

I blinked away the fuzziness of my thoughts and shook my head. "What happened? Did I just pass out?"

"Yeah, you did," he replied softly. "I caught you before you hit the floor, but I admit I wasn't prepared for it." He tilted his head to the side, observing me closely. "I'm going to go out on a limb here and assume you have low blood sugar?"

I clenched my tingling hands into tight balls, my mind still a bit sluggish. I hated this feeling when it came on. "How did you know?"

"My friend Greg has the same problem. He usually

warns me before he drops to the floor though."

I closed my eyes, feeling exhausted. After a bout of my sugar crashing, I was practically useless. I tried to muster some energy, but none was available to me.

"Jamie," I heard him call to me.

"Mm-hmm…"

"Open your eyes and look at me."

I obeyed him, even though all I wanted to do was sleep.

"You need to eat something."

"I'm not hungry."

"Tough," he said, taking me by the arms and lifting me to a sitting position. He pulled me closer to him on the couch and steadied me. "I hope you don't mind, but I took the liberty of rummaging through your kitchen for food. Here." He tore open the wrapper of a chocolate covered granola bar and shoved it in my hand. "While looking for this, I also found about five take-out menus from Thai joints. I assume that means you like Thai, so I ordered us some. It should be here soon. In the meantime, drink some orange juice. Again, I'm taking a stab here, but is that what I chased all those oranges for?"

"Yeah." A sudden smile pierced my lips as I remembered Joseph's hot pursuit down the hall. "Oranges help to maintain sugar levels once they're back up."

Joseph laughed. "Oh, now you decide to be all smart and doctor-like. Where was this woman who should've remembered this while drinking tons of coffee with nothing to eat all day?"

That woman was totally preoccupied, I thought inwardly, recalling the immense fun I had in his company. I made the decision not to give him an answer and save face. I drank the entire glass of the freshly-squeezed juice and glanced at him over the rim. I noticed he was still watching me closely.

"I'm fine," I insisted. "You don't have to keep doing that."

"Doing what?"

"Monitoring me like I'm some helpless child you need to keep an eye on."

"Maybe I like keeping an eye on you."

I rolled my eyes. His statement would have sounded so much better to my ears had I not made a spectacle of myself beforehand.

The buzzer erupted through the apartment, splitting my head in two.

"That was fast," Joseph said, standing. He gave me a quick once-over. "Will you be all right while I'm gone?"

I crowded my brows in confusion.

"Thai's here," he said pointing toward the door. "I gotta go let the guy in the building and pay him. You all right?"

My memory came back to me. Right. Joseph ordered take-out. I nodded my head and took another bite of the granola bar.

He backed out of the living room and pointed at me, his boyish grin tickling my insides. "Don't go anywhere."

I feigned a smile on the outside, but inside I was darn near humiliated. Why did this man have to see me in my most vulnerable state, and why in the world was he sticking around?

During his absence, those questions continued to roll through my mind, especially after knowing his childhood sweetheart decided to give up on their friendship. I didn't know that much about Joseph, but I assumed he wasn't as strong as he was acting. If someone had done that to me, I would have been devastated. From the look on his face when I had opened the door and found him about to knock, he looked quite upset by the turn of events.

I then recalled what he'd said to me thereafter. *I was going to tell you something, but I completely forgot what it was. You do that to me, you know? Make me lose my head.*

I couldn't help but feel special. I'd made this guy lose his train of thought. He didn't appear to be a man who'd let anyone get into his head on such a profound level, no matter who they were. He had too much self-assurance to be that weak.

Yet, he admitted to being wounded. *Seeing you...helps.*

Again, I felt exceptionally special to have alleviated whatever strife he was going through, even if I had no clue what he really meant by the statement. Realizing the mammoth smile on my face, I quickly took another bite of the granola bar. The last thing I wanted to do was have him catch me in the act of enjoying his downfall.

Thank goodness I took control of my emotions when I did, for he walked in unannounced, a large white sack in one hand, keys in the other, and a small bag hanging from his teeth. He smiled the minute he saw me and kicked the door shut.

"Dinner is served," he muttered, still clenching the bag between his lips.

He sat beside me, and I reached for it. "What's this?"

"Extra fortune cookies," he winked. "I figured there's nothing wrong with stocking up on a little more luck."

"More luck?"

"Yeah," he said, tearing into the take-out bag. "I lost one friend and gained another all in the same day. How many times does that happen to a person?"

I knew the question was purely rhetorical, but I silently agreed with him. If anyone was lucky this weekend, it was me. When it came to good fortune, most times it would pass me right by. Someone must have slipped Mr. Sandman a missive. Either that or he tripped and spilled his magic dust all over me by accident.

"Don't worry," he interrupted my thoughts. "I'll share with you."

"You think I need some added luck in my life?"

"I know you do," he concluded. "You're contending with me in your life, all of a sudden, and I doubt it was something you planned. If that isn't bad luck, I don't know what is."

I opened the Styrofoam container and regarded Joseph's choice of words. "I wouldn't call it 'contending.'"

I watched as Joseph helped himself to a set of chopsticks and deftly lifted his first bite to his mouth. He proved to be skilled with the utensils and a sense of wonder overtook me. I, on the other hand, had never gotten the hang of them despite my many futile attempts.

"So, what would you call it?" he asked.

I speculated whether to try the chopsticks in front of him or just concede to using the fork provided for me by the sympathetic owners of the Thai restaurant. I chickened out. I ripped open the sheer plastic covering on the fork and dove in. "I call it opening a door for a friend in need."

Joseph nodded, but he seemed lost in thought, toying with his rice and vegetables.

"You don't believe me?" I asked.

His eyes landed on mine in a way that froze every muscle in my body.

"No, I believe you, Jamie. But I can't help but think if

you hadn't known about Caroline walking out on me yesterday morning, you wouldn't have opened that door at all. You wouldn't have picked me up off the hallway floor and put me into my bed after my drunken binge. And I doubt you would have invited me in for coffee the next morning."

"You think I did all that out of pity?"

"Honestly, I don't know why you did it."

I took a deep breath and prepared my response in my head. Truth be told, I couldn't say I had a logical explanation for why I helped him in so many ways. Sure, assisting a beautiful man like Joseph had its perks, especially for a single woman looking to score a new man, but that was not me. I didn't lend a hand to him because I aimed to cut forward in line of all the other women in his life. Just thinking that had me cringing.

"Well?" he encouraged.

I straightened my back and looked him square in the eye. "I did it because that is how I'm made. I don't turn my back on those in need." I stuck my fork deep into the pile of spicy goodness, on the verge of saying more. I bit my lip, hesitating to open the dam of my convoluted mind. I had so much in my head he didn't need to hear, but I decided to at least unplug a small portion of it. "I don't know if you've figured it out yet, but I'm not like Caroline."

As soon as I said it, I regretted the words. I couldn't look at him anymore and, frankly I wondered where in the world that daring side of me came from. I certainly hoped I hadn't insulted him. Caroline was someone he cared for, and, by attacking her dignity, I might have overstepped my bounds. Then again, I wasn't the insensitive wench who had attacked his heart with no concern for his feelings.

While two wrongs shouldn't make a right, I wanted him to realize that not all women were heartless and self-absorbed.

"No, you're nothing like Caroline," he admitted. "In fact, you're nothing like any of the women I've known."

I was not aware of the exact number of females he had encountered, but with Joseph's striking good looks and charming personality, I assumed they could at least fill a small stadium. "Coming from you, I'll take that as a compliment."

"Contrary to what you might think, I know enough about women being the only male amongst three sisters. Probably more than a man *should* know."

"Somehow, I don't think that was your only means of knowing the female mind."

He looked at me askance, a half-cocked grin lighting up his face. "Should I take that as a compliment as well?"

"You should. You're a very thoughtful, charismatic, handsome man. I can't imagine you having any trouble meeting women or keeping their interest, with or without your sisters' help."

His hearty laughter filled the room, which made me want to laugh with him, though I didn't find much humor in my flattering remark. I meant it. Joseph was every girl's dream, including mine had I been searching for a perfect mate.

"You need to eat more, Jamie," he said, gently elbowing my arm. "That sugar of yours is still too low, and you're talking out of your head again."

I giggled and picked up the small bag of fortune cookies. "Let's see what Confucius has to say about it." I dug into the bag and pulled out the first one. "You know how to read these, don't you?"

"There's a wrong way to read a fortune cookie?"

"Not a wrong way," I corrected. "Just a better way. It adds more spunk to the average philosophical crap they write on these things."

"Oh, yeah?" His face lit up as he swiveled his body in my direction. "How do we do that?"

I enjoyed how he assumed this would be a partnership in order to enhance the general, ambiguous predictions of a crunchy vanilla treat. I broke my cookie open and pulled out the slip of paper. "It's really quite simple. You just add 'in bed' at the end of the fortune."

"In bed," he repeated skeptically.

"Here, just listen to mine." I read it silently to see if it worked. Some fortunes didn't make sense with the addition, but most times it added a whole new take on the prophecy. Mine worked perfectly.

He who controls others may be powerful, but he who has mastered himself is mightier still...in bed.

Joseph almost choked on his food. His reaction was priceless as he beat his chest, trying to clear his airway so he could continue laughing.

"See, I told you it made them better."

"You weren't lying," he concurred. Excitedly, he reached for his fortune cookie and cracked it open. I watched him glance over it, reading it ahead of time with the additional word choice. His brow lifted and a devilish grin took shape. I sat transfixed in his gaze. "Oh, this is a good one. I think it might even be better than yours."

"Let's hear it."

He cleared his throat as if he were about to give a presidential address.

Any activity becomes creative when the doer cares about doing it right, or better...in bed.

Had I not been battling hypoglycemia, my reaction would have been a bit more spirited. He was definitely correct...his was better than mine, and I think he worried that I would've been embarrassed with his insinuative fortune. Maybe in time he'd realize I was not a prude, like I envisioned his Caroline to be.

"Guess you'll never look at a fortune cookie the same again, will you?" I resumed eating while he continued to smirk at the tiny paper.

"You got that right." He tucked the fortune in the front pocket of his jeans and watched me as I chewed. "Is it good? Did I order the right meal?"

Remembering my manners, I didn't want to talk with my mouth full. I simply nodded and hid my massive chews behind my hand. Before I could fork another hearty portion, he handed me the other set of chopsticks.

"Try eating with these. It tastes so much better."

I took a few seconds to finish chewing and swallowed. "I've tried a thousand times and can't figure them out."

"That's because you never had *me* show you. Here." He took hold of my hand in his, and placed my fingers properly on the sticks while giving me tips on how one stick stays stationery in my grasp. I tried to listen to his expert advice, but all I focused on was the feel of his warm hands on mine. His touch felt exquisite against my skin, and I couldn't keep myself from enjoying its effect on the rest of my body.

"You're trembling," he noticed. "You cold?"

"No," I dismissed too quickly, wishing I would have conceded with his observation.

"What's wrong?" he badgered sweetly, his eyes gazing into mine.

I had to look away. Normally, I could stare into Joseph's eyes forever, but this time he had my insides in complete turmoil. "It's my sugar, I think," I fibbed.

He seemed to believe me and gave me back the fork. "I'll let it slide this once because you need to eat. But the next time we have Thai, you're using chopsticks. Got it?"

Next time? There's going to be a next time?

My heart did a summersault triggered by the exuberant fluttering of butterflies in my stomach. I passed over his offer as though it were a normal, everyday proposal and included one of my own. "Fine. I'll use chopsticks from now on, if you promise to let me ruin your coffee the next time you're in my shop."

He extended his right hand immediately without hesitation. "Deal."

I accepted his hand, and we shook on it, his grip strong and compelling. Somehow, I felt as if we were shaking hands on a different pact all together. In securing two 'next times,' he seemed to welcome whatever the future might hold for us.

Chapter Ten

Within an hour, my sugar rose to its appropriate level, but my energy took a nosedive. By the time Joseph and I finished our meal, I had sunk to a state of exhaustion. I could no longer keep my eyes open, and I slouched into the cushion of the couch. Playing host was no longer in the cards.

"All right," Joseph stated soundly. "I'm outta here. It's obvious I'm boring you."

My head felt like a two-ton boulder, but I managed to open my eyes. "You're not boring me. I'm just sleepy."

I felt his hand on my knee, and my breath caught. "Don't think you're getting out of going out with me so easily. Clearly tonight is not the night, but I'm holding you to it, you hear me?"

"I hear you," I said, smiling from ear to ear.

"Tomorrow is Sunday, and I have plans, so I can't do it then. How about next weekend? You free?"

I had absolutely no idea what I was doing next weekend, but I was darn sure I could move things around if I had plans. No way was I going to let this opportunity slip through my fingers. And not because I wanted to suddenly pursue him. Undoubtedly, we were two different people who wanted different things in life. I enjoyed his friendship, the conversations, and the company—nothing more.

"Next weekend sounds great. Should I knock?" I jested.

"No, we're passed that now. I'll pick you up at seven on

Friday."

I repeated the time and date in my head. Between Joseph's hand still on my knee and the fogginess of fatigue, I made a serious mental note not to forget. "Got it."

I felt him stir on the couch and lifted my eyelids just enough to catch Joseph reaching for the blanket on the nearby chair. He spread the afghan over me and winked. "Sleep tight, Sutherland."

The synapses in my brain were no longer firing at optimum speed, but I could tell by the tone of his voice that he didn't really want to leave. Knowing what I'd heard between him and Caroline this evening, I worried he would go off and do something stupid again, like drink himself to death.

"Are you okay?" I asked as he approached the door.

He glanced over his shoulder for a brief moment then turned around to face me. "Yeah," he said with a pleasant smile on his face. "I'm good."

He stood there gazing at me, his thumbs finding a home in his front pockets. If I could have taken a picture of Joseph, it would have been right now, second only to the moment when he had donned the towel. I loved the casual poise of his character, the squared confidence in his shoulders contradicting the laxity of his grin.

"This very well could have been the second worse day of my life," he explained, looking down at his feet for a second. He took a deep breath, as if fighting off an emotion he likely wanted to keep buried, before he raised his head with conviction. "But you, Jamie, turned this day around. Thanks for…" He searched for the right words. "For everything. For being you."

My eyes remained open. There was no way I could

close them now. I couldn't say I understood what just happened, but something definitely changed between us. Not being very skilled in the ways of men and women, I couldn't discern between casual friendliness and potentially connecting on a whole new level. I just knew I felt a foreign emotion taking root in my heart, and I think he did too.

He glanced down at the bag of fortune cookies and impulsively snagged one before backing up toward the door. He cracked it open, popped half the tasty cookie in his mouth and read the inscription to himself, his devilish smile reaching all the way to his eyes.

Curiosity got the better of me. "What's it say?"

He shook his head. "It's my fortune, not yours."

"That's not fair."

"Some other time, maybe," he said, tucking the strip of paper into his jeans pocket. "You need to sleep."

I hadn't the energy to argue with him. I felt my eyes begin to close.

"See you Friday, Jamie," was all I heard as he left the image of his glorious smile branded on my brain upon his departure. After the door closed, I fell into a deep sleep with the image of Joseph Alexander Scarbrough holding me in his arms.

* * * *

The next morning was like any other, except that my first thoughts were of Joseph and not coffee. I sat up and stretched the stiffness in my neck and back, cursing myself for sleeping on the couch instead of in my own comfortable bed. Lesson learned. Never crash on the couch when a two-thousand-dollar, pillow-top mattress is but a few feet away.

Walking to the kitchen, I prepared to make my morning java. Joseph's lovely male voice unreeled itself in my head as I relived yesterday's key moments. The first that came to mind was his innocent grin the moment I opened the door before he could knock. His hair was adorably disheveled and his eyes bloodshot. It made me want to reach out and tame his silky, brown waves, to brush that pesky unruly lock away from his right eye.

The second memory was waking up from my hypoglycemic episode with his face inches from mine. Still groggy from my restless sleep, my overactive imagination led me past the boundaries of reality and into the realm of fantasy. Before I knew it, in my mind I had pressed my lips to Joseph's and kissed him.

The moment our lips met, I gasped and rewound myself to the present. I touched my mouth. The feel of Joseph's, or rather what I imagined his lips to feel like, lingered on mine. I could almost smell him.

Until the phone rang.

Irritated, I picked up my cell and answered. "Hello." I tried not to sound miffed, but darn it, it was difficult to break away from my morning reflections, even if they were fictitious.

Donna, my weekend college employee from the shop, divulged the madness she had endured upon opening, blathering on about how the espresso machine was not working properly. Rubbing my temples, I assured her that I would be right there to look at it. She seemed relieved to know I was coming but continued to apologize for calling on the weekend.

After a few moments of reassuring her, I hung up and

threw on some clothes. Nothing special—just sweats and a T-shirt. Within ten minutes, I had brushed my teeth, combed my hair, slipped my arms inside my coat, and walked out the door.

As soon as I stepped into the corridor, something hard and unforgiving rammed into my leg. The awful sound of metal crashing resounded around me. I'd collided into someone passing by. I nearly buckled from the blow, but a pair of strong arms caught me before I went down.

"Oh, my gosh. Are you all right?"

I looked up and there stood Joseph, cradling me in his embrace. He looked just as handsome as he always did, but this time he wore jeans, work boots, and a tan Carhartt jacket. He smelled of soap and aftershave, yet the stubble on his face proved it was just for the aroma.

"I'm so sorry," he apologized, standing me on my own two feet. "We've got to stop meeting like this."

I glanced at the floor in the hallway. His faded-red, metal toolbox lay toppled on its side and I finally realized what had hit me. Until I looked away from Joseph, I hardly felt the pain in my thigh. Now it throbbed and burned. I reached down and gave it a good rub.

Joseph dropped to his knees and shimmied the elastic hem of my sweat pants halfway up my leg to inspect the damage. His fingers brushed the sensitive skin behind my knee, and my stance faltered a second time. I backed away from him. "I'm fine, Joseph. Really."

"You've got a welt the size of Antarctica on your thigh and a bruise already forming."

"It's okay," I assured him. "I bruise easily."

He stood and ran his fingers through his hair. "I'm serious, Jamie. I think I need to take you to the hospital.

Those Champion toolboxes are made to take a beating."

I hopped on my injured leg, demonstrating that he'd not broken any bones and a trip to the hospital was unnecessary. "I'm not going to the ER for a bruise, Joseph. Now quit worrying." Ignoring the ache setting in, I bent to pick up his toolbox. It was a lot heavier than I expected and the lift became more of a heave. "Where are you headed?"

Joseph immediately seized it from my possession, his concern still visibly present in his eyes. "To my sister's farm. She's got a leaky barn roof."

This was the first I'd heard of his family. I couldn't help but be intrigued. "Your sister lives on a farm?"

"My whole family does. They're in the horse boarding business. It's pretty lucrative in Lexington."

"Is that where her farm is?"

He smiled, almost as if I were the first person to have taken an interest in his family's life. "Yeah, you want to come with me? I could use an extra hand."

My brain instantly crumbled to pieces in my head. I stumbled on my words and my tongue felt like it had been sailor-knotted. I couldn't believe he invited me to go to his family's residence. Most men are reluctant to take a new woman into their comfort zone, but Joseph didn't appear to care.

"I-I wish I could," I stammered. "But I've got to go into work. Espresso machine is pitchin' a fit today."

"I could take a look at it," he offered. "Got everything I'd need for the job right here."

For some reason, Joseph looked so much larger today. It might have been the bulky coat he wore or the extra inch of tread lining the bottom of his boots, but I swear he towered over me in this hallway. I stepped back to keep my head from tilting at such a steep angle.

"Oh, that's all right. You've got your hands full already. Besides, it might be a complicated job. I'll just call the repairman."

"On a Sunday? Seriously, it's no trouble."

I tried to dissuade him with another pitiful excuse, but he wouldn't budge.

He placed his hand on the small of my back and ushered me to the elevator. "Look, it's simple. We'll drive down to the shop and take a look at the machine. If it's an easy fix, we can be out the door and at my sister's in less than two hours. If it's a job above my qualifications, then you can call a repairman and decide what you want to do with your day from there. At least, let me give you a ride to work."

I broke. It was so easy to give in when it came to Joseph. Honestly, he could have threatened that spending the day with him would result in head-to-toe splinters, and I'd still want to come along.

Chapter Eleven

I'm not certain why I felt embarrassed about walking into my own coffee shop with Joseph at my heels. If anything, I should have felt proud to have this caliber of man in my company. Any woman would.

Not me.

All I felt was everyone's eyes on me, judging me, callously calculating how a guy like him could be with a girl like me and betting on how short the relationship would last. Little did they know there was no relationship to wager against.

I ignored the looks from all the female clientele sitting at the café tables and ushered Joseph behind the counter, removing my coat and gloves. Donna's eyes lit up when she saw me, but didn't remain on me for long. Her gaze automatically lifted above my shoulder to Joseph. She didn't say a word, but I could tell she longed for an introduction.

"Donna, this is Joseph," I said out of politeness. "He's my neighbor and pretty good with his hands."

She tore her eyes from his and gawked at me.

"I mean, he's good at fixing things," I corrected immediately. I pinched my nose, trying to gain some sort of composure in front of my hired help. "He's offered to look at the espresso machine."

Donna held out her hand and smiled warmly. "Wonderful," she said, shaking Joseph's hand. "I hope it doesn't give you as much trouble as it's given me this morning."

Joseph didn't look intimidated. If anything, he looked more determined than ever to repair the temperamental appliance. I directed him to the back counter and acted the informant, pointing out the fussy apparatus in question.

Joseph removed his jacket and handed it to me. My eyes fell over his broad shoulders and the muscles of his arms bulging beneath his tight cotton shirt. He didn't notice me staring, thank goodness, and for a short moment I got to take in his little Wrangler behind as he looked over the machine. That is until I noticed Donna waving her hand in front of her face as if too cool herself.

"Oh. My. Gosh," she mouthed.

I agreed with her silent, yet exaggeratedly expressive outburst. We exchanged a collective biting of our bottom lips and pretended to carry on with other duties, all the while sneaking glances at his beautiful body. I was taught better than to treat a man like a piece of meat, but I couldn't help it. Men like Joseph didn't come along every day, nor did they often award us with opportune moments of unabashed ogling. I told myself that one day he would move on to other more important escapades and our platonic relationship would fall by the wayside. I was only gorging my undue fill of him while I had the chance.

Donna slithered up next to me at the cash register. "Where did you find *this* guy?" she whispered as she wiped the already clean counter.

I glimpsed over my shoulder in Joseph's direction, hoping he hadn't heard her nosy inquiry. He had already unscrewed the back portion of the machine and was checking the hoses and the other intricate parts of the pesky contraption's innards. "Like I told you before, he's my neighbor."

"I wanna live where you live," she replied enthusiastically. "Course, I'd be purposefully running out of condiments just so I could knock on his door every night. Is he dating anyone?"

I looked at her curiously. Donna never had much to say to me in the past given the age gap between us. She was in her third year of college and I was in my early thirties, not to mention that I was her employer. But today, I didn't think I could shut her up if I duct taped her mouth closed.

I noticed the peculiar twinkle in her eye as she waited to hear about Joseph's availability. I was not a jealous person by nature, but something inside me hatched and chipped away my fragile exterior, daring to emerge. An inherent fem fatale-like possessiveness urged me to claim Joseph for myself. I cleared my throat and suppressed my sinister compulsions. I would not be guided down a gluttonous path. Though it pained me to remember his timely fall out with Caroline, I spoke the truth. "No, he's not dating anyone."

Donna sucked in a sharp breath and moved closer. "You think he'd go out with me?"

Her frank question took me by surprise. I didn't know Donna well enough to know if she was the type of girl Joseph went for. On the flip side, I didn't know Joseph well enough to know what kind of woman he desired. I would have liked to say he was into me, but as I checked Joseph's progress, he seemed more enrapt by the internal workings of my coffee machine than listening to two hormonal women swooning over him. "I have no idea, Donna. You'd have to ask him."

She apprehended my wrists as if we'd been best friends for years. "You think so? Oh, my gosh, I can't. What would I say to him? He'd probably say no anyway, wouldn't he?"

She was too busy casting quick covert glances toward Joseph to notice my distress. The longer she held on to me, the more I felt my blood thickening in my veins. I pulled away and stepped back, forcing an amiable smile to hide my distaste.

The door of the café swung open, interrupting my ridiculous plot to fire her because of some mysteriously missing bills from the register. What can I say? I'm human. I turned away. "I'm going to check on a few things in my office. Call me if you need help," I said, gesturing toward the three new patrons.

I think Donna took the hint that I was not ready to be her BFF on such short notice. I walked past Joseph and around the corner to my small office, the sound of Donna's disappointment radiating from her practiced "Welcome to I Like You a Latte" greeting. It was a sweet song in my ears.

I dropped into my chair and studied the large calendar staring me down. Donna's name, written on every Saturday and Sunday square, jumped out at me, taunting me. Like the envious overlooked woman, I itched to take a bold Sharpie marker and black out her name in ebony scribbles. If that were not enough, I wanted to paint over the hideous, unforgiving scrawls with many layers of Wite-Out to hide my sinister jealousy.

I yanked open the middle drawer of the desk, just to check whether those weapons of choice were available to me, but slammed it shut before I did something foolish. I rolled my eyes and scolded myself for thinking such childish things. If anything, Donna could sue me for discrimination, if I'd removed her from the schedule without a viable reason. And she'd win. I'd lose everything over coveting a man who wasn't even mine to covet.

I drilled my palms into my eye sockets and shook off all thoughts of Donna and Joseph. Instead, I flipped the page of the calendar and set my sights on something more productive. I barely had time to go over next month's schedule when a tentative tapping brought my attention to the door. Joseph stood leaning against the frame, his arms crossed at his chest and a smug look on his face.

"You fixed it?"

I didn't mean to sound surprised. It wasn't that I didn't think Joseph *could* fix the espresso machine. I just didn't think he'd have the right tools for the job. Even as I sat there, I couldn't imagine one common thing between leaky barn roofs and broken coffee machines.

"Yeah, it was just a clogged water filter."

"And you had one of those in your trusty, rusty toolbox?"

He laughed aloud, loud enough for Donna and the rest of the place to hear. My heart soared.

"I actually found a spare in the cabinet below the machine. I think the guy who was here the last time left you an extra on purpose, so he wouldn't have to miss another one of his daughter's soccer games to fix it."

"Smart man."

"No," Joseph amended, shutting the door. He strolled into my office and plopped his cute, little behind on the edge of my desk. "I'm the smart man who found it and installed it, even under the pressure of your employee's constant gaping. She really needs to learn the art of nonchalance."

Heat infused my cheeks. "I am so sorry. I'll say something to her."

Joseph waved it off. "Don't even worry about it. She's young. She's got the rest of her college years to smarten up." He clasped his hands together and grabbed his knee, hiking it up. His face scrunched in an odd sort of way. "Did you put her up to asking me out?"

My mouth fell open. "She asked you out?"

"Mm-hmm."

"Wow, she doesn't waste any time." I leaned back in my chair, inwardly wishing I had that kind of courage.

"Aren't you the least bit curious if I accepted?"

Curious didn't come close. Chomping at the bit was closer to what I felt, though a woman of my age would never give him the satisfaction. I picked up a pen, idly playing with it as I spoke. "Who you choose to date is your own business. Who am I to reprimand you for going out with a girl a decade younger than you?"

"So, you wouldn't approve."

"I didn't say that," I rectified. "I just think you need to remember that you don't have to rebound on every girl who comes along. You can have any woman of your choosing, and jumping into the dating scene again with a college girl who's barely over the legal drinking age is not one of your wiser decisions."

Joseph seemed to be enjoying himself, although I couldn't say I harvested much amusement from the matter.

"Don't worry. I let her down easy. I told her I was flattered with the offer, but I was too old for her. And that I had the hots for you."

The pen fell to the floor and my heart jumped in my throat. I had no way of knowing if he meant what he said or was just playing around. I dared him to come clean despite the meekness of my voice. "You didn't..."

He leaned across the desk, daring me back. "What if I did?"

I closed my eyes, imagining how difficult it now was going to be to work under the same roof with the girl. I heard the laughter in his voice and realized the joke was on me. I stiffened my chin. "No, really, what did you say to her?"

He stared at me for a moment, as if taking pleasure in my angst. "I told her that the guy who was checking her out as she filled his order was better suited for her."

"And she was okay with that?"

"Over the years, I've learned that desperate girls on the prowl have the attention span of gnats and will jump at anything that takes a second look at them. I bet if you asked Donna right now, she'd not be able to tell you my name, even though you introduced us. Now, you on the other hand, could probably list the number of men versus women patrons in the shop and what each is wearing."

"Is that so?" I asked, wondering if that was his idea of a compliment.

"Tell me I'm wrong," he stated, crossing his arms. "Better yet, I'd put money on the fact that you can tell me what I was wearing the first time we met."

The image of Joseph in a towel, bare-chested and delightfully muscled, came to mind. "Anyone who's not legally blind would remember what you were wearing. I don't think that counts."

"Fair enough. How about the second time we met?"

I sighed and looked toward the ceiling, drawing to mind that same evening when I came home from the grocery with my arms full. "You had on a tie and dress slacks. The tie was blue with navy stripes, the pants were khaki, and your shoes were shiny black like they were recently polished."

"See? I knew you're the type to take notice of these things."

"All right, smarty pants, what was I wearing?"

"Which time are we talking about?"

I crossed my arms, thinking he'd never get this right no matter which one I chose. Knowing he'd been too caught up in Caroline leaving him that one fateful morning, I decided on the most unlikely moment he'd recall his own hand in front of his face. "The first time we met."

Joseph pretended to think, scratching his head for theatrical purposes. "You were…not in a towel. Although that would have been nice to see."

My face probably flushed ten shades of red due to his charming little compliment. I bit my lip, hiding my absurd reaction over his flattery and waited for him to try again.

"You were dressed in jeans, winter boots trimmed in brown fur, a matching *Land's End* down parka, black leather gloves, and a red scarf. I'm going with handmade by your grandmother."

I stood in awe. My brow rose to heights beyond my hairline, if that were possible. I could not believe he rattled off what I had worn that day and with so much detail. Simply put, he defied the laws of the virile man-code. "How in the world did you remember all that?"

"I shall not reveal my secrets," he said, hand over his heart. "Come on, let's get out of here."

Still stunned, I followed Joseph out of the office and noticed the warm smile on Donna's face as she locked eyes with him. He stealthily pointed toward a table of three men chatting it up about tonight's football game and gave a thumb's up. She mouthed "thank you" and shimmied around the counter to clean the nearest table and work her magic. Judging by the way she innocently tossed her long blond hair off her shoulder as she tidied up, I knew she'd have a lock on a future date before her shift ended. She was that good.

"You ready?" Joseph asked, handing me my coat and gloves. Another one of his irrepressible grins lit up his face. I then realized he was not the overly perceptive man he'd made himself out to be. I wore the same ensemble of winter apparel this morning as the first day we'd met.

I shook my head, feeling the fool. "You think you're so clever, don't you?"

"Hey, I remembered your red scarf, didn't I? You're not wearing that today. Surely, that should count for something?"

"I don't think so." I slipped my arms in the sleeves and shrugged into my coat.

He put on his coat as well, but stopped to fasten mine. "Just answer me this," he said shooing my hands away and sliding the zipper up my midline. "Did your grandmother crochet your red scarf?"

Quoting him verbatim, I gave a satisfied smile. "I shall not reveal my secrets."

He tipped his head back in laughter. "She did and you know it."

Chapter Twelve

Riding with Joseph to his sister's house was the most fun I'd had in years. He talked on and on about his younger days and the typical, boyish trouble he'd gotten himself into on the family farm. From what I gathered, he had a memorable childhood filled with as many inexhaustible adventures as a curious country boy could find.

Now all grown up, I imagined the daring, exploratory lad had not left him completely. Just listening to the way he described the labyrinth of trails winding through his parents' woods, and the day he and his buddies built a tree house with his father's 'borrowed' tools they never returned, was proof he'd do it all over again.

I never had a family farm to while away my time on or a lake in the back forty to swim in on a hot July afternoon. We lived in the urban areas of Kentucky where the closest thing to a farm was Trauth Dairy in Newport.

As Joseph drove further south on I-75 and onto I-64, the panorama of fast food restaurants, gas stations, and franchised hotels drifted away. The view of concrete streets and traffic lights slowly faded into a scenic landscape of rolling meadows, black board fences, and fancy Thoroughbred horses.

From there, until we pulled into his sister's drive, I sat mesmerized by the beauty of the land. The trees had lost most of their leaves to the harsh approaching winds, but I could envision a paradise of red, orange, and gold blazing between lush green meadows and blue skies on picturesque autumn days.

Joseph dropped gears as we turned the bend and drove beneath a huge, rusty, wrought iron sign proudly welcoming me to *Pride & Joy Farm*. After descending a hill and turning another crook in the road, he slowed to a halt and killed the engine. For the first time since we left the expressway, I gazed at my handsome driver.

"This is where your sister lives?"

Joseph smiled as he took in the two-story farmhouse and the impressive tan and black barn with symmetrical gables in the distance. He released a long breath. "Yeah. This is it." He pointed beyond the barn to the outlying crop of hills and trees. "And that's my parents' place. On the other side of that is my other sister's farm, but she's not usually in town. She travels the States in search of rescue mustangs."

I took in the impressive scenery, combing the vast estate with astonished eyes. "How could you leave such a grand place to live in downtown Cincinnati?"

"Caroline," he replied.

"What?" At first, I thought he called me by the wrong name.

He opened the door of his truck and shut it with a hard slam. As he walked around the front of the vehicle, I noticed the deep furrows in his brow. He opened my door for me and divulged the rest of the details. "Caroline had me move so I could be closer to her. She hated driving an hour and a half to see me. Said it was too far and inconvenient for her busy schedule. Like the sucker I am, I gave into her petty whims and thought it would be better for our relationship."

He let out a scoff, displaying his final take on the matter.

"I'm sorry, I shouldn't have pried."

"It's all right."

His truck was a large Ford diesel, so hopping out of the cab became more like BASE jumping. He steadied me as soon as my feet hit the blacktop. I tried to ignore the thrilling sensation of his strong hands grasping my arms, albeit covered by a thick down coat. But no way could I disregard the slightest touch given by Joseph. Every contact he made with me sent my heart skyrocketing toward the moon.

"I don't know about you, but I'm starving. That chronic temperamental espresso machine of yours depleted all my gumption for the day. Let's get some grub first," he suggested, "and then we can attack the barn full force."

I followed him up the sidewalk to the house and was floored when he didn't even knock. I wasn't used to the *mi casa es su casa* approach. My family was much more formal. We always called before visiting and knocked when we arrived.

He entered the home, as if he lived there, gave a shout for his sister, who didn't answer back, and continued his trek to the kitchen. Immediately, he opened the refrigerator door and began searching for something to eat. "What do you like? Turkey? Bologna? There's not much here. Look's like she's got some fried chicken…I could heat that up for us."

I suddenly felt like I was imposing. "I'm fine. I don't need to eat your sister's food."

His eyes landed hard on mine. "Don't hand me that crap. I know about your sugar issues. You're eating something and that's final. I'm not going to get you up on a barn roof, so you can pass out on me and plummet to your death. My sister would kill me."

"You're *giving* me a reason to kill you now, Joey?"

From behind the refrigerator door, a tall brunette in jeans, flannel shirt, and chaps walked into the kitchen. She resembled Joseph in many ways, but looked nothing like a man. She was all feminine—petite waist, small hands, and noticeable curves. But the unmistakable hardness in her eyes proved she was not a woman to mess with. I imagined she and Joseph often went round and round as children.

"Don't call me that," Joseph complained, shutting the fridge door. "You know I hate that name."

She glanced my way and smiled. I assumed the pleasant welcome was not for cordial reasons, but because she took pleasure in making her little brother squirm in front of a female guest.

"Well, Joseph, it's good to see you finally came to your senses and got rid of Caroline." She held out her hand, and when I accepted, she gripped it like a man and gave one hard pump. "I'm Candace. And you are?"

"Jamie," I offered. She seemed very delighted to meet me, although I think it stemmed from Joseph bringing someone else besides Caroline to her place.

"How long you two been dating?" Candace inquired, glancing between us.

For poor Joseph's sake, I felt compelled to speak right away. "Oh, we're not dating." I caught sight of him closing his eyes in embarrassment. "We're just friends."

Candace nodded, though she didn't look convinced. "Right."

Joseph cleared his throat and changed the subject. "I'm

sorry my sister doesn't seem to have much to eat. As you can tell, she's got plenty to munch on with her big fat foot in her mouth."

Candace slapped the back of her brother's head and the unruly lock I'd grown fond of fell into his eye. "He's just bitter because he let a woman emasculate him, and he's yet to grow a pair after all these years."

"Unlike you who runs off every guy who's even remotely interested in you, with his tail tucked between his legs," Joseph added, raking his hair back into place.

"I can't help that I'm choosier than you." Candace shot me a quick apologetic look. "No offense."

I grinned at her. "None taken."

"Don't you have something to do?" Joseph pleaded earnestly.

I couldn't look at them with a straight face anymore. The sibling rivalry between them, even at their age, was beyond comical. I never had that with my sister because of our age difference. She moved out of the house before any kind of rivalry could exist.

"So, what did Joey bribe you with to get you to come out here?" Candace asked, leaning against the counter.

"He didn't bribe me with anything," I confessed, keeping a close eye on his reactions. "I wanted to come."

Joseph held my gaze as he crossed his arms. "I had to fix your espresso machine first before you accepted."

"Well," I said, biting my lip nervously. "Had it not needed fixing in the first place, I wouldn't have gotten the offer. I have a nasty bruise on my leg to prove it."

"Are you saying if I asked you to come with me, you would have?"

"Sure, why wouldn't I?"

We seemed to have forgotten about Candace being in the room, for neither of us could take our eyes off each other. I felt trapped in his gaze, the intensity of his private thoughts speaking volumes. I was not a mind reader, but I think I made the man happy by being here with him. My presence at his sister's farm, with no strings attached, seemed to mean more to him than anything I could have chosen to do with my day.

I wanted to let him know how much it meant for him to invite me, but something inside me told me it was better left unsaid. It was too soon to start divulging such emotions with Joseph, and I could imagine him tucking tail and running, just like Candace's boyfriends, the second I did.

"Okay…" Candace said, breaking up our quiet bonding moment. "I've got to get back to work. It was nice to meet you, Jamie." She patted me on the back as she crossed the kitchen. Before she exited, she shouted a warning over her shoulder. "Be careful on that roof today. It can be a slippery slope."

I wondered if her cautionary, cryptic words were for me, or if I was reading too much into them. I didn't have long to ponder. Joseph turned and dove into the refrigerator again. He reached in and selected the lunchmeat packages, cheese, and mayo.

"Bread's in the cabinet." He gestured toward the one behind me as he set the items on the counter.

I fetched the loaf, and together we made sandwiches. We didn't say much, but the occasional smiles and glances continued as we filled our stomachs. About half an hour later, we made our way to the barn.

The journey to the building was longer than I expected. From his truck, everything looked extraordinary, and I suppose actual distances didn't register then. My eyes remained on the ground, and eventually our pace fell into step with each other's. I felt like the band members from the iconic sixties slapstick comedy TV show, *The Monkees*, though our arms were not intertwined. Joseph realized our synchronized stride as well and gave a little chuckle.

Despite the smile on his face, he looked as though he was plagued with heavy thoughts.

"Are you all right?" I asked, shielding my eyes from the glaring sun as I looked up at him.

"Yeah," he played off. "I'm fine. But I should probably apologize for my sister. She's kind of a hard nose and forgets that some of us have feelings. I hope she didn't make you feel uncomfortable."

"No, not at all. She's funny actually."

Joseph's brow rose. "You're joking, right?"

"Look, you don't have to coddle me because your sister brought up Caroline. I know she was a big part of your life, and, whether your family agreed with that relationship or not, she was your friend. I get that. I hope you realize I'm not trying to step into her place by being with you."

"Your shoes are too big anyway."

"What?" I looked down at my size six feet. "Caroline's feet are smaller than mine? That's impossible. She's almost as tall as you."

Joseph averted his eyes and searched the open sky. "Don't be so literal, Jamie. That's not what I meant."

"What did you mean then?"

Joseph stopped walking and blocked my forward motion with his arm. He turned his entire body to face me, hands on his hips. He took a deep breath and held it, words failing him. The color of the bright, cerulean sky behind him was no match for the vivid swirls of blue dancing in his eyes. They nearly entranced me as he stood there fighting the urge to express his mind.

I saw his Adam's apple bob, and I almost believed he was about to say 'never mind.' Then he took another long breath of courage and spoke. "If Caroline tried to stand in your shoes, Jamie, she would fail to fill them. You are so much bigger than she could hope to be. And I'm not talking bone structure here. I'm talking about good old-fashioned charisma, character, and kindness. You have all those qualities and more, and not because you're trying. It's just the way you are…what's inside you."

He glanced at his feet, giving me a small moment of reprieve from his dazzling eyes. I couldn't begin to predict the next words that would fall from his lips or the sight of welled-up tears threatening to fall when he looked back up at me. My heart melted to see such emotion in Joseph. I treasured it. But honestly, I had no idea how to deal with the sudden outpouring.

"I didn't know I needed someone like you," he began slowly, "until you showed up. I was perfectly fine being me. The playboy without a heart. Caroline's accused me so many times of not having one, I began to think she was right. Then you came along, and…"

"And?"

His voice grew quiet. "And…something stirred inside me. When I saw you that morning, in the hall, you made me forget all about the darkness in my world. And trust me," he whispered, striking his chest with a fist, "there's so much in here…you don't even know."

I watched as he came to terms with himself for sharing that little bit of information. He looked as if he were trying to convince himself that I could be trusted with the rest of his innermost feelings. I wanted to assure him that he could. Under normal circumstances, despite my diminutive physique, I could be a solid rock upon which to stand. But honestly, the ground beneath my own feet was shifting, and I couldn't gain a firm stance for myself, let alone Joseph.

He shuffled his boots on the pavement. "You probably wouldn't understand, but lately I've had a hard time. I've been in a fog, and I can't seem to find the joy in life. I-I've just been running on autopilot. You know, the-world-must-go-on kind of mentality. And then I met you."

He laughed at himself, as if he couldn't believe what was coming out of him. "Short of sounding like a cheesy, hopeless romantic...you were like a ray of sunshine. And for the first time in a long time, I actually felt the warmth of someone's smile. Your smile."

He fidgeted some more. "I don't wanna lose that feeling. And I certainly don't want to lose you." He hung his head and stroked the heart tattoo on his wrist. "Like everyone else I ever cared about."

Chapter Thirteen

I trembled like the lone leaf on a tree, enduring the brunt force of Joseph's words. At any moment, depending on the might of the next gust, I felt like I would be bowled over and swept away. My mind had already gotten caught up in the whirlwind. The chaotic circulation of my thoughts was too random for my brain to select just one and process it. If I tried to speak, I knew I'd only end up looking the fool.

Joseph continued to stare at his wrist, tracing the script-like initials inked on his skin. I had never suffered the loss of a sibling, or anyone in my immediate family, so I had no inkling of what he was going through or what I could say to comfort him. All I knew was I hated this awkward silence.

I was certain this wasn't the first time he'd dealt with someone being uncomfortable in this situation. I imagined he had gotten that a lot at the funeral. But the last thing I wanted to be was the typical individual who tried to smooth things over with misguided words and impersonal encouragement.

I reached out and touched his hand. His skin was warm against mine. He lifted his eyes to me, the pain and weariness of his long-term grief etched in the tiny lines around them. I prepared to say something—what exactly I had no idea—but he dropped his arms to his side and retreated from my touch.

"Can you give me a sec?"

I had no time to answer. He had already removed himself from the piss-poor effort on my part and made a beeline for his truck parked in front of the house. He had plenty of time to gather his wits and shake off the blues. When he returned with his toolbox, he feigned a smile.

"Before you say anything," he said, squeezing his eyes shut and sighing. "I just want to say I don't tell everyone about...this. I just...I want you to know I'm telling you the truth."

"I know that, Joseph," I agreed, rocking back on my heels. "You've always spoke the truth, and that's one of the many things I like about you. I'm glad you felt comfortable enough to share your feelings with me. I'm honored, and you can rest assured that it's safely tucked away in here."

After patting my chest, I clutched my trembling hands together. I had more to say and needed to find a way to speak as forthcoming as Joseph had. I brought to mind the courage he had found moments before he escaped to his truck and seized the proverbial bull by the horns. "You're not going to lose me, Joseph. No matter what happens, I'll never stop being your friend."

This time, the smile that lighted his face was sincere and genuine. I'd brought joy to him with a few simple words, words I meant and would uphold. He needed me. Strangely enough, I needed him too. Like him, I didn't know it until we met.

Life had a funny way of reminding a person of what was needed. I thought I was the self-sufficient woman and coffee-house owner who didn't need a shoulder to lean on. I had gained all I had without the help of anyone. What I didn't realize until now was that the fruits of my labor were all for nothing.

What good were a successful business, a growing bank account, and a promising future if I had no one to share it with? I wasn't thinking about marriage or a committed lovers' relationship. I was ruminating over the importance of companionship and an honest camaraderie with someone I could trust.

I'd never before felt this way about any man. To me, men were nothing but lying, cheating, unreliable SOBs who sucked us in with their charm, weaseled their way into our hearts, and tore it out of our chest at a moment's notice with no regret.

Joseph was not like that. Sure, I'd said that about several hopeful suitors in my past, but this time I knew differently. He was a man who knew what it meant to be forsaken. He knew what it felt like to be helplessly sunk in bottomless sorrow. He knew the pain of loss and grief and would never put someone else through the same anguish. No matter what Caroline had claimed, Joseph had the biggest heart of any man I'd ever known.

My beliefs about Joseph were immediately confirmed the second he dropped his toolbox to the ground and wrapped me in his strong arms. The strength of his solid embrace knocked the wind from my lungs. I saw stars, fireworks, and lightening streaks behind my eyelids. My heart pounded against the boom of my bubbling emotions. I had imagined so many times what his hugs would feel like, yet the real thing was so much more. It was safe. A sanctuary. Heaven.

I relished this wonderful moment, taking in every splendid sensation of his hand climbing up the back of my neck and splaying into my hair as he pulled me tighter against him. His fingertips gently cradled my head and I took a deep breath, memorizing his intoxicatingly masculine scent. Though blanketed with a thick winter coat, the heady aroma of his warm skin permeated around me. Thick Carhartt canvas never smelled so good.

Tentatively, Joseph released me. His face was alight with happiness and appreciation. Together, we overcame a huge obstacle, and it seemed we were no worse for wear.

He cleared his throat and clasped his hands together. "Okay," he muttered, taking another step back.

Amazingly, I was grateful for the space as much as he. Had he held me any longer, I might have sequestered him from his duties and stowed him away from the rest of the world with no remorse.

I was so screwed. I had promised myself I'd never fall for another man ever again and here I was considering the idea of handing myself to Joseph on a platter.

"As much as I hate to say this," he pointed over his shoulder, "that barn is screaming my name."

"Right. I hear it too. Or maybe it's Candace," I searched for her in the fields, "groaning in agony from our little public display of affection."

Joseph glanced around the farm with a devious grin. "I don't care. Let her groan. She'll get over it. Besides," he said, cocking his head to the side. "I think she'd like you to stick around."

"You think?"

Joseph blew out a sardonic breath and bent to retrieve his toolbox. "Trust me, if she didn't want you around me, you'd know it. There's one thing about Candace, she's more honest than I am."

"Should I take that as a fair warning?"

His hearty laughter carried in the breeze, whisking

through my hair. "Oh, yeah."

Chapter Fourteen

In the course of a few hours, I learned many important life lessons. Don't look down once atop a two-story barn roof. Don't assume the gutter will catch anything other than rain. (We lost many screws to this principle—or to be more precise, I lost them.) And don't forget that cordless drills slide down a six-twelve pitch metal roof rather quickly.

What I had put Joseph through today, would have made the typical man blow a gasket. A two-hour job ended up taking twice as long because I was not accustomed to manual labor twenty feet in the air. Joseph didn't seem to mind. In fact, it was the most I'd ever heard him laugh.

Don't get me wrong. I received my share of I-can't-believe-you-just-did-that kind of cringes from him, especially when I accidentally bumped the ladder with my foot and it slid sideways down the face of the gutter until it crashed to the ground. However, I was fortunate that Joseph had a soft spot for my expression of apologetic desperation. "Timmm-ber" was my timid attempt to make light of the hefty mistake.

Once we replaced the old ring-shank nails with modern rubber washers and hex-head screws, and Candace came to rescue us from our lofty prison on the tin roof, Joseph whisked me away into the thick of his family's pine tree forest. We followed a narrow dirt path, which Joseph explained was a worn deer path, until it opened up to a recently-plowed hay field and a massive crystalline lake sparkling in the sunlight.

We walked its perimeter for a while, discussing the things we enjoyed most as kids. My stories were not as interesting as Joseph's, and I found myself enthralled with his memories of the days on this very lake.

"So, your parents used to own this part of the farm too?"

"It was one huge plantation until they divvied up parcels for each of us kids. When I moved to Cinci, I sold my piece of property to my sister, Miranda, the one who rescues wild mustangs. Dad wasn't all that happy about it, since I was his only son, but she needed it more than I did. At least, I kept it in the family. Anyway, this lake was my favorite place as a kid. If I still owned my land, it would butt up against Candace's on the west side."

I looked out over the water and watched the dried-up cattails sway in the breeze. I pitied Joseph that he'd given up his piece of heaven for someone as unworthy as Caroline. The more I found out about her, the more I resented what she'd done to him. He didn't deserve it, and she definitely didn't deserve his loyal friendship. If wishes could come true, I'd wished he had never met her.

As much as I could muster, I pushed away my dark thoughts of Caroline and returned to Joseph's lovely haven he chose to share with me. "I can see why you liked this place so much."

Joseph found my hand and dragged me down toward the east side of the lake. "Come on. I want to show you something."

I ran with him, having no idea what could be so important. The cool wind rushed past me in our exuberant jog, but all I could feel was the warmth of Joseph's grasp. The thrill of his enthusiasm radiated through me, and I realized at that very moment how much I appreciated the strength of a working man's hands.

I had never dated a guy who made an honest living from manual labor. Most of the men I attracted were paper-pushers, IT guys, or lazy I'll-just-let-you-bring-home-the-bacon losers. There was much to be said about the responsible men of this decade who still aspired to support themselves by the sweat of their brow and not by the handouts of a sucker girlfriend.

As I continued to savor the feel of Joseph's calloused hand, we finally stopped at the base of an age-old tree at the edge of the lake. Its trunk was about as wide as I was tall with rungs of weathered wood planks nailed up its face. Joseph looked up and reached for the lowest branch.

"Come on," he urged, bracing his foot on the first step. He hoisted himself onto the limb and continued to climb.

I glanced up at the dizzying height of the tree and saw the decrepit, makeshift, childhood tree house balanced on a limb three branches up. "You've got to be kidding. I can't get up there."

Joseph glanced down after he successfully secured himself in the V of the next bough. "Sure you can. If you can hang out on a twenty-foot high barn roof, you can climb a tree."

"There's a difference," I said, crossing my arms in defiance.

"How so?"

"The surface area of a roof, no matter how high, is considerably larger than the bottom-most branch of this tree. You do remember the many things that fell from the roof, don't you? If you haven't realized, I'm a bit of a klutz." I shifted the weight of my body on my other foot for emphasis. "No way am I getting up there."

Joseph outstretched his hand to me. "I won't let you fall. Promise."

The pledge he made, on top of the sincerity in his voice that he wouldn't let me descend to my demise, had me agreeing to this ridiculous feat in less than a flash. Although my skittish heart pounded in my chest, I huffed away my fears in one hasty sigh and prepared to make my ascent.

"Grab hold of that limb with your right hand," Joseph instructed, "and put your left foot on the rung. At the count of three, you're going to push up and grab my forearm."

I gave him one last look of trepidation, hoping he'd say to forget it. Evidently, I didn't sell it well enough. "Trust me" was his response.

Putting all my faith in Joseph's powerful grip and his strapping body wedged in the fork of the tree, I counted aloud and reached as high as I could for his arm on 'three.' He groaned and growled as he tugged me higher.

"Use your feet," he gritted through his clenched jaw, his face turning red.

As he ordered, I stepped from plank to plank until I reached the height of his chest.

"The limb beside you. Use it," he said in a labored, breathless voice. Taking hold of the branch allowed for the dead weight of my body to release the strain on his. We had further to go, but at least I stood atop the first branch.

"You okay?" he asked, panting.

Still shaking like a leaf, I nodded an affirmative.

"The next part is easier since the limbs are closer," he

reassured. "You just have to reach and hold tight to me, once I lug you across. Balance is everything, got it?"

Balance. Right. I wanted to laugh. If he knew the catastrophe I had caused in ballet school when I was ten, he wouldn't be risking his life just to get me into a warped, childhood camp that had seen better days.

"Are you sure it's safe?" I asked, clutching the trunk with the fervor of a stubborn two-year old and her security blanket.

"You can do this." He patted my tensed arm and tilted his head in the most adoring fashion. That cursed lock of hair fell across his brow, and I was smitten. "Just lunge for me, and I'll catch you."

Under the direction of Joseph's practiced tree-climbing skills, I did exactly as he said and sprang from my limb to his. My arms snaked around his torso like a boa constrictor, and I screamed as we teetered together in a tight embrace. I saw the ground, who knows how many feet down, and shut my eyes.

I felt one powerful arm across my back, and I assumed he had his other anchored firmly around the girth of the trunk. After a few more grunts from the male chest into which I had resorted to burying my face, the struggle to stay on the limb ceased. I slowly opened my eyes and peeled my cheeks off the safety of his coat.

Joseph looked at me with pride, his face smeared with a handsome roguish grin. "Piece of cake."

With my heart in my throat, I attempted to ascertain the height of my idiotic upward hike, but Joseph stopped me. His palm cupped my jaw in the most delicate manner, as if the bones of my face would break under his touch.

"Don't look down," he whispered. "Just keep your eyes

on me."

Awestruck by the indigo ring encircling the light fissures of blue irises, I was incapable of looking elsewhere. Long, midnight lashes fell on high cheekbones as his gaze lowered over my mouth. I absorbed the beauty of his face, his full, sensual lips outlined by a manly shadow of scruff. His mouth was the perfect medium for kissing.

Pressed against him, I swore I could feel the beating of his heart through the padding of our coats. I wondered if he could feel mine. I felt lightheaded, lethargic in his embrace as I waited for his next move.

Joseph let out a huge breath and withdrew his head. His arms loosened around me, and I felt the tenseness of his muscles relax. "We're almost there."

I blinked rapidly, trying to shake away the fog of our near-kiss moment. Disappointment racked my whole body, but I pulled as much contentment as I could from somewhere deep in my soul.

I tore my eyes away from his gorgeous face and geared myself up for the next hike up the tree to the nearby platform, sided with battered wood slats and a hanging rope ladder. The wind whipped against us at this height, but I felt hot and sweaty. I tugged at the zipped-up collar of my parka, overheating in its downy sheath.

"Go ahead," Joseph ushered, holding out his arm to steady me as I snagged the line dangling from the limb above my head. "I got you."

Reminding myself not to look down, I climbed the last steps to our destination with Joseph quickly following behind me. Frightened about the wood floor giving way beneath my weight, I waited for him to give me the go-ahead.

Sifting past me, he stepped out and seized the rickety railing. His eyes searched the distant horizon. I assumed he was letting it all come back to him—the memories, the emotions, the nostalgia. He glanced over his shoulder and extended his hand. "Care to join me?"

I put my hand in his and allowed him to lead me forward. I took in the breathtaking view of a colorful sunset hovering over pillows of far-off rolling hills. The lake mirrored a sheet of glass, reflecting the setting sun in its soft ripples. The treetops stood at attention, saluting a fine ending to another blissful day in their existence. I forgot all about the disenchantment I'd felt removing myself from Joseph's arms moments ago.

I looked at Joseph. The profile of his sharply chiseled face boasted one more added bonus amid the stunning picture. Feeling the weight of my stare, he looked at me. His smile beamed brighter than any noonday sun.

I drew in a huge breath, taking in the clean country air.

"This," he claimed proudly, "was where I spent most of my boyhood days. I used to pretend the treehouse was a pirate ship, sailing over tumultuous seas in search of buried treasure and bonny lasses."

A wave of courage rushed through me as I contemplated the nostalgic place to which Joseph brought me. "Did you bring any of your dates aboard?"

He chuckled and shook his head. "Nope. You're the first girl who's ever been up here."

"Caroline didn't chase you up this tree?"

He looked at me askance, as if I should know better. "I couldn't get her up here, if I'd paid her." He drifted back in thought. "I take that back. My sister came up here once. But only once."

"Candace?"

He shook his head.

I tried again. "Miranda?"

His eyes fell to his wrist. "Lindsey."

I reached out and gingerly touched his tattoo. "Are these her initials?" Technically, I knew the answer since I'd overheard his conversation with Caroline about her in the hall, but I played dumb.

He smiled and gave a tender nod of his head.

I suddenly recanted my castle-in-the-sky type wish about Caroline and decided it would be better to cast one in favor of sparing Joseph the loss of his sister.

"She was dating the high school jock, and, to impress him, she brought him here. She told me secretly that she wanted to win his heart by showing him that she was worthy of his affections. Between you and me, though," he sneered, "the guy was an ass."

I couldn't help but laugh with him. I watched him closely as he continued the story of his beloved sister.

"She got him to climb the tree and dared him to swing from that rope." He pointed to the thick-knotted strand of boat line hanging a few limbs up. My heart fell like a stone as I imagined when Joseph had climbed higher to secure it back in the day.

"Did he take the dare?"

"Like the typical beefcake who had more muscle than guts, he made up all kinds of excuses not to. Said he was putting his professional football career on the line and his coach would kill him."

The laugh lines in his face grew deeper as he told the rest.

"Lindsey finally realized he wasn't all that and a bag of

chips and left his sorry ass in the tree house. She commandeered the rope and swung out. She even finished with a perfect dive just for kicks. She and I swam the rest of the afternoon while Mr. Wannabee Brett Favre spent his day trying to figure out how to get out of the tree without falling and breaking his neck."

A bout of companionable silence overtook us. While Joseph probably used the moments to reminisce about his time with his deceased sister, I exhausted mine wondering how I could get him to tell me more about her.

Finally, I caved. "You don't speak of her much, do you?"

"Not if I don't have to." He idly spread a pile of leaves around with his boot. "It's hard for me to open up about stuff like that. It hurts to think about how she died."

I covered his hand with mine. "I don't need to know that stuff. I would never want you to have to relive that day over anyway. But…" I said, dragging out the word long enough for me to get my thoughts in line. "I'd love to hear about her. Only when you're ready though, Joseph. We have time."

He turned and captured me with a look I hadn't expected. His eyes pierced through me and tethered my heart to the hope of knowing all there was to know about his life, past and present.

He gestured toward the wood floor of the tree house and lowered himself in a cross-legged position. "Sit down. I'll tell you all about her."

I sat across from him, elated beyond words that he was about to let somebody in on his treasured memories—and that someone was me.

He inched closer and took my hand as he spoke.

"There was this one time when Lindsey came to see me when the band play at Bogart's. The place was packed, and she shows up right when…"

Chapter Fifteen

I stood in the hallway of my apartment complex, struggling to unlock my door. I had spent the entire day with an amazing man and was not looking forward to saying goodbye. When I woke up this morning, I had no idea I would fix a barn roof, climb a hundred-year-old tree, and watch the sun go down from the observation deck of an imaginary pirate ship. Joseph had breathed more life in me today than I'd ever drawn in during the course of my nonexistent life, and he made me laugh more than any clown who'd hit the Barnum and Bailey circuit.

My hands trembled as I fumbled with the few keys I had left on the ring. I then realized it was not the amount of keys that had kept me from inserting it into the slot, but Joseph. From the moment I met him, he made such an impression that I seemed to lose all hand-eye coordination.

"Here," Joseph offered, setting his toolbox down and taking over the task. "Let me help you." With deft hands, he slid the key into the lock, turned, and shoved the door open. He dangled the keys above my hand and dropped them into my palm with cool casualness. "There you go."

"Thanks."

I rocked on my heels, squeezing the jagged metal in my grasp. *Say something*, I demanded of myself.

"We still on for Friday?" Joseph asked, as if he possessed telepathic abilities.

"Friday?" I could barely get a grip on today, let alone try to recall plans five days from now.

He seemed to enjoy my sudden onset of dementia and jabbed his thumbs in his jean pockets. "Yesterday you accepted my offer to take you out this weekend. Changing your mind? 'Cause it's okay, if you are. I won't hold it against you."

The events of the weekend all rushed back to me. "I'm not changing my mind. I look forward to our date." As soon as I heard the term come out of my mouth, I backpedaled. "I mean…our evening together as friends."

"You don't have to dance around the word. I don't mind, if you call it a date. It is what it is. Some might even call today a date. Like your detail-greedy friend, Melissa, for instance."

I had to agree. Melissa would so call this a date, especially once she found out about the near-kiss moment in the tree house. "I guess we can't dodge that bullet, can we?"

He leaned against the wall and braced his arm on the doorframe. "Only if we tried. But I'm not so eager to move out of the way. Call me a thrill seeker."

I reckoned I'd be one too, if the thrill ride included Joseph in the seat next to me. I tucked a loose strand of hair behind my ear, trying to collect one ounce of bravado. All day, we never ceased to run out of conversation, but now when it mattered most, I couldn't come up with a single word to say to this guy.

I wanted to tell him how grateful I was he'd invited me to his sister's farm and taught me how to reinforce roof slats under a tin covering without replacing the whole thing. I wanted to thank him for sharing his precious memories of Lindsey with me. I wanted to praise him for assisting me out of the tree house without letting me fall to my death. I wanted to let him know how thoughtful he was to run through the drive-thru on the way home, making sure my sugar levels were up. I wanted to admit how much it meant to me just to be near him. But I couldn't verbalize any of those thoughts into sensible sentences, if my life depended on it.

All my life I've always been the one to ruin a good thing in the start of a relationship. Too many times I said things that I thought were considerate and somehow I gave the impression I was ready to plan a wedding. Guys freak out when you say things like "I had a really nice time. We should do this again" or "That was so sweet of you of you to think of me. You're definitely a keeper." Chickens.

So, yeah, it was my turn to be a chicken now. This was the beginning stages of something too good to be true, and I wasn't about to mess it up with stupid words of appreciation. He'd have to come out and ask me if I enjoyed myself before I'd ever burst that dam.

Joseph dropped the casual façade and pushed off the wall, stepping toward me. Out of instinct, I drew back. The opposite side of the doorframe halted my retreat and my keys clinked against the wood as my hands coupled behind me, bracing myself for his approach.

"I had a wonderful time today," he declared, his body inches from mine.

"Me too," I squeaked before I could clear my throat.

"Would you go back, if I asked you again?"

I tried to pretend the close proximity of his muscled body, even hidden behind a winter coat, didn't bother me. "Do I have to sabotage something at the coffee shop before you'll extend the invitation?"

He faked giving it thorough consideration. "I don't think that's necessary."

"Good." I heaved a fake sigh of relief. "It could get pretty costly for me otherwise."

Joseph ignored my joke and brought his hand up to my face, brushing the back of his fingertips against my cheek. His eyes traced a course across the contours of my brow, down the crooked edge of my nose, and over the curves of my lips.

"You'll have to forgive me, Jamie."

He slid his hand along the slant of my jaw and closed the distance between us with a final momentous step. His head dipped and the tip of his nose grazed mine.

I felt his warm breath skim across my skin. "F-forgive you for what?"

His eyelids lowered with shameless desire and the stringent muscle in his jaw clenched. "For wanting to do this all day."

By the time his confession fell from his lips, he had taken mine in a light, sensual kiss. His mouth pressed tenderly upon my upper lip while the prickle of his scruffy face tickled my chin. His lips were, by far, the softest I had ever felt, warm satiny flesh wreaking havoc on my pathetic, athirst body. I'd waited so long—yearned for a man as perfect as Joseph. Were we moving too fast?

He pulled me closer, wrapping his other arm around my back, securing me in the strength of his mighty embrace. His tongue caressed the sensitive plateau of my bottom lip, testing me, teasing me.

He tasted of sweet menthol from the lingering flavor of mints he'd offered on the way home. I then realized he had planned this all along, and I forgave him of the offense. Admittedly, I was guilty of the same.

As abruptly as the kiss began, he ended it, stepping out my arms before I was ready. Still shaking from the wonders of everything that made Joseph the man he was, I stared at him for what seemed like forever. And he let me.

"What was that for?" I asked, feeling my knees buckle.

"I'm just doing what my fortune told me to do." He pulled his wallet from his back pocket and slipped a tiny rectangular piece of paper from behind his credit card. Taking hold of my hand, he pressed it into my palm and closed my fingers over it. He brought my hands together, and raised them up to his lips. He pressed a long, blissful kiss on my knuckles and backed away.

"Goodnight, Jamie," he said, picking up the toolbox at his feet. With another devilish smile, he winked and strolled down the hall to his apartment door. "See you Friday."

As soon as his door closed behind him, I opened my hand and saw he had left me a fortune reading from a cookie with yesterday's date scribbled on the bottom. Thinking back, I had vaguely remembered him snatching a cookie from the table and tucking it into his pocket before he left. Our conversation filtered into my memory…

"What's it say?"

He shook his head. "It's my fortune, not yours."

"That's not fair."

"Some other time, maybe," he said, *tucking it into his jeans pocket. "You need to sleep."*

Realizing that Joseph had given me a chance to read the prediction he'd acquired the day before, I promptly flipped it over and read what was written.

At this very moment you can change the rest of your life.

I gasped, my eyes lifting to the distant door down the hallway. Joseph's door. The door to the most unpredictable, charming, and generous man I'd ever had the privilege to meet.

Coiling my fingers around the sentimental paper, I held fast to the anticipation of Friday evening, wondering what other fates we might embark upon. As I stepped into my apartment, something unusual happened—an optimistic thought entered my mind.

I stepped into my apartment, something unusual happened—an optimistic thought entered my mind.

This could be the start of something good.

The Road to Something Better

Chapter One

Mondays can take a toll on any responsible, taxpaying citizen. Rising before the crack of dawn to cater to most of them is especially trying when your hopping coffee shop is nestled in the midst of Fountain Square in bustling downtown Cincinnati. Everyone needs their double espressos and soy lattes to help them start their work week, and who am I to deny them?

But this Monday was different for me. No matter how outlandish the order, my fellow Cincinnatians were greeted with a cheery smile and unfailing courtesy, whether they liked it or not. Nothing could destroy my exuberant mood today.

I had just spent the entire weekend with my gorgeous neighbor, Joseph Scarbrough, and given that he'd topped off our time together with a cherry of a kiss upon our farewell, I was darn near giddy this morning. And I typically didn't do "giddy."

In the past, I had often worn my heart on my sleeve, which inevitably crushed it short of irreparable more times than I could count. Because of that, I'd perfected how to hide my emotions where men were concerned. But after last night, "giddy" was my new getup, and I wasn't hiding it under superhero-alter-ego-nerd glasses either. I was proudly displaying my Superwoman S-shield on my chest—though mine would be represented with a capital G for Giddy—with no desire to look for a phone booth.

Like the happy geek I was, I forged through the crazy Monday morning serving the best coffee in Cincinnati to my fellow, working-class citizens. I even tried to remedy the scowls of those who had clearly wakened on the wrong side of the bed by handing out free coffee certificates for their next visit. Nothing was going to spoil my day.

What made this Monday even better was being on the receiving end of Melissa's constant surveillance. While she was my best friend and the most loyal, dedicated employee I'd ever hired, she was also very perceptive. She could smell peculiar like a bloodhound on a coon's trail.

I sensed her hovering just inches behind my right shoulder. I ripped my last customer's receipt from the till and handed it to him along with my usual *Thank you a latte and please come back and see us* departure speech and turned around.

"All right, spill it, Jamie."

"Spill what?"

"Really?" she sighed and pulled me away from the counter. "You're working your hind end off with a smile no one could remove with a crowbar. What's up?" Her eyes lit up like a teenager who'd just opened a Christmas present and found the newest 5G iPhone complete with unlimited texting capability sitting in a bed of tissue paper. "You saw Joseph this weekend, didn't you?"

She left me no time to respond, cutting in with a squeal that could break glass.

"Oh, my gosh! I knew it! How did it happen? What was he wearing this time? Don't tell me a towel again, my heart can't take it. Did you invite him into your apartment? Oh, my gosh, you did! I can see it on your face. Did he spend the night?"

"Whoa, whoa, whoa, Annie Oakley. Before you start shooting off about things that never happened, how about you take a breath…and I'll tell you."

She pointed at me sternly. "Details. Not the *CliffsNotes* version."

"Oh, God forbid," I dished back, rolling my eyes. I let out a huge sigh and mentally ran through the multitude of events that had occurred this past weekend, not knowing where to start. Her face held such a glow of anticipation I hoped my tale would live up to her expectations. I mean my weekend with Joseph was momentous to me, but maybe she'd think it was pretty tame by her standards. However, since I knew she dated about as often as I did, I suspected she was about to live vicariously through me. Maybe she did the same thing in high school when her BFF then shared her sweet sixteen kiss with the high school jock. I never had a BFF in high school nor kissed a jock, but I've watched *Sixteen Candles* about a hundred times, so I had an idea.

"Well, I arrived home from work Friday with an armful of groceries, and I tried to unlock my door. Just as I was about to insert the key, Joseph suddenly showed up to help and scared the bejesus out of me. My bags ripped and produce went rolling down the hall. But Joseph…" I added, recalling Melissa's fetish for his attire, "now sporting khakis and a tie, took off after my oranges and collected them for me."

As if I'd just revealed some to-die-for details about a romantic kiss, she clutched her heart and closed her eyes. "Oh, what a gentleman. He's so dreamy."

Dreamy for chasing fruit down a hallway, huh? And I thought I was Captain Giddy.

"Go on...." she encouraged me, fanning herself. "This is good stuff."

If I didn't know better, I'd think Melissa might be on the verge of euphoric bliss. 'Course it had been ages for me, so I could've been wrong. "Anyway...we gathered up the last of the groceries, had a really awkward conversation about our plans for the evening, which I'm going to leave out for the sake of time and irrelevance, and then said our goodbyes."

"What? That was your big weekend with Mr. Terrycloth?"

"I'm not finished. And it's Scarbrough. Joseph Alexander Scarbrough." My voice took on a British intonation as I spoke his full name. I was proud of my improvisational accent, and if the Queen of England were here, she might have been impressed as well. Or not. All that mattered was that Melissa enjoyed it.

"Oh, that's even better than Maxwell," she gushed behind her steepled fingers. "Okay, now get to the good parts."

"I thought you wanted all the boring details?"

She flapped her hands back and forth in front of her so fast she resembled a hummingbird. "Not those boring details. I want details like you read in *Harlequin Blaze*. The stuff you'd leave out when talking to your mother." Her feet did a little jumpy move and she nailed the landing with a few happy claps. "Come on. Don't keep me waiting!"

I grasped her by her upper arms, made eye contact, and spoke in calm tones. "You *do* know we have decaf available."

"Quit stalling, Jamie."

Melissa knew me too well. "Fine." I then told her how he'd come home from his "guy's night out," passed out in the hall, and how I struggled to get him back on his feet and into his apartment. When I mentioned helping him into bed, I thought Melissa's head might explode. I'd never seen her get so stirred up hearing a simple story, which was by no means a steamy Harlequin romance. Secretly, I feared her reaction when I *did* get to the kissing part.

My tale continued with our Saturday coffee and conversation, Thai food, and fortune cookies. I purposely left out eavesdropping on Joseph and his former girlfriend, Caroline, and, of course, my sugar-plummeting episode as they were not my best moments. As I moved into Sunday with Joseph fixing the shop's faulty espresso machine, our mishaps upon his sister's barn roof, and my death-defying ascent into his childhood treehouse, I came to the part where he stood at my door and gazed into my eyes.

I must have been under the same magical spell as Melissa for neither of us heard the jingle of the bell over the coffee shop door. She took a step closer as my words had almost become a whisper. "And…." she encouraged softly.

"It was the most amazing—"

From behind me, an impatiently rude customer had cleared his throat and interrupted the best part of my epic saga. I wasn't one to return a customer's impoliteness, no matter how belligerent he proved to be, but I was about two seconds from a Poltergeist head spin.

Until I saw the shock on Melissa's face.

She swallowed hard, glanced wide-eyed at me, and back over my shoulder at the patron with a forced smile. "We'll be right with you."

"Take your time."

I closed my eyes. I knew that voice. I had heard that voice all night long in my dreams. I clenched my teeth. "Melissa…."

"Yes?" Her voice cracked under the pressure of that tiny word.

"Please tell me that is not Joseph."

Chapter Two

I picked up my bottle of Lipton Green Tea Citrus from the back counter with a shaky hand and downed half the liquid to soothe my suddenly parched gullet. I spun on my heel and pasted on my most congenial smile. "Hey, Joseph. How long have you been standing there?" I feared his answer but knew it all the same.

"Long enough to know the juiciest tidbits were about to unfold."

His smug little grin reached all the way to his eyes. The tiny crow's feet that parenthesized the sparkle in his baby blues made the casual confidence of his demeanor all the more alluring. That damn unruly hank of hair fell haphazardly into his right eye as he leaned on one elbow across the counter. Complacency looked divine on him.

"And you must be Melissa," he said, extending his right hand toward her.

"In the flesh." As she accepted his handshake, her nervousness disintegrated before my very eyes. "And you must be Joseph. Welcome to *I Like You A Latte*."

How does she do that? I am never that composed when meeting a hunky guy for the first time. While I stand shaking in my shoes, not having the faintest idea what to say to the man, *she* crosses the Rubicon without looking back.

Joseph leaned closer, as if he and Melissa were about to have a private conversation, despite the fact that I was looking right at them. "So, is Jamie the type to kiss and tell?"

"We'll never know now, will we?"

"Yeah, bad timing on my part. Sorry about that." He actually sounded sincere, though I knew it was a load of crap. "I suppose I'll call ahead next time."

I couldn't take this conversation anymore and butted myself up to the counter between them. "So, why are you here, Joseph?"

He straightened, a slight tinge of surprise highlighting his sharply chiseled face. "To make good on our deal. Don't tell me you forgot?"

Melissa elbowed me. "What deal? You didn't say anything about a deal?" She swiveled her head toward Joseph, directing her inquiry to him as if they were now best buds. "What's the secret pact?"

"It's not secret," Joseph and I said in unison.

Our eyes met and held at the uncanny sound of our simultaneous reply. His smile returned and his thumbs found a home in the front pocket of his jeans.

There it was again. That cool, casual confidence accompanied by the sexy slice of hair dangling across his eye. He'd either have to visit a barber soon, or I was going to lose my heart to him solely on the basis of his hair.

I'd never met a man who had fantastic hair and who was also a diehard heterosexual. With one look, you knew Joseph never stepped foot in a salon. His brows, though distinctly a pair, looked as virgin to hot wax as a kindergartner was to trigonometry. His nails were a manicurist's nightmare. But that's what made Joseph sexy. He was a man's man who was blessed with unadulterated sex appeal without the high dollar GQ price.

"All right, you two. One of you better come clean. I'm dying here."

Joseph cocked his brow and leaned against the counter toward me. "You weren't lying, were you? Melissa lives for details."

"Hey." Melissa was so cute when she feigned hurt feelings. Though I knew it was all a ruse, I decided to let her off the hook.

"It's not a big deal," I professed. "He just promised to let me ruin his coffee the next time he was in here, if I promised to use chopsticks the next time we ate Thai."

"Next times, huh?" Melissa held up her fist and the two of them automatically bumped knuckles as if they'd done it before. "Great way to score another future date, Mr. Terrycloth. You're good. Can I steal your technique?"

Joseph's face went white and mine turned a shade of red, I do believe. By the nickname she used, I knew Joseph was wrapping his head around the fact that I spilled the beans on his half-naked breakup with Caroline in the hall last week.

"Thanks, Benedict," I said, playfully shoving her aside. "That will be all."

Oops, was all I heard from behind me as Melissa began organizing the various syrups and cup lids that littered the back counter.

"So, you *do* kiss and tell," he teased.

Evidently, being slapped in the face with the true nature of women imparting secrets gave Joseph a strange sense of pleasure. I changed the subject at once. "How can I ruin your coffee today, sir?"

"Well, let's see…" He pretended to scan the many blends of coffees and lattes. The way he lifted his chin and narrowed his eyes on the banner behind me sent a thrill rippling through my tummy. I keyed into every little gesture he made. But I had to get a grip. I was too old to be acting this immature.

"So many choices," he muttered, breaking me from my reverie. "I guess I'll just have what you like. I think it's called Sugar Coma with extra whipped cream?"

"Coming right up."

I left the proverbial hot seat of being in Joseph's presence and began making the best cup of coffee he'd ever have. Melissa, like I expected, slithered up next to me.

"I'm so sorry. It just came out."

Her whispered apology made me smile. There was no way I could ever hold her indiscretion against her. I knew she meant no harm. "Chill out. He'll get over it."

"But what if I spoiled a *next time* for you?"

I snorted. "Trust me, he's not that insecure. He grew up with three sisters, so I'm sure he's used to *girl talk*."

I reached for a lid to cover the mountain of whipped cream I sprayed atop the rich-brown liquid and changed my mind. Joseph wasn't used to drinking coffee with cream and would most likely obtain a small dollop on the tip of his nose without his knowledge. I'd seen it many times from first-time buyers and it never ceased to be funny. He had no qualms about embarrassing me in my comfort zone, so why not reciprocate the favor?

I returned to the register and handed him his cup of heaven. "Heading off to work?"

He took his first sip with tentative lips. Upon testing the temperature, he tipped the cup further and drank one hefty gulp. Licking his lips, he smiled. "Not bad, Jamie. I could get used to this." He took another generous swallow and nodded his head, examining the cream that had already begun to melt in his cardboard cup. "Yeah, I'm headed to work now. What time do you get off?"

I pretended not to notice the bead of white resting on his nose. I purposely looked away so my grin didn't come bursting through. I wiped the counter with a dishrag and faked the busy work I had ahead of me. "Hopefully, I should be out of here by seven. Why?"

"Just wondering. Thought maybe you'd like to catch a movie?"

"A movie?"

"Yeah, why not? You like chick flicks?"

My brows lifted in bewilderment. "Do you?"

"The occasional."

My mind fast-forwarded to the two of us watching some guy meets girl, guy breaks girl heart, girl forgives guy and they live happily ever after kind of movie. While those sappy films were fine for a group of gals and their Graeter's ice cream, I didn't care for the awkwardness two *friends* would undoubtedly be forced to endure when the credits rolled. "How about an action flick instead?"

"Perfect. My place?"

I had to laugh. Mr. Terrycloth *was* good. "Mine."

"Fair enough. I'll bring the movie." His smile lit up his eyes again as he backed up toward the door. "Eight?"

"Eight it is."

The chimes on the door jingled with his happy departure and I turned to face Melissa. We both giggled like college sorority girls over the globule of whipped cream Joseph sported on the end of his nose.

"I'm so cruel."

Melissa shook her head. "No, he's cruel for coming in here dressed in those jeans. Did you see that butt? Wrangler and Carhartt never looked so good. What the hell does he do for a living anyway?"

"No idea. Does it matter?"

Again, we chuckled at our girlie fetishes of men who knew how to rock a pair of jeans. Though we didn't speak anymore on the subject, I knew the image of Joseph was embedded in both our brains for the rest of the day.

And who could blame us?

Ask any woman in this coffee shop who witnessed Joseph standing at the counter, and I guarantee every one of them hated to see him leave but loved to watch him go.

Chapter Three

Just as I expected, at eight o'clock sharp Joseph knocked on my door. I tried to tamp down my excitement as I removed a pan of lasagna from the oven. Thanks to Melissa who offered to close the shop, I had time to race home and prepare dinner. I had long forgotten about Melissa's slip up with Joseph, but she insisted she make it up to me by closing and letting me get "prepared" as she called it. Joseph never said anything about us sharing a meal along with his movie invitation, but I figured once he caught on to my childish, whipped-cream prank, I'd owe him some sort of cease-fire offering.

I threw a few pieces of garlic toast on foil and placed them on the top rack of the oven. Setting the timer, I skipped through my living room and threw open the door. Instead of my neighbor, a scowling blonde all decked out in designer clothing—Joseph's ex—stood on the threshold.

"Hi." My voice betrayed me and disappointment hung heavy on that one little word.

"Do you know where Joseph is?"

Her curtness took me aback. Not a "hello" or a "Hi, I'm Caroline. I'm the low-life, materialistic ex-girlfriend who enjoys ripping Joseph's heart out every chance I get" greeting. And why would she think I knew where Joseph was?

"I'm sorry, I don't."

Her eyes scanned passed me as if she suspected I was hiding him. By sheer instinct, and because my total distaste for this woman rose like an overblown helium balloon, I grabbed the edge of the door and pulled it tight against my side, lessening her line of sight within my apartment.

She took the hint pretty well, for the thoughtless blonde that she was, and straightened her back. Her nose flared in vexation. My mind conjured up images of a spitting cobra, rearing up in a threatening display before ejecting a stream of venom at its enemy.

"Well, if you see Joseph, tell him I stopped by."

She turned to leave and I couldn't help myself. I hung my head out the door. "And you are?"

I knew exactly who she was. She was the type of person who assumed everyone knew her name. From Joseph's description, I knew she was an up-and-coming model. From my perception, she thought, because she spent time in Milan and Paris behind the lens of a camera, the whole world should bow to her prowess. Giving her that satisfaction was the last thing I wanted.

She ground her teeth and forced a polite smile. "I'm Caroline. That's all you need to know."

Kill her with kindness. Kill her with kindness.

I heard my conscience reminding me of my mother's advice from long ago. I flicked Jiminy Cricket off my shoulder. "Oh, I recognize you now. You're the woman from last week. I believe you and Joseph were arguing in the hall as I was on my way to work that morning."

Seeing her fidget uncomfortably was priceless. "Yes, that was me."

"I'm sorry. There's so many women that pass through here, it's hard to tell them apart. But I'm sure he'll remember you." From the corner of my eye, I saw her mouth open to speak, but I didn't wait around to hear it. I slipped behind the door and shut it soundly. Leaning against the cold, hard wood, I suddenly felt frigid and hard-hearted as well.

But only for a second.

Joseph deserved better. Not to say that I was better, but I knew with every fiber of my being that Caroline was the last person he needed in his life.

I had the privilege of seeing the real Joseph this weekend. The man with a huge heart to give, if only someone was thoughtful enough to handle it with care. Part of me wanted to be that person. Part of me thought I wasn't his type. And the other third of me hoped he'd realize that sometimes the best things in life come in surprise packages with familiar wrapping.

* * * *

Just as I burned my finger taking the bread out of the oven, a cheerful, repetitive knock resembling the end of a jingle sounded upon my door. I cringed to think it might be Caroline again, but the manner in which the knock was delivered had Joseph written all over it.

I didn't take any chances though. If I peered through my peephole and saw her grimacing, painted-on, Clinique face, I was *not* going to answer. I didn't owe her anything, and I certainly wasn't about to give her suspicious, coal-black soul another chance to invade my privacy with her probing eyes.

I stood on tiptoes to peek through the eyehole and breathed a sigh of relief when I saw Joseph standing there in jeans and an old faded T. It clung to his chest and upper arms like a second skin but was loose enough in the torso to be comfortable. I glanced at my attire—also jeans and a T, but my shirt was a brand new one from *Aeropostle* that was purposely made to look old and outdated. Joseph wouldn't know the difference.

Taking in a breath, I swung the door open. "You're late."

He lifted his nose and sniffed. "You're cooking."

"Nothing gets past you, does it?" Noticing his casual confidence wasn't seeping from his body as usual, I eyed the odd placement of his left hand. "What's behind your back?"

He smiled like a Cheshire cat and revealed his secret stash. Sitting on a silver tray were two chocolate cupcakes, mounded high with whipped purple icing, an unmarked DVD case, and two fortune cookies.

"What's this?"

"A truce."

"You're allowed to be late, Joseph."

He shook his head slowly, his hair refusing to fall into his eye, thank goodness. "It's not for being late," he corrected. "It's for the little game of get-even we seem to be playing."

The dab of whipped cream on Joseph's cute little nose this morning flittered into my brain and the looks he must have gotten on the walk to work. "I don't know what you're talking about."

Joseph playfully pushed his way inside. "Careful, Pinocchio. I'm armed." His eyes fell to the platter of loaded cupcakes balanced on his fingertips as he kicked the door shut.

For every foot I backpedaled, he reciprocated a step forward, keeping the space between us at a minimum until I slammed into the divider wall of my kitchen. Helplessly pinned with Joseph mere inches from my body, I swallowed hard. "I accept your truce."

"Of course, you do *now.*" He set the treats on the counter without taking his eyes off me. His stare held me immobilized. "But what happens when the opportunity presents itself again?" He gestured toward the chocolaty desserts sitting like two plump piles of tremendous temptation. "Can you refrain from shoving one of these cupcakes in my face after dinner?"

I no longer felt trapped. Without him realizing it, Joseph had revealed an escape route with his good, clean game of double dog dare. "You going to give me a reason to shove them in your face?"

"Not if I can help it."

"Are you saying you may lack willpower, Joseph?" My challenge hit him square in the gut. It would stun any red-blooded man who prided himself on being completely in control. I reveled in this moment.

I watched his mouth twitch and his eyes glaze over in thought. He lowered his head and his mouth opened slightly. I froze. He looked as if he were about to kiss me. My head spun and my heart skipped. Maybe I wasn't cut out for this game of double dog dare after all.

He brought his hand up and lifted my chin with an index finger coiled into a loose fist. "I guarantee, Jamie, I have more willpower than you."

I planted my hands on his chest—his wonderfully broad, hard, warm chest—and playfully shoved him backward a half step. I stuck out my hand to shake on the deal. "Game on."

He accepted with a firm grip that nearly swallowed my whole hand. My stomach summersaulted when his calloused hand pumped mine while he gazed at me with those self-assured smiling eyes.

I will lose this bet for sure.

Joseph was the first to break eye contact, his attention shifting toward the stove. "Did you make lasagna?"

My breath escaped me as I shifted around the counter and pulled open the silverware drawer. "I hope you're hungry."

"I'm always hungry for lasagna." He joined me behind the counter and took a huge whiff of the bubbling layered noodles. "How the heck did you have time to make this?"

"I got off work early."

"Let me guess…Melissa felt bad about her big mouth?"

I laughed. "Something like that."

Joseph eyed me like a hawk, trying hard to read me. "You know I don't care, right?"

I pulled two oven mitts over my hands and carried the hot baking dish to the dining room table. "I know that you have no reason to care. I didn't tell her anything about your private conversation with Caroline."

Joseph was on my heels carrying the plates and silverware. "You mean the private conversation you'd eavesdropped on?"

I edged by him to retrieve the garlic toast. "Yes, that one." I felt the skin on my face flare up. I truly felt guilty for doing such a thing, but what girl could ignore a dripping-wet man of pure muscle garbed in a towel?

"So, what *did* you tell her?"

Here we go. Why couldn't he let this one drop? I knew he was only baiting me. I plopped a piece of bread on each of our plates. "I only told her about the scenic view I had on my way to work that morning."

"And that the view had a name." He watched me gather two Cokes and glasses from the cupboard.

"Most recognizable landmarks do." I tried to act nonchalant and show him his inquiry didn't fluster me. "You like a lot of ice?"

"I'm a landmark now?"

I filled his cup full of ice cubes whether he liked it or not. "You're a wealth of nosey questions for someone who doesn't care."

His deep, hearty chuckle was the bomb. He had no idea, but his laughter sent my spirits soaring. I loved making him laugh. I never considered myself very funny or even witty. So, when a guy like Joseph laughed at my comebacks, I chalk one up for myself.

"Shall I?" he asked, taking hold of the spatula and hovering it over the pan of lasagna.

"Again, another question. Do you always do this when you're nervous?"

His hand paused in cutting the first serving and he looked at me. "Me? Nervous?"

The two of us burst out laughing, and I didn't even have to say a thing. The fact that he answered me yet again with two more questions was hilarious.

He flopped a stack of lasagna on my plate. "You want more?"

"Okay, stop!" My sides hurt now. We were both laughing so hard I felt tears gather at the corner of my eyes. "Don't make me get the cupcakes, Joseph."

We settled down after a few moments and suddenly the room went deathly quiet. He sat at the opposite end of the table, his fork and knife in hand, looking over his plate of food. Finally, his eyes lifted to mine. "Thanks for this."

"Oh, it's not a big deal. My grandmother's recipe is pretty easy—"

"No, I mean this," he said, waving his fork back and forth between us. "The…jokes. The…comfortableness of it all. The fun." He dropped his head. "I needed this. I've needed this for a long time, but I've never felt comfortable enough with anyone to just let loose. To just be me."

"Not even your guy friends who took you out last Friday?"

"Nah, that's different. I've known them all my life."

He set his utensils down and snatched up his Coke. Like a man dying of thirst, he popped the tab and drank heavily. I watched his throat bob with each swallow. Why I found that alluring, I didn't know.

He poured into his glass what was left of his soda and seemed to ponder his next words. "I meant with someone who's…"

He looked so adorable struggling for the right words that wouldn't sound incriminating. I decided to help him. "Of the opposite sex?"

"Something like that, I guess." He rubbed his palms down the length of his long thighs and leaned back into his chair. The casualness was there, but his cool confidence had taken a hiatus.

I preferred the marginally haughty Joseph to the mega serious one. When he was at ease and having a good time, so was I. This awkward moment so needed to go away. "Joseph?"

"Yeah?"

"You don't have to explain. I get it. I'm like...one of the guys...but with...feminine parts."

Joseph brought his fist to his lips and snorted, trying to hold back his laughter so he wouldn't choke. "That about sums it up—in an apt, yet strangely perverse way."

"Sorry. It was all I had." I reached for my fork and stared at my plate.

"Nah, it was..." he paused, taking his utensil in hand too. "...perfect. Well said."

In my mind, I chalked another dash next to my name. Jamie—two. Joseph—zip.

"Eat your food, Mr. Terrycloth. We've got a movie to watch.

Chapter Four

"Speaking of movies…what are we seeing tonight?" I never could postpone gratification. I am a tell-me-now type of gal.

Joseph chewed and swallowed his first bite, then cleared his throat. I watched him twist his face into some sort of weird smolder and garble, "James Bond. Double O Seven. *Dr. No.*"

"Was that your idea of a Scottish accent?"

"Come on, I nailed it." He screwed up his face and tried again. "It was bloody great."

I snorted this time. "Says who?"

"Don't tell me you're not a Sean Connery fan?"

"Oh, I love the man. It's the amateurish attempts at impersonating Sean's sexy Scottish brogue that make me cringe."

"Man, tough crowd tonight. You always this critical, Sutherland?"

"Only when it comes to people butchering the Hot Scot. Nobody does James Bond like Sean Connery."

He shoveled another fork of lasagna in his mouth. "And nobody does lasagna like you. This is the best I've ever had."

"Flattery'll get you nowhere, Sport."

"I'm serious. Can't you take a compliment?"

"Sorry. I'm just not used to getting one."

He cocked his brow in surprise. "Haven't you ever cooked for someone before?"

"Once or twice, I guess."

"Well, if they didn't compliment you on your cooking, then they must have lacked taste buds. This is fantastic."

I could tell by the way he scarfed his dinner that he was totally enjoying the meal. 'Course men aren't too hard to please when it comes to food. If it's home-cooked and he didn't have to turn on the stove, it was always *the best I've ever had.*

I wondered if Caroline had ever cooked for him. *Ha! Who was I kidding?* She'd probably consider having to chop, dice, measure, and work over a heat source beneath her. Just her standing near a stove with all that product in her hair was a fire hazard. I imagined her going up in smoke and bit back a sigh of satisfaction.

"Who taught you how to cook?" Joseph asked, as he used the tines of his fork to soak up the residual tomato sauce on his empty plate with a buttery sponge of garlic bread.

Recollections of my grandmother, who never worked from a recipe, flooded my memory. My eyes prickled a little bit as I remembered her adding a *pinch of this* and *dash of that* by memory alone. "Just add a little and taste it," she'd say. "You'll know if you need more." As hard as I tried though, I could never imitate her culinary expertise, even when I was able to convince her to write down a recipe for me. It never tasted as good as hers. Maybe grandmothers just have that touch or maybe memories have a way of coloring the truth.

"My grandmother. She's the best cook this side of the Mississippi." I'm sure Joseph heard the pride in my voice as I named my teacher.

"Is she Italian?"

I finished my helping and took a sip of Coke. "No. German actually. Her best meal is hash."

"Hash?"

"Yeah. It's what she makes with leftover roast beef. It's potatoes, shredded roast beef, and onions in a thick gravy. The best!" My mouth watered just thinking about it.

"Sounds delicious. You making that for me tomorrow?" He stretched his legs again beneath the table and looked at me with challenging eyes.

"You wish."

"You're thinking about it."

Damn him, I was. *How did he know that?* I took another swig of my drink and rose from the table. "You finished?" I picked up my plate and silverware. I ignored the fact that he continued to smile and stare at me as he, too, gathered his dirty dishes and followed me into the kitchen.

I rinsed my plate at the sink and did the same to his. The silence between us was deafening as the water swirled like a top down the drain. I wondered how long he was going to stand beside me and watch me load the dishwasher.

I was about to suggest cueing the movie, when the draining water gurgled and burped and filled the bottom basin. I fished beneath the greasy water for what might be the culprit of my clogged sink, but found nothing.

"Dammit."

"What's wrong?" Joseph asked, leaning against the counter.

"Sink's clogged. Again."

"Again?"

"Yeah, it did this a couple nights ago."

Joseph peered inside the sink nonchalantly. "You didn't put anything down it, did you? You know it's not a food disposal."

"Yes, Mr. Obvious. I know it's not a food disposal. I scrape leftover food into the garbage not the sink."

"Why don't you call the super?" he suggested. "That's what he's there for."

"I know, but maybe I can just go buy some Draino tomorrow."

Joseph threw me a sideways glance. "Don't do that. Do what your landlord would want you to do and get it fixed right. Do you need the number?"

"No, I got it here somewhere." I began searching through my junk drawer, beneath lots of Thai restaurant menus, scotch tape, loose batteries, and pens until I found my lease agreement with all the important phone numbers listed at the end.

I glanced at Joseph as I flipped through the papers. His grin stopped me mid-flip. "What?"

"Nothing," was all he said before slipping back to the dining room table.

I stared at him as he brought the leftover lasagna to the counter. He rummaged through my cabinets for a Tupperware container. "I assume you want to save this?"

"Yeah," I agreed, pointing to the cabinet door behind him. "Lids are in the drawer below."

I shook off Joseph's peculiar behavior and went back to finding the superintendent's number. I typed in my text, along with my name and apartment number then resumed cleaning up our dinner mess. I had no idea how long it would take before the man got back in touch with me. Based on past experience, probably a few days.

Joseph and I bumped around in the small kitchen space and laughed each time we collided. Despite the innocence of our continual run-ins, I couldn't help but feel uncomfortable. I was not used to someone in my apartment, in my space, doing the things I did on a regular basis. "How about you start the movie. I'll make popcorn."

"Sounds good to me." He practically ran around the counter and snagged the DVD off the tray he'd brought in. "Don't forget, we've got cupcakes too."

I smiled at the cute little way he waggled his brows, as if daring me to withhold from smashing them in his face. "Salt first, then sweet. Get your priorities straight, Joseph."

His laughter echoed from the living room. I peeked around the corner and saw him drop to his knees, placing the DVD in the player. "Never thought I'd know someone else who likes her snacks in the same order I do. Finally, someone gets it."

Intrigued that he lumped my freaky food fetish in the same neurotic category as his, I retrieved a bag of microwave popcorn from the pantry. My heart did flips over the concept of him pairing up with me. I'd never had much in common with men in general, so finding a man like Joseph had the same crazy tastes as I did was beyond thrilling. *Am I really that needy?*

"Where did you get the cupcakes?"

He slid onto the couch and clasped his hands behind his head. "Some mom and pop store a few blocks from your coffee shop. I think some cute, little old lady owns it. You should try them. They're awesome."

"All in good time," I replied, pushing the buttons on the microwave. I refilled our glasses with more ice and retrieved two more Cokes from the fridge. I set the drinks on the coffee table and joined him on the couch. I was very conscious of the space between us. I didn't want to appear too eager. I think he noticed my mindful behavior because I swore I saw his lips quirk up in a cocky smile as I poured our drinks.

"So, does your grandma live near here?"

I kept my eyes on the foam rising in my glass. "No. She lives near your parents' place actually. In Paris."

"Really? We should go visit her the next time we're in Lexington."

His candidness was off the charts tonight. Only Joseph could get away with those assumptions without seeming too bold. I still had to call him out on it. "We? Next time?"

"Sure, why not? You said you had a great time. Were you lying to me again?"

I felt my face start to heat up. "No." *Will that microwave never beep?* "I just didn't assume you'd take me with you the next time you go."

"Fair enough," he said, reaching for his drink. "But for the record, I've already planned for you to accompany me next time, so don't let me down."

The wink that punctuated his sentence made my stomach flutter. And the way he ran his hand through his hair, taming the falling chunk of hair with the rest of his gorgeous locks, sent a flash of warmth through my soul. I watched his lips part as he lifted the glass to his mouth. The dark, carbonated liquid slipped passed his perfect lips and down his throat. With each subsequent swallow, I was hypnotized. The only thing that saved me from looking like an idiot was the high-pitched beep of the microwave signaling our popcorn was ready.

Jumping up from the couch, I nearly tripped over the coffee table.

"You all right?"

Can I be any bigger dork?

I could tell by his tone that he found amusement in my clumsy trot.

"Yeah, I'm fine. Just start the movie."

"Yes, ma'am."

At the moment I returned to the couch, still leaving a foot of space between us, he cursed under his breath and pulled his cell from his pocket. He stared at the screen and sighed.

"What?"

The look on his face didn't resemble someone who'd received a simple text. I threw a handful of popcorn into my pie hole to keep from saying more.

He scratched his head and sighed again. "I'm so sorry."

"Wharrt?" I asked again, my mouth full.

"I have to take this call." He glanced at his cell again, as if trying to convince himself to ignore the person who messaged him. "Can I get a rain check on the movie?"

As if I had a choice....

I forced a smile as I tried to swallow. *Caroline.* I knew it had to be her. The look on his face screamed her name.

"Sure, no problem." I hid my disappointment and picked up the remote from the coffee table, hitting STOP.

Without so much as a thank you, Joseph jumped up from the sofa and made a beeline for the door. As he was about to disappear, he peeked around the wood. "I promise I'll make this up to you, Sutherland."

I waved him on and shoved another handful of popcorn in my mouth. And to think I was about to enjoy a nice evening alone with Joseph. In my convoluted, overactive, imaginative mind, visions of Caroline, grinning with satisfaction, knowing she'd just interrupted my plans, unfolded. Names I'd love to call her, modified by the four letter words of a sailor, abounded.

It took every bit of self-control I possessed not to run after him and make him realize she wasn't worth his time. That he didn't have to go chasing after her the second she beckoned. I really wanted to safeguard his heart, sure to be broken again if he took her back into his life. But who was I to get involved in Joseph's personal affairs? What he did with his heart was his own business. If he chose to entrust it to her razor-sharp, soul-slicing talons again that was his mistake. It'd be no sweat off my brow. I barely knew him.

Who am I kidding? I'd be crushed to see Joseph hurt.

Though I didn't have much invested in this blossoming friendship with Joseph, I could tell Caroline would ultimately be the death of me.

Polishing off the bag of popcorn seemed to be my only solace. I was one of those girls who found comfort in food, and I also found even more comfort when I balled up the empty bag and tossed it in the trash.

All I wanted to do was go to bed and close my eyes until morning. I was hardly sleepy, but I didn't have the energy for much else. I blamed the extra-processed butter sitting like a rock in my gut.

Just as I padded across the floor toward my bedroom, a knock came at my door.

So help me, if that's Caroline I'm going to….

Kill her with kindness. Kill her with kindness.

I rolled my eyes at my conscience's relentless determination to keep me from confrontation. If my conscience was truly a visible figure like Jiminy Cricket, I'd have to strangle him. And then, because choking him wouldn't be enough, I'd rip open the door and cram him past Caroline's flawlessly-lined, Floozy Fuschia lips and down her throat before kicking her posh, porcelain butt to the curb.

I exercised my unruly anger with a deep cleansing breath and peered out the eyehole to the hallway. My visitor was not the person I thought it would be.

Chapter Five

I opened the door in a flash. "Joseph?"

He stood dressed in light blue, denim coveralls and holding his red Champion toolbox in his right hand and his cell in his left. He glanced down at his phone and back up to me. "I believe I have the right address. Are you the one with the clogged sink?"

I crossed my arms at his game. "Joseph. What are you doing?"

"I'm here to fix your sink. I got a message from a woman in Loft B. Would that be you, ma'am?"

He lifted his phone for me, so I could confirm the text on his screen. I had to grab it and pull it closer. "I texted *you?*"

"Yes, ma'am, you did."

His polite manners exuded the southern charm I'm certain he grew up with. "What, are we role playing now? I don't think we're quite there in our relationship, Joseph."

His laughter reverberated down the hall. "I'm serious. I'm here to fix your sink. Look," he said pointing at the name tag on his left breast pocket. "Joseph, Superintendent. That's me. Now do you, or do you not, have a clogged sink?"

"You know very well I have a clogged sink." I stepped aside and ushered him in, still processing it all. "But what's with the theatrics?"

He casually strode into my kitchen and set his toolbox on the counter. His eyes lit up again in amusement. "Why is it so hard for you to believe I'm the superintendent of the building?"

I closed the door and gave it thought. "It's not hard for me to believe. You just never told me."

"I did tell you. The morning after we met. Over coffee, remember?"

My mind drifted to that memorable morning. I recalled Joseph and the pitiful hangover he'd endured because of his drunken recklessness the night before. I remembered our conversation about Caroline and how he claimed he couldn't fall in love no matter how hard he tried. On the flip side, I also recollected how I doggedly tried to resist him and the temptation to fall in love. I struggled to keep from picturing myself in his arms and being the object of his affection. Since then, I'd been failing outright. But I didn't remember a single thing about his career choice.

"You asked what I did for a living. I said I was a Jack-of-all-trades kind of guy. Whatever comes up."

"And I was supposed to assume you're a super from that vague description?"

He unlocked the hasps on his toolbox and pulled out a wrench. He pointed it toward me. "The important question is not what you failed to understand, but what you felt when I left to take that call. You were upset, weren't you? You thought I ditched you."

The room temperature seemed to spike. A tingle of sweat prickled across my skin. "I was not upset."

He peeked into the garbage can. "That crumpled bag of popcorn says differently. Did you really eat the whole bag by yourself?"

"Shut up," I said, hiding my smile. "Okay. So I was disappointed. A little."

He cocked his brow, challenging me.

"Fine. A lot. But you left in such a hurry...I just thought...."

"You thought what?"

I stretched the neckband of my T-shirt. *Why did he have to go here?* "It doesn't matter. I was mistaken and you redeemed yourself. Moving on...."

"You're not getting off that easily, Sutherland." He leaned across the island toward me and looked deep into my eyes. "Tell me. Whose text did you think was so important that I would ditch you?"

I sighed and crossed my arms, finding serious contempt in saying her name. "Caroline."

His head retracted and his face puckered. "Caroline? Why on earth would you think that?"

"Because you two have history."

"So?"

"So, it's not unlike her to text you, right? Besides," I added, stumbling on my next words. "She did come looking for you tonight."

Again, his face furrowed in surprise. "Looking for me? Here?"

I nodded my head. "Yes, here. I think she thought I was hiding you in my apartment."

"What did she want?"

"What? Am I your secretary now?"

He laughed, but I could tell Joseph wasn't so at ease with this turn of events. "I wish you would've told me, Jamie."

"Well, to be honest, I didn't really care to bring up the subject of your ex. It's not my forte to bring rain showers to a sunny evening."

He laid the metal wrench against his forehead and closed his eyes. "Okay. So my timing was bad when it came to surprising you. I didn't mean to make you think I was ditching you for her. I would never do that. I just wanted to make you smile, when I showed up at your door in my work clothes."

His apology was the sweetest. I couldn't let him think I was even the slightest bit upset with him for his little charade. In fact, it was adorable that he went to so much trouble to make me smile. He could've just fixed the sink after dinner. Instead, he let me dig up his number, go through the steps of leaving a message, all the while playing the ruse of the superintendent showing up at my door with his worn-out, rusty toolbox.

While it was certainly endearing, he did trick me. This called for drastic measures. Maybe not a cupcake-in-the-face, but radical enough that he'd know revenge was upon him.

Looking as innocent as I could, I walked around the island counter and faced him. "Don't worry about it. I know you meant well. So, you gonna fix that sink or what?"

"Get me a large pot," he commanded. "I'll have your sink unclogged before you know it."

I fetched a pot and handed it to him. He sat crossed-legged at the open cabinet doors, placed the pot beneath the drain pipe, and made quick work of loosening the trap.

Now was my chance to set a trap of my own. Taking scotch tape from my junk drawer, I quietly pulled a strip and wrapped it around the depressor of the sprayer hose to the right of the faucet. That way when he turned on the water, the nozzle would be primed and ready to spray at his unsuspecting self.

"How's it going down there?" I asked, diverting any possible focus from myself.

"Um…it's as I expected," he muttered. "The person who lived here before you seemed to have used the drain as a disposal. Nasty stuff."

"What's clogging it?"

"You don't want to know. Can you hand me a paper towel?"

"Sure." I couldn't wait until Joseph was finished. Watching him get sprayed was going to be incredibly satisfying. I wiped the smile from my face before handing him the towel. "This enough?"

"Yeah. Almost done…" I heard him groan and ramble on about idiot tenants and the ridiculous things they did while renting. "You can bet your bottom dollar if they *owned* their place, they would never do half the shit they do. Boggles my mind how people just don't care anymore."

I pretended to care about the conversation, affirming my take on the matter with a few subsequent "yeah's" and "mm-hm's."

"Okay, I think we're good now," he announced from the floor. "Turn on the water and see if she drains."

Crap.

I quickly pulled the extension hose out and held it down into the sink. Turning on the faucet, I kept my fist around the hose so he couldn't see the tape should he look up. The water circled and drained in a speedy fashion. "Yep, I think we're good." I replaced the hose in its upright position.

"Awesome." He stood up and pitched the paper towel that I assumed contained the mass of greasy, hairy indefinites in the trash. He held his hands up and mimed a grotesque look. With the fuse lit, the sparks would soon fly when he washed his hands.

Standing back from the line of fire, I grinned from behind him. And waited.

"You ready to watch that movie now—" was all he had time to say before the stream of pressurized water hit him in the stomach. "What the—!" He lunged to shut off the faucet, then stood there dumbfounded and soaked.

I laughed like there was no tomorrow.

"You think that's funny?"

"Yes, I do." I was so tickled I could barely talk. Who would ever think I could be so diabolical.

He shook his head. "No willpower, huh?"

"Sorry. I couldn't help myself. You so deserved this and you know it."

"It's possible."

With a look that would stop traffic, he reached up and unzipped his coveralls, revealing the warm smooth skin of his bare chest. With careful precision, he peeled the wet fabric from his shoulders, one by one, and stepped out of his coveralls.

My mouth dropped open. I did not expect him to be shirtless beneath his work attire. His jeans hung low on his narrow waist and the ripple of washboard abs rose like hard waves toward a perfect pair of pecs. His shoulders were broad. His biceps naturally bulged as his thumbs sank casually into the front of his pockets. If I didn't know any better, I would have thought he was a Greek god who'd stepped straight out of a marble statue in the middle of my kitchen.

I swallowed hard.

This wasn't the first time I'd seen him half-clothed, for we'd met this way in the hallway when he stood in nothing but a towel. But this was even better. He was within my reach, within the privacy of my own home.

Shirtless.

Yeah. This was way better.

Eat your heart out, Caroline.

Chapter Six

"How's your willpower now, Jamie?"

"Wh-what? My what?" My gaze jumped from the droplets of water glistening on his stomach to the sparkle of blue in his eyes. I didn't mean to stare so blatantly, but who knew that wet skin and hard muscle could be so enthralling?

He seized my wrist and picked up a cupcake from the tray. "Game on, Sutherland."

My eyes widened in panic and I jumped backwards, ripping my arm from his grasp. "Joseph, no!" I screamed and ran from him, sprinting through the living room and around the coffee table. He proved to be more agile, catching me, and tackling me to the floor. I landed on my stomach, his body on top of mine.

I felt his strength as sure as I smelled his cologne enveloping me in a waft of heat, citrus, and spice. Face down, I fought to be free, but he captured my arm and restrained my other with his leg. Straddling me, he smashed the cupcake in my face. The sweet smell of sugar and frosting invaded my nostrils as my nose was impacted with icing and moist cake.

"Are you serious?" I shouted, hearing his laughter vibrate through me.

I felt him shift off me. I rolled over and stared up at him. In the course of our battle, some purple icing had smeared across his jaw. He swiped it away with his hand and brought it to his mouth.

"The taste of victory is so sweet, don't you think?"

I let my head fall back to the floor in submission. "You are such a child."

"Me? Who taped their sink hose?"

Visions of Joseph wrestling with the onslaught of spraying water came to mind and I snickered. I sat up on my elbows, chunks of squished cake falling off my chin. I licked my lips, finding a portion that clung to the corner of my mouth.

Joseph made a gesture across his own cheek and nose, indicating where the smashed cupcake still lingered on my face. "You missed a spot."

"You think?" I said, knowing it was everywhere. I hooked a piece with my finger and placed it in my mouth.

"Good, isn't it?"

Actually, he was right. This was the best cupcake I'd ever tasted. I'm sure it would've tasted even better had I not had to eat it off my face.

"We have another one if you're still hungry," Joseph teased.

"I'm good, thanks. You eat it."

Like a gentleman, he stood and pulled me to my feet. The muscles in his arms flexed and inwardly I smiled. I had no idea defeat tasted this heavenly.

He bent to retrieve a couple tissues from the Kleenex box on the table and handed them to me. "You're not mad, are you?"

I cleaned what I could feel and snorted at his paranoia. Globs of icing flew from my nose and plopped on the floor. "Does this look like a face that's mad?"

Joseph chuckled. "It's hard to tell amongst all the icing."

He took another tissue from the box and gingerly wiped the bridge of my nose. I averted my gaze as he cleaned me up. I could hardly look at him all bare-chested, sexy, and thoughtful. I swore I felt the heat of his skin burn through my shirt even though we were a foot away from each other.

"There we go," he muttered, balling the tissue in his fist. "Now this looks like a face that's...that's so...beautiful."

My gaze returned to his. He held me riveted to the floor with his stare and my chest burned with anticipation. I saw his eyes drop to my lips and my breath caught.

His hand came up to cradle my jaw. "There's only one thing left to do."

"Mm-hmm," I mumbled. "What's that?"

He bent down on one knee in front of me. "We have to clean your floor. You don't want ants."

I released a breath that I didn't know I held. I watched him gather all the crumbled cake in the tissue, all the while feeling relieved and disappointed at the same time. He had the power to hypnotize me with barely a look and every time he did, I felt so foolish for doing so.

I walked away for a moment, distancing myself from the hot shirtless man playing Molly Maid. The kitchen was far enough away to allow me to gather my wits and catch my breath without him seeing my struggle.

"You okay?" Joseph asked from behind me. I heard him toss the wadded tissues into the garbage can.

I feigned indifference. "Of course. I'm just..." I turned on a dime and dove into my kitchen cabinet for some cleaner. "...getting some spray for the floor."

I tried to circumvent him, but he stepped in front of me. I nearly collided with his bare chest. He held out his right hand to me. "Truce?"

I clenched my jaw, trying to decide if I was capable of touching this Adonis again without throwing myself into his arms. The thought was there, given the sight of toned, male muscle before me and I couldn't erase it from my brain if I tried. I recalled the strength of his arms yesterday when I had climbed into his treehouse. His embrace was the best I'd ever felt, despite the thick winter coats between us. I could only imagine just how glorious it would feel to hug him without clothes.

"Jamie?"

I shook my head to rattle the lovely visions from my mind. In an instant, I shook his hand. "Truce—for now," I offered, faking an aloof smile. "I'll even throw in another bag of popcorn since you didn't get any."

"Aww...aren't you thoughtful."

I turned toward the pantry and retrieved another bag. "How about you reciprocate the thoughtfulness and put on a shirt?"

"If that's what you want, Sutherland. I aim to please."

Ha! He only aims to torture me.

I watched him dash out of my apartment—well, I watched his cute little tight butt in Wranglers, if truth be told. And enjoyed every moment of it. Melissa would be proud. I could just imagine her excitement tomorrow morning when I dished about my evening.

The microwave beeped just at the moment Joseph reentered with the same gloriously tight-fitting T he'd sported earlier and an even bigger smile. "Finally, my timing is back on track."

I handed him the steaming bag and slumped into my soft couch. He snagged the last cupcake from the counter and sat next to me—very close to me, I realized, for his long thigh rested against mine.

He offered me the last cupcake and I accepted, smiling as he carefully tore open the bag. He caught sight of me staring and teasingly hoarded his buttery, salty snack. "I don't think so, Sutherland. You already had your fill of salty."

Like the mature woman I was, I stuck out my tongue. "And to think I was going to share this cupcake with you." I exaggerated the enjoyment of the first bite and hummed my satisfaction. "Not anymore."

Joseph smiled. "Don't worry. I'll get my dose of sweet later."

"What?"

"Shut up and watch the movie," he said, playfully shoving me. He filled his mouth with popcorn and pressed PLAY on the remote. I tried to keep my mind on the opening scene, but couldn't help but wonder how he'd *get his dose of sweet later.* Maybe he meant he'd get his second helping of sweet with a goodnight kiss. He kissed me last night. Why wouldn't he do it again tonight? The thought of him tasting sweet sugar from my lips had me quivering with anticipation. Or maybe, he just had another stash of cupcakes in his own apartment and planned to eat another. *Yeah, that's what he probably meant.*

I finished off my cupcake in silence and several minutes later, despite what he had said before, Joseph absently shared his open bag of popcorn without taking his eyes off the TV.

"I'm good." I waved the bag away. Any more salt tonight and I'd look like a puff frog tomorrow.

I had to grin at how easily absorbed he became in a movie I'm sure he'd seen a thousand times. While my allure for him came from the fact that he was a hard man to predict, he was certainly a very typical man in other respects. I loved that about him. It was a comfort to know he wasn't so different he'd be a challenge to get along with. In fact, hanging with Joseph was as natural as breathing, which was definitely a first for me. Never had a relationship with a guy been so easy.

His words at dinner floated to the top of my attention: *The…comfortableness of it all. The fun. I needed this. I've needed this for a long time and I've never felt comfortable enough with someone to just let loose. To just be me.*

I suppose the true comfort was that Joseph seemed to feel the same way I did. That our thing—whatever it was—was a nice change of pace and something we both longed for, whether we consciously knew it or not.

"Why are you smiling?"

His voice made me jump. "I'm smiling?"

"Yeah. Like a fiend," he replied, his eyes glued to Sean Connery calmly kicking ass in his classic black tuxedo. "What's so funny?"

"Nothing's funny." I stumbled to find the right words without freaking Joseph out. "I'm just happy, I guess."

For the first time since the movie began, he tore his gaze from the screen and looked right at me. He stared, reading me, burning a hole in my vulnerable soul with his intense Montana-blue-sky eyes.

"Me too."

Chapter Seven

Joseph's lips curved in a smile, reflecting the giddy grin I must have had on my own face. I felt the knuckles of his hand innocently brush mine as he ran his palm down his thigh. I left my hand where it was, unable to move a muscle. His index finger extended and he lightly stroked the sensitive skin of my pinkie.

"Thanks for saying yes to my movie-night suggestion," he said. "And for being such a good sport about taking a cupcake up the nose."

"Yeah, well, let's not make a habit of it."

Joseph reached across the coffee table, pressed PAUSE on the remote, and stood to fetch the two fortune cookies from the tray on the counter. He plopped back down next to me and held them both in his palm for me to choose. "Why don't we find out what Confucius has to say on the subject?"

"Okay...."

"Go ahead. Pick your fortune, Jamie."

Women's intuition told me to choose the one on the right. I ripped the wrapper and broke the cookie open.

"Don't read it ahead of time," Joseph warned. "Just read it on the spot."

"If I must."

"Yeah, you must."

I cleared my throat and read.

Old habits are hard to break. It's more fun to form new habits with someone who's bound to stick around. In time, they'll soon be old ones impossible to get rid of.

"In bed," he quickly added.

I had to laugh at his enthusiasm for adding the wistful twist at the end of the fortune. "Right. In bed. Cute. But I wonder if by 'old ones impossible to get rid of,' the fortune meant the new friend or the new habits."

"Hmm...," Joseph murmured, hiking up one knee, and turning toward me. "Good question."

"All right. Your turn. And no reading ahead of time either."

"Fair enough." He broke open his cookie and read immediately.

If the person beside you is still beside you, then there's a good chance you both are on the road to something better.

I sat astonished. If I didn't know better, I would have sworn Joseph had made these up and somehow inserted them inside the cookie. It was uncanny for us to have these kinds of random predictions back-to-back like this. Was Confucius a mind reader now? Normal fortunes were just the luck of the draw and most times a load of bull.

"Oh, almost forgot! In bed," he again added with a mischievous grin.

I crossed my arms, taking in the smirk on Joseph's handsome face.

"What?"

He actually had the audacity to look innocent. "Either the Asian restaurant industry has upped their game with their fortune cookies or…you wrote them."

"Now, how could I get them inside the cookie *and* the wrapper, if I wrote them?"

"Yeah, well, I thought of that too. But then again, you are full of surprises and very capable of pulling something like this off. I mean, you do write songs…so why not fortunes."

Joseph's laugh echoed around me and his lock of hair finally flopped over one eye. *Damn his sexy hair.*

"Just like compliments, you can't help but be skeptical with everything else in your life, can you?"

"What's that supposed to mean?"

"It means you think too much, Jamie." He signed off with a wink and snatched the remote. Before he could hit PLAY, I stole it from him.

"You think you're fooling me?"

"Nah, you're too smart for that. But you're easy to ruffle."

"Ruffle?"

"Yeah, like ruffle your feathers."

I held the remote further away as he tried for it. "You're not ruffling any feathers."

He leaned across me, reaching further, but never took his eyes from me.

"Come on, Joseph, fess up."

"Fess up to what?"

"That you wrote them."

"Is that all you want to know?" His eyes fell over my lips and back to my gaze. His tilted body froze inches from mine and his arm proved to be longer than the one I'd extended. I felt the warmth of his hand wrap around my fist. I swallowed and my breath squeezed from my lungs in laborious, little-by-little gasps. I could barely think, much less answer him.

"Jamie?" he probed in a husky voice.

I struggled to think back to his actual question. *What the heck did he ask me?*

Before I could answer, he planted a quick kiss on my forehead and stole the remote from my grasp. "Just as I thought. So easily ruffled. Now watch the movie."

The film came back on and I was left stunned, in the wake of Joseph's casual confidence and charm. I felt like an idiot, hot and bothered and, yes, ruffled. It drove me crazy that he was right.

I sighed, wiggled into the couch until I was comfortable, and watched Sean Connery save the world and charm beautiful women for another ninety minutes. When the movie was over, Joseph extended his long arms above his head and stretched his whole upper body while the closing credits and Bond theme song played. "Great movie. Never gets old."

He stood and left my comfy couch, throwing the empty popcorn bag in the trash. I watched him, adoring every agile move he made, but said not a word. When he returned to the living room, he took both my hands and pulled me to my feet.

"Thanks for dinner, Jamie."

"You're welcome. I'm glad you enjoyed it."

"I enjoyed your company more," he claimed, pulling me into his arms. His bold move had me stiffening my spine. I wasn't prepared for it. "Relax, I won't hurt you."

I blew out a breath and tried to soften my body in his embrace. *Don't let him ruffle you.* "Sorry. I'm just…"

"Full of questions?"

"Yeah, I guess."

"Fire one off, then. But you only get one." His smile lit up the whole room as he waited.

Trying to clear my thoughts, I asked the one question that burned in my brain. "Did you write those fortunes? Or not?"

He pondered his answer. "For the record, that's actually two questions."

Frustrated, I tried to wiggle from his embrace, but he pulled me closer. "I think we all have the capability of writing our own fortunes. How's that for an answer?"

"You still didn't answer the question."

"Maybe not, but I know many of *my* questions were answered tonight."

"And what questions would those be?"

"Nope, sorry. Can't answer that one, else I'd be letting you violate the one question per night rule."

As he stared at me, I thought I would incinerate on the spot. His face neared mine, slowly, tentatively. His nose touched mine in a gentle nuzzle until his mouth brushed across my upper lip. I felt my knees buckle and my stomach twinge as his soft lips covered mine.

I heard him draw in a deep breath. His arms tightened around my back and his fingers wound into the ponytail hanging down my back. He tenderly tugged, angling my head backward to receive more of his hot kiss. I was completely oblivious to anything but Joseph. The way he smelled. The heat of his body blazing through mine. I didn't want this to end. I wanted to kiss him all night.

I felt his lips tighten in a smile before he pulled away. Until that moment, I had no idea how close I had pulled his body against mine. Very aware of my boldness now, I loosened my arms around his waist.

"Goodnight, Jamie."

"Goodnight." My voice squeaked and he chuckled all the way out the door. Once it closed behind him, I collapsed onto the couch and giggled like a school girl. Even with every question I could think of left unanswered, this night would go down as the BEST night ever.

Take that, Caroline.

Chapter Eight

The next day began with me hitting SNOOZE too many times on the alarm clock, which made for a very hectic morning. I wasn't late for work, but I wasn't my usual perky, perceptive self. I had thrown my hair up into a chaotic bun and somehow wore two different colored shoes. To my defense, they were exactly the same brand and style, but one was navy and the other black.

Of course, Melissa noticed right away. But she assured me no one else would. Personally, I think she was just placating me, so I'd forget all about the fashion faux pas and get on with the real reason I'd lost my head when dressing.

Like the good friend I was, I told her every little detail. From the cupcake fight to the goodnight kiss after the movie, I divulged my entire evening with Joseph in between customer orders, all the while keeping a sharp ear on the door chimes. I refused to have another episode of Joseph walking in and eavesdropping on my conversation.

"I am so green with envy, Jamie," Melissa said, fanning her face. "What I wouldn't give to have a neighbor like Joseph take interest in me. Oh, my gosh, can the man get any yummier?"

I thought about her choice of words: *a neighbor like Joseph taking interest in me*. It was hard to believe that a man as suave and sexy as Joseph could be the slightest interested in a gal like me. I wasn't anything special. I didn't have a lot to offer him except for a splendid cup of coffee and some of my grandmother's special recipes. While it might appeal to him now, I feared eventually it wouldn't be enough to keep him.

Keep him...

I suddenly realized I was doing exactly what I swore I would never do again—leave my heart unguarded for a guy who was destined to break it.

I recalled our conversation over coffee the other morning when he confided that he wasn't able to fall in love. If the beautiful, successful Caroline couldn't get this man to fall, what made me think I could?

I squeezed my eyes shut and turned from the over-worked espresso machine. I needed to clear my head. In private.

"You got this?" I asked Melissa.

I could sense her concern, but she didn't push the issue. "Sure. No problem."

"I'll be in my office." I wiped my hands on my apron and opened the door to escape. Images of Joseph sitting casually on the corner of my desk the other day invaded my thoughts. No matter where I looked, he was there. The espresso machine he fixed. The doorway he always used as a leaning post. Even the stupid jingle of the door chimes had me salivating like Pavlov's dog in the hopes it might be Joseph. But I didn't want to see him at every turn. I wanted a reprieve. I wanted things the way they were before, when I wasn't so caught up in him. When I wasn't thinking of him every minute of the day. When I wasn't counting down the hours at work so I might see him again. When my heart was shielded by the wall I'd built around it to keep it safe from catastrophe.

At least, that's what I kept telling myself.

I plopped down in my office chair and gawked at the desktop calendar. Friday, December 12th stared back at me—the day he and I were supposed to have our first date, or whatever we called it. A day for two friends to hang out and get to know each other.

A date.

A day of doom.

I closed my eyes and reclined in the chair, my head falling back against the leather cushion. Why was I suddenly dreading this day? For days, I had been so excited about it and now I was fretting.

You think too much, Jamie.

Just as I considered Joseph's words, my office door flew open. A hesitant, yet lightheartedly-silly smile split Melissa's lips. "You have a visitor." Then she mouthed, "It's Joseph."

My goodness, the man has impeccable timing.

My first thought was to say I was too busy with scheduling and ask Melissa to take care of his order. But I knew she wouldn't accept that excuse. She'd drag my sorry butt out of the chair and throw me out of the office. I imagined her and Joseph fist bumping again.

"Tell him I'll be there in a moment."

"Tell me yourself."

My heart gave a little flip as Joseph weaved around Melissa in the doorway. As if he owned the place, he just came in and took a seat in the straight-back chair against the wall.

He and Melissa exchanged smiles as she left. I made a mental note never to play soccer with her if she was the goalie. She sucked at blocking incoming balls.

"Good morning," he said, all chipper and cute. "I'm glad to see you're so happy this fine Tuesday morning. It's funny, 'cause I woke up the same way."

I hadn't realized my lips betrayed me with a beaming grin until he mentioned it. "You did, huh?" *Yeah, but did you find yourself second guessing everything you've done up to this point? Doubt it.*

"I did. And I like it. I feel…giddy." As soon as it came out of his mouth, he scrunched up his face. "Hmm…I believe I just turned in my man card with that little statement."

"You think?"

"Yeah, I feel like I should follow that up with a manly groin shift and me chugging a beer."

I snorted. "Totally not necessary. Especially the groin shift. We're in a public place with Melissa standing guard. I can't have her passing out today. She about blacked out when I told her about the kiss—" I stopped immediately, realizing what I was about to divulge. "…the…kick-ass coffee promotion we've got coming up."

Joseph wasn't buying it. His lips had already begun to purse as if he were holding back a huge belly laugh.

"Kick-ass coffee promotion? Really? What the heck is that?"

I burst out laughing and dropped my head in my hands. "I have no idea. It just came out."

Joseph guffawed right with me. I'm sure our laughter carried all the way into the café. What made it even better was that neither of us could talk when Melissa peeked in for a quick second.

It took a few moments for us to finally settle ourselves. I wiped tears from my eyes as Joseph moved from his chair to my desk, sitting his Wrangler derriere on its corner.

"Kudos on the quick thinking there, Sutherland."

"Thanks, but like your giddy remark, this too shall be forgotten. Right?"

"I think that's only fair," he nodded. "But I have to ask, did Melissa enjoy all the sordid details of the," he hooked his fingers in quotation marks, "kick-ass coffee promotion? 'Cause that's what's important here."

My face burned. I didn't know which was worse: Joseph knowing I told Melissa about our goodnight kiss or the fact that he called me on it in such a crafty, smart-alecky way. "I believe she did."

"Did Jamie?"

I could hardly look at him now. "Yes."

He picked up my sharpie marker and circled the number 12 on my calendar. Beneath the date, he wrote 7 p.m.

"Are we still on for Friday? Or are you getting cold feet?"

My gaze grabbed his. *How did he know that?*

"Melissa told me you were in here pondering. But don't make her work overtime again. It wasn't her fault. I probed. She caved."

"Neither surprises me."

"If you'd rather not…"

I cut him off. "No, I want to go. I do."

Joseph's face lit up. "Great. Should I pick you up here or at your apartment?

"I have to work 'til seven, so here would be fine."

"Here it is, then." He capped the marker and flipped it up in the air, catching it with ease. "Oh, and dress warm. We'll be outside—weather pending, of course."

I couldn't hold back my smile. It seemed my worries about Friday had all but vanished since he barged into my office. I was back to being excited about the evening and what he had in store. It was like the man emitted positive energy that attacked my negative neurons on a constant, perfect time-release basis. He was like a prescription of Zoloft, but in an easier-to-swallow-capsule.

"Where are we going?"

"You'll see."

"Will I enjoy myself?" I quizzed.

He took my hand and helped me stand. "That depends. Do you like freezing cold water, flinging animal feces, and the occasional risk of being mauled by a lion?"

"Uhhh…no!"

"Good. 'Cause we're not going ice skating at the Cincinnati Zoo or for the Festival of Lights like every other Tom, Dick, and Harry. So, you should have a great time where *we are* going. And don't eat dinner. I've got that covered. Well," he backpedaled as we made our way out of the office. "Eat a little something to hold you over, so you don't go sugar droppin' on my watch again."

Oh, how I wish I could erase that day from both our memories. "Deal. Want some coffee before you go?"

His hand touched the small of my back as he skated passed me. My mind leaped back in time to when I had helped Joseph to his bed after his drunken night out. His hand rested on that exact place, begging me to stay.

"I think I will, actually," he said interrupting my thoughts. He searched through the selections of coffee names for a few seconds and, damn, if his touch didn't linger on my back the whole time. "How about that kick-ass coffee you're looking to promote in the next couple days?"

Melissa gave me a sideways glance. "What is he talking about?"

He pointed to her. "Buckle up for that long haul, Melissa."

"Just ignore him," I waved off and began whipping up his coffee. "He thinks he's funny."

I handed him his order, and he leaned toward me. "Is that what you're trying to be with your mismatched shoes...funny?"

I'd nearly forgotten all about them. I palmed his sexy, smiling face and shoved him away. "Don't you have some emergency sinks to fix somewhere?"

He ignored me and took one look at his java piled high with cream. "I'll need a lid for this, Ms. Thinks She's Coy."

I rolled my eyes amid my evil grin and placed a lid on his cup. He handed me a twenty and I pushed it away. "Put that toward your joke fund. It's pretty scarce right now."

Without a good comeback, he turned to leave—all giddy and grinning—while tucking the bill in his front pocket of his jeans.

Melissa and I, however, had our eyes locked on his back pockets as the door jingled and closed behind him.

Chapter Nine

All afternoon, it was difficult to concentrate on my job, thanks to the double dose of Joseph-juice I drank this morning. On one occasion, I had completely forgotten a customer's order as soon as I left to fill it. On several others, I had a serious case of butterfingers. Cleaning sticky cream and various flavored elixirs from countertops and cabinet faces was not my idea of fun, especially when they flooded into every available crack and crevice that I. Just. Cleaned.

Though Melissa did her best to make up for my numerous mishaps, I think she, too, fell prey to the intoxication of Joseph-juice. Despite charging someone's order on another patron's charge card, her blonde blunder seemed minor compared to my coffee catastrophes.

At seven o'clock sharp, I gladly locked up and went home. Eager to forget about my exhausting day, I made haste to toe-off my pair of mismatched shoes as soon as I walked in the door. I grimaced at them lying there on my foyer floor and gave them a little kick, Mia Hamm style.

A bottle of Pinot Grigio was just what I needed to feel better and relax. I strolled barefoot into my kitchen, and yanked open the pantry. To my delight, I found two full bottles. I felt very clever for stocking up the last time I was at the local winery.

I stepped around the kitchen island to get the corkscrew out of the side drawer. My foot snagged on something. I looked down. On the floor lay Joseph's discarded uniform coveralls. Instantly, a smile played upon my lips remembering how he shucked them in front of me. Images of Joseph's strip tease danced in my brain like Channing Tatum's strip solo in *Magic Mike*.

I picked the coveralls up and pressed them to my nose. They smelled of wood with a slight hint of sweet, the same tinge of sweet that came from the cologne I once smelled in his bedroom. I had no idea what brand Joseph wore, but I loved it. I found myself gyrating around my kitchen to the sexy, thumping beat of "Pony" with the wine bottle still in hand, above eye level for effect.

I looked at the bottle. Of course! No sense drinking alone tonight. What better person to invite over to help me kill the bottle than the very man responsible for my rollercoaster ride of a day.

Hip-swaying toward the door, I brought along my unopened liquid courage and his clothes. Dancing into the hallway, I beared left and ran right into Caroline carrying a box.

We struggled to keep the items we each were carrying from hitting the floor.

"Excuse you," she barked. Her eyes glared with contempt.

I hadn't the patience for Caroline's blatant rudeness, but I rose above my disgruntled self and made a sincere effort to be apologetic. "I'm so sorry. I didn't see you there. I was just on my way—"

I stopped midsentence. Considering she was Joseph's ex, I couldn't very well tell her I was heading to his place. But then again, it was obvious to even a blind person where I was going. *Save face and explain yourself, Jamie.* "I was just

returning his work clothes. He fixed my sink last night."
Oh, great. Now she thinks he stripped naked at my house.

She adjusted her grasp on the box and frowned. I couldn't help but notice the contents—designer clothes, assorted women's hygiene products, toothbrush, and a frilly, carnival teddy bear. They were clearly the evidence of a "been kicked out" Caroline.

Looking down from the bridge of her perfect, probably cosmetically-corrected nose she noticed the bottle of wine in my possession.

Busted.

"Right. Well, he's not home," she snapped.

I tried to hide my disappointment and feigned a smile. "Some other day then."

She shifted her burden to her other hip and narrowed her eyes at me. "Look, I don't know what's going on between the two of you, and frankly, I don't care. But I feel I should let you know that no matter what Joseph says, we are not finished. He always comes back to me. *Always.*"

Figuratively, I felt the cold, hard slap of Caroline's open palm across my face. I stood there stunned. She shouldered past me and marched down the hall to the elevator. I barely felt her last hostile blow for the sting of her words hurt more than anything she could've done. I had no way of knowing if she was being cruel or honest.

The elevator dinged and broke me from my trance. I looked down at the crumpled denim hanging over my arm and the bottle of wine. It was going to take something stronger than fermented grapes to soothe my aching heart.

Like a tail-tucked puppy, I walked back into my apartment and collapsed against the closed door. I shut my eyes and let my head thump against the wood. Caroline was right. She had her claws so deep in Joseph, there was no way he'd ever truly leave her out of his life. They had history. They had a comfort level of familiarity that comes with a couple who've spent most of their lives together. I didn't have that with Joseph. All I had with him was a weekend and a couple weekdays. That's wasn't enough time to get to know someone. That wasn't even enough time to break in a new pair of shoes.

I took one last sniff of Joseph's coveralls and threw them over the nearest chair. I wasn't daring enough to prove Caroline wrong, nor was I strong enough to handle getting dumped by Joseph *over* Caroline. She had too much power over me for that to end well. I'd rather he fell in love with my best friend, Melissa, than choose Caroline. Anything to keep her from getting the last laugh.

I could almost hear her cackling, Wicked-Witch-of-the-West laugh. The sound was like fingernails scratching down a chalkboard. I forced my mopey self to the pantry and stared at my alcohol choices. *Jameson* and *Feckin'* stared back at me. I was not one to shoot straight whiskey and they knew it, but I chose the *Feckin'* anyway, solely for the name, reminiscent of the feckin' mood I was in.

I brewed a pot of decaf coffee and assembled my most treasured ingredients to go with the *Feckin'*—Bailey's and whipped cream. Most women would head for the freezer for a pint of Butter Pecan or Rocky Road. In this instance, I preferred the ways of the Erin folk who drank their troubles away instead of gorging on frozen dairy treats.

I took my first sip of whiskey-burning, creamer-dousing goodness and looked out the window toward the city skyline. The backdrop of the midnight-black sky garmented a serene view of the nearby skyscrapers dotted with random square-lighted windows and colorful business signs. It was utterly peaceful outside, unlike the clash of emotions warring in my heart.

I sat at my dining room table and pulled out my cell. The only person I longed to talk to was my grandmother. She always knew what to say to make me feel better.

It took five rings for her to answer. By the sound of her chipper voice, I knew I'd made the right choice where my breaking heart was concerned. "Grandma?"

"Well, hello, Jamie. How are you?"

"I'm good," I fibbed. "Just busy with the coffee shop."

"Did you call to lie to me or are we going to have an honest conversation? Because if we're playing that lying game, then you'll be happy to know my arthritis is gone and I'm training for the *Flying Pig* marathon this May."

I shook my head and smiled, imagining my elderly grandmother hobbling down the streets of Cincinnati for the annual 5K jaunt with a walker. "Cute, Grandma." I took another sip and brought my knees up to my chest, snuggling in for the long talk. "I don't know what to do. And I need your advice."

"Oh? Man troubles?"

"Kinda. You got time?"

I heard her snort on the other end. "Does a rolling stone gather no moss?"

I paused to ponder her question. Perhaps a little too long. She sighed and finally gave her affirmative the way normal people do. "Of course, I have time. I always have time for my grandkids. What's on your mind?"

I told her the long story. Everything. Probably more than she needed or expected to hear, but I wanted her to know it all. From the way Joseph and I first met, how I tried hard not to fall, our incredible weekend, how I began falling for him, his past relationship with Caroline, and finally to how frightening it was knowing I'd fallen for a man who could very well break my fragile heart without meaning to.

"You know what I think, kiddo?"

I prepared myself for some tough love. "What?"

"I think you should take a leap of faith."

"At the risk of my heart?"

"The way I see it, a broken heart only lasts so long. Regret, on the other hand, lasts a lifetime. Do you really want to spend the rest of your life wondering if you might have missed your one-true-love because you were afraid to take a chance?"

"Yeah, well, that all sounds well and good, Grandma, but considering my past love life, I've never been lucky enough to find Mr. Right. I've always come out with a broken heart."

"Even a broken clock is right twice a day, honey."

I was my turn to snort. "You're on a roll tonight."

"That just means I remembered to take all my meds for the day. Tomorrow's another story, honey."

I drank more of my coffee, letting the soothing burn of the whiskey do its thing on my scattered brain and tense muscles. In combination with chatting it up with my grandmother for another half hour, I was well on my way to relaxation junction.

"Sleep tight, Jamie. And make sure you finish that Irish coffee I know you're sipping. That stuff's too good to waste."

"Thanks, Grandma. For everything." I ended the call and took another gander out the window, rehashing the advice in my head. I felt a twinge in my chest, which was probably my heart reminding me of its unwillingness to endure another tragedy. That, or the alcohol had finally seeped into my bloodstream, surging through my vital organs like the catatonic cure for restlessness that the Surgeon General continually warned the masses about.

Chapter Ten

Wednesday and Thursday passed like a slow dripping faucet; one grueling hour at a time. During those two days, I never saw or heard from Joseph. Though I took advantage of the time spent without him—so I could at least think things through with a clear head—I couldn't help but wonder why I hadn't at least gotten a text from him. Was he avoiding me? Had Caroline worked her magic and got to him before I even had a chance? Was he getting cold feet about Friday, and hoping with his disappearance I'd back out so he didn't have to?

I tried not to get ahead of myself. I tried not to think too much and worry over what I'd ultimately do when it came to our relationship. On one hand, I hated to think what would happen to me if I took that leap of faith and got shot down because Caroline had better weapons than I. My heart couldn't take it, if that happened. On the other hand, I stressed over backing out and letting my one chance at Mr. Right slip through my fingers. Love had a strange way of making the impossible seem possible, and after a while, I found myself leaning toward the big jump. At least, if I tried and failed, I wouldn't have to contend with any regrets. That was my decision on Thursday.

When Friday rolled around, I wasn't so sure anymore. It wasn't like Joseph to not communicate in some way. A call, a simple text, anything. But he gave me nothing. I couldn't help but think the worst. Something was up, and I could only wait for the other shoe to fall.

That morning, just as the sun was coming up, as I stepped out of my apartment, I heard Joseph's door shut beside me. My heart leapt and, in a split second, I realized I wasn't ready to give up on him. I swiveled my head expecting to see Joseph's handsome face. Only it wasn't his...but Caroline's.

Like a two-ton boulder, my heart plummeted. I felt the hard, painful drop in my stomach. I couldn't bring myself to acknowledge her as she locked up. Or the fact that she was leaving Joseph's apartment at such an early hour. I had no idea blood-sucking vampires could walk among us in broad daylight.

Then it hit me. Joseph's avoidance...Caroline's departure at the crack of dawn...

She'd spent the night.

Or maybe even a few nights. Either way, it hurt.

I stared at my key inserted in the lock as she walked past me. I was relieved she, at least, had the decency to keep her big mouth shut and not say 'I told you so.' My heart felt like it had been ripped from my chest and stomped on by her seven-hundred-dollar, four-inch-high, Prada heel pumps in Classic Black. My whole body shook. I didn't know if I trembled from nervousness, anger, or just plain sorrow.

The ding of the elevator signaled her departure and a sense of relief washed over me. I closed my eyes and leaned my forehead against the door. Why should I be this upset? Joseph and I were not in an exclusive relationship, nor had he ever promise one. Heck, we were barely friends. So why did it hurt so badly? And why were these pathetic tears running down my face?

I hated this. I hated that I was so weak I'd let this man get under my skin and affect me in such a way that I felt betrayed and used. Though I knew Joseph would never mean to hurt me, he had.

The crazy thing was it wasn't his fault. He'd warned me he couldn't fall in love. I should've taken the hint and saved myself this anguish. Instead, I took Joseph's thoughtful, caring nature and read too much into it. I had no one to blame but my stupid, hasty self.

Inwardly, I chalked another failed relationship on my tally board. There was nothing left to do but suck it up and go about my day. I wiped away my tears, dropped my keys in my purse, and walked to work.

A headache came on and all I wanted to do was run back home and curl up in bed, lights off, covers pulled up over my head. I wanted to be alone. I wanted to avoid the world, not serve coffee to a sixteenth of its population. Unless I was willing to lose my business over a silly heartbreak—that I could've *so* prevented had I listened to my women's intuition in the first place—I had to put aside my grief and carry on.

I unlocked the door to my café and flipped on the lights, I checked the clock on the wall. I had fifteen minutes before opening. Just enough time to compose myself and freshen my eye makeup. I couldn't let my patrons know I'd been crying, because some of my regulars actually cared about me. Plus, I sure as hell didn't want Melissa to know either. There would be no hiding my sadness from her, but I couldn't let her see that her boss was a sappy, sobbing weakling.

I turned the lock on the front door and headed for the bathroom. Before I could stop myself, my brain conjured up the beautiful, flawless Caroline. She'd know just the right product to hide the puffiness around my eyes and spruce up my tired, outdated makeup.

Wench.

Even down, she still found a way to kick me.

* * * *

"So, what are you going to do?" Melissa asked after the evening rush finally died down.

I looked again at the clock on the wall. Six o'clock. An hour before Joseph was to pick me up for our 'date.' I sighed and leaned against the back counter. "I don't know."

"You're not still thinking of going through with this date tonight, are you?"

The last thing I wanted to do was pretend my heart wasn't broken by a man who'd unknowingly broken it with a woman I despised. "I don't know."

"Jamie," Melissa soothed, taking hold of my hand. "You have to tell him how you feel."

"Right, 'cause that's going to help me."

"Well, you can't avoid him forever. He lives right next door to you. And he should know you don't appreciate being led on. He owes you that much."

"He doesn't owe me anything. We're just friends," I reminded her. Or maybe that was to remind myself.

"If you're just friends, then why has he kissed you? On several occasions."

"It wasn't that big a deal. Not like it was ever an open-mouthed kiss."

"Jamie, quit making excuses for his piss-poor behavior. He's obviously a guy who wants his cake and to eat it too. You've got to make him understand that doesn't fly with you."

Melissa was right. But I was a chicken. I don't like confrontation, no matter how important the issue.

Melissa crossed her arms. "You know what? I'll do it for you."

I shook my head. "That's not necessary."

"You go home, and I'll wait for him to show."

"This isn't high school, Melissa. I'm a thirty-year-old woman. I can do my own dirty work." *No, I couldn't. But it sounded good.*

"With me doing it, I can make sure you don't cave and go on this date with him. You deserve better. A man who is sensitive to how he treats you."

At that moment, my cell vibrated in my pocket, signaling an incoming text. I pulled my phone out and stared at the screen. It was Joseph.

"What?" Melissa asked.

"Speak of the devil.…"

"Give me that," she snapped, grabbing my cell from my hand. She read the text back to me aloud.

Running a bit late. About 10 min. Errands took longer than I thought. Wait for me.

"Is *he* serious?" Melissa made a growling sound and handed my phone back to me. "Is he so self-centered he thinks you have nothing better to do than to wait around for him?"

"It's only ten minutes."

Melissa frowned at me. "He was probably stuck with Caroline somewhere and couldn't get away. Yeah, you are *not* going on this date. For once, this guy needs to know what true rejection is. And you," she said, pointing at me for emphasis, "need to stick to your guns. Even if he comes knocking on your door tonight, you do *not* answer it. Got it?"

She didn't wait for me agree. She grabbed my coat and purse from my office, shoved them into my arms, and pushed me out the door.

"Remember. No answering the door."

"But—"

"No buts. If he shows up at your door, you know he's going to give you every excuse in the world to make you change your mind. Be stubborn. Be strong. And for goodness sake, be smart. Don't give him his cake. He already eats it on the side. Right under your nose and he doesn't care. Remind yourself...he's that kind of guy. A man-whoring douchebag."

Was he really that kind of guy? He didn't seem to be. My heart didn't want to accept that he was.

"Go. I got this."

I took one peek in the café and it seemed the few last stragglers of the night had listened in on our conversation. When our eyes met, they nonchalantly went back to gazing at their laptops and iPhones. My little drama was probably the most interesting thing that had happened to them today. I couldn't blame them for eavesdropping. I was a die-hard people watcher too.

"Jamie?"

Melissa's voice broke my reverie. "Yeah?" I asked, slipping my arms into my coat.

"I'm sorry." She pulled me into a tight hug, and I felt my eyes burn with the tears that were dying to fall. "I know how much you wanted this. There's other fish—"

"Don't," I interrupted. I didn't want to ruin this hug with foolish idioms. "Just don't. I don't want to hear that."

Melissa said nothing more, but I could see the tears that welled in her own eyes. She was that good of a friend. A friend who felt my pain as if it was her own. And somehow, knowing she was in tune with my emotions made the pain lessen a little.

But only a little.

Chapter Eleven

Just as Melissa had predicted, a knock sounded at my door. I glanced at the alarm clock on my nightstand. A quarter after eight. *Wow. Melissa must have given him an ear full at the coffee shop.* It was over an hour past the time he said he'd be there to pick me up, so either she kept him that long or he drove around the city wondering what to say to me.

The knock came again, this time a little harder.

I stayed in my nice, warm bed, beneath the heavy quilt my grandmother made for me. All the lights were out in my apartment. Maybe he'd think I wasn't home. I prayed he'd think that and give up.

"Jamie?" I heard him call through the door as he knocked again. "I know you're in there. Open up. Please. I need to talk to you."

I cringed. His voice sounded sincere. Serious. Joseph was hardly ever serious. Could he be sincere? Every fiber of my being wanted to jump up and open the door. Melissa's voice burst into my head.

If he shows up at your door, you know he's going to give you every excuse in the world to make you change your mind. Be stubborn. Be strong. And for goodness sake, be smart.

Melissa would hunt me down and kill me if I gave in, so I held my ground. I tried to ignore the temptation to answer the door, throwing the covers over my head as if they'd drown out the knocks—which had now become pounding.

After a few more pleads and several repetitive, hard thumps, silence finally followed. I drew in some much needed air and let it escape in a long, drawn out respire. He'd given up. And I felt both at ease and disappointed.

"Jamie?"

I shot upright in my bed. Joseph's voice came from the direction of my bedroom door. I gasped to see his silhouette against the moonlight streaming in from my windows.

I grabbed the blankets and pulled them closer to my chin. "What are you doing in my apartment? How did you get in here?"

The lights flipped on, blinding me. I flung my right arm over my eyes. "Arrggghhhh!"

I could hear the uncertainty in Joseph's voice. "I'm sorry to just barge in like this, but I have to talk to you."

"By breaking and entering?"

"Well, technically, I didn't break and enter your apartment. I'm the superintendent. I have a key."

I squinted at him, letting my eyes adjust to the bright lights and the startling fact that Joseph Scarbrough was standing in my bedroom. Whether he broke the law or not, he still entered uninvited.

My mind whirled with crazy stories of stalker boyfriends going all Charles Manson on their unsuspecting female neighbors. Was I about to make tonight's eleven o'clock news? "What do you want?"

"What do I *want*?" He took three huge steps toward my bed and knelt at the side. "Jamie, I want to know what's going on. I came by your shop to pick you up like we planned and Melissa started spouting off about me shacking-up with Caroline. What the heck is she talking about?"

I inched further away, taking the covers with me. I wasn't ready to do this. I thought Melissa said she'd handle Joseph. I was so ditching her as best friend tomorrow.

"Sutherland. Talk to me."

I relaxed a little hearing him use the name that only he called me and the way he begged me to open up. There was a tenderness in the way he spoke, a deep sincerity registering in his tone. I could at least rest assured knowing I wouldn't be plastered all over the news tonight. Ax murderers didn't usually take time for endearments or idle chit chat.

"Why does Melissa think I'm back with Caroline?"

The look in his eyes was of utter bewilderment. Either Melissa did a crappy job of explaining or he was a practiced actor. "Look, Joseph, I know you and I are only friends, but surely friends don't need to hide behind lies."

"What lies? I've never lied to you."

"Okay. Well, maybe you've never lied to me, but you didn't exactly tell me the whole truth."

"And that is?"

Was he being obtuse on purpose? "That you still have feelings for Caroline and she spent the night with you last night."

"She did?"

"Really, Joseph? Do you think I'm that dumb? I saw her leave your apartment at five this morning on my way to work."

"Believe me, this is all news to me. I wasn't even home last night. I spent the night at my sister's."

I crossed my arms. "Then why was Caroline in your apartment?"

"I have no idea." He chewed his lip. "Wait a minute. She has a key. Maybe she thought she could convince me to take her back."

"Take her back?" It was hard to fathom Caroline begging Joseph. Or her even having to beg for anything. In my eyes, she was a woman who got anything she wanted with just a flick of her silky, fake-blonde hair and pout of her irresistible, Diva Devil-red lips.

"Wednesday she showed up at my apartment wanting to give *us* another chance. I told her it wasn't going to work and it was best she get her things and go. I left before she did so she couldn't prolong the debate. I stayed busy at work just in case she waited for me to come home. I purposely worked late that night to avoid her. When I came home, I saw she had packed up her stuff. Then Thursday came and work kicked my butt. I wanted to see you, but your lights were out. I assumed you were asleep early. Knowing we had big plans for Friday, I headed to my sister's farm and spent the night so I could get an early start."

"Doing what?"

Joseph sighed and tilted his head. "I don't want to say. It'll ruin the surprise."

I looked at him. I mean, really looked at him. Everything he said lined up with the timelines of the week I had. "You weren't avoiding me?"

"No. Why would I?" Joseph scoffed. "Granted, I was avoiding Caroline. But not *you*." He reached out and took my hand into his. "Look, I have no idea why Caroline came out of my apartment this morning. I can only assume she was searching for me, but I wasn't there. I swear. I was at my sister's. You can even ask Candace."

Joseph's hands felt so warm against mine. I had no idea how cold my hands were until he clasped one of mine in both of his.

I wanted to believe him. I wanted to think he hadn't just circled the block in his truck, dotting all his I's and crossing his T's before coming to me with this elaborate story. My heart wanted to believe, but my head wasn't so willing.

Joseph moved from his knees to the edge of my mattress and sat beside me. "I know you're having a hard time believing me. And I don't blame you. Caroline is a pro at messing with people's heads. But you have to trust me, Jamie. If you come with me right now, I can prove to you that she means nothing to me. I can show you why I was late picking you up. Please...just get dressed and come with me."

"Why can't you just tell me?" My voice came out as a squeak. I wanted to bury my head in a hole. How could I have allowed my emotions to surface in front of this man? I hated feeling this weak and needy.

"I *could* tell you. But it will ruin everything I worked so hard for." He brought his hand up to my face and stroked my cheek. I felt his thumb wipe away a tear. "Trust me, Sutherland. I can make this all better, if you just come with me. Please."

Chapter Twelve

I sat in Joseph's big Ford truck, staring out the window and watching the world pass by as he drove south on I-75. The radio played a Jason Aldean song and absently I listened to the words as the street lights of the busy highway lit the way due south.

I had no idea where we were headed, and frankly, I didn't much care. I'd go anywhere with this man, especially after the way he'd redeemed himself in my apartment. The way he looked at me so earnestly and wiped away my tears, as if he truly cared, made me feel like I was the most important woman in his life. I felt special knowing he'd gone to so much trouble for this 'date' and that he wanted to keep his plans a surprise. Most men would've given in and dished up the details. But not Joseph. It was clear he had a thing for surprises, and I couldn't help but love that about him.

I thought of all the pleasant surprises I had with Joseph, whether planned or by happenstance. There was the way we first met. The many unexpected run-ins in the hallway. The day he caught me in his arms when I collapsed from hypoglycemia and carried me to my couch. (That one I wish I could've been coherent for.) The way he fixed my temperamental espresso machine. The way he shared his feelings about me for the first time in his sister's driveway. The amazing stories he shared when we were sitting cross-legged in his treehouse. The kiss goodnight at my door...the list went on and on.

"You're awful quiet, Sutherland."

I looked at Joseph in the driver's seat. His wrist rested casually on the top of the steering wheel and he wore his boy-next-door grin. His Carhartt jacket hid the sinewy bulge of his muscled arms, but I knew they were there. His long thighs stretched across the leather seat, spread wide to accommodate his ever-present, cool confidence. Sitting in his truck, reminiscing about our odd relationship, I found comfort here. Joseph, whether he knew it or not, had a way of making me feel like I belonged in his world.

"I was just trying to figure out where we're going."

He glanced at me. "We're going to my sister's farm."

I furrowed my brows in confusion. "Is Candace's barn roof leaking again?"

Joseph chuckled. "Nah. There's no way that roof's leaking now. We fixed her up right."

I scoffed. "You remember the barn roof a whole lot differently than I do."

His laughter echoed above the radio playing in the background. "Oh, I remember the ladder blunder, don't you worry. So does Candace. She made sure to point it out for my parents at dinner last night when I told them about you."

"You told your parents about me?"

"Yeah, why wouldn't I?"

"I don't know." I sat embarrassed to think I was the topic of his family's conversation. Inwardly, I cringed, wondering what else was said about me.

"Look, I like you, Sutherland, and I want my parents to meet you. I think they'd really like you too. I know Candace does and that's a plus."

I stared out the window. Inside, I smiled with ridiculous joy but didn't have the courage to do so in front of him. Though I often gave the impression I was independent and self-assured, there was still a big part of me that harbored insecurities.

"By your silence, I'm going to assume you haven't mentioned *me* to your family."

I cleared my throat, the awkwardness of this conversation strangling me. "I told my grandmother all about you. Does she count?"

"Depends. When did you tell her about me?"

The impact of his question hit me solid in the chest. I winced. "Wednesday night."

Joseph rolled his eyes and took a firm grip on the steering wheel. "Great. Now she thinks I'm a jerk. What did she say?"

"Actually," I replied, remembering the benefit of the doubt my grandmother gave him. "She said I should take a leap of faith. That while a broken heart heals, regret lasts a lifetime."

Joseph turned his mouth under in thought. "She should write fortune cookies. I like her."

"Don't get too excited. I haven't decided whether or not I'm taking her advice."

"Oh, yeah?"

"I'll let you know after tonight."

Joseph's smile beamed with confidence, as if he knew something I didn't. "You do that."

The rest of the ride to Lexington passed in silence. At least for me. Joseph kept himself busy singing a few refrains from country songs that played on the radio. He even strummed a few of them on the steering wheel in between downshifts and turns. Unbeknownst to him, I hoped one day he'd feel comfortable enough to whip out his ol' flat box and play for real. His voice, I realized, would sound absolutely beautiful accompanied by an acoustic guitar.

Upon arriving at *Pride & Joy Farm*, he killed the ignition and engaged the brake. "You ready?"

I bit my lip. "I think so." Inside, I was ready to burst.

He reached across me, opened the glove box, and pulled out a flashlight. "We'll be needing this, for sure." He jumped out of the truck, ran around the front of the vehicle, and opened my door before I had a chance. Like last time, he snagged my hand and assisted me to the ground.

With my hand still in his, he led me through the woods in the direction of the lake. The beam of the flashlight highlighted the narrow deer path we followed, for the moon wasn't quite high enough to light the way. Like myself, it seemed to emit its own shyness, hiding behind the leafless trees.

In the dark, I couldn't make anything out, though I assumed at this point, we were following the familiar trail to his favorite, childhood place. My heart skipped, anticipating another death-defying climb.

"Watch your step," he said, indicating an upraised root along the way. I felt his grasp tighten around my hand and I reveled in his manly, protective nature.

"Okay, we're here."

I looked around. The shadowy darkness hindered my ability to really discern whether we were at his treehouse or not. Outside the beam of the flashlight, I could barely see Joseph, much less our destination. I played the sarcastic card. "Wow. You did all this for me?"

"Shut up," he joked. "You can't see shit yet. Give me a minute."

I heard him rustle around in the leaves a few feet to my right, shining light on a semi-large, red and black square object on the ground. He pulled what looked like a choke and turned a key. The quiet rumbling engine of a generator hummed to life and instantly the world around me brightened.

Tiny white Christmas lights, draped among the tree limbs above, shone like twinkling stars in a midnight sky. They also roped around and in between each spindle on the railings of the treehouse and circled the entire trunk on the way down. At the base of the tree was a table draped with a white tablecloth, two place settings of fine china, two crystal wine glasses, and a covered silver platter. The table legs and chairs were also strung with the tiny lights, illuminating a spectacular, private table for two with a bottle of white wine chilling in an ice-filled toolbox—his rusty-red, Champion toolbox. I smiled. The old relic was soon becoming an iconic symbol of our relationship—trustworthy and multi-functional.

Next to the table, stood a lampshade-style, propane, patio heater for warmth and an old '90's boom box, complete with a CD player. Joseph lit the heater, then reached into his jacket and pulled out a CD case, rattling it in his grasp.

"Is that my Frank Sinatra Greatest Hits?"

"Yeah, well, I noticed it when we unpacked your stuff last weekend," he explained as he inserted the compact disc and pressed PLAY. "So, I stole it tonight while you were getting dressed." He strolled casually toward me with his thumbs in his jean pockets, his devilish grin inching higher up his cheeks. "I already added breaking and entering to the list of things I did wrong this week. What's a little theft?"

Old Blue Eyes started singing *I've Got You Under My Skin*, and all I could do was shake my head. "You did nothing wrong. Everything's just right." My gaze traveled up the elevation of the tree, taking in the height of the lights that hung from its limbs. "How in the world did you get those up so high?"

He followed the direction of my scrutiny. "That, my dear, is what a ladder and sheer determination will get you. Although, I made certain *not* to kick the ladder over once I was up there."

I adored his sarcastic humor, but still freaked out about him hanging lights at such a dangerous height. "Seriously, Joseph. Those lights are about ten feet above the treehouse. Tell me you didn't put the step ladder on that dilapidated platform?"

He planted his hands firmly on his hips. "Yeah, that's called reckless courage, right there."

"You think? You could've killed yourself." I punched his gut, though my blow was cushioned by his thick coat. He pretended to stagger backward.

He came back to me, took my hand, and pulled me into a dance embrace. His arm held me tight around the small of my back and his warm hand swallowed mine. "It would've been worth it."

His eyes bore into my soul as he swung me around his makeshift woodland dance floor. I wanted to look away, but couldn't. His intense gaze mesmerized me, as did the palpable pull of his body to mine. Like a magnet, I was drawn closer. I was the negative electron attracted to his positive. For the entire length of Frankie Baby's hit melody, we slow danced beneath the dangling lights, dressed in winter coats, boots, and scarves. Not even a sudden winter blizzard could ruin my most perfect evening.

"Am I forgiven then?" he finally asked, when the music momentarily paused between songs.

I felt foolish for thinking Joseph could ever be so merciless as to break my heart. Here was a man who'd had his share of heartache with the loss of his sister, Lindsey, and the relentless shenanigans from his she-devil ex, Caroline. He'd endured grief and pain firsthand and would never purposely push that kind of hurt on anyone. I felt guilty for thinking he could. "If anyone needs forgiving, it's me. Not you. I'm sorry I doubted you, Joseph."

He let go of my hand and wrapped both arms around my back, linking his hands at my waist. "I don't blame you, Jamie. I blame the countless assholes you dated before me who made you feel guarded and suspicious."

His words took me aback. "Are we dating now?"

"You tell me, Sutherland. Would that make you happy?"

My answer came out with a blush. "Yes."

"Good. That's exactly what I wanted to hear." He led me toward the table. "Shall we eat, then?" He pulled out my chair, and after I sat, he draped a cloth napkin over my lap.

"What's for dinner?"

"The only thing that's delectable at both hot and cold temperatures, especially on a chilly December night like this one." He lifted the silver dome cover from the platter and revealed our dinner choices. "Cold, left-over pizza—everything but anchovies," he added. "Gourmet cupcakes—but only for eating this time," he warned. "And lookie there…two little fortune cookies."

I smiled as he took his seat across from me. "You've outdone yourself."

He shook out his napkin and folded it neatly on his lap. "Have I?"

"Yes." I took another sweeping glance at the magical place where I sat. The music, the outdoor heat, the glowing effect of the numerous white lights all around me, the china and crystal, the spread of conventional, bachelor take-out food, and what seemed to have become our sentimental dessert-fetish—fortune cookies and cupcakes. I felt like I was living in a whimsical fairytale, my chivalrous knight in shining armor sitting with me.

Tears welled up in my eyes and I looked down at my lap to keep Joseph from seeing them. Unfortunately, one escaped and rolled down my cheek before I could catch it.

"Hey, now," I heard Joseph say two seconds before I felt his hand on mine. I opened my eyes and found him kneeling before me, his other hand brushing my hair from my face. "I didn't mean to make you cry. I wanted to make you happy."

I laughed at his naiveté. "I am happy, Joseph. These are tears of joy."

"There's such a thing?"

I melted. How was it that this poor man never knew what tears of joy were? Then I remembered the wicked witch he used to date. I pitied him for all the wasted years he spent with that cruel, self-absorbed woman. I took his hand from my face and held it tightly. "Yes, Joseph. There is such a thing. And it's wonderful. *You* are wonderful. Everything you did for me...I...I just..."

"What?" His Montana-blue-sky eyes pleaded with me. "You just what?"

"I just keep asking myself...why? Why did you do all this?"

Joseph drew in a deep breath and leaned back on his heels. "Because of all you did for me. Sutherland, you have no idea what a difference you've made in my life. I thought I was as happy as I could possibly be, and then I met you. My whole outlook changed. My whole life changed. I never really knew what it meant to enjoy a woman's company until you came along and brought this crazy, I-can't-stop-thinking-about-you kind of happiness. I never had that with Caroline. I never had that with *anyone*. I don't know. I guess this is just my way of saying thanks. And hopefully, maybe...you might find yourself feeling the same way about me...as I do you." His voice faltered and he waved his hand to dismiss the point he was trying to make. "It's stupid—and probably a little too over-the-top this soon in—"

"No, it's not stupid," I said, pulling him back. "Or over the top. It's...it's sweet. And unexpectedly...reassuring. 'Cause I feel the same."

"You do?"

It floored me that a gorgeous man like Joseph would ever doubt a woman falling head-over-heels for him. His sincere humbleness was like a breath of fresh air to my polluted, falling-for-the-wrong-guy, heart-broken past. "Yes, I do."

His eyes locked with mine. He moved from his haunches to his knees, positioning himself between my bent legs. My heart leapt as he brought his hands up to my face. His warm thumbs caressed my cheeks as his gaze fell over my lips, my eyes, my nose, my lips again, and back up to my eyes. When he got his fill of looking at me, his fingers slid into my hair on each side of my head, pulling me slowly toward him. His lips parted and pressed against mine with the gentlest of care. The aroma of wood, musk, and that vaguely familiar sweet scent I remembered from his bedroom enveloped me. I felt his tongue slide across my bottom lip. For a moment, I tensed. He tasted me, his mouth moving slowly and cautiously.

I focused on the way he cupped my face in his gentle hands. The way he held his breath as I was. The way he waited for me to give consent.

I was ready to go further than just a touching of lips. I was ready to kiss him the way a lover would. The way a woman who knew exactly what she wanted would. I'd waited so long to feel the essence of this man's genuine affection and for the first time in my life I wanted to know what virility tasted like.

I wrapped my arms around his back and pulled him closer. I parted my lips and his tongue met mine, sliding and twisting with slow, deliberate strokes. I savored the taste of Joseph and the skill of his passionate, heated kiss. I floated as if I had wings.

I heard Joseph make a noise. A small moan, perhaps, and I had to smile. Did that mean he liked my kiss as much as I loved his? I opened my eyes and a semblance of bliss and restraint encompassed the look on his face.

"Sorry…" He pulled on the collar of his jacket and ripped open the top snaps as if he were suddenly feeling overheated in his insulated coat. "Damn. Your kiss is amazing, Jamie."

Heat enflamed my neck and cheeks. I could not believe what I heard. In my mind, I chalked up another score on my tally of things Caroline had lost out on.

"I think it's time for you to open this," Joseph said, dropping one of the fortune cookies in my hand.

I looked at him, wondering who the real author of the fortune would be—him or Confucius. I tore the clear wrapper and broke the cookie in half, anxious to read the words on the concealed slip of paper. I unfolded it and smiled at the message printed in all caps.

I am your Confucius, if you'll still have me.

"So, you *did* write those last fortunes." I pressed the slip of paper to the table and ironed it with my fingers, treasuring it as I had all the rest. "But how? How did you do this? The cookie was sealed."

"It's amazing the things you can find on the Internet. There's this site that lets you write your own fortunes and they'll stick 'em in the cookie, seal 'em, and send 'em."

"When did you do this?"

"Sunday night…after we kissed goodnight."

My mind flashed back to that night at my door. I recalled the nervousness that had possessed each of us as we stood there, trying to decide the right way to say good night. I remembered Joseph apologizing and how he approached me, backing me against the doorframe right before he kissed me. It was the best, first kiss I'd ever experienced.

I shook my head clear of these thoughts and returned to the subject at hand. "But how did you get them so fast?"

"Overnight shipping," he said matter-of-factly. "It cost me a pretty penny, but so worth it after seeing your smile. You have such a beautiful smile, Sutherland."

I could feel his gaze on me as I reread the message. I wondered if he meant to write the fortune in such a way that adding 'in bed' to the end made it that much more interesting.

"What are you thinking about?"

"This fortune. I just added 'in bed' after it, and I'm contemplating your offer."

"My offer?"

"If you'll still have me *in bed*."

Joseph laughed. "Well, then now's the perfect time to open the other cookie."

"Okay...." I tore it open immediately and read the second note.

Life's too short. Say all there is to say.
Do all there is to do.

"In bed," he added quickly.

I lowered my chin and raised one eyebrow. "Is this your convoluted, romantic way of trying to get past third base with me?"

"Hey, this may be the last night you get all of this," he said motioning over the length of his body.

Since he offered, I took a nice long look at Joseph's muscular form, mentally picturing his bare chest beneath his coat. "You come with an expiration date?"

"I'm just saying…I may not be around come morning."

I sat there dumbfounded. I had no idea what Joseph was getting at. "Why do you say that?"

He leaned across the table and looked around, as if to make certain his confession would only be heard by my ears. "'Cause Candace's going to kill me when she can't find all of her Christmas lights."

My jaw dropped. I looked up and estimated the number of lights it took to create this elaborate, yet elegant, fantasy world. "Joseph Alexander Scarbrough! You didn't!"

He snagged a piece of pizza and bit off a huge chunk, smiling like a Cheshire cat. "I did."

Chapter Thirteen

I stood in the upstairs hallway of Candace's house. It was about two in the morning and Joseph had left me momentarily to let his sister know we'd be crashing in her spare bedrooms. I waited in the dark, careful not to make a sound. But inwardly, I was squealing and reeling from the most magnificent date I'd ever been on. I could hardly stop smiling.

As I heard Joseph come up the staircase, I wiped the crazy, giddy-girl grin off my face. I wanted to end the night on a good note, not a scary one. I rocked back on my heels in nervousness and pretended I was calm and poised. If he could hear my heart, he'd know I was a sprightly mess on the inside.

"Okay, Candace is cool with it," he whispered. His hands automatically reached out and clasped my elbows. "Would you like something more comfortable to sleep in? One of my shirts, maybe?"

The man could've offered me chain mail. As long as it was his, I was willing to sleep in anything. "Thanks, that'd be nice."

"Give me a sec." He disappeared into the room beside me. I heard a drawer open and close, and his footsteps coming back to me. "Here you go. See if this'll fit. It's my lucky shirt."

It's my *lucky shirt now.* "I'm sure it'll fit just fine." I held the soft cotton jersey with reverence and imagined how great it would be to sleep in it, second only to sleeping with Joseph.

He pointed to the rooms across the hall from each other. "You can sleep in there, and I'll sleep in here." I barely had time to peek inside my room before he wrapped his arms around me and pulled me close. "There's extra blankets in the closet, if you get cold."

I liked how he seemed to worry over me. "I'll be fine."

"Okay. Well, I guess this is goodnight."

I nodded and bit my lip, hating for this night to end.

"Sleep well, Sutherland." He pressed his lips to mine, smiled, and pulled away. We caught and held each other's hand, neither of us wanting to let go. I watched him back up into his room with reluctance, our arms extending far enough to keep our fingers locked. Once our fingertip grasp broke, we entered our separate rooms. I clung to my door, not wanting to close it. He left his open and all I wanted to do was follow him. I yearned to kiss him again and feel his hands on me. He had the best touch of any man I'd ever known and it was all I could do to separate myself from him.

I heard him rustle in the darkness and I saw his coat land on the floor at the foot of his bed, then his shirt. I heard boots tumble. Two seconds later, I heard the quick rip of his zipper and the swish of denim as he yanked them from his legs and tossed them on the pile.

I swallowed hard at the thought of Joseph in his boxers—or maybe briefs...whatever he wore—climbing into bed. The sound of springs squealed under the weight of his muscular body had my heart aching with need. A vision of him lying in bed with his hands behind his head, his biceps flexing, had me darn near salivating. But who knew what the man really did after he took his clothes off?

As my mind attempted to wander off toward less than innocent, I closed my door and changed out of my own coat and clothes. I slipped his jersey over my head and shimmied it down over my body. Joseph's aroma enveloped me. I was in heaven knowing this oversized shirt once laid against his smooth, warm skin and now it was against mine.

* * * *

I snuggled deeper into the soft mattress and relished the unusual heat radiating from beneath the heavy duvet of Candace's spare bed. All night, I dreamed of Joseph—his goodnight kiss, the way he looked at me with mad desire as we entered our separate bedrooms. I even dreamed he called to me, in that sexy husky whisper of his, and I sneaked across the hall to join him in his room. My brain had so vividly conjured the steamy scenario of him lifting the covers so I could slide into his hot, naked embrace that even now, I could feel the sultry heat of his chest against my back as we lay spooned.

Oh, how wonderful this would be if it were real...

Not wanting to open my eyes and wake from the magnificence of my dream, I rolled toward my make-believe Joseph and snuggled against him. I reveled in the way his short, crisp hair tickled my fingertips as I lay my hand against his muscled chest. I drew in a deep breath of satisfaction and let his potent, sweet aroma waft around me. I felt his embrace shift and tighten.

Half asleep, I spoke to Joseph as if here were actually lying in bed with me. "I'm not one to linger in bed, but you could certainly talk me into it."

Inwardly, I sent up a prayer of thanks for the incredible ability of my subconscious mind to recreate moments of pleasure without much coercion. It amazed me how real my dream seemed to be.

I felt my fantasy deepen, going so far as to feel Joseph's leg drape over mine. Consumed with the feel of utter contentment, I murmured praises to my pretend Joseph. "You are so warm..."

"So are you."

I scoffed, half-stunned at how real his voice sounded to my drowsy self. Without realizing, my eyes fluttered open and a blurry sight of Joseph sleeping on my pillow emerged. His arms lay draped around me, his enticing lips inches from mine. That unruly lock of hair I loved so much had fallen over his brow. The sexy shadow of scruff along his strong jaw dared to be touched. He was a heavenly vision in his sleeping form.

I blinked languidly, preparing myself for when this beautiful delusion would dissipate into thin air and I'd be left clutching a pillow. Only that pillow never appeared.

I blinked again, this time a little more energetically to clear my vision.

The scene was the same. Joseph. Still there. In my bed.

A sleepy grin spread across his handsome face when he saw me staring. "Good morning."

I gasped and bolted upright. "What do you think you're doing?" I smacked him on his bare arm as he stirred.

"Ow! What the heck was that for?" he asked, now fully awake and scowling.

I gripped the blankets and pulled them up around me. "Why are you in my bed?"

He rubbed the sleep from his eyes and rolled onto his

back. "Why am I in *your* bed? Think again, Sutherland. You're in mine."

The Gift of Something Grand

Chapter One

"Why am I in your bed? Think again, Sutherland. You're in mine."

Joseph Scarbrough's words hit me like a ton of bricks. My eyes scanned the room. I fell asleep in a mint green room last night and woke up this morning in a blue one. I was, indeed, in his bed.

But how'd I get in here? Did he really beckon for me in the middle of the night and I succumbed? I wouldn't do that. *Would I?*

I watched him run his fingers through his bedhead crop of hair. His bare chest looked richly appealing against the crisp white sheets. I now cursed my overactive imagination because now was not the time to be weak.

"Seriously, Joseph. Why am I in this room?"

"Hell, if I know." He propped himself up on one elbow. "It was about four in the morning when you came in, and I was too tired to care."

Sheer panic tightened its vise around my heart. "I sleep

walked?" What if I had also talked in my sleep? What if I said things to him? Things I'd never divulge this soon in a relationship. Scratch that. I didn't want to know. I just needed to get away.

I jumped from the bed and took the covers with me. "I can't believe I did this. I'm so sorry." Brisk air met my bare legs, and I fumbled to cover them with the blankets. I knew I should've slept in my own pants and not just the oversized T-shirt Joseph had given me. "Why didn't you kick me out?"

"Yeah, 'cause that's what we men do. We wine and dine women in hope you'll climb into bed with us—just so we can kick you out."

I heard his quiet laughter as I hustled toward the door right before he leapt from the bed and caught me at the threshold. In his boxer briefs. At least I didn't have to wonder anymore.

"Hey, you don't have to be sorry. Trust me, I didn't mind."

I squeezed my eyes shut. My face flamed with embarrassment. I was not one of those girls who jumped into bed with a guy. To me, an intimate relationship was something further down the line, when both parties were committed and ready. Sure, I was committed and ready, but I was pretty darn sure he wasn't. "That's not the point, Joseph. I'm not like this. I don't hop into bed with men— *especially* this soon and—"

"Hey," he interrupted, brushing my tangled hair from my face. "Nothing happened. I promise. I was a perfect gentleman."

I gritted my teeth and forced a smile. Maybe he was, but what was I? I had no recollection of my actions and I feared I may have come on too strong. "I'm not worried about what you did or didn't do. I know you wouldn't take advantage of me but what did I—"

"Jamie, breathe." He gave me a little shake and looked deep into my eyes. I relaxed at the sight of that calm Montana blue sky staring back at me and sighed. His lovely blue eyes could ground me every time.

"That's better. Now listen. I was taught never to wake a sleep walker. God only knows why we're taught that, but, frankly, I wouldn't have wakened you up anyway. It was obvious you had no idea what you were doing. You were cute."

"Cute?"

"Yes, cute. Especially when you snuggled your little butt against me."

I sighed even heavier this time. "Great. Just great." I tried to walk away, dragging the blankets and my shredded dignity with me, but he stopped me again.

"Sutherland, wait. I know you're embarrassed about this, but you don't have to be. Nothing happened."

"I know, but it's your sister's house."

"And my sister's house gets drafty. You were cold. Besides, she probably has no idea this even happened in the first place. You're freaking out for nothing."

"I guess."

Joseph must have heard the skepticism in my voice. He pulled me into his arms, blankets and all, and hugged me. "It could've happen to anyone. In fact, I can think of no better person I'd want sleep walking into my bed. In the words of Keith Urban, you look *good* in my shirt."

I felt his hand on the bare skin of my thigh where the blankets had failed to cover me. I pushed him away and hobbled into the bedroom across the hall. I tried to keep myself shielded with the swath of blankets wrapped around me, but was failing miserably.

He blew out a perfect construction worker's whistle. "Nice legs, Sutherland."

I slammed the door and collapsed against it, beaming with delight behind the safety of the wood. My brain was in a complete whirlwind, and I couldn't have been happier. The sexiest eligible bachelor I'd ever known had just favored me with a sexist whistle and I loved it.

Chapter Two

A light knock sounded on the door behind my head.

"You want to take a shower?"

My breath caught. Instant pictures of Joseph and me, all wet and soapy, filled my brain. Surely he didn't mean *with* him…

"Separate, of course," he added after I hadn't responded.

I breathed a little easier. "That would be nice."

"Ladies first," he offered.

"No, you go ahead. I've got to….um…." I needed time to myself. To get a grip. A serious grip. "I need to call work and see if everything's okay. Make sure they don't need me to come in."

"If you say so." I know that was disappointment I heard in his voice. "I'll set out a towel and washcloth for you when I'm finished."

"Thanks." I didn't really need to call work. Donna, my college weekend crew leader, had my number and never hesitated to call if things went haywire. I did, however, want to call my grandmother. She'd given me such good advice about taking that risk with Joseph that I thought it only fair to let her know how the date went.

I heaved my blanket-cocooned self from the door, shuffled to the edge of the bed and plopped down. I reached for my purse and dug out my cell. As I swiped the screen on my iPhone, I heard the water from the shower turn on and figured I had about ten minutes.

I continued to scroll for my grandma's thumbnail and tapped it. I gave her plenty of time to get to the phone. She wasn't as quick as she used to be. After six rings, her cheery voice sounded in my ear.

"Hey, Grandma. It's me."

"Well, hello, Jamie. How are you this morning?"

I fiddled with a loose string on the hem of the blanket draped over my lap. "I took that leap of faith last night."

"You did?" She sounded like she pretended to be shocked, all the while knowing darn good and well that I would. "How did it go?"

I flopped to my back and grinned like a baboon. I had no intention of telling her about how I sleep walked into Joseph's bedroom. Given how important it was to her for a young lady to preserve her reputation, it was probably best to leave that part out. "Oh, Grandma, he pulled out all the stops." I used an expression I knew she'd be familiar with. I seemed to do that often with her as she enjoyed hearing her vintage vernacular still in use.

"This is that Joseph fellow, right?"

"Yeah, that's the one." I imagined her taking a seat on the antique, upholstered chair next to the entryway table that held her black, rotary phone and stain glass lamp.

"So, what made you decide this all of a sudden? Last I heard, you gave up on men. Protecting your fragile heart and all that. What makes this gentleman caller so special?"

I loved the way she referred to Joseph. Just hearing her talk of gentlemen callers and courting made me wish some things were still the same. Back in her day, men were held to gentlemanly standards. It was part of their upbringing; opening doors, standing when a gal entered the room, and pushing her chair in as she sat at the table. It was all second nature. Nowadays, guys barely even walk a girl to her door. In my opinion, not since before the whole equal rights thing started in the nineteen sixties had men been gentlemen. Grandma wasn't the only one who believed times had changed and not necessarily for the better.

"Well, let's see. He's kind and he's funny." I rolled over onto my stomach and crossed my ankles as I continued to tick off his most endearing traits one by one. "He loves his family. He's a musician. He can fix a lot of things, too—he's the building's superintendent. Oh! And he loves your lasagna recipe."

"All good qualities. But what does he look like? Attraction's important too, you know."

I had to laugh. My grandmother may have been in her eighties, but she wasn't a prude. I tried to remember my days watching old black and white movies with her, so I could come up with a handsome actor who most resembled Joseph. "Name some leading Hollywood men, Grandma."

"James Dean? You youngins still think he hung the moon."

"No, too bad-boy looking."

"Okay, how about Clark Gable?"

"No, not him. Can't get passed the mustache."

"Hm. You're a tough cookie. All right, how about Archibald Leach."

"Who?"

I heard Grandma sigh. "Cary Grant, child. Cary Grant."

"Close…Joseph definitely has his casual confidence, but Grant's eyes are too dark. Joseph's are blue. Dreamy blue, like a Montana sky."

"Blue, huh? How about Peter O'Toole then?"

"No, too thin in the face." I twirled a strand of hair around my finger and pondered hard. "Hey, what's that movie we watched with Ava Gardner I really liked?"

"Oh, you mean *The Snows of Kilimanjaro.*"

"Yeah, that's the one."

I could almost hear my grandmother's thoughts churning. "You say your Joseph looks like Gregory Peck as Harry Street? Well, now there's a striking man. I'm going to have to meet this Joseph and judge for myself."

"Personally, I think you'll agree, Grandma. He's got that suave demeanor, a chiseled face with a little bit of scruff around his lips, and a darling chunk of hair that always seems to fall over his forehead, just like Harry Street on safari."

"Good hair, you say?"

Grandma was a fan of men with thick hair, claiming she married Grandpa for that very reason. "Oh, the best hair," I crooned. "The kind you can run your fingers through endlessly—"

"Ahem."

Startled, I whirled on the bed and saw Joseph leaning against the doorframe, his arms crossed—a classic young Gregory Peck look—if Peck had ever sported snug Wrangler jeans and a white T. I marveled at how it stretched and fit ever so deliciously across his broad shoulders. He looked like an angel trapped in a bad-boy, Harley-biker body. And his devilish smile said he'd heard every word of my conversation.

I felt my skin flush as I heard Grandma still chattering on the other end. I was pretty sure she was going on about Grandpa's thick head of hair in his younger days, before he went off to war and they buzzed it all off regulation style.

"Um, Grandma," I stuttered, inch-worming off the bed. I kicked at the blankets to free my feet. "I gotta let you go. Can I call you back later?"

"Sure. Is everything all right?"

I heard the concern in her voice and didn't want her to worry. "Everything's fine. Something…pressing just came up." I laid my fingers over my lips to signal Joseph to be silent.

"I hope it's nothing serious," I heard my grandmother say as he sauntered up closer to me, tugging me in his arms.

He murmured in my ear, making me shiver. "Am I really that pressing? I thought I was suave and chiseled with great hair."

I covered his mouth with my palm and widened my eyes at him for emphasis. "No, Grandma, nothing serious at all. Promise."

"If you say so, dear. Stop by and see me sometime."

I hated to rush her, but I needed to get off the phone. Joseph was nibbling my ear and I was extremely ticklish. Holding back a giggle, I pushed him away from my sensitive lobe and told my grandmother I'd visit soon. Ending the call, I tipped my head back to get a good look at Joseph's face.

His gorgeous, blue eyes twinkled amid a bright toothy grin. His hunky boy-next-door smile was definitely his best asset. That and his muscled chest and arms. And derriere, if we were breaking him down into pieces.

Joseph must have realized I was ogling. "What?"

"Nothing," I lied, delighting in the clean manly smell of the body wash he used. "Just admiring you."

"Oh, yeah?" He gave his head a good shake, causing his too-sexy-for-his-own-good hair to fall over his eye. "Want to admire my darling chunk of hair that you could run your hands through endlessly," he mocked in his best swooning Jamie Sutherland voice.

"Shut up."

Without warning, he dipped his head and I dodged him. "What are you doing?"

"I was going to kiss you."

"No, you're not. I haven't brushed my teeth, Joseph."

"I don't care."

"I do. There's some things a woman doesn't like to reveal."

"Like she has dragon breath in the morning?" He laughed. "It's quite common, Jamie. Everyone has it. Even me."

"I know, but—"

"Here," he said, pulling a brand new toothbrush out of his back pocket. "Brush up, if it'll make you feel better."

I looked at the dental instrument in his hand, still sealed in its package. I accepted it. Hesitantly. "You keep a stash of these for all your girlfriends, whenever they sleep over?"

He crossed his arms. "No, they're Candace's. So, I can only assume *she* stashes them for all her *boyfriends* who sleep over. If any of them has ever made it that far."

His joke about his hard-nosed sister had me giggling. I poked him with the brush. "You're cruel."

"According to you and your grandmother, I'm Gregory Peck."

"I see it's also in your nature to eavesdrop." I didn't bother to hide my snide tone. I headed for the bathroom down the hall with his laughter following me.

"I guess that makes us even, now doesn't it, Sutherland?"

Chapter Three

I stepped out of the comforter and left it in a heap on the shag bathroom rug. I took a long hard look at myself in the mirror. My hair was a tangled mess and my makeup was near nonexistent, save for the mascara still stuck to my lashes. Joseph's bright blue University of Kentucky jersey made me look paler than normal too. I couldn't believe he woke to the sight of *this* monstrosity and wanted to kiss it.

Glancing at the toothbrush in my hand, I realized I'd walked away from Joseph without asking where Candace kept the toothpaste. I sighed.

"Side drawer on the right," Joseph called, as if he knew I was standing there wondering.

I yanked open the drawer and a tube of Crest 3D White slid to the front. "Thanks," I yelled over my shoulder. I squirted a good amount on the bristles and went to work on my fuzzy teeth, gawking at my appearance again in the mirror.

"You look fine, Sutherland," I heard him say.

"Oh, my gosh," I said, my mouth full of white foam. "Do you have a camera in here or something?"

"I just know you."

I finished brushing, spit, brushed again for good measure, rinsed and spit again and dropped the toothbrush on the counter. "You think you *know* me?"

"I know you well enough to know you're in there bashing yourself."

I glanced into the mirror and scowled. "No, I wasn't." But my lie only encouraged him to intervene instead of drop the subject. The door handle turned and I leapt forward to block him from entering. "Do not come in here, Joseph," I said, peeking through the ajar door. "I'm not dressed to receive."

"Oh, cut the act, Ava Gardner."

I tried to slam the door shut, but his palm blocked it and he barreled in anyway.

"Tell me you weren't in here picking yourself apart in front of the mirror, and I'll leave."

Feeling very self-conscience about my bare legs, I yanked down the hem of his jersey. It drove me crazy that I could be so transparent. "All right. Maybe a little."

He shook his head. "This, coming from a woman who's independent, knows what she wants in life, and has worked hard enough to build her own thriving business."

"That has everything to do with my character, not my looks."

"Well, I think you're stunning."

I looked away, finding his words hard to believe. Sure, I could look in a mirror and see that I had some pleasing features. My teeth were perfectly straight and I smiled a lot. But to say I was stunning seemed a far stretch.

Joseph turned my face toward him. "Wanna know why I think you're stunning? Because you don't know you are. And that makes you the most beautiful woman in the room."

"Not if I stand in a room with Caroline. I can't hold a candle to her." I saw his eyes widen ever so slightly and his shoulders straighten as if hearing her name pin pricked something deep inside him. I regretted my words immediately. "I'm sorry. I shouldn't have said that."

"No, I'm glad you did."

"You are?"

"Yes, because it proves my point. Caroline is a very attractive woman. I'll be the first to admit it. However, she *knows* she's gorgeous, which means that's as far as her appeal goes. Skin deep. Go beneath that and there's nothing worth a second look. You, on the other hand, *can't* see how beautiful you are. There's not an ounce of conceit in you and that's what makes you a total bombshell."

A comfortable warmth spread through me and I couldn't contain my joy.

"You're smiling. So, we good here?"

"Yes."

His deep voice dropped to a husky whisper. "Good. Now, kiss me."

My body trembled with excitement and my brain went blank. He tasted of refreshing mint and something richly masculine that could only be described as Joseph. An overwhelming numbness swept over me as if this were our first kiss. Only this wasn't our first. Not even the second, third or fourth. I'd lost count after last night.

I was assuredly falling for this man. And for the first time in my life, it felt safe to do so.

"You're smiling again."

"I'm happy," I claimed, unwilling to end the kiss. I wrapped my arms around his neck and pressed my lips harder against his. All I wanted was to get closer to him.

I felt two strong hands cup my bottom. Callouses scraped against the satin of my panties as he lifted and hiked my legs around his waist. He crushed me against the open bathroom door and it gave way. Swinging back on its hinges, it slammed into the rigid stopper behind it. The sudden jarring clacked our teeth together.

"Ow!" we both exclaimed simultaneously, then laughed.

"Are you okay?" Joseph asked.

I ran my tongue across my front teeth to make certain I hadn't chipped them. "Yeah, I'm good. You?"

I watched him do the same and I felt my stomach somersault at the sight of his tongue moving so skillfully. "All good here too."

"Who knew kissing could be so dangerous."

He laughed at my joke and I loved him for it.

"Next time we kiss," he said, reaching above my head and knocking, "I'll have to remember to utilize a wall, not a door."

"More 'next times,' huh? You're good at planning those."

"So, I've been told." He snickered and staked his thumbs in his front pockets. He leaned against the bathroom vanity, contemplating something. "You know...you're actually the first girl I enjoy having 'next times' with. I find myself looking forward to them."

"Is that so?"

"Mmm-hmm. It is." He snagged my hand and pulled me to him. "And speaking of next time...you are so wearing this jersey again." He brushed my hair back and revealed the number on the front, his eyes full of lust. Full of promise. "Thirty-three is definitely my lucky number."

I slowly leaned forward and kissed him one last time to savor this moment. I drew in a long breath and released it. "Now get out, so I can get my shower."

Another chuckle shook his body. "Yes, ma'am. Need any help?"

I touched his prickly cheek. "I think I got it. Left is hot. Right is cold."

He cleared his throat and pushed himself from the vanity. "Yeah, I've got to get out of here before I need another one."

"Another shower?"

He stepped into the hall and respired heavily. "I don't think the first one was cold enough."

Chapter Four

I stood in the shower, letting the hot water cascade down my back. Steam filled the bathroom as happiness filled my heart. It had been a long time since I'd felt so elated, this high on life. It was almost as good as the day I'd opened my coffee shop, but without all the stress of its potential failure.

Normally by now, I'd be second guessing the direction of this new relationship because things were going too well. I'd fret about how long it would last, almost betting against myself. Being a serial, ruined-relationship survivor does that to a person.

But with Joseph, I didn't feel so cynical. I felt confident in the days ahead and looked forward to having him involved in every aspect of my life. He was good for me and it seemed, I was good for him.

Though we came from different worlds, in time our lives had meshed. My independence and lack of self-absorption was as much medicine for him as his honest and sincere camaraderie was for me. My heart felt whole again. Stitched back together by the tender thread of Joseph's casual yet notable existence.

Deep down, I knew we were perfect for each other and nothing could come between us. Not even Caroline.

"Hey, Jamie."

His deep voice broke through the happy fog of my roving thoughts. I peered out of the shower curtain and projected my voice so he could hear me. "Yes?"

"Candace made breakfast for us. You got time to stay?"

"Sure."

"Everything's okay at the coffee shop?"

I remembered I'd told Joseph I needed to call in, even though I hadn't. "Oh, yeah. Things are fine. I can stay."

"Perfect. I'll wait for you."

"I'll just be a minute." I squirted shampoo in my hand and lathered up. I washed my hair and body as quickly as I could. I dried off and stepped out of the shower. The mound of blankets lay on the bath mat. *Crap. I forgot to bring in my clothes with me.*

There wasn't much chance Joseph hadn't waited for me, but I wished this once he would've gone on down to breakfast. I wrapped a fluffy mint green bath towel around my body and laid my lips against the bathroom door.

"Joseph?"

"Forgot something, didn't you?"

I tipped my head back and sighed, squirming my toes into the bath rug. "Yes…"

"I've got your clothes right here."

I cracked the door open and peeked through. Joseph stood, casually leaning against the frame, with my clothes neatly folded on his palm. "Here you go."

"Thanks." I snatched them out of his hand and ripped the towel from my body, throwing it at him. I saw it wrap around his grinning face before I slammed the door.

"So not fair, Sutherland."

I giggled and turned the lock for good measure.

I dressed as fast as I could and ran my fingers through my damp hair. I didn't dare look in the mirror again for fear Joseph would call me out. When I stepped out of the bathroom, he lunged at me and pulled me into his arms.

"You think you're something else, don't you?" Joseph said huskily. He tickled my ribs to underscore his point. I wriggled out of his arms, our laughter knitting us together like a fuzzy, warm sweater. Yes, we were a great pair.

His hand clasped mine and he led me down the hall toward the kitchen, his smile still beaming.

"I think I heard my other sister downstairs. Her name's Miranda. You'll like her. She's not as rude as Candace, but she's twice as tough."

I trotted down the steps with Joseph leading the way. To my surprise, he stopped at the base of the staircase, keeping me one step higher. I was eye level with his handsome face and a tremor of anticipation raced through me as he blocked my path. His long arms braced the wall at one side of me and the railing at the other.

"Don't be nervous. Miranda's harmless."

I pretended to be nonchalant. "Okay."

"I don't want you to feel overwhelmed."

"Why would I feel overwhelmed? I've already met Candace."

"Yeah, but I should warn you. Candace is in a mood."

"Because of me?" I hated to think I'd ticked her off by spending the night with her brother.

"Nah, she just gets this way every so often and for no good reason. Just do what I do. Ignore her."

My stomach knotted up. If Candace was in a mood, I worried what she might have said about me to Miranda. It would be two against one, and I sucked at contact sports.

"Hey," he soothed. "Don't let Candace scare you. Trust me, her bark is worse than her bite."

I tried to shake off my nerves and pep talked my wary

self from inside the batter's box. "Right. Okay. I can do this."

His eyes shimmered like blue diamonds. "I know you can." He draped his arm around my shoulder and pulled me off the step. Tugging me close against his side, we walked together into the kitchen where his two sisters sat at the table.

A hush came over them as we made our entrance, conjoined as if we'd been close all our lives. With the peculiar looks we received, I felt safer near him.

"Miranda, this is Jamie," Joseph blurted out. "Jamie, Miranda."

Miranda exchanged a surprised smile with Candace. I assumed she expected Caroline to accompany her brother.

"Please, call me Randi." She stood to shake my hand across the table. "It's nice to meet you."

I extended my hand as well and, like Candace, calluses scraped against my soft palm. I tried not to get hung up on the fact that we came from totally different worlds. I only hoped she didn't think less of me because my hands lacked the feel of rough sandpaper.

"Sit, please. Make yourself at home." Miranda gestured toward an open seat.

Joseph and I chose the pair of chairs next to each other and sat down. I noticed the old fashioned china and silverware and realized they were the same ones used to set the table in the woods last night. Maybe that's why she was in a mood. Her brother had "borrowed" them, just like he had the Christmas lights.

"Can I get you some coffee?" Miranda asked.

I dismissed my thoughts and played innocent. "Yes, please."

"Me too, Sis," Joseph called over his shoulder.

As Miranda rounded the table to get the coffee pot from the counter, I glanced in Candace's direction. "And I appreciate you letting me stay last night."

"It's no trouble at all. You're welcome to stay anytime."

Okay, that was a good sign. It seemed Candace's mood was not because of me. And it couldn't have been from Miranda since all was well between them when we entered. That left only Joseph.

"So, what were you two doing in the woods so late?"

Oh, there it is. The bait. I squirmed in my seat and made myself busy. I took the napkin from under my place setting and laid it across my lap. I wondered how Joseph was going to break the news to her.

"Yeah, about that," he began tentatively as Miranda poured coffee in both our cups.

"Save it, Joey. I already know what you did. And you better make sure those lights come down—today—or I'll kick your ass."

Miranda chuckled as she sat back down. "What lights is she talking about, Joseph?"

He rolled his eyes, but before he could answer Miranda, Candace out spoke him. "My Christmas lights. My china. *And* my brand new propane heater that Dad bought me. All carted off to his stupid treehouse down by the lake."

I watched Miranda as she scooped a spoonful of scrambled eggs onto her plate, trying to gauge her reaction to Candace's gripe session. "What was all that stuff for?"

Joseph first looked at me and smiled, as if he were recalling the wonderful night we had together, and then back at Randi. "I wanted to surprise Jamie with a special evening. Dinner for two at the place where we first got to know each other. But I wanted to make it something she'd never forget. Thus, the lights."

As the food made its way around the table, I filled my plate, taking in the two sisters' reactions. Miranda smiled with pride at her little brother, while Candace glared at him. I quickly determined that Randi often found delight in the off-the-wall things her little brother did, while Candace was not so approving. I figured it had a lot to do with the age difference.

Randi was much older, in her early forties, putting her as the sibling who had helped to raise the younger ones of the family. A mother hen. While Candace, on the other hand, was closer to Joseph's age and probably had to compete with him all her life. Given he was the only son, I imagined he was a momma's boy and could do no wrong, leaving Candace resentful growing up. It was obvious her bitterness carried over in her adult years.

"Call me curious, Jamie," Miranda said as she spread her toast with jelly. "But what did my little brother make for dinner?"

I peppered my hash browns and passed the shaker to Joseph, meeting his gaze again. "Pizza. Carry out."

Candace scoffed. "Real romantic there, Jocy."

"Hey, I was limited in my choices given the weather. Cut me some slack."

Miranda chimed in and I was glad for it. I felt bad that Joseph was taking some serious heat for something he'd done for me. "Don't you think you're overreacting a little, Candace? I think what he did is cute."

Candace piled her plate with bacon. "Cute? I don't think so. He comes to my house on Wednesday, claiming he's here to help me get things done on the farm, when all the while he's stealing my stuff. He's a regular con artist."

"A romantic con artist it seems," Randi insisted.

"You'd feel differently if he used *your* china and *your* Christmas lights."

"I would've used Randi's, but they're all packed." Joseph elbowed me gently, gaining my attention. He didn't look at all concerned with Candace's protests. I, on the other hand, was still trying to figure out my place in this discussion and what was appropriate for me to say on Joseph's behalf, should I speak at all. "Randi's moving out west."

"Oh, how exciting," I said, hoping to direct the conversation elsewhere.

"Yeah it is pretty cool. Spencer's work is transferring him to Colorado, and I'll be that much closer to my rescued 'stangs. My daughter, Evelyn's not too happy about it, but the twins are. Henry and Hunter are like their father. Up for an adventure with no ties to hold them down."

"How old is Evelyn?" I asked, eating my eggs first.

"She's fifteen, so she's pretty upset about leaving her high school and friends behind. But she's a tough girl. She'll adjust soon enough. I've heard they have a great school system out there."

"Speaking of relocating, Joey," Candace intervened. "I assume you'll be relocating my Christmas lights from your treehouse to my house—today?"

"Yeeees, Candace," Joseph droned. "I'll even do one better. I'll cut down a pine tree and set it up in your living room, lights and all. How's that sound?"

Candace nibbled on her toast, pondering his offer. "Fine. But no mistletoe. You hang that crap up, I'm tearing it down."

I nearly choked on my food hearing Candace be so direct and objectionable at the breakfast table. It's no wonder the woman was single. I imagined Joseph was the only man alive who could deal with her prickly personality.

"Cross my heart, Ms. Scrooge." He gave her shoulder a mild shove. "See? Little brother always takes care of you."

"Shut up and eat." Candace glanced at Miranda "And wipe that smile off your face. Don't encourage him."

Miranda kept smiling despite her sister's reprimand. "I don't think I'm the one encouraging him."

All eyes, even Joseph's, landed on me.

The weight of their stares caught me off guard. It was time for me to speak and God only knows how I found the words. "For what it's worth, I can't take credit for any of Joseph's behavior, good or bad. But I did appreciate the lengths he went to surprise me with such a magical evening. No man has ever done that for me. And your lights and china were beautiful, Candace."

"He's never done that for anyone," Randi added. "Not even Caroline."

Candace cringed, setting her fork down as if the mere mention of Joseph's ex ruined her appetite. "Really? Did you have to mention *her* name at my table?"

"Admit it. It's nice to see Joseph go the extra mile for someone other than—"

"I got it," Candace interrupted. "And, yes, I'm super thrilled my brother has finally come to his senses and found someone I can actually get along with. So there. I said it. I approve my brother's choice of…"

Candace stopped and looked to Joseph for assistance.

I swallowed hard, wondering how he'd publically acknowledge me. I dabbed my napkin at the corner of my mouth and waited.

"Girlfriend," Joseph finally stated matter-of-factly. "If that's okay with Jamie."

The term echoed in my head.

Girlfriend.

I drew in a deep breath, unprepared for the way Joseph punted the ball to my side of the field. *Girlfriend.*

Again, I heard it rattle around in my brain, though it did little to ease the weight of everyone's stare. I tried to block them all out. How *did* I feel about being his girlfriend?

I made him laugh on a regular basis and he made me feel wanted and loved. So, at the present, I felt pretty darn good about it. I wanted to rejoice in the term he referred to me, but now wasn't the time to be sappy.

Recollections of the night we first kissed came to mind and how we both stumbled on the right words to call what we planned a "date." Almost verbatim, I chose the same phrase I said then and lifted my coffee cup in a toast. "I suppose we couldn't dodge this bullet, if we tried."

He picked up his cup and clinked it with mine. His free hand came up to my cheek and he leaned forward to kiss me. I froze, feeling the sweet demand of this man's impulsive behavior. I almost forgot his sisters were still in the room.

"Okay. Now I'm officially grossed out." Candace pushed her chair out and removed herself from the table to eat in the living room.

Joseph's rumbling laughter tickled me, though I was still concerned that Candace was disgusted with me as well. I hated to think she cared for me as little as she had cared for Caroline.

To my surprise, she gave me a reassuring wink as she

exited down the hall. "Remember Joey. No mistletoe or I'll shove it where the sun doesn't shine."

Chapter Five

After breakfast, Joseph and I gathered our belongings from upstairs. I made sure both beds were made, the bathroom towels hung up, and the rooms were in better condition than I found them. There was no way I'd do anything to bring the wrath of Candace down upon me.

I checked my cell for any missed calls. No one had called me from the coffee shop. No news is good news, I always say. I shoved my cell in my purse and slipped into my winter coat and hat. If I stayed to help Joseph, I wouldn't have to go home soon. I opened my bedroom door and met Joseph in his Carhartt as he came out of his room. A huge smile radiated on his lips. His arms immediately enveloped me.

"You got everything?"

I patted my coat and purse strap. "I think so."

"Good." He laid his forehead on mine and brushed the tip of his nose along my cheek, closing his eyes. "I've had so much fun."

"Joey! You're burning daylight! Those Christmas lights aren't going to take themselves down!"

Candace's voice resounded from the first floor, interrupting the kiss Joseph was about to initiate. He straightened his back and calmly lifted his index finger. "Excuse me a minute." Leaning away from me, he averted his face over his shoulder. "I'm on it, Candace! Quit yer bitchin'. I'm doing you a favor!"

I laid my hand across my mouth to keep from laughing. At their ages, it was quite comical to hear them bicker like little kids. When he angled himself back into our embrace, he caught sight of my amusement.

"What?"

"Nothing," I insisted, ushering him down the hall. "Come on, we need to get those lights down before she has a conniption."

"No, there's no *we*."

"Yes, I'm helping you take them down."

At the top of the stairs, he took hold of both my hands. "I appreciate you wanting to, but this is my responsibility. Besides, there's no way I'm letting you climb a ladder again."

He was right. Ladders and I didn't get along.

"I'll tell you what," he proposed as he descended the steps with me in tow. "I'll drop you off at your grandmother's so you can spend some time with her while I *tend to my chores*." He punctuated the last four words with his fingers crooked in quotations. "And when I'm finished, I'll pick you both up. We'll go to dinner or something."

We stopped at the bottom of the staircase and I had to lift my chin to meet his eyes. "I don't feel comfortable leaving you to climb a tree and—"

"I'll be fine. This ain't my first rodeo."

I planted my hands on my hips. "What if you fall?"

"I'll call you."

His nonchalance hardly humored me. "I'm serious, Joseph."

"So am I," he said, cupping my face. "I'll be fine."

I could do nothing but let him kiss me. He could easily convince me of anything with those lips. I swear the man could talk me into skydiving over a cactus field.

After our kiss, he yelled to Candace to let her know where we were going and we made our way to his truck. Like a gentleman, he opened the door for me and helped me climb inside. As I buckled myself in, I relished the lasting scent of his cologne infused in the vehicle's upholstery.

He shut the door, unaware of my delight over his compelling manly aroma. He rounded the front with a swagger only Joseph could pull off and climbed into the driver's seat. Clicking his seat belt, he gave me a look that would stop a woman's heart.

"You ready?"

I cleared my throat, shaking the shivers from my spine. "Yep." Inwardly, I wondered what I'd done to deserve him. After countless heartbreaks, had I finally found the one?

"Paris, Kentucky, right? That's where your grandmother lives?"

"Yes. Right off Duncan Avenue."

He thought for a quick second and shook his head "Gosh, I haven't been to Paris in years, but I know exactly where it's at." He turned the key and fired up the engine. The vehicle seemed to rumble with as much testosterone as its driver. The two were a perfect fit. Popping the clutch, the 4-wheel-drive diesel lunged forward. Joseph spun the steering wheel, sending the truck into a spin in Candace's gravel drive.

My hands immediately braced against the door and seat. My body leaned into the turn driven there by momentum. Joseph laughed as we tore down the laneway. "Hang on!"

I squealed as I was thrown back against the seat. "Candace is going to kill you."

"I know," he said, looking over his shoulder out the back window. I glanced over my shoulder too to see whether Candace was standing there shaking her fist at us. She wasn't thankfully, but I could just imagine her reaction when she finds out Joseph had thrown gravel all over her front lawn.

Dust billowed behind us as we sped along. I shook my head and laughed. Joseph enjoyed poking the bear as much as Candace did, only he did it with actions instead of words. He was an instigator from the word go. I wondered if he and Candace would ever grow up.

We passed beneath the wrought iron *Pride and Joy* sign, and Joseph shifted again. The truck bounced from the gravel onto the pavement. If not for my seat belt, I'd have hit my head on the cab roof.

Joseph laughed at me and shifted gears. The truck accelerated and we roared down the road. "Fun, isn't it?"

Good grief. Boys and their toys.

"Tell me that wasn't fun, Jamie." He glanced at me, taking his eyes off the road momentarily, willing me to agree with him. "It's even more fun in a hay field."

"*Not* Candace's hayfield…."

Joseph's hearty laughter filled the cab. "No, not Candace's. I know better than that. But I have been known to rip up Randi's field. Well, before I sold it to her anyway."

"You think Randi will sell the property back to you? I mean with her moving out west, she'll have to give up her home here, won't she?"

His wrist rested casually on the steering wheel as he spoke. "I imagine. I told her if she was ever ready to sell, I'm her man."

I thought about how selfish Caroline must have been to

even think of asking Joseph to sell his plot of land, so he could move closer to her. The fact that she didn't appreciate his sacrifices, made me dislike her even more. How could she live with herself?

I turned and looked out the window so Joseph couldn't see the grimace on my face. I pushed her out of my mind. As I watched the blackboard fence speed by, I forced myself to think of pleasant things, like Joseph's strong arms and savory lips.

"You know, I was thinking," Joseph said, interrupting my reverie. "This has been the first time I've ever had a girl over at my family's place and it not be uncomfortable."

Well. How about that? Chalk one up for Jamie. *Nada* for the she-devil.

"I think Candace and Randi really like you."

"You think so?" I hoped so. I wanted their approval badly, and I believed I may have succeeded. It was difficult though to tell whether they were just relieved he moved on from Caroline or if they truly liked me.

"Oh, yeah, definitely. Trust me. You'd know if Candace didn't approve."

I laughed at the dig on his sister. She was a lot like *my* sister—headstrong, opinionated, and unreserved. Maybe that's why I felt more inclined to want her favor than Miranda's. "I'm glad I didn't embarrass you."

"Embarrass me?" He downshifted and slowed into the turn onto I-75, before looking my way. "Heck, no. You were great. Really. It was nice having you with me. It's weird actually being able to say that and mean it."

Hearing Joseph talk about me with such high regard never got old. I soared every time he whistled at me, praised the look of my legs, or remarked about how good I kissed.

"Call me crazy, Sutherland, but I could get used to this."

"What?"

"You and me. Together. All the time." He settled into the cushion of the truck seat. "I used to think my friends were nuts for trapping themselves in serious relationships. I could never understand why anyone would want to settle down with one person for *their whole life*. To me, that was ludicrous."

I swallowed hard, listening to Joseph bare his soul. Was this that pivotal moment just before my world came crashing down? That split second pause just before the rug was jerked from under me? I wasn't certain I was prepared for this because I already allowed myself to dream that I'd found the one person I could settle down with. My breath hitched in my throat while I waited for the other shoe to fall.

Joseph reached for my hand. "And then you came along."

Chapter Six

The blue in Joseph's eyes shocked me as he turned to deliver that line. Maybe it was the sunlight streaming through the windshield that made them so brilliant, but all I saw was a cerulean blue sky over a picturesque Montana afternoon with a picnic blanket and Joseph sprawled next to me, feeding me chocolate covered strawberries. My perfect world.

"You're so different from all the other women I've met. For one, you've never thrown yourself at me." He chuckled. "In fact, you always seem to resist me."

How he thought that was beyond me. The way I recalled it, all he had to do was look at me and I was putty.

"I like that you make me work for it, Sutherland."

"You do, huh?"

He nodded reminiscently. "Yeah. That's why I can't stop thinking about you. I like knowing that at any minute, I could say or do the wrong thing and possibly lose you—which for the record, is the last thing I want to do. But with you, comes this challenge. That maybe for the first time in my life, I might fall in love with someone who may not fall in love with me. Do you understand what I'm getting at?"

Actually, I didn't. I wanted to assume I knew, but because of my past boyfriends who said one thing and did another, I couldn't begin to fathom what he really meant.

I watched him run his hand over his scruffy jaw. The lines on his face told me he struggled to find the right words. I couldn't help him this time. I had my own relationship issues.

"What I mean is," he finally said, taking hold of the steering wheel with both hands, "I like being with someone who's impossible to take advantage of."

Obviously, he did not know me. "Oh, it's been done."

"No, I get that—your past and all. But it's impossible...for *me*. I can't begin to imagine taking advantage of you or your friendship because it means so much. I know we've only known each other a few weeks, but it's been the best few weeks of my life."

He reached over and laid his hand on mine. The heat from his touch warmed me. I flipped my hand over beneath his and interlaced our fingers. "Mine too."

The strength of his grasp soothed me in ways he couldn't possibly understand. Being a man who'd never felt the gut-wrenching, near strangling choke hold of love before, he couldn't know what it felt like to be head-over-heels with someone who'd eventually rip the rug out from under you and tear your heart out in one fail swoop. I'd been the recipient of so many BS lines about finding their soul mate that I'd always been leery of men who seemingly spoke from the heart.

But Joseph was different. Somehow, he had a way of making me feel like he wasn't just saying all these things for the sake of an ulterior motive.

I looked down at our conjoined hands. You couldn't even see mine beneath the breadth of his. Only my fingertips resting between each manly knuckle. It was a weird fetish, but I loved large, masculine hands. His, by far, were construction worker's hands; callused, banged up, and brawny. Nothing about his hands said *I sit at a computer desk for a living.* And yet this macho, bone-crushing, man hand held mine with delicate care.

What made it even more special was knowing he felt just as comfortable holding hands. Though it was an unpretentious public display of affection, it still had an audaciousness about it that proclaimed 'I'm taken. Don't even try to hit on me.'

I loved holding his hand, but we'd both gone deathly silent. I didn't want him to suddenly feel awkward and let go. I spoke to lighten the mood. "So, you said you'd hadn't been to Paris in years. What took you there?"

Joseph grinned. "Our band played at Varden's all the time on weekends. I think it's called the Grey Goose now."

"Oh, yeah. On Main Street."

"Yep, that's the one."

I thought back to my college days when everyone else was out with their boyfriends and I was spending the weekend with Grandma, sipping hot tea, assembling jigsaw puzzles and learning how to crochet. I remembered our nights spent on her back patio, listening to the faint sound of a rock band and 'chewing the cud' as she liked to call our gab sessions. "I probably was listening to you guys and didn't even know it."

"You were at Varden's?"

"Not when you played, 'cause I would've surely recognized you. But I used to sit on my grandmother's patio and hear music coming from across town. Like I said, I might have heard you playing there."

"Well, it's probably better you didn't know me then. I was your typical lead singer, charming all the groupies hanging around the stage mic."

"How'd Caroline feel about that?"

He laughed heartily. "One time we were playing there, and I had a few too many. At a song change, I pointed to some blonde in the crowd who I thought was Caroline and I said 'this one's for *you*, babe.' She was not happy."

Joseph drawled out the 'not.' Dang, I wish I'd been there to see Caroline's face.

"Especially since the chick I called out bought the band a round of beers. Luckily, though, my drummer saved my butt that night. He told Caroline he had the hots for the blonde and the dedication came from him. Which wasn't a stretch from the truth since he took her home that night. But without him, I wouldn't have had a ride home. Caroline was ready to leave me behind at two in the morning."

"I'm sure some other girl in the bar would've taken you home."

"Yeah, well. No one worth losing your dignity over." He gave my hand a squeeze and shot me a dazzling smile. "Now, if you'd been there, I would've let *you* drive me home."

"Who says I would've offered?"

"Ouch, Sutherland."

I loved that we could joke around and cut each other up without fearing the other might take offense. We often laughed together, and in my mind, I memorized that sound. Everything about Joseph's laughter was noteworthy. The way his whole body shook. The way his beautiful, straight teeth gleamed behind perfect, kissable lips. The way his eyes sparkled like sunlight over a rippling river.

We spent the rest of the ride to my grandmother's house pointing out how much things had changed from when we were younger. It wasn't so astonishing for me since I visited Grandma on a regular basis and had seen the modifications to the quaint little town over time. But we shared stories of places we recalled as teens. I especially enjoyed Joseph's recollections of where he went on his first date and the exact spot he stole his first kiss, which thankfully didn't involve Caroline.

As we passed the Grey Goose and finally turned a few corners onto Duncan Avenue, I directed Joseph down the little country lane bordered with tall, old oak trees. In the middle of summer, this historic street was a dazzling display of colorful perennials, lush green lawns, and magnificent shade trees embellishing some of the most charming Queen Anne style houses in Paris, Kentucky.

"Right here," I pointed. "This is it."

He pulled the truck in the drive, and I regarded my grandmother's Folk Victorian home. The L-shaped, two-story cottage hugged a semi-spacious porch adorned with fanciful white spindles, posts, railings, and angle braces. The bluish gray siding offset the whimsical trimmings and scalloped bargeboards along the gables of the house.

"Wow, what a neat place," Joseph remarked as he killed the engine. "I bet you loved coming here when you were little."

"Still do." I glanced at the upper, front window where I'd room on certain occasions. A memory washed over me of sitting there on the cushioned dormer bench on breezy summer afternoons with a romance novel and a cup of coffee.

Without hesitation, Joseph opened his truck door and got out, his gaze still fixed on my grandmother's house. I opened my door, and he quickly rounded the truck and assisted me to the ground with a smile. "Are you nervous?"

I furrowed my brow. "Why would I be?"

"Because you're introducing me to one of your family members. I don't know much about your past boyfriends, except that the majority of them were assholes. I imagine you probably regretted bringing them around."

"*All* of them were assholes and huge regrets. But I don't think you have anything to worry about in that department. My grandmother's going to love you."

"'Cause of my hair, right? How's it look?" He smoothed his sexy, unruly lock away from his forehead with his fingers and struck a GQ pose.

I elbowed him as I passed by. "You look fine, Fonzarelli."

He chuckled and took my hand. We climbed the porch steps together. A nostalgic smell of weathered wood and wet pine hit me. It made me smile knowing Grandma still applied a layer of pine needles as mulch around her landscaping bushes. Being a citizen of the Depression, she reused common items for multiple purposes. It was a habit impossible for her to break.

I rang the doorbell and crossed my arms behind my back. Rocking back on my heels, I looked at Joseph standing beside me.

"You are nervous, aren't you?"

I sighed. "Okay, maybe a little."

He wrapped his left arm around my shoulders and tugged me close. "Don't worry, I promise I won't embarrass you. I'll be on my best behavior. Scouts honor."

I leaned into his hug and tried to steal every ounce of confidence from him. I loved how calm and collected he was all the time. He made life, with all its trials and tribulations, look so easy. Given Grandma was one of the most important persons in my life, I wanted to finally make a good impression. I wanted to prove that Jamett Penelope Sutherland could actually pick a quality boyfriend and keep him.

After what seemed like five whole minutes, my grandmother's voice sounded through the door. "Who is it?"

Relieved she remembered to check before letting a visitor enter her home, I took a step forward so she could hear me. "It's me, Grandma. Jamie."

"Jamie?" she asked, cracking the door open. Her blessed face lit up when she saw me smiling back at her through the old screen door. "Come in, come in. What a wonderful surprise."

Joseph held the screen door open and ushered me in first. I held out my arms and embraced my grandmother carefully. I felt her scoliotic spine with its frail, boney protrusions, and I couldn't help but wonder why she'd lost so much weight over the last year. She always assured me it was just old age, but in the back of my mind, I worried it might be more.

"You said you'd visit soon, but I didn't know you meant today. Or did we make plans? I may have forgotten."

"No, Grandma. You're fine. I didn't say anything about coming over today." I looked at Joseph, including him. "We just decided to visit."

I slipped my arm around his, emphasizing the 'we' part. "Grandma, this is Joseph Scarbrough."

Chapter Seven

Grandma's eyes lifted toward Joseph, and I could see her measuring him up. "Jamie's told me a lot about you, Joseph."

He took her outstretched hand, sandwiching hers between both of his in a gentle grasp. "All good things, I hope."

He gave her that charming boy-next-door smile, and I knew Grandma was as taken with him as I'd been the first day I met him. Lucky for Grandma, though, he was fully dressed. I imagined she'd have suffered cardiac arrest, if she'd seen him wearing nothing but a towel and a smile.

I looked down and saw she had yet to let go of Joseph's hand. He didn't seem to mind and kept the conversation going.

"You have a lovely home here, ma'am. So much character and warmth. I feel right at home."

I couldn't agree more. Inside was an eclectic combination of mahogany hardwood floors, high ceilings, and decorative crown molding. Each inner door was solid wood and arched, complete with crystal knobs and skeleton keys, a veritable old-world fantasy realm for the young at heart.

Grandmother blushed at his compliment. "Well, I do try to keep things tidy. A clean house is a happy house, I always say." She patted his hand with as much fervor as her arthritic hands could handle. "Come, sit down. How about some coffee?"

"I would love to, ma'am, but I have some work to do on my sister's farm in Lexington."

"Oh, that's too bad." Grandma's puckered her lips in disappointment.

I touched her arm. "I'm going to stay though."

"Yes, Jamie's going to stay here with you while I finish up, and then later this evening, I'd love to take you both out to dinner."

Joseph's voice was deep and soothing. Grandma stood there staring at him as if he was the second coming. He gave her hand—still tucked in his—a little squeeze. "It would be an honor."

A small nervous laugh came out of my blushing grandmother as her hand came to rest on her bosom. "Oh, how sweet of you, dear." She looked at me and spoke out of the side of her mouth. "Hang on to this one, child. He's a keeper."

Joseph leaned toward my grandmother and looked right at me. "I keep trying to tell her that, but you know Jamie. She's hard to convince."

She winked at him in the most flirtatious way. "I'll put in a good word for you."

"That's most generous of you, ma'am."

"Please," Grandma insisted. "Call me Rose."

I stood astounded at the way my grandmother gushed over Joseph. She'd always been a good judge of character, so I derived from her blatant swooning that I had nothing to worry about where Joseph was concerned. This was good. Very good.

"All right, dear, you shuffle off to your sister's and get your work finished and Jamie and I will catch up over coffee." She finally let go of his hand, but I could tell she would have rather not. "Do you have a hat? You need a hat, Joseph. It's cold out there."

I smiled as she fretted over him. As a child, it was the one thing she fussed about whenever we went outside—to make sure we wore a hat over our ears and never sat on the ground with an "R" in the month. Her blood thinner medication made her cold all the time now, so her nagging about dressing warmly had escalated, even in mild temperatures.

Joseph reassured her he had one in the truck and would put it on just for her. I was grateful he went the extra mile to ease her mind. I supposed he learned how to with a house full of women.

He reached for my hand and pulled me toward the door. "I'll be back to pick you gals up around five-thirty." He hugged me and whispered in my ear. "How'd I do?"

I gave him a huge smile and replied to him in code. "Five-thirty is *perfect*. I couldn't ask for a better time."

"Actually, five would be better," Grandma interjected, "if we want to beat the Saturday night dinner crowd."

Joseph gave me smile, knowing my grandmother didn't comprehend my cryptic message. "I'll do my best, ma'am."

"Rose," she corrected, shooing him out the door. "And don't forget that hat."

I watched Joseph jog down the steps with a skip to his swagger. Grandmother also watched him like a hawk, and I had to smile at her overzealous behavior. When he reached his truck, he opened the back door, pulled out an old knit cap and held it up for Grandma's sake before pulling it over his head. I confess I didn't believe he had a cap in his truck, but I enjoyed the fact that his promise wasn't just a bunch of mollifying gibberish.

Joseph was definitely a keeper.

As he climbed in the cab and pulled away, my grandmother closed the door with a satisfied look on her face. "He's a nice boy."

It cracked me up that she referred to Joseph, a grown man in his thirties, as a boy. "Yes, he is."

"That's a big truck he's got. Will we be going to dinner in that?"

I realized she was probably worried over the high climb. "I'll help you get up in there."

She scoffed. "All one hundred pounds of you? I'd like to see that. But I'm betting your Joseph can hoist me up. A working man always has a strong back." She shook her head as she shuffled down the hall to the kitchen. "He's going to need it."

I followed her, eager to have coffee with my Grandma. "We'll get you in safe and sound."

"I'm not so worried about getting in as I am falling out. I don't need a broken hip."

I patted her gently on the shoulder. "Joseph won't let you fall."

"Speaking of falling," she added, "I can see why you're so taken with him. He's quite the looker."

There was that outdated vernacular again. "Yeah, he's a good looking man. Hard to believe he's into me."

"Oh, you shush." She flapped one hand at me as I retrieved two coffee cups from her kitchen cupboard. "You're a beautiful young lady and any man would be lucky to court you."

"You're family, Grandma. You're supposed to say that."

"Pour that coffee and button your lip."

I obeyed my Grandma, taking particular notice of how slowly she eased into the kitchen chair. "Your arthritis acting up again?"

"This damn weather. I'd be better off living in Florida. You know, your mom and dad are thinking about moving there."

I recalled their conversation at Thanksgiving. "I heard they already found a condo in Destin. Some gated community thing."

"That's what they say...."

I detected a tinge of insinuation in Grandma's voice. "You thinking about moving there, too?" I kept my eyes on her as I sat down across the table from her. Her lips pursed and her eyes blinked rapidly. She suddenly seemed anxious.

"I'm giving it thought. Like your mom said, it would be good for me. And better for them."

"Better for them? How?"

"Well, I'm no spring chicken, Jamie. There's a lot of things I can't do anymore and it's only getting worse as time goes on." She rubbed her hands together, easing the ache in her fingers.

"What do you need done at this house? I can help you. Just tell me. Housework? Vacuuming? I can come down once a week and do all that for you."

Again she waved me off. "You're not coming all the way down here and cleaning for me. You've got your business, and you don't need to waste gas money making the drive from Cinci just to scrub my floors. That's silly."

"Grandma," I said, laying my hand over hers. "I wouldn't mind at all."

"I know you wouldn't, dear, but I would. Besides, it's

only a matter of time before this heart stops ticking."

"Don't talk like that."

"Jamie, it's true. I'm eighty-six years old and it's bound to happen sooner rather than later. If I moved to Florida with your mom and dad, I wouldn't be a nuisance for everyone."

"You're *not* a nuisance."

"I am when the closest family member is two hours away. What would happen if I fell and I couldn't get to a phone?"

"Okay, so we'll sign you up for that Life Alert thingy." My mind was spinning. I could hardly fathom my grandmother living in Florida, and I sure as heck didn't like the idea of having to fork out airfare every time I wanted to see her. Now *that* would be silly. Sure, it wasn't all that convenient from Cinci to Paris, but at least it would be more cost efficient than flying to and from the Gulf Coast. Money aside, there'd be no more 'just stopping in on a whim,' if she moved south. I could kiss my close relationship with my grandmother goodbye. I knew I wouldn't be able to afford a plane ticket every week.

"I'm not plopping money into Life Alert's pockets. That money belongs to you grandkids and whoever is left taking care of me."

"Grandma...." All this talk about broken hips, heart attacks, and nursing homes knocked the wind right out of my sails, as Grandma would say.

"And if by some chance I *do* end up in a nursing home, I need to get out from under this deed. Your grandfather built this house and the last thing I want is to hand it over to the government. They took enough from him in the war."

"What? You'd sell the house too?"

Grandma lifted her cup to her lips and took a sip. "I can't move it with me, Jamie. I have to sell it."

"To who?"

"To whoever the hell wants it."

I lifted my palms in surprise. "You can't just sell to anybody." Recollections of Miranda talking to Joseph about his part of the farm came to mind. "You have to keep it in the family."

"I'm the last of my siblings, Jamie. And your mother and father at their age don't want it, and your sister sure as heck doesn't need another mortgage when she's got a husband and a good life in D.C."

"What about me? I'll buy it." I said the words before I really thought about what it would take to purchase it.

"Jamie, be realistic. You can't afford to buy this house when you've already put everything into your coffee shop business. That means too much to you to let it go under. I'll not hear of it."

I ignored her crooked finger pointing at me. "Actually, Grandma, I have a nice little nest egg saved up *because* of that business. I could very well buy this house with cash and be just fine."

"You do that and it'll piss me off," Grandma snapped.

I stuffed my laughter down my throat. Hearing my little old grandmother curse sounded comical to my ears—until I really looked at her and realized she was serious. I calmed my voice to a low, soothing tone. "I'm sorry, Grandma. I didn't mean to upset you."

The harsh lines of Grandma's face softened. "I know, honey. But you have to understand how hard it's been for me to get to this point. In a perfect world, I'd live here until the day the good Lord calls me home, but we both know that's unrealistic." Her trembling hands cupped her coffee mug and her eyes stared at the steam rising from the brim. "It's for the best that I move in with your parents where they can keep an eye on me. Besides, my memory is isn't what it used to be and some days I can't remember if I took my medicine or not. Your mother could monitor that for me."

I couldn't argue with her there. I'd noticed her memory slipping from time to time, but hated to bring it up. I took a long sip of coffee and let the idea of Grandma moving settle in. Convincing her to stay in Kentucky would only be for my benefit, so I had to try to look at the situation from her perspective.

"Seems your mind is made up, huh?"

Grandma regarded me with a grave look. "It is."

I took a long look around me. The antique china hutch that displayed all the mismatched dishes and cups Grandma had bought at yard sales, the assorted crocks and metal cooking utensils that sat above her cabinets, the lacey curtains she'd had since her wedding day hanging at every window, hand-made quilts and afghans draped over nearly every chair—they were all things as dear to her as they were to me.

"How are you going to ship all your belongings?"

"I'm not taking anything with me. Just clothes."

My mouth dropped open a little. I couldn't speak.

"Jamie, there's no room for all my stuff. Your mom says the condo's fully furnished so I won't have to worry about it."

"But you love your—"

"They're just material things. Nothing I can't live

without."

I heard the catch in her voice and stopped myself from pushing the issue. The last thing I wanted to do was make my dear, sweet grandmother cry—or make me cry in front of her. Inside, I knew how important her things were to her even though she brushed them off as insignificant possessions. I made a mental note to call Mom when I got home and find out if there was a way for her to take some of them. At least, her bed. She loved her sleigh bed, and it was the very reason I'd bought one too.

Grandma cleared her throat and topped off our coffee cups. "So, let's talk about something else. How's that apartment of yours? Did you get all settled in?"

I forced a smile and shoved the matter of moving to Florida to the back of my mind. "Yeah, I'm unpacked now and it feels nice to have all that turmoil behind me. I put that quilt you made me on my bed. And the pillow cases you cross-stitched. I love them so much."

Grandma's shaky hand came across the table and squeezed mine. The coolness of her touch warmed my heart. Ever since I could remember, she had poor circulation and cold limbs. It was what made her different from my mother, whose hands were warm and strong.

Grandma, despite her limitations, seemed to know me better than anyone. She saw right through my idle chit chat and said, "I love you so much too, Jamie."

Chapter Eight

After coffee, Grandma and I moved into the living room to do a little crocheting. She showed me a new stitch she'd been working on and I, of course, stuck to my beginner's chain. For hours, we talked and looped, and I, being distracted by my depressing thoughts, took a few moments here and there to text Joseph. Without him realizing, his little messages helped me get through the afternoon, especially once I found out Candace's Christmas lights had been successfully taken down without injury. Part of me wished I was there helping him pick out his sister's Christmas tree. But no sooner than I wondered about his progress, he texted me two pictures and asked me to choose the one I thought Candace would prefer. Even though we were apart, I felt I was there with him.

At four thirty, my grandmother looked up from her crocheting at the chiming grandfather clock and tucked her yarn and needle in the basket at her feet. "I should freshen up before Joseph comes."

She labored to get out of her recliner, and I dropped everything to assist her. It didn't go without its reprimand as she insisted she didn't need help. I allowed her to stand on her own, but kept my hands inches from her body in case she fell backward.

She shuffled toward the bathroom. "I'll just be a minute."

I cleaned up our empty coffee cups and cookie crumbs

and did the dishes for her. Afterward, I ambled around the house, looking at old pictures hanging on the walls. Each photo led me closer to her bedroom and I eventually made my way inside.

If Grandma was anything, she was a clean freak. Her bed was made, her dresser tidy, and not a speck of dust could be seen on the furniture. I wondered how long it took her each day to dust and clean her house given every movement she made was slow and painful.

I sat on the edge of the bed and ran my hand across the quilted fabric of her comforter. So much love and care had gone into those stitches, and it made me sad to think she'd leave it all behind—just to keep from being a nuisance to her loved ones.

My heart ached as I thought of all the things my dear grandmother was about to sacrifice. As a woman who lived through the Depression, watched her husband go off to war, and worked for minimum wage to help make ends meet, she'd given up so much already. It hardly seemed fair she should be made to do without in yet another chapter of her life.

I placed my face in my hands and cried. I cried as silently as I could so Grandma in the bathroom wouldn't hear me. A gentle knock sounded and I jerked my head upright. Joseph stood at the bedroom door, his face full of concern.

"You all right?"

I sniffed and wiped away my tears, feigning a smile as I scooted off the bed. "Yeah, I'm fine. I didn't hear you pull up."

He thumbed behind him. "Your grandmother let me in. She said you might be in here." Joseph approached me and placed his hands on my shoulders. "What's wrong?"

"Nothing," I lied, trying to shrug off his grasp.

He halted me and tugged me back into his arms. "Don't lie to me, Sutherland. You suck at it." His eyes bored into my soul. "Seriously, what's wrong?"

I tried to keep my emotions in check. I glanced out the doorway, checking to make sure Grandma wasn't within earshot. His hand cupped my cheek and directed my eyes toward his.

"What is it?"

I laid my hand over his and felt the comfort of his large knuckles press into my palm. My eyes burned as I struggled to get the words out. "Grandma just told me some news after you left that's hard to swallow right now."

"Is she all right? Is it her health?"

"No, nothing like that." My voice didn't sound convincing. I felt the hard lump in my throat swelling. "She's selling the house and moving to Florida with my parents."

His eyes widened. "What? Why? She loves this house. What would make her decide to do that?"

Joseph's rapid fire of questions made me smile a little. At least I could say I wasn't so distraught that I couldn't recognize his defense mechanisms. "She told me the cold weather is getting to her and she's decided to take my parent's up on their offer to move where it's warmer. She doesn't want to be a nuisance, she says."

"Nuisance? She's eighty-some years old, for crying out loud. She's earned the right to be a nuisance."

I shushed his rising voice. "No one called her a nuisance outright. She just feels that way because some things are getting more difficult to do on her own. I told her I'd come down here on a regular basis to help her, but she won't hear of it. Her mind's made up, and I have to respect that."

"Okay, so…she's selling and…."

I saw where he was going with this and stopped him. "I already offered to buy the house, but she doesn't want me to. I told her I could afford it, but she's right…I can't commute two hours to work every morning. Traffic would be horrendous, not to mention the two-hour drive back each evening. It's just not feasible." My voice cracked under the weight of this realization. I hadn't wanted to accept it, but in talking aloud about it with Joseph, the conclusion became quite clear. Saving her house was impossible.

His thumb made a delicate swipe across my cheek, catching a falling tear. "Jamie. Don't cry. We'll figure out something."

"There's nothing to figure out. It is what it is, and I just have to come to terms with it." I straightened my back, sniffed away my sadness, and put on a happy face. "I'll get through this."

He feigned a smile just for my sake and pulled me into his embrace. "You have to look at the bright side. At least your grandmother is still here. You haven't lost her forever."

I was glad my face was pressed against his chest. I couldn't bear for him to see me after he delivered those poignant words. Knowing he referred to the pain of a loved one's passing—as only he could attest—it took me a minute to get past pitying him and see his point for what it was.

He was right. I wasn't losing her. She was just moving further south. There were worse things to deal with, and I should be grateful my time with her had not come to an abrupt end.

I squeezed my arms tighter around his body, his thick Carhartt jacket cushioning the vice I had on his ribs. He returned my hug and I could've stayed in his strong, protective embrace all night.

Forcing myself to step back, I lifted my chin to meet his gaze. "Thank you."

"I didn't do anything," he said humbly, his hair falling over his eye.

I clutched his hand and locked my fingers with his. "Yes, you did. More than you know." I gave his arm a little tug, leading him into the hall. He followed without resistance and awarded me with his sweet smile. If we'd been in the privacy of my own home, I might have kissed him senseless. As it was, we were about to take my grandmother to dinner, and as much as I knew she liked Joseph, she wouldn't stand for me to 'get fresh with him' in her home. Her words, not mine.

"Are you two kids ready to go?" I heard her call from the entryway. By the time we turned the corner, I saw her digging into the hallway coat closet. "Joseph, will you be a dear and help me."

He rushed forward, his hand resting protectively on her back. "Sure, what do you need?"

"That thing there, in the back on the left. It's stuck on something." She looked at me accusingly as I walked up beside them. "Probably your Grandpa's work shoes. That man sure had big feet."

"Is this what you need?" Joseph asked, finally freeing a poster-sized metal frame with two legs. As he turned it around, the telltale black and fluorescent orange colors of a

FOR SALE sign flashed before me.

My breath caught. Joseph and I exchanged looks, and I could see his was one of sincere empathy. Neither of us could've foreseen this bombshell.

"Yeah, that's it," Grandma said, unaware of my shock. "Your grandfather made that sign when he was selling that old Cadillac he fixed up. Remember that car?"

I shook my head mechanically, still staring at the seven capital letters taunting me as Grandma continued with her story.

"You used to love to lie down in the backseat of that car and stretch out. 'Course, you were only six years old and no bigger than a minute." I heard her laugh as she segued to the story of how I used to be little enough to scrunch down into a beer box and scare the bejesus out of Grandpa's friends.

"Oh, Joseph, you should have seen it. Her Grandpa'd be outside having a beer and when his friends would pull up, he'd say," –and this was when I came out of my trance because Grandma's sweet voice turned deep and loud as she imitated Grandpa– "Get ya a beer there and sit down. They're nice and cold." She laughed, whether at the memory or maybe at the stupidity of his friends who constantly fell for the joke, I didn't know. "And right when they'd reach down to grab a bottle, Jamie here would jump out of the beer box, arms in the air. Like to give ol' Arlin a heart attack that one day, you remember that, Jamie?"

Again, I nodded and faked a laugh over the three-decade old memory. It was good to see Grandma smile, and I realized I needed to buck up. What kind of granddaughter would I be to rain on her parade? Granted, it wasn't a Macy's Thanksgiving Day Parade, but she was happy nonetheless. It was obvious she'd come to terms with selling and I, in my own pessimistic way, needed to as well.

Chapter Nine

We ate dinner at the Grey Goose on Main Street. I tried my best not to dwell on the image of Joseph staking the FOR SALE sign in my Grandma's front lawn before we left. Or how she'd asked Joseph if he would mind fixing her drippy bathroom sink faucet the next time he was in the area. But it was all so overwhelming. Hearing her talk about repairing incidentals so would-be house buyers couldn't whittle her down on the final sale price had me near the breaking point again.

I ate my salad in silence, listening to Joseph accept the job, without pay of course, and how he'd also rid the squeak in her front door while he was there. For the duration of the meal, I hardly partook in their conversations, allowing Grandma to gush and praise Joseph at every turn for being such a gentleman. It wasn't often she let her hair down and enjoyed the company of a young, attractive man, especially one who was going to be practically at her beck and call now that she suckered him into some minor renovations. As a widow, she had every right to cut loose, laugh, and even swoon—if she cared to—over a handsome man's attention. Her innocent flirting and blushing had me valuing her lighthearted spirit that much more. I was definitely going to miss her.

"Jamie, honey, can you help me with my coat?"

Grandma's request brought me back to reality. I looked up and saw Joseph paying the bill as my grandmother flipped her napkin from her lap to the white-clothed table. I jumped up and helped her scoot back her chair, giving her ample room to brace herself and stand. Joseph joined in, sandwiching her between us, in case she staggered.

He and I locked eyes and I mouthed the words *thank you*. I meant for both dinner and for being so attentive to Grandma's needs, though I think he assumed the tab. He smiled, until she yanked on his arm and wound her own around his elbow. His laughter tickled my insides as he accepted his role of being her escort for the evening.

"Don't forget your coat and scarf, Grandma," I reminded her, wrapping them around her snuggly. She barely surrendered her death grip on Joseph as she sifted her arms through the sleeves.

Patting his hand with hers, she smiled up at him. "You're a nice young man, Joseph. Should I leave the tip?"

He picked up her purse from the chair and swung it up on his shoulder. "Your money's no good here, Rose. I took care of it already."

She harrumphed and walked arm-in-arm past the other patrons in the restaurant. I trailed behind them, unable to see Grandma's face but I imagined she was eating up all the envious glances from the other mature ladies in the place. Joseph was naturally a sight for sore eyes in any room. Coupled with his dashing smile and attentiveness to the elderly, tonight he was twice as fetching.

Walking out into the street, Joseph continued to speak to my grandmother with his arm still buried between hers and her bosom while she cooed over every charming thing he said. If she'd been anyone else on his arm, I might have been jealous.

As the three of us walked a few car lengths down the

sidewalk to Joseph's truck, my eyes happened to drift downward. His sexy, tight little Wrangler butt was all mine to ogle. I took advantage of the moment—I certainly needed the distraction—and studied how his jeans hugged him with just the right amount of give in the fabric to accommodate the alluring bulge of his ever so sculpted, taut behind. Mesmerized by his perfect physique, the zigzag stitching on the back of his pockets lulled me into a lazy stupor. My brain drifted to thoughts of me slipping my hands into both said pockets and cupping that perfect butt like nobody's business. And then I'd—

"Jamie!"

The sharp snap of Grandma's voice cause my head to jolt upright. Joseph was peering over his shoulder at me, his brow cocked. "Whatcha doin' back there?"

"What?" All coherent brain function scattered.

"Do you need to borrow my hearing aids, honey?" Grandma joked. "I said, take my purse so Joseph can hoist me in this truck."

"Right." I circled around them and hefted her purse onto my shoulder, the weight of it surprising me. "What the heck you got in here, Grandma? The kitchen sink?"

"Just a lady's necessities, dear."

All ten pounds of it, I imagined. *Criminiddly, it was heavy.*

I watched as Joseph stood directly in front of Grandma, his hands on either side of her waist, and gently lifted her body enough so she could place her foot on the running board. Straightening her leg, she slid herself onto the seat of his single cab truck.

She let out a 'whoo' and a sigh to follow, patting Joseph's hand. "Thank you, good man."

"My pleasure, ma'am."

"Rose," she corrected with a smile.

I placed her purse on her lap and told her I'd buckle her in from the other side. Closing the door, I met Joseph's eyes. His grin foretold of a devious thought, one that looked especially sinful under the dim white glow of the street lights.

He wrapped his arm around me as we made our way around the front of the truck. "Did you enjoy the view?"

"What?"

"The view. My ass."

"I was not looking at your ass."

"Right."

"I was just daydreaming, Joseph."

His laughter carried in the night as he opened the driver's side door for me. "I believe you."

I stepped up onto the running board and smiled back at him. It was all I could do after being caught red handed.

"Might I partake in the same shameless goggling? It's only fair," he added and gave my rump a firm slap.

I jumped at the playful spanking, quickly plopped myself on the front seat, and slid over to the middle. I pointed at him and flashed him a look that said 'Behave. My grandmother's watching.'

He climbed into his seat and winked. He inserted the key and the engine roared to life at the same moment he complimented my derriere.

"What did he say?" Grandma asked, handing me her seatbelt buckle.

"Joseph was just remarking about how good the food was tonight." Where I came from, white lies were not sins, especially when they were said to protect my grandmother's delicate sensibilities. After hearing the click of her seatbelt,

I turned to retrieve mine.

"It was *so* good," he boasted, grinning like a sly fox. "Wishing we had leftovers."

I elbowed him as a warning before Grandma caught on. "Just drive."

He chuckled, peeking into his side-view mirror, and pulled away from the curb. His leg rested against mine as he shifted smoothly through the gears, and the warmth of his body heated places in me that were far too scandalous to mention with my grandmother sitting beside me.

In a matter of minutes, Joseph turned the corner onto her street and that darned FOR SALE sign caught me off guard again. I stiffened at the blow and clenched my jaw. I'd forgotten about it for a few blessed minutes given Joseph's grand scheme of distracting me. But there it stood, like an ostentatious nudist on a non-nudist beach, flaunting its bold message in all caps.

Joseph must have felt my reaction. He switched hands on the steering wheel and laid one on my knee, giving it a reassuring squeeze. Pulling into the drive, I closed my eyes. I could barely look at my grandmother's house knowing this might be the last time I'd be allowed in it. I didn't think the new buyer would be all that willing to let me frequent the rooms I loved as a kid.

Grandma reached down and unbuckled her belt, slapping her heavy purse in my lap. "Well, Jamie, it was so nice of you to come by today."

I wanted to say we'd do it again, as that was my normal response, but I clamped my mouth shut. Instead, I just faked a cheery smile.

Joseph had already exited the truck and made his way to the passenger-side door. When he opened it, brisk night air sifted inside and stole the little warmth left in the cab. I watched as Grandma rotated in her seat to allow Joseph to help her descend. With the debonair of a true gentleman, he set her on her feet and guided her up the driveway to her porch steps.

I scurried from the truck to meet them, digging in her purse for the keys. I unlocked the door and held it open so Joseph could walk her inside. I enjoyed how he took the time to help her out of her coat and hang it in the hall closet. No other boyfriend of mine had ever been so attentive to my grandmother, especially without prompting. I suppose it was all natural to him growing up in a predominantly female household where good manners were important. I made a mental note to thank him for his courtesy on the drive home. Maybe even give him "a little sugar" for his trouble, as my grandmother would say.

"Now you make sure you lock up behind us, Grandma." I set her purse on the entryway table and gave her the tightest hug her osteoporotic bones could handle without them crumbling to dust in my arms. "I love you so much."

"Oh, Jamie, you know I love you too. And don't you fret about me moving to Florida, you hear? Everything's going to be just fine."

"I'll try."

Sounding convinced was not my forte when I had to sell something I didn't believe. How would everything be just fine when I was not only losing the house I'd adored for as long as I could remember, but my precious grandmother as well? I teared up thinking about the hundreds of miles that would soon separate us.

"Now, don't you start that," she remarked, shaking my

arm. "We still have Christmas to celebrate together. We can cry then."

I laughed a little and stepped toward the door. As Joseph said his goodbye, her eyes twinkled like I'd never seen before. Not only was Joseph good for me, but it seemed he was twice as therapeutic for her. I'd remember this night and how happy she'd been in our company for the rest of my life.

Chapter Ten

"You're awful quiet, Sutherland. You okay?"

Joseph's tender voice broke through the haze of my depressing, woe-is-me thoughts. I couldn't even tear my gaze away from the starry night outside my window for fear I'd break down. I took a deep breath and blew it all out before choosing my words.

"Yeah, I'm fine. Just wish there was some way to save Grandma's house. She's not even taking her stuff with her," I added in frustration. "How can she walk away from all her precious possessions?"

"Maybe they're not as precious to her as you think. Maybe they're reminders of who she used to be. A wife. A mother. A grandmother to you. Taking them with her might only hark back to a place and time she'd rather be. Sometimes parting from everything you've ever known is easier than bringing it all with you. Clean slate, you know?"

Joseph's words did little to soothe my aching heart. In time, I'd probably look back on his wise words and realize just how sensible they were. Right now, I was content to sulk.

"Hey," he said, stretching his arm toward me. "Come here. Slide over."

Reluctantly, I unbuckled and skimmed across the seat toward him. After securing the other seatbelt, his strong arm tugged me closer until my body nestled right against his. I leaned my head on the pocket of his shoulder and relished the security I felt in his embrace. Just nestled up to him made a world of difference to my mood.

"Thanks for all you did this weekend," I finally said. "You have no idea how much it all means to me."

"I've got a pretty good idea."

I heard the smile in his voice without looking up. Joseph's handsome smiling face had been the one thing that struck me on the day we first met and it would forever be the warm sunshine on all my cloudy days. "I know I didn't say much about our date last night, but I hope you know how happy you made me. No one's ever done anything remotely close to that. The lights, the dinner, the dancing…I'll never forget it, Joseph."

"Neither will I. Speaking of," he said, reaching into his coat. "I believe this is yours."

I watched him pull out a CD case from his breast pocket and hand it to me. I smiled as I held my Frank Sinatra greatest hits—the one he stole from my apartment. "Oh yeah, I almost forgot about it." I had to laugh as I remembered how he'd waltzed into my bedroom uninvited and begged me to just get in the truck with him. To trust him enough that he'd make everything all better. Little did he know I'd trust him enough to walk through broken glass, if he needed me to.

"Why don't you put it in, DJ? We could use a little pick-me-up right now."

I plucked the CD from its housing and slipped it in. Ol' Blue Eyes started singing one of my favorite tunes and I snuggled back into my spot under Joseph's arm. Nothing else was said as we made our way up I-75 North and that was fine with me. I think after all that had happened to us in the past twenty-four hours, we both welcomed the peace and quiet.

As we finally crossed the Brent Spence Bridge, the downtown lights of Cincinnati, combined with the nostalgic Sinatra melodies playing in the background, welcomed me home. As much as I loved visiting with my grandmother, the sight of familiar landmarks brought an unspoken sense of comfort to me. The PCN Tower, the Great American Tower with its top inspired by Princess Diana's tiara, the Carew Tower, and so many other architectural wonders of the Queen City lit up the night. They stood proud and tall as if saluting my safe return.

Weaving through Cinci's streets, Joseph gave my body a little squeeze. "You asleep? We're almost home."

Hearing him say that made it sound like we shared a home—which we did in a sense since we lived in the same apartment complex. But my brain took it further. I liked the sound of living with Joseph, though I'd never mention such a thing to him. Previous relationship faux pas warned me of that mistake, and I'd be darned if I was going to give Joseph a reason to back out now.

"No, I'm not asleep. But I'm ready to."

He parked the truck in the side lot and killed the engine. Without hesitation, he leapt from his seat and held out his arms for me. I retrieved my purse from the floorboards and slid across, taking his hand. I heard the hard slam of the door and the beep-beep of the lock mechanism engage before he wrapped his arm around my shoulder. We walked together into the building and stepped onto the elevator.

I looked up at Joseph after he pressed the button for our floor and the doors closed. For a few seconds, we were shut away from the rest of the world, except for maybe the guy on the other end of the hidden camera. He turned his head and smiled down at me. "What?"

"Caroline is so wrong about you," I said. "You've got the biggest heart of any man I've ever known."

His deep chuckle echoed around me. "Glad you think so. And while we're on the subject of Caroline...I'll be changing my locks this week. We don't need another surprise visit from her."

I was relieved he'd go to such lengths to keep Caroline from entering his life again. It proved to be a very bold act of finality on his part. And I was ever so happy for it. "You think that'll keep her from trying?"

The elevator doors opened and we stepped out, still in conversation as we walked down the hallway. "It'll be a start. Maybe she'll finally take the hint."

I baited him before I realized the impact of my words. "And that would be...?"

We stopped at my door and he leaned his shoulder against the wall. That cool casualness of Joseph's demeanor returned as he crossed his arms and gazed upon me with a shrewd grin. "That I've moved on. That I've found someone who makes me happy and accepts me for who I am."

I looked away. Anywhere besides the lure of his handsome face. He was right. I didn't take compliments well. I dug in my purse for my keys.

"Allow me," he said, pulling his large ring of superintendent's keys from his coat pocket. With quick precision, he found and inserted the correct key in the door. He turned the door knob, swung the door open, and gestured for me to enter.

I flipped on my lights and turned around to face him.

"Thanks for a wonderful weekend."

"It's not over yet."

I smiled at his attempt to stretch the night a few hours longer. "Well, if it's all right with you, I'd like to be alone for a while." Which really meant turn in early. Eat a whole pint of ice cream. Cry myself to sleep. The usual female eccentricities.

He nodded casually and shoved his thumbs in his pockets. "Sure. Whatever you want."

I began taking off my coat, but he snagged the sleeve and pulled me to him. His long arms trapped me in a comforting hug, his mouth turning up in a scheming smile. "Realize if you decide you need company, or if your room gets drafty, I'm right next door. You could always sleep walk your way over to mine."

My laughter mingled with his, though I imagined he wasn't necessarily joking. "I appreciate the offer, but I'm pretty certain I'll be warm enough in my own bed."

"Can't blame a guy for trying, right?"

"I'll give you points for effort." I relished the way he looked at me with such want. I could never tire of it.

"Are you busy tomorrow?" he asked, taking another swing in the batter's box.

"No, why?"

He crinkled his nose in a frown. "I'm a little behind with my Christmas shopping, and considering how well you chose Candace's tree—which by the way, she loved—I thought maybe you could help me buy gifts for the family."

"You want me to go Christmas shopping with you?" I had to ask because, frankly, I was a bit surprised.

For one, men didn't seem to enjoy that kind of thing. I often recalled my father and brother-in-law grumbling on

Christmas Eve about the crowds, the rudeness of so-called *gift-givers* ripping sale items right from a person's grasp, and the fact that it was ultimately a waste of time given their wives would return whatever they picked out anyway.

Secondly, Christmas shopping as a couple projected all the signs of a committed relationship. Surprise, surprise. My pessimism crept forward. I couldn't help it.

"Yes, I do," he reassured. "I could use your help—if that sounds like something you wouldn't mind doing on a Sunday afternoon."

I'd give this man a lifetime of Sundays. "I'd love to. What time you thinking?"

"Noonish?" he pitched. "We'll grab some lunch first and maybe head up to Kenwood?"

"Sounds good to me."

"Great." His gleaming smile met his Montana-blue eyes. Mesmerized by the intensity of his gaze, I watched with eager anticipation as his mouth neared mine. He stopped just short of my lips, his arms hugging me tighter against his chest. "Sleep well, Sutherland."

Our mouths touched and my knees buckled. Ice cream and a good cry no longer held their appeal. Josephs' kiss was much better for the soul. Beyond compare. No denying, the man knew exactly what he was doing when it came to physical touch. His hands, his lips, the way his body moved forward and connected with mine in all the right places. Every part of him worked together in perfect harmony to deliver the best kiss imaginable.

He smiled as he pulled away and stepped out of my embrace. He backed up into the hall, clenching his jaw as he held my gaze. The look on his face displayed the pain he endured at parting from me. I wondered myself how long I could keep up this charade of celibacy. It had been a long time since I'd wanted a man this badly. Heck, it had been a long time since I'd had any kind of desire—period. And Joseph, with all his chivalrous qualities and drop-dead gorgeousness, only made it twice as hard to resist that temptation.

"Goodnight, Jamie."

I sighed and nodded in disappointment. It was best that I let him leave, though my entire body screamed otherwise. I stepped forward and clung to the door, forcing myself to close it. "Goodnight, Joseph. I'll see you tomorrow."

I heard a small, manly groan escape him, though I know it wasn't meant for my ears. Until I heard his door open and close, I held mine open just a crack in case he changed his mind.

I waited to the count of five. No such luck.

Chapter Eleven

I tossed and turned the entire night. Between thoughts of Joseph sleeping in nothing but his skin-tight boxer briefs and my grandmother moving, I barely got any sleep. The next morning I lugged my tired self from bed at six o'clock and stalked to the shower. A cold one would do me good for multiple reasons.

Afterward, I made a pot of coffee, cleaned the apartment, and caught up on my laundry knowing I'd be gone all afternoon shopping with Joseph. At ten o'clock, I resorted to calling my mother about Grandma. I plopped down in the dining room chair and waited for her to answer. I stared out my windows. Funny how the gray sky hovering above the Ohio River mirrored my mood. I brought my legs up to my chest and hugged them tight as I sipped my third cup of coffee.

"Hey, Mom," I said drearily.

"Well, hello, Jarnett."

I cringed every time she called me by my birth name. "How's Dad?" I said out of habit.

"Oh, he's fine. He's practicing his golf swing in the living room again. The man acts like he's going to play Tiger Woods one day." I heard her cover the phone before yelling to him about her precious lamps. "I'm serious, Roger! You break one thing and I'm going to break that club over your head."

I heard Dad reassure her and my mother moan in

response. "I'll be glad when we move to Destin and he can practice his swing—on an actual golf course!" she shouted, loud enough that Dad could hear.

"Yeah, about that, Mom. Is it true that Grandma is selling her house and moving to Florida?"

"She said you paid her a visit yesterday and that you brought a special someone with you. You never told me you were dating anyone. What's his name?"

Leave it to my mother to redirect the conversation to other subjects. "His name is Joseph Scarbrough and I think he may be around for a while." I tried to alleviate the possibility of a long conversation about my personal life by combining points of interest so we could get back to the original topic.

"Well, that's nice, dear," she said in her very predictable, very complacent voice. "How did the two of you meet?"

I assumed her inquiry was solely for the sake of small talk and not because she cared. "He's my next door neighbor."

"It doesn't sound all that romantic, but I suppose convenience has a way of introducing couples just as well as any other approach."

I realized at that moment where my pessimistic side originated.

"Your grandmother said he's a keeper and a looker. He took you both to dinner and paid, I heard?"

Knowing my mother was probably shocked at Joseph's generosity, I made sure to sell that point. "He comes from a well-off family and knows how to treat a lady with respect."

"It's about time you found someone like that. What does he do for a living?"

Here we go. We've arrived at the part of the conversation where she gets to belittle the man I'm dating and offer her opinions as if I wanted them. I could date a prince of England and she'd still find something to remark about. "He's the building's superintendent."

"A blue collar worker, huh?"

The skepticism in my mother's voice rang loud and clear. I drummed my fingers on the table, anxious to make this interrogation as painless as possible. "He's very handy around the house, a veritable Mr. Fix It." My mind flashed back to the day Joseph unclogged my kitchen sink in his 'shirtless' uniform. I couldn't help but smile. "He's even going to repair some things at Grandma's house." I figured I'd sneak in one last attempt at talking Joseph up before she delivered her final ruling on my incompetence to attract a nice, young man with prospects.

"That's what she says," mother replied, unimpressed. "She also said he's a farm boy. Big truck and everything."

I giggled as I could just hear Grandma raving about Joseph's jacked-up truck and how he had to lift her inside. "His family lives in Lexington. They're into boarding horses so a four-wheel drive vehicle is a necessity on the farm."

"I see. He's sounds quite different from your other boyfriends. Which is a good thing, but I remind you that while his country lifestyle may be appealing, it could be the very thing that separates you. You're not used to farm life with its mud, horses, and manual labor."

I expected this from Mom and waited for her to belabor her point.

"What I'm saying is, be yourself with this guy. I know how you are. You think you have to be the person he wants you to be just so you can keep him interested long enough to fall in love with you, but that's not how it's supposed to happen. You want a man who's interested in the real Jamett Penelope Sutherland."

Ugh, there it was again. That name would be the death of me. "Don't worry, Mom. I'm not starting this relationship off with lies." Recollections of how Joseph came to witness my hypoglycemic episode came to mind. "He knows exactly who I am and what my limitations are."

"Does he know your real name?"

I rolled my eyes. "No, Mother. He doesn't. And what does it matter?"

"It matters because that is you."

"Whether I'm Jamie or Jamett, I'm still me."

"Are you?"

My mother's voice raised so high it sounded like the shrill chirp of a referee's whistle. "I think so."

"Well, all I'm saying, honey, is if you can't be honest with something as simple as your real name, then what about the important stuff like how you cherish your independence. Or how you might very well be the breadwinner given his meager occupation. Some men are put off by that stuff."

"Joseph's not like that," I reassured her as much as myself. "And besides, it's not like we're getting married next month. We just started dating for crying out loud."

"I just want what's best for you, Jamie. Don't let this guy change who you are or make you forget what you've accomplished on your own. A Sutherland woman doesn't need a man. We just enjoy their company should they tag along."

I scoffed aloud. "Is that the line you used to score Dad back in high school, Mom?"

"Hey, he knew exactly what he was getting when he first asked me out. And considering he couldn't stay away means I did something right."

In the background, I heard Dad's rebuttal. "You and I both know that's *not* how it went down, but you keep dreaming, Glenda."

"Don't listen to him, Jamie. He's just bitter because I made him work for that second date. He practically begged for it."

"Begged for it?" I heard him say. "The shit's getting deep now. Where are my waders?"

"Go back to your golfing, Roger. Like your memory, your putting's a little off. Anyway, dear, just take your time with this one and be upfront. In the end, he'll appreciate it."

"Right." I took another sip of coffee in hopes of washing down the dry, cynical advice that was my mother's signature. "So, back to Florida, Mom."

"Oh yeah, we kind of got off-track, didn't we?"

Leave it to my mother to never accept blame for something she'd done. "Is Grandma really going with you?"

"I'm pretty sure that's what she's decided. Believe me, I was as shocked as you, but it only makes sense for her to move with us. Surely, you've noticed her memory slipping from time to time."

"I have," I admitted. "And I know the warmer temps will be better for her arthritis, but I just don't understand why she's not taking any of her belongings."

"Honey, there's really no room for them. Have you seen the amount of stuff she's collected over the years?"

"I know, Mom, but she loves her antiques and yard sale finds. Can't she at least take some of it?"

"Jamie, if I give her an inch, she's going to take a mile. I don't want to be put in a situation where I have to limit her. It's bad enough she has to sell the house."

"Exactly. So, why not let her at least take her bedroom suite with her. You know how much she loves that bed."

"Did she put you up to this?"

I hiked my shoulders up around my ears at Mom's accusing tone.

"I know how manipulative she can be, Jamie. She is my mother, after all."

I sighed loud enough that my mother could hear. "No, she did not. I just hate to see her give up so much of what she cherishes. She may be your mother, but she's not like you. Some things are just plain sentimental to her. Believe me, I'd love to convince you to let her take more, but I know who I'm dealing with. You are *my mother* after all."

I felt a small sense of satisfaction in being able to feed her exact words back to her.

"And don't think I haven't thought of ways to buy Grandma's house so—"

"Jamett Penelope Sutherland, don't you dare. You buy that house and you'll be making the biggest mistake of your life, aside from that one idiot, computer guy you dated who almost stole your identity and took you for everything you had. What was his name? Ficklestein? Mickenschtein?"

"Mom!" I grumbled. "It doesn't matter what his name was." Truth be told, I forgot it anyhow. "Anyway, I'm not going to buy Grandma's house because I know it wouldn't be sensible, but the point is you're family. And you should realize how important some things are to her. I'm not asking you to ship everything she owns to Destin. Just give her a little piece of happiness and let her bring something with her besides her clothes."

"Fine."

I paused, feeling skeptical of my mother's change of heart. "Fine meaning…"

"I'll have her bedroom suite shipped to Destin."

"And her handmade quilt that's on it." Since I had my stubborn mother surrendering, I figured I'd better throw in a few extras.

"Anything else?"

I stretched my legs beneath the table, feeling a foot taller. "Well, if you're asking, how about Grandma's china hutch?"

"Don't push it, Jamett."

I talked to Mom for another half hour about Christmas Eve and how they'd be driving down the day after. I offered to have Christmas Eve at my apartment since all their things would be well on their way south in a moving van. Mom couldn't exactly have company over when there was no furniture to sit on.

She agreed wholeheartedly and I think I heard a little excitement in her voice when I told her she'd get to meet Joseph. After finalizing plans, I hung up feeling better about Grandma's move to Florida. At least for her sake, I was able to extract her bedroom suite from my mother's leave-it-all-behind plans. I may not have been able to buy her house, but I at least sold my point to the queen of pragmatism.

My grandmother would be most pleased.

Chapter Twelve

After I folded the last of the laundry and put it away, I selected a purple sweater, and black leggings for today's attire. Every time I'd been with Joseph, I was wearing a T-shirt and jeans. I decided to get a little dressed up for this occasion and maybe show him another side of me that didn't include a ponytail.

I curled my hair and slapped a little makeup on my face, finishing up with a light layer of lip gloss. I spun one last turn in front of the mirror and smiled at my appearance. Satisfied with my casual, but stylish look, I slipped on a pair of fur-lined, knee-high boots to complete the outfit.

With ten minutes to spare, I grabbed my purse and keys from the entryway table and locked up. I knew I'd be early, but punctuality was always my thing. Joseph seemed like the type of guy who'd admired that in a woman, given the countless times he probably had to wait for Caroline to get ready.

I walked toward Joseph's apartment and knocked. My heart picked up speed as I waited for him to answer. The door swung open and Joseph smiled. My gaze drifted downward over his beautiful, muscled chest and the bright white towel that hung so alluringly on his narrow hips. His hair was wet and my mouth went dry as I noticed a few droplets of water resting on his wide shoulders.

"Hey," he said in his distinctive husky voice. "Don't you look nice."

"Hey," I squeaked back. I cleared the frog in my throat. "And thanks. You look pretty good yourself."

"This old thing?" he joked.

I giggled and blushed at the same time.

"Come on in." He gestured towards his living room. "I'm almost ready."

I sneaked a peak at his lower half as he shut the door behind me. *Ready for what,* I asked myself. *A good shagging?*

I tried not to stare, but he looked so delicious in terrycloth. I could certainly get used to seeing this on a regular basis.

"Make yourself at home," he said, waltzing back into his bedroom.

With Joseph out of my field of vision, I forced myself to take in other things around the room. I noticed his guitar still leaning against the wall same as it had a few weeks ago when I helped his drunk-ass into bed. I wondered if he'd picked the instrument up since then.

"Did you get a chance to talk to your mom about your grandmother?" he called from the other room.

I whirled around, hoping I'd get the privilege of seeing Joseph in his towel again. To my disappointment, he was further into his room and, unless I blatantly entered his 'private chambers', he remained hidden.

"Yeah, I did. And good news! I convinced her to ship Grandma's bedroom suite."

"Did she tell you how soon they're moving?"

"It looks like Christmas Day."

"Wow," he said, poking his head out. "That's just around the corner."

We locked eyes for a few seconds and my heart skipped. He had such a way of looking at me that caused all brain function to come to a screeching halt. He broke our gaze and went back to dressing.

I turned back toward his guitar and reached out to touch the strings. I plucked a couple, thinking how much I longed to hear him play. "Written any songs lately?"

"Nah. Not since a few weeks ago."

I knew the week he spoke of; the night before Caroline ripped his heart out. I felt foolish for bringing it up. "Sorry. I wasn't thinking."

"Don't be," he said, sounding preoccupied.

I looked over my shoulder just in time to see him walk around his room in his boxer briefs. He opened his chest of drawers and pulled out a pair of jeans. I watched mesmerized as his biceps flexed and bulged while he worked to slide each long leg into his pants. He made zipping and buttoning his fly look like a regular strip tease, only in the opposite order.

As he turned to retrieve his T-shirt from a different drawer, our eyes met again. Embarrassed that he caught me staring, I whirled around and pretended I hadn't seen him. I heard him chuckle, but, thank goodness, he didn't call me out on it.

I cleared my throat and walked further into the living room where I wouldn't be tempted to peek into his bedroom again. His couch was black leather, sitting between two oak end tables and their respective lamps. A single photo album, bound in black leather, sat on the coffee table beneath a TV remote.

Curiosity killed me. I wondered what pictures a man like Joseph kept. I cringed thinking he might have a few of Caroline in there. I didn't dare look.

"Okay, I think I'm ready now," he announced as he

came into the room. He shoved his wallet into his back pocket and strode right past me to the kitchen. "Want a drink before we leave?"

"No, thanks."

I watched him open the fridge, reach inside for a bottled water, and shut the door behind him. He twisted the cap and chugged the whole thing in one huge gulp. "You sure?" he asked again, holding up the empty container.

"I'm fine."

He smiled and threw the bottle in the trash. "That you are." In a few strides, he came to me and tugged me into his arms. "You okay? You seem a little uncomfortable being in here with me. Are you afraid I'll bite?"

I wasn't befuddled because I was in Joseph's apartment. I was befuddled because I was in his presence after seeing him half-naked. No amount of trying could make my brain forget the smooth skin and strong muscles of his body. Add that to being trapped in his embrace while his amazing cologne made my mouth water and I was definitely a woman who'd been irrefutably knocked off kilter.

"Hello in there…" he said, bumping his nose with mine. "Are we needing food?"

I ran with his suggestion as it was the best excuse. "Yes, I'm starving."

He kissed me quick on the lips and flashed his debonair smile. "Then let's get going before that sugar of yours drops." He tugged me toward the door and lifted his Carhartt from the coat hook. "Where's your coat?"

Forgetting it was mid-December, I sighed. "It's in my apartment."

"You goof. Here, take mine." He handed me a deep

brown, bomber jacket. Immediately, the smell of leather and Joseph wafted around me. I slipped my arms inside and pulled the coat over my shoulders. I swam in it.

Joseph laughed at me. "You look cute."

"I look ridiculous."

"Ridiculously cute," he added, zipping me up.

I held out my arms, displaying how the sleeves extended past my fingertips. "I'll just get mine on the way out."

"I'd rather you wear mine."

"Why?"

"I'm hoping when you give it back, it'll smell like you." He leaned in and tucked his nose just under my jaw. I heard him inhale. "I love the way you smell."

Sold! I felt like a fortunate buyer at a highfalutin auction. *Sold to the woman in purple who's a pile of putty in that man's arms!*

"You really like how I smell?"

"I like everything about you," he stated, wrapping his arms around my back. I felt him tug on the ends of my hair as he smiled down at me. "I really like your hair today. I don't think I've ever seen it down."

He strung his hands through my curls and let them cascade around my shoulders. His eyes followed the tresses that hung around me in loose waves and the corner of his mouth inched up. I wondered what he was thinking.

I let him marvel me and I enjoyed every minute of it. To hold this man's attention was like winning the lottery.

I saw his Adam's apple bob as he swallowed hard. His eyes blinked in repetition until they eventually landed on mine. "Shopping," he reminded aloud, stepping back. "We're supposed to be shopping today."

"Yes, we are," I agreed. It was nice to know he was

having the same issues I was when it came to being this close.

"Okay," he said, clapping once, as if to preoccupy his hands. "Shopping it is. After you."

We walked down the hall and into the elevator. We stood side by side, gazing up at the numbers lighting up as we descended to the first floor. Before the doors slid open, his hand clutched mine. Swallowed up by his large grasp and oversized coat, I felt so small around him, yet on top of the world. We looked at each other and smiled. These moments when we did nothing in particular would be the things imbedded in my soul.

It was official. I was in love with this man.

Chapter Thirteen

We drove north toward Kenwood Town Centre, heading straight for the Cheesecake Factory. After spending almost two hours eating lunch, laughing, and eating some more—because you can't go to the Cheesecake Factory without ordering cheesecake for desert—we finally arrived at the mall.

The place was packed with people, hoping to score the deal of the season. Crowds never bothered me though. I was used to swarms of eager patrons anxious to get their hands on a sale-priced item. At my coffee shop, we always had a seasonal deal to get people in the door. That was Marketing 101.

While I was there to buy gifts for his family, I could arguably say I was there more for the company. I could do anything with Joseph Scarbrough—watch paint dry, wait for water to boil, count toothpicks—it didn't matter. I'd be the happiest woman in the world, whether we were productive in our gift search or not.

Having to shift around countless shoppers and their bags only made it more necessary for me to cling to his side. With his arm wrapped around me, we browsed through many clothing and shoe stores, Yankee Candle (because I just love the smell), the Apple Store (for his teenage niece—big surprise there), the Disney Store (for his twin nephews), and even the Sunglass Hut just for laughs. We tried on pair after pair, sporting our best poses for every occasion imaginable.

Once we tired of that, or rather the store attendants tired of us, I caught sight of one of those instant photo booths. I tugged him toward it and we crammed inside and pulled the curtain. With our hoard of shopping bags surrounding us, there was no place left for me to sit except on Joseph's lap.

He patted his knee with a devilish grin and I accepted. We put in five dollars, chose sepia for the color and a cheesy heart designed frame that would enclose our four random photos.

"Okay. Serious smiles first," I demanded.

"Fine. Then what?"

"We just make it up as we go."

I felt Joseph's gaze on me and when I turned to look at him, his arms snaked around my waist. "I like spontaneous."

He had slipped his hand beneath my coat and I flinched as I felt his warm fingertips brush against my bare skin. The sensation of his hand running along the small of my back felt far too intimate for such a public place.

I reached behind me and grabbed his hand.

"What? No one can see. My hand's off camera." I could do nothing to stop him and his mischievous grin lit me on fire. While holding my gaze, he hit START.

Snap!

The first picture captured us staring into each other's eyes. I gasped. "Wait, we were supposed to do smiles first."

"Too late now. Smile!" He tickled my ribs and sent me into a fit of giggles.

Snap!

"Joseph!" I said, trying to scold him. But he didn't let

up. This time, he buried his nose in my neck and kissed under my jaw. The prickle of his five o'clock shadow tickled me even more. I squirmed and tried to pry him away, to no avail. Our laughter mingled and our bodies mashed. His arms held me tight and my hands clasped his scruffy face as the third picture clicked.

Snap!

"Oh my gosh, Joseph! Stop it! We only have one picture left!"

Joseph glanced at the numbers counting down on the screen in front of us. "Three seconds. Better make it good."

I panicked. "We need a serious one. Hurry!"

"You want serious?" he asked.

But before I could answer, he framed my face with his hands and pulled me to his lips. I froze, feeling the sudden demand of his warm, sweet mouth on mine.

Snap!

I barely paid attention to the final click. I was kissing Joseph Scarbrough in a very confined, very private photo booth and nothing else mattered at this moment. Until I heard a little girl's voice from outside the curtain.

"Mommy, they're kissing."

Joseph laughed against my lips and my heart dropped. "They can see us?" I asked in horror.

"Every bit," he murmured. "There's a screen outside the booth."

I pushed away and scrambled from his lap to see if he was jerking my chain. I tripped on the way out and caught myself just as a mother was yanking her daughter away. Sure enough, anyone who happened to walk by could see everything that went down inside the booth.

"I'm sorry," I called to the bitter parent, but my

apology landed on deaf ears.

Joseph climbed out with our bags in hand, his gorgeous smile reaching his blue eyes. "You mean you really didn't know everyone could see us?"

"No, I didn't." I unzipped my coat and fanned my face. "Is it hot in here?"

"It's a little warm, but I don't think it has anything to do with the coat you're wearing."

I slugged his arm. "You're the devil."

He inclined his head and kissed my cheek. "And you love it, Sutherland."

I didn't care to admit it, but I did, and smothering a smile proved futile. "I cannot believe we just did that. You know we pissed off a mother."

"It's not the first time I've ever pissed off a parent. Doubt it'll be the last."

"Well, you better bring your game face at Christmas. You're going to need it with my mom."

"She doesn't scare me," he said, leaning casually against the booth.

"You say that now…"

"And I'll say it the morning after we meet." With a casual glance toward the slot, he winked. "Our pictures are ready."

I sighed and pulled the narrow strips of photo paper from the aperture, anxious to see the evidence of our inappropriate behavior captured on film. I scanned each of the four pictures and had to smile. Each one was better than the last, and I couldn't pick a favorite.

"Let me see." Joseph pushed himself off the booth and hovered over my shoulder. A few seconds of silence followed as we admired the thumbnails. "We look good together."

"You think?" I turned my head to the left and my nose bumped his chin. His lips were right at eye level and I couldn't help but look at them. The smell of Joseph and leather and his warm skin enveloped me as I waited for his answer.

"Nobody looks better with me than you. Nobody."

That statement deserved a kiss. More than a kiss, truthfully, but I was restricted to the amount of reward I could give him in the mall without being arrested for public indecency. I pressed my lips to his and held them there. I inhaled his rich, husky scent. I found myself lingering longer than I'd planned, the sound of footsteps and intermittent conversations from passersby drowning out the thudding of my heart.

I wanted more. So much more. Kissing Joseph felt like splurging on a chocolate volcano sundae and heading straight for the hot drizzle of caramel sauce. Much more of this type of behavior and I couldn't be held responsible for what came next.

I pulled away breathless. "Shopping," I reminded.

Joseph closed his eyes and nodded, blowing out his sexual frustrations in one heavy sigh. "Right. Shopping. Where to now?"

"Spencer's," I said with a smile.

He cocked his brow. "Spencer's? What do we need there?"

A layer of suggestiveness coated his question. "Truth or Dare Jenga."

He narrowed his eyes at me. "Who's that for? Your parents?"

"No, silly. Us."

He grunted once like a caveman and followed on my heels like an eager puppy.

Chapter Fourteen

After a long day of shopping, we dragged our sorry butts to his truck and stuffed his cab full of presents, wrapping paper, boxes, and bows. Before climbing inside, I glanced up at the dark clouds above and thanked our lucky stars the wintery mix of rain and snow the meteorologists predicted hadn't arrived yet. I could only hope the nasty weather held off long enough for us to get all this stuff inside our apartment complex.

On the drive home, we ran through the list of gifts to make sure we hadn't forgotten anyone, while Jason Aldean sang *When She Says Baby* on the radio. I had reached into my purse and pulled out a pen and paper to jot down names for the sake of organization. I tapped my pen to the beat of the song as I checked the list twice.

"I think that's everybody." I looked at Joseph, who was strumming the catchy melody on his steering wheel.

"Everybody but you," he stated.

"Me?"

"Yes, you." He sneaked a curious glance in my direction and shook his head. "You didn't think we were exchanging gifts?"

I stammered. "I—I mean—I—sure, I thought about it but—"

"Let me guess. You once exchanged gifts with one of your past boyfriends and it didn't meet his expectations?"

"Try exceeded." I sighed and slumped into the seat. I

hated explaining my past mishaps to him. I would've rather dismissed the whole subject entirely but I could tell from his inquisitiveness that he wasn't about to let this one go.

"See, there was this guy, Michael Dougherty. We'd been dating for about seven months and everything was going great. Close to Christmas, he started making a big deal about the gift he bought me and how excited he was to see the look on my face when I opened it. I, being a woman, assumed it might be a ring."

I glanced at Joseph again. He wore a smug little smile as if he already knew the gift was nothing close to what I'd envisioned. Must be some innate guy code I wasn't familiar with because it never occurred to me that it'd be something else. "I know it sounds foolish, but for the record, things were going great. A ring wasn't so far out of the picture."

"Yeah, you said that already." He turned down the radio so he wouldn't miss a gory detail. "Go on…"

"Anyway," I continued, "I decided to get him something that would equal his gift—assuming it was a ring," I justified, "to show how I really felt about him. So, I bought him an engraved watch. A Roger Dubuis. Excalibur."

"Holy crap!"

"I know but, in my defense, I bought it on eBay for only two grand."

"You do realize those babies are worth thirty grand. You sure it wasn't stolen?"

"I don't know. I didn't run the serial numbers."

Joseph was laughing at me now. "This is good. Continue."

Seeing his delight over my predicament made it hard for me not to enjoy my own plight right along with him. I never really laughed over this before, but I had to admit it was kind of comical. Smothering my own smile, I dished out the rest. "So, on Christmas Eve I opened his gift first and…"

"And…" he coaxed, anxious for the punch line.

"It was RUSH tickets."

He exploded with laughter, a hearty bout of guffaws that echoed in the limited space of the truck cab. "He gave you concert tickets?"

"Yes. And I hate RUSH."

He pounded out his delight on the steering wheel. "This is just classic, Sutherland! Concert tickets. How funny is that?" He finally caught my glare and realized his reaction might have been a little over-the-top. He cleared his throat and wiped a tear from his eye. "Sorry. I shouldn't have laughed so hard, but surely, by now, you have to see the hilarity in it?"

"Ha, ha. Yeah, it's so hilarious," I mocked.

With a huge smile, Joseph reached over and took hold of my hand. "I didn't mean to poke fun at you."

"Could've fooled me."

"No, seriously, I get it. Exchanging gifts can be awkward."

"Yes, thank you," I said, relieved to know he understood the point I tried to make. "Especially since we've only known each other a few weeks."

"Okay, so how about this?" he prompted, squeezing my hand gently. "We don't spend any money on each other. The gifts we exchange should be something we already own."

I'm sure I looked thoroughly confused. "You do realize I'm a woman, Joseph. I don't have anything in my possession that a man would want or need—and just so you know, Michael Dougherty kept the watch. If you're looking to score an Excalibur, it's not gonna happen."

"I don't want a watch," he reassured. "And besides, I'm a man. I don't have feminine things in my possession either. But I know we're both creative. We can figure this out."

"I don't know." I grimaced at the thought of making a Christmas gift for Joseph. The first thing that came to mind was a dreaded mixed tape. And yes, I've been there and done that before, with disastrous results. "I think setting a price limit would be easier."

He lifted my hand and kissed my knuckles. "Christmas is about giving from the heart. I'm sure you can come up with something without digging into your wallet."

"You have a lot of confidence in me, Joseph."

"Yes, I do," he agreed. "And I think this will be fun. You and I…exchanging gifts that require a little ingenuity."

Ingenuity sounded like such a typical guy word. Ingenuity, like giddy, was something I did not do.

"So, what do you say?"

"We can't spend a single dollar?" I asked, just hoping he'd reconsider.

"Nope. Not even a penny." He winked at me and held out his hand. "Deal?"

I looked at his hand with reluctance. Finding something I already owned that Joseph would want was going to be a serious challenge. Finding something to give him from the heart would be next to impossible. Thinking I had a little over two weeks to come up with the perfect gift left me with a feeling of utter terror. But if he could do it, so could I.

I think.

I surrendered and shook on it, feeling my world caving in. With a satisfied look on his face, Joseph replaced his right hand on the wheel and drove in silence. By the way he rubbed his whiskered jaw, I knew he was lost in thought, coming up with some ingenious, heartfelt present that would totally put my idea to shame.

My mind was rapidly running through every last thing I owned and evaluating it as a possible gift.

"Did you go?"

"What?"

"Did you go to the RUSH concert?"

I averted my gaze from him and stared out the window at the winter scenery zipping by. "No. He freaked out and took some other chick."

I hoped my answer would be enough for him to drop the darn subject. But no. He had to keep pecking.

"What did the engraving say?"

I whirled my face around, smiling. "Really?"

He couldn't help but chuckle. "Yes. I want to know what you thought appropriate to engrave on his watch."

I scrubbed my hands up and down my face. "Fine. It said *My love for you is timeless*. Happy?"

Joseph stared straight ahead, grinning like I'd never seen him grin before.

* * * *

Just as I expected, sleet bombarded us with icy needles as we unloaded the truck. Somehow we managed to secure all the bags and rush upstairs in one trip, Joseph carrying the most.

I dug his keys from his coat pocket and unlocked his apartment door. We set the packages on the floor and took off our coats.

"You hungry?" Joseph asked as he hung them up.

"Not really. You?"

"I'm a guy. I'm always hungry," He headed toward the kitchen patting me on the butt as he passed me.

I followed him and watched as he took a beer from the refrigerator, screwed off the top, and downed a few gulps. "Wanna beer?"

Crinkling my nose, I shook my head. I hated the taste of beer.

He gazed into his fridge and named the other drinks he had to offer.

"I'm good."

Determined to find something for me, he opened his cabinet. "I've got a little Southern Comfort?"

Feeling a bit chilled from the outside weather, and a little mortified from my dating demise story, a little shot of alcohol seemed the right way to go. "Sure. I'll take that."

Joseph smiled at me, as if he relished the idea of my hidden daring side, and poured me a shot of the amber liquor. He handed the glass to me and clinked his bottle against the side. "To us."

I nodded once and lifted the glass to my lips. I started to sip it, but thought otherwise. I tilted the glass higher and swallowed like a champ. I slammed the glass on the counter and squeezed my eyes shut against the sweet burn in my throat and chest. When I opened them, I saw Joseph staring at me with his bottle resting on his lips.

An easy grin turned up the corner of his mouth. "Get 'er done, Sutherland. Want another?"

"One more," I said without hesitation.

Again, I shot it back and reacted the same way. I clapped my hands once and rubbed my palms together, ready to take on the world. "Truth or Dare Jenga?"

Joseph eventually let out an edgy laugh, still contemplating my unusual mood. "Sure. If that's what you want to do."

I turned to walk into his living room and he snagged my elbow, whirling me around. "Hey. You okay?" He set his beer down and pulled me into his arms. "You're not yourself right now. Is this about exchanging gifts? 'Cause if it is, we can skip it altogether. I don't want you to feel like we have to do this. I'm good with anything. Gifts or no gifts."

I opened my mouth to speak, but clamped it shut. I didn't know how I felt about the whole secret Santa thing. I didn't want to make a big deal over this or make Joseph feel like I wasn't into the idea of a committed relationship—especially if he was. On the same token, I didn't want to make the mistake of assuming how he felt and come up with something that was, like my past blunders, a little too over the top. The last thing I wanted to do was send the guy mixed signals and have him running scared like all the others.

"How about we just play Jenga, and I'll let you know how I feel about it tomorrow."

He nodded, reading me carefully. "We can do that."

"Okay," I said, pushing out of his embrace. His muscled body was getting me all worked up again. "You get something to eat, and I'll set up the blocks."

I didn't wait for him to offer a better suggestion. I turned and dug the game out of one of the shopping bags on the floor. I aligned the stack of red wooden blocks in a tower on his coffee table and sat back on the couch to wait for my handsome opponent to join me.

His photo album stared back at me.

Taunted me.

I moved it to his end table. I hadn't drank enough to open it and see what pictures were inside. I wasn't sure there was enough alcohol in the world for that.

Within a few minutes, he entered the living room with his beer, a plate with a PB&J and chips, and another shot of Southern Comfort. He handed me the glass, set the dish on my end table, and picked up his sandwich. I set my drink aside and watched him shove the last of his sandwich into his mouth as he took a seat beside me.

"Who goes first?" he asked, running his tongue along his teeth. He downed his beer and placed the empty bottle on the floor.

"I will." I assessed the tower and spotted an easy block. With as much stealth as my shaking fingers could manage, I began sliding the little bugger out.

"Any rules I should be aware of?"

I halted immediately, unable to talk and slide at the same time. "It's truth or dare, Joseph. Anything goes."

"Is that the alcohol talking or you, Sutherland?"

I ignored him and finished slipping the block from between its vertical lodging. The tower barely moved and I held my prize with pride.

"Read it," he commanded. "It's not yours 'til you complete the task. You fail to do what it says, it's mine."

"I know how to play the game."

He seized my hand before I could read my block. "Did you play with Michael Dorkerty?"

"Dougherty," I corrected. "And no."

He laughed and shimmied back on the couch. "Just checking."

I stuck my tongue out playfully and read the block. My smile faded.

"What's it say?" Joseph asked eagerly.

"It's a dare."

"Well? Come on…read it."

I drew in a deep breath. "Demonstrate your favorite sexual position."

Chapter Fifteen

Joseph's laughter erupted and he clapped in his excitement. "Perfect. This I gotta see."

I take back what I said before. There was not enough alcohol in the world for me to do *this*. Asking him to reveal the photos in his album suddenly didn't sound like a walk on the wild side.

"Come on, Sutherland. Strike a pose."

I bit my lip. "I think we need a new rule."

Joseph tilted his head to the side. "What's wrong? You having a hard time with this one? It's only the first block. I've never played the game before, but I imagine they don't get easier."

I've never played the game either. I only heard about it from my college days, but no one ever mentioned just how personal the dares could get. I figured they'd be physical challenges or tasks of a comedic nature. Weren't the truths supposed to be of the intimate sort?

"I can't do this one," I exclaimed, flipping the block in his lap. "You win."

Joseph picked up the block and reread it to himself. "Fair enough. This one is pretty personal and given we just started playing, I think we should add a rule. Each player has the ability to forfeit a truth or dare of his or her choosing without getting docked for it." He held the block out to me. When I reached for it, he tightened his grip on it and didn't let go. "Is this the one you're forfeiting?"

"Yes, definitely," I affirmed.

"All right, so what do we do with it?"

I took the block from him. "We add it to the top. Your turn."

I watched as Joseph selected and glided his block free with ease. With an air of haughtiness, which was ever so sexy, he rolled the game piece in his palm until the words appeared. He read it to himself, glancing at me, and then back to the block.

"It's a truth," he confessed. "Describe your worst kiss." He thought for a few minutes and came clean. "I suppose that would have to be with Irene Jacobson."

I was hoping it was with Caroline because that would certainly put my mind at ease if she ever came around again. And I *knew* she would one day. Contagious diseases always had a tendency to reappear once they were in your system.

"It was back when I was a junior in high school. Irene was a little...how do I put this nicely...a little malnourished. And she was the only senior from her class that didn't have a date for the prom."

I listened intently as Joseph continued his story.

"I guess being raised with all sisters, I sympathized with the whole female thing about how important it is to have a date for the senior prom. I hadn't asked anyone yet, and I figured I'd make her dreams come true. So, I asked her and she accepted. I think she might have even peed her pants a little that day. Or so the rumors had said. Fast-forward to the evening, I met her folks and she came staggering down the stairs in her frilly, puffy, lacey dress. I didn't think much of it because she wasn't exactly the most graceful girl in school and chalked her unsteadiness up to nerves.

"We arrive at the prom. We dance. She jets off to the bathroom. We talk. She disappears again to the bathroom. This happens all night long, but again, I don't think much of it. I'm just a naive teenager. Hours later, I'm standing on her porch saying goodnight, never thinking that all her stumbling or hiccuping throughout the entire night was due to her sneaking shots of vodka from a flask in her purse. I thought I'd be a gentleman and end the evening with a nice, peck on the cheek."

I could already tell this story was about to head south real quick. A smirk started to inch up on my lips before I could stop it.

"I bent to kiss her and she lunged forward, locking her lips with mine. At first I was stunned, but then as the kiss wore on, it wasn't so bad. Until…"

"Oh no," I murmured, my face puckering at the thought of what the lush did next.

"Yep. She threw up in my mouth."

I didn't mean to laugh, but it was so disgusting I couldn't stop myself. "What did you do?"

"What do you think?" Joseph said, laughing right with me. "I ran off the porch and vomited too. Her father came outside, hearing all the commotion and after he saw the two of us puking our guts out, he accused me of getting his little girl drunk so I could take advantage of her. As if…" he waved.

"What did you say to her father?"

"I took one look at that poor girl, knowing the humiliation she felt was enough to kill her, not counting that she'd have to confess to confiscating a bottle from her parent's stash on prom night. So I went ahead and took the blame."

My laughter died slowly and I looked at Joseph with budding admiration. "That was really sweet of you."

"Whatever. It sure taught me a lesson, if nothing else."

"Oh, yeah? What's that?"

"Never listen to my sisters." He jumped up from the couch and headed toward the fridge for another beer, probably to wash the seventeen year-old memory of vomit from his mouth. Upon returning, he chugged a couple swallows and plopped his block on the top. "Your turn, Sutherland."

I turned my attention to the tower and plucked one from the bottom middle, hoping this one would be an easy play. I read it and my head fell back on my shoulders. "You've got to be kidding."

Joseph held his beer bottle to his lips. "What's your doom now?"

"Blow a raspberry on someone's tummy."

He set his beer down on the coffee table and yanked up his shirt, revealing a luscious rippled plane of rock-hard abs. "Pucker up, Buttercup."

Maybe it was the two shots of courage I'd downed moments ago, but for some reason I wasn't nervous about planting my lips on Joseph's flat stomach and blowing to my heart's content. In fact, I don't think wild horses could've stopped me.

I leaned over, bracing my hands on his thighs—my, my, they were warm from beneath his jeans—and I pressed my lips just above his cute little navel. I giggled at first, failing to make a good connection.

"Do over," he said, his muscles tensing. "Come on, Sutherland. You can do it."

Drawing from his encouragement, I tried again, this

time crushing my mouth to his smooth, warm skin. I took in a deep breath and blew for all I was worth. The silly sound we both longed to hear erupted like someone passing gas, and we laughed until we cried.

He high-fived me, and I sat back on his couch. Between the alcohol, embarrassment, and hysterical laughter, I felt hot and triumphant at the same time. I fanned my shirt to stir some much needed air against my clammy skin.

Joseph rubbed his jaw, looking at me oddly. "My turn."

I gestured toward the tower. "Good luck, Giggles."

"Nah," he said, slanting toward me. "I don't mean it's my turn to play. I mean it's my turn to blow a raspberry."

I looked at him, hoping he was only joking. But the second he leaned toward me, I scooted further along the length of the couch. He followed my movements until I hit the armrest and had nowhere to go. Joseph braced his arms on either side of my body, trapping me in a semi-reclining position. I pushed on his shoulders as he threatened to lower his mouth to my stomach. "Joseph, that's not how you play. You can't steal an opponent's dare."

"Who says I can't?"

"It's in the rules," I bartered emphatically.

"I let *you* make up a rule on the fly. So here's *mine*."

His arms flexed and he lowered himself along my lap. "Joseph...." I tried to sound stern, but the rest of the words failed me. I stared at him as he nudged my sweater up with his nose. Chills ransacked my body, followed by another wave of heat, as I contended with the erotic image of his handsome face at my navel.

I felt like a scared cat, ready to spring at a moment's notice. I lay tense and trembling, my eyes glued to him as he gazed at my bare stomach. A sea of dazzling blue flashed before me as he looked up from his sprawled position. His sexy, devious smile replaced his boy-next-door grin, and I knew I was in serious trouble.

I tried to speak one last warning, but his name came out in the most strangled fashion. Barely a whisper. He held my gaze as his mouth pressed ever so tenderly upon my flesh. The scruff of his beard prickled me, while his warm, steady breath caressed my skin.

I felt him draw air. It was so slow and so deep that I wondered if he was inflating his lungs or relishing the scent of my skin. Without warning, he sank into the softness of my tummy. Ridiculously ticklish vibrations assaulted me as he blew. I squirmed, and yelled, and giggled, and squirmed some more, trying for all I was worth to push him off me.

"Joseph, Joseph, please! I can't take it any—" My useless pleading was cut short by my silent, stomach cramping, heaves of laughter. We writhed and thrashed upon his couch until he finally withdrew his face.

I lay panting in a heap of exhaustion, my eyes closed. When I opened them, I found Joseph looking at me, his face inches from mine. His hair was a tousled, darling mess. His chiseled face was edgy and serious. His eyes grew dark as our breathing settled one ragged breath at a time. I fell entranced by his silent stare. The look of unadulterated desire in his eyes mixed with the lingering scent of cologne and Joseph played havoc with my senses.

I swallowed. Hard. I brought my hands up and cupped his face, unable to look away from the beautiful sight that lay upon me. I could feel myself shaking and I didn't know if I had the guts to initiate what my body craved to do with this man.

I closed my eyes and went in blindly. Our lips met and

every muscle in my body relaxed. My heart melted as I felt the heat of his kiss. Passion ran amuck the minute his tongue touched mine and together our bodies entangled like balled-up yarn. On their own volition, my legs wrapped around his back and I pulled myself closer to him. The weight of his body pressed me further into the leather cushions. I was tingling all over and only Joseph could remedy my yearning.

Suddenly, he pulled away, winded and red-faced. His eyes bore into mine as he seemed to struggle with something. I could almost hear his thoughts churning. Should he continue? Should he stop? Should he get up and slam his erection in a door?

"Joseph," I whispered, wanting to alleviate the ethical questions running through his mind. "I think we need a new rule."

He cleared his throat, taken aback. "Another one?"

"Yes." I played with the soft hair on his nape as I tried to find the right words. "I think you and I should stop fighting the inevitable."

"The inevitable being?"

Dang him. Was he really going to make me spell it out? "Being that I want you to—"

He pressed his finger to my lips and silenced me. "Don't say it," he commanded huskily.

"Why?"

I saw his throat bob as he swallowed. "Because I don't want to." He squeezed his eyes shut and recanted. "I mean, I want to. Like, *really* want to. But I can't do that to you."

"Do what?"

He sighed. "Take advantage of you."

"But you're not. I want this." *I think*. Well, ninety-five

percent of me wanted this. The other five percent was my wary heart. Majority rules, right? "I'm giving you full consent, Joseph."

His face softened and he smiled. He stroked my cheek ever so tenderly with the back of his hand as he looked at my entire face. My eyes, my lips, my nose, my eyes again. "And you have no idea how much that means to me," he whispered. "But you've had a couple shots. Your inhibitions are gone. I refuse to take advantage of that fact."

My heart plummeted, though I believe with relief rather than disenchantment. The rest of me fell limp beneath him. While I totally gave this man kudos for adhering to the gentleman's code, I was still left disappointed. Combine that with my pessimistic mind and I couldn't help but think perhaps he didn't want me like I wanted him.

"Jamie, please don't think I don't want you. You have no idea how hard this is for me to turn down your offer. It's killing me. I want you more than I've ever wanted anyone." He emphasized his point by crushing his lips to mine and breathing me in. "But," he exhaled, "the last thing I want is for you to wake up tomorrow morning and regret what we've done. I don't want you to have one single doubt in your mind. And I know you. You have doubts that number like the stars."

A guilt-ridden smile eased upon my lips. He was right. I probably would second guess the night and what had happened. I'd relive it over and over in my head, wondering if I'd made the right call. Wondering if those two little shots of courage had anything to do with it. Wondering if Joseph accepted because he knew I was under the influence and this might be his only chance.

Yeah, he was right. It seemed he knew me better than I knew myself. But still the fact remained. I was disappointed and embarrassed and unsure what to even say now. I felt I'd ruined a perfectly good night.

"I'm sorry I came on to you like that," I said, sitting up.

Joseph followed my lead and leaned back into the couch, stretching his legs. He pulled mine across his lap and toyed with the zipper on my knee-high boots. "You don't have to be sorry. I enjoyed it. A little too much, I'm afraid."

I smiled at his admission. "Now what?"

He glanced over at the tower of red blocks. "We could continue to play...."

"Or?"

"Or call it a night. You know we both have to work in the morning."

After all that had happened, I was pretty tired. "I guess we should call it a night."

Joseph fetched my hand and lifted it to his lips, kissing my knuckles. "Not just any night. But one of the best nights of my life." He paused. "You know...I don't think you have any idea how happy you've made me. Being with you has been so different and so...amazing. I've never had this much fun with a woman. With anyone. And I don't ever want it to end. I like believing you and I have something special. Something I've never had before. You're all I can think of. No matter what I'm doing. Your beautiful face is all I see, and it's like sunshine. Warm sunshine." He snapped his fingers. "I think I just wrote a song."

I giggled, letting the warmth of his hand and sweet words caress my soul. As I sat with my legs across his lap, my thoughts were as clear as crystal. I knew I said it before, but some things bear repeating.

I was wholeheartedly, absolutely, without a doubt in love with Joseph Alexander Scarbrough

Chapter Sixteen

"Jamett Penelope Sutherland, what is that on your face?"

My pen paused mid-sentence as I looked up from the calendar on my work desk. In the doorway of my office stood Melissa, her arms crossed, her foot tapping with impatience. Absently, my hand came up to my cheek. I wondered if I'd missed a dab of strawberry sauce from the Danish pastry I'd eaten this morning.

"Not your face," Melissa corrected, frowning. "Your *face*." She waved her hands in a large circle as if to indicate my aura. "You have the look of someone in love."

I pressed my cold palms against my face to cool my burning cheeks. "Is it that obvious?"

"Honey, Helen Keller could see it." She took a seat on the corner of my desk. "But how is that possible? The last time I saw you, you were near tears over Joseph and his bitch of an ex. Heck, *I* was near tears too." She glared at me sternly. "Don't tell me you went on that date with him after I specifically told you not to?"

I cringed. "I did..." I confessed. "But I had good reason."

"Oh, Jamie..." I could hear the disappointment in her voice. "I knew he'd get to you. You're such a softy."

"Just hear me out, Melissa. Trust me. You're going to love this."

She shook her head. "This better be good."

I pushed next month's scheduling aside and ditched the pen. I sat back in my chair and got comfortable. I knew this would be a long conversation, considering all that had happened since Melissa and I saw each other last Friday night. I sighed. "Gosh, where do I start?"

"Friday night after you left here would be good." The sarcasm in her voice was palpable.

"Okay, so Friday night I went home and got into bed, determined to ignore any of Joseph's attempts to get me to listen to him. And I did," I reassured Melissa. "At least, until he came barging into my bedroom."

"What?"

"Yes, he let himself into my apartment."

"You gave him a key?"

"No, he has a key. To everyone's apartment. He's the superintendent of the building, remember?"

"Oh, my gosh," she said, pinching the bridge of her nose. "I forgot."

"Yeah, well, me too."

"I can't believe he just broke into your apartment like that. I would've called the cops."

"The thought certainly crossed my mind. But I think the shock of him standing in my bedroom in the dark rendered me senseless."

"So anyway...." She churned her hand in a "get on with it" motion.

I reorganized my thoughts and continued. "I sat there in my bed, with the covers pulled up to my ears, and he came to the side of my bed, begging me to talk to him. I told him about Caroline coming out of his apartment early Wednesday morning, and he said he wasn't even in town. He'd been at his sister's in Lexington and had no idea what

Caroline was doing there."

"Of course, he's going to say that, Jamie. Men don't just admit they're sleeping with their ex when another chance to score some tail comes their way."

"It wasn't like that at all. He really was in Lexington. His sister confirmed it and she hates Caroline. There's no way she'd lie for Joseph. Besides, wait until you hear why he was in Lexington and what he did for me."

"Well, you better hurry this along. We open in fifteen."

Anxious to fill Melissa in on all the beautiful details of the weekend I had with Joseph, I commenced the long, drawn-out story of our date, how I'd ended up in his bed the next morning, how he'd taken my grandmother and me to dinner, how he'd consoled me over the news of my grandma moving to Florida, how we'd gone Christmas shopping together, and lastly, how we'd played Truth or Dare Jenga. Seeing the look on Melissa's face when I described how I blew a raspberry on his stomach was the best, but seeing her swoon over the fact that he didn't want to take advantage of me once we started making out was priceless.

"I don't know what to say," Melissa uttered as she fanned her face. "What a weekend. What a gentleman." The joy on her face matched the delight on mine as she ruminated over all the glorious details. "I bet you're exhausted. I know I am just listening to you." She clasped my hands in hers. "I'm so happy for you. My little Penelope has finally found true love."

I squeezed her hands and we squealed in unison like immature school girls. Sharing this news with Melissa felt so good. It was twice as gratifying having someone to open up to about the developments in my pitiful dating life, especially when they involved someone like Joseph Scarbrough.

"I could barely fall asleep last night," I conveyed shyly. "My mind kept running through last night, over and over. If only I hadn't had those two drinks."

"I know," Melissa agreed, slugging my arm. "What were you thinking?"

"I don't know. I could just kick myself. But then again, he saved me from the dreaded *morning after*," I said, striking quotes with my fingers. "You know as well as I do that you would've found me in a fetal position under my desk had we done the dirty. Joseph saying no was for the best."

Melissa giggled. "Yeah, you're right. Finding you grinning from ear to ear was much better." She closed her eyes and sighed, relishing my story all over again. "Where can I find a man like Joseph?" Her eyes popped open. "Does he have a brother?"

I slapped her knee as I stood from my chair. "Nope. Sorry."

"Cousin? Distant cousin? Once removed?" she probed, following me out into the coffee shop. "I'm desperate here. I'll take anything."

I unlocked the door and flipped the window sign to OPEN. As I turned to walk back behind the counter, the chimes rang aloud. Melissa's eyes widened momentarily.

"Speak of the devil," she murmured.

I spun and caught sight of Joseph entering with his to-die-for smile plastered on his face. He wore his normal work attire—jeans, boots, and his Carhartt jacket. His chunk of hair was on its best behavior today, but I was hard pressed to forget how messy it had looked last night. Naughty had never looked so good.

I cleared my throat and met him halfway, standing on my tiptoes to kiss him good morning. His arm wound its way around my back as he whispered in my ear. "Good morning, Sutherland." He sneaked a peek in Melissa's direction, noting the huge grin on her face. "I take it she's been briefed."

"I left no detail untold," I said, drawing an imaginary circle on his chest above where his coat gaped. The hard swell of his pec beneath his T-shirt had me itching to tug his cute little self into my office for a little private one-on-one. But I didn't scratch that itch. That would be far too cruel in front of my loyal friend. "So," I finally breathed. "What are you doing here?"

He released his hold on me and eased his way up to the counter. "I just thought I'd grab a cup of coffee before I headed to your grandmother's to fix her stuff."

I walked behind the counter to fill his order. "I thought you were going to do that this coming weekend?"

"Well, I was, but my sister, Randi, called this morning and asked me to help her load some furniture in the U-Haul. Spencer's flying in from Denver to help her pack. Thought I'd just kill two birds with one stone while I was down there."

"Oh, I see." I didn't mean to sound disappointed, but I was looking forward to going with him to see my grandmother. "I wish I could go with you, but Monday's are Donna's night class at Northern. There's no one to cover for me."

"No problem," he said, leaning over the counter. "As long as you don't mind me hanging out with your grandmother without you."

"No, I don't mind." I thought about how Grandma had

gushed over him this past Saturday. "I'm sure she wouldn't mind having you all to herself either. I saw her wandering eyes when you weren't looking."

"Nothing like the way her granddaughter looks at me though."

I caught his charming little wink as I looked over my shoulder and blushed. I couldn't argue with him there and poured some extra frothy cream into his steaming cup of mocha. I didn't bother asking how he wanted his coffee today. I figured I'd give him something to remind him of me for his long drive south.

"You dating anyone, Melissa?" I heard him ask. Without turning around, I knew he'd just piqued her interest with that little question.

"Who's asking?" she replied with a tinge of flirtatiousness.

"A friend of mine. I told him about you and he seemed interested to meet you."

"Is that so?" I saw her eyes light up. "Is he as cute as you?"

"Can't say I ever looked at him that way, but I'd be happy to give him your number, if you're so inclined."

"Oh, I'm inclined," she said in haste. I watched her scratch her number on a slip of paper and hand it to Joseph. "What's his story?"

He tucked her number in his back pocket and smiled. "The usual. Can't find a decent woman to save his ass. Tired of gold diggers and one-night stands."

"Sounds like my kind of man."

I handed Joseph his cup and shook my head at his twenty-dollar bill. "You're doing me a favor by helping my grandmother. Keep it."

He took a sip of coffee and leaned in for a kiss. "I'll see you tonight."

"Okay." I heard Melissa giggle as she turned to help the next customer who walked in the door. "Be careful," I commanded protectively.

"Always." He turned on his heel and almost bumped into the person standing behind him. He apologized and sifted around the long line that had already started to form at the register.

As usual, Melissa and I watched him walk out the door, our eyes glued to his tight Wrangler butt. When the door chimed upon his exit, we both sighed with utter contentment. Having our 'Joseph fix' for the day meant nothing could ruin the start of our manic work week.

Chapter Seventeen

Fourteen grueling hours later, I dragged my dog-tired self from the elevator of my apartment complex and turned the corner of the hallway. Joseph was kneeling at his door, a screwdriver in hand and his trusty Champion toolbox at his side on the floor.

"Hey," I said in surprise. "Watcha doin?"

He glanced up and smiled. "Hey. Just changing my lock. How was your day?"

Mondays always prove to be busy and tiresome. A great thing for an entrepreneur like myself. But hearing Joseph was changing his locks, because of the stunt Caroline pulled last week, totally made my day. No one could erase this self-satisfied smile off my face.

"It was good," I tried to say without much enthusiasm. I didn't want Joseph to know that I was practically dancing a jig on the inside. "How about you?" I slid down the wall beside him. "I didn't expect you to be home so soon."

He looked at me askance. "It is eight-thirty at night."

"Oh, I know," I sighed, closing my eyes. "I just thought you'd still be down at your sister's. How did it go today?"

He made the final adjustments on the new door knob as he spoke. "Great. Your grandma's sink doesn't drip anymore and her door's been squeak-proofed."

"And Randi?"

"The first truck load is on its way to Colorado."

I sat in awe. Joseph was the first guy I ever knew who

could be so productive in a single day. Just hearing about how much he'd accomplished had me wondering how the man did it all. Not to mention, drive two hours back to Cincinnati and still beat me home.

He tossed his screwdriver into his toolbox and latched it shut. "You look exhausted, Sutherland."

"I am." He snagged my hand and helped me stand, all the while grinning at me. "What?" I finally asked.

"You haven't said a thing about me changing the lock. You do realize I'm not doing it because it's broken, right?"

I laid my head against his chest, hiding the grin on my lips. "I know why you're doing it."

"And?"

"And I'm thoroughly happy."

He pushed me away from his chest just enough to look in my eyes. "You are?"

"Well, any other woman might run outside, climb the Purple People Bridge and shout it for all the world to hear. But I'm not one to gloat. I'll just celebrate in my own quiet way the day Caroline comes back and finds her key doesn't work anymore."

"Speaking of keys...." He reached into his back pocket. "This would be yours." He took my hand and planted a shiny new key in my palm. "It's only fair since I have a key to your apartment."

I squeezed it tightly. "You sure about this?"

"I've never been so sure in all my life."

He dipped his head and kissed my lips softly. I wrapped my arms around his neck and kissed him back, letting him know just how happy he'd made my evening. When he ended the kiss, I staggered backward.

"Let's get you off to bed," he said, picking up the

toolbox from the floor.

"You're going to tuck me in?"

His snicker vibrated through me as he followed me to my door. "If that's what you'd like."

I'd like him to do more than tuck me in, but I wasn't about to confess my most darkest desires to him. I was still a bit mortified about coming on to him last night to traipse down that wicked path again.

I let us into my apartment and turned to flip on the lights. Joseph's hand closed over mine. I heard him set his toolbox on the entryway floor and he kicked the door shut. Holding my hand, he spun me into his arms and kissed me again in the dark. He picked me up in his arms and carried me to the bedroom.

My heart raced. My thoughts whirled. I tensed in his arms and I could feel the sharp edges of his key digging into my palm. I didn't want to let go of it or him. Together, they were such a special gift that I would cherish always.

When we reached my bed, he laid me down. I watched him curiously, wondering what his intentions were. Like a gentleman, he took off my shoes and set them as a pair on the floor. Next, he unzipped my coat and slipped it off me. In seeing my pajamas on the chair, he brought them to me.

He knelt on the floor, between my legs. He reached up and released my ponytail, letting my hair cascade around my shoulders. He played with a curly strand, caressing it between his fingers. "I hope you sleep well, Jamie."

The husky sound of his voice was the best lullaby in the world. Whether he called me by my first name or my surname, I loved the sound of it on his lips. I clutched my pajamas along with his key against my chest. His unruly lock of hair dared me to thread it through my fingers, but I didn't reach out to hold him. I feared I'd not be able to let go.

"Jamie," he said, looking downward.

My voice squeaked. "Yes?"

He looked puzzled or nervous, I couldn't tell. But something consumed him. "Never mind," he recanted, moving to stand.

I snagged his wrist to keep him from leaving. "What is it?"

He brushed back the hair from my face. "I just had a lot of time on my hands today. Thinking, you know. And…" He paused, sitting beside me on the bed. "And I guess I just missed you, that's all."

Amid the dark shadows of the room, I held his hand and gave it a loving squeeze. "I missed you, too. We've spent so much time together lately, it was kind of weird not having you around today."

"Which leads me to my next thought."

"And that is?"

He cupped my hand in both of his. "While I was down at your grandmother's house today, I found a lot of things that needed urgent repair."

"Okay…" I wasn't sure where he was going with this. "So, can you fix them?"

"Sure, I can fix them," he said, tilting his head in thought. "But it's going to take some time. What I mean is, I'm going to be staying with Candace for the next two weeks so I can get them finished on time. You know, before your grandmother moves. I've talked to my boss here and he's fine with that."

"Oh," I said, contemplating this news. "In other words, I won't see you much after tomorrow."

"Right."

"Well, I could always come down on the weekends and help you."

"Actually, I work better alone." My face must have shown my disappointment because he amended his statement pretty quickly. "I'd love to have you there with me, Jamie, but…" His mouth twitched upward in a crooked smile. "I'm afraid you'd only be a distraction for me. I mean, when you're around, I can't seem to focus on anything but you."

His compliment lifted my spirits. A little. "Okay, I get it. I think."

Joseph cradled my face in his hands. "I'll certainly miss you."

I felt bad knowing he was only helping my grandmother because of me. What's worse was knowing he'd not take a cent from her for it and that he was giving up his vacation time to do it. No one was better for the job, but I hated knowing he'd not get anything for his trouble. "I don't expect you to do this, Joseph. I have money. I can hire someone else to do it."

"You're not hiring someone else. I told your grandmother I'd do it for her. I'm not going to back out now."

I could tell there was no convincing him otherwise. "Two weeks, huh?" Saying it aloud sounded more like forever. Being away from Joseph for a few hours was hard enough. Whether he realized it or not, I craved his company.

"Two weeks," he repeated, frowning. "I should get back in town the day before Christmas Eve. Want to get together then?"

"It's a date," I said, already longing for this two-week hiatus to be over.

He wrapped his arm around my shoulder and tugged me against him, kissing my forehead. "In the meantime, you can be thinking about my Christmas gift."

I elbowed his ribs playfully. "What if I've already decided what I'm giving you?"

He laughed. "You so suck at lying, Sutherland." He palmed my face and shoved me. I fell back into the pillows for effect, still clutching my PJs and his key.

"You're so beautiful, Jamie."

"Thank you," I said, reeling inside.

He finally stood and walked to the bedroom door. The longing I felt watching him leave was greater than anything I'd ever felt before. I wanted him to turn around and say how hard it was for him to leave. I wanted him to suggest he stay. I wanted to invite him to spend the night so he'd know what was running through my head.

"Joseph," I called in haste, bolting upright in bed.

He rotated on his heel and braced his arms casually on the doorframe. "Yeah?" His dark silhouette filled most of the opening. He was so gorgeous. What if he turned me down again? I couldn't bear another disappointment.

"Don't forget your toolbox," I said at last.

Despite the shadows masking his features, I could still see the wicked grin on his lips. "Goodnight, Jamie."

Chapter Eighteen

"How long has it been already?" Melissa asked, bumping my hip with hers behind the coffee shop counter.

I cleaned the last of the mess around the espresso machine and tossed the coffee-stained dishcloth into the small sink beside the Styrofoam cups. I sighed and crossed my arms. "Three days."

She gave me a sympathetic smile. "You going to make it?"

"Do I have a choice?"

"I don't see why you just don't go down there this weekend and surprise him. You know you want to."

"I can't. I promised him I wouldn't."

"You don't have to stay all day," Melissa persuaded. "Just for a few minutes. Sneak a little lovin' while he's bent over the table saw."

My brow kicked up. "The table saw? That could get a little dangerous."

She dismissed my literal interpretation with an eye roll. "You know what I mean. Besides, don't you think your grandmother would like to see you?"

"She's not even there," I explained. "Evidently, Joseph is tearing into the walls and there's a lot of dust. He asked my mother if Grandma could stay with them for a while so she's not breathing all that in."

I pushed myself from the back counter and ambled toward the door, my thoughts roaming in the same direction as Melissa's. I wanted more than anything to surprise Joseph with a quick little visit, but I also didn't want to upset him. He made it perfectly clear that I was a distraction, one he didn't need if he was going to get anything done. I turned the lock and flipped the sign in the window to CLOSED.

"What if you surprised him by being at Candace's house?" Melissa suggested. "He's not working there and maybe once he comes home on Friday night, he'll *want* that distraction. He is a man, you know."

As good as that sounded, I was not about to have our 'first time' in his sister's guest bedroom. "I don't think so. I'll just go home and watch some TV. Eat a whole pint of Graeter's."

Melissa laughed at my joke. "Well, if you need anything…someone to help you binge on Black Raspberry Chip or what not, call me. I'll be right over."

"Thanks," I said, hugging her.

"Come on, I'll give you a lift home." We collected our purses and coats and headed out the door together. We walked a couple blocks to the parking garage and climbed inside her cherry red Camaro with black stripes running the length of the hood. I always thought this vehicle had too many horses for her to handle, but they didn't scare Melissa. She lived to test the limits, just short of breaking the rules. I, however, was content to live vicariously through her.

She fired up the engine and pulled out, the deep rumble of the motor echoing against the concrete walls of the near empty garage. In no time, she circled the block and turned down Sycamore Street. She pulled in front of my apartment building and slid the shifter into park. I hugged her from across my seat and got out, waving as she sped away.

Knowing I had nothing to come home to, I entered the historical building in a funky mood. I couldn't believe I had eleven more days of this. I decided then I needed a hobby. Maybe I'd finish that afghan I started crocheting a few years ago. Surprise my grandmother with it for her birthday.

Who was I kidding? Crocheting would only remind me of Grandma, which in turn would remind me of Joseph laboring to repair her house, which then would remind me of how much I missed him. I concluded that I didn't need a hobby after all. I needed more ice cream. Tomorrow, I'd pick up a dozen more pints on my way home from work. Problem solved.

As I stepped off the elevator and turned the corner, I stopped short. Caroline stood just outside Joseph's door, punching an angry text on her cell. I could only assume Joseph was at the receiving end of that stabbing finger. I stepped back and hid behind the corner wall, suppressing a smile. It seemed she wasn't all that happy about the sudden lock change.

Coincidently, my cell vibrated in my pocket. I pulled it out and read the screen.

Caroline is at my door. Don't go home yet.

I texted back.

2 late, already here.

As soon as I hit SEND, I heard the heavy stomps of her designer boots marching down the corridor. I panicked and dashed for the elevator. I pressed both buttons repeatedly. *Come on. Come on.* I glanced up at the floor indicator lights. The elevator was stuck on the first floor. I made a mad dash for the stairwell.

From behind me, I heard the disgust in Caroline's voice. "Uuuugh. You."

I whirled around and manufactured a pleasant smile. "Well, hello. Clementine, right?" I purposely chose a ridiculous name. I was not about to give this woman the satisfaction of thinking she was memorable.

"Caroline," she snipped, planting her hands on her hips.

"Oh, that's right. I'm sorry. I'm terrible with names."

"Cut the crap, Judith." Amazed that the woman was smart enough to dish the name game back at me, I couldn't hide my amusement no matter how hard I tried. My pursed grin only infuriated her. "Do you have something to do with this?" She held up her key between two French-manicured fingernails.

I played dumb. "What's wrong with your key?"

"It doesn't work," she snapped. "Why is that?"

I stuttered, not knowing how to fend off this charging bull. Without a figurative red cape, I felt like an ill-equipped matador. "I don't know. You'd have to ask Joseph about that."

"Oh, I will. Don't you worry. And if I find out you had something to do with this—"

"Are you threatening me?" Somehow, amid all her posturing and hoof scratching, I found my back bone. Standing toe-to-toe with this walking Clinique counter didn't seem to intimidate me anymore.

She glared at me with fire in her eyes. "Where's Joseph?"

As much as it would've pleased me to slap this pompous princess with a full explanation of where he was and why, I wasn't about to divulge such personal information. If he wanted her to know where he was, he would've informed her himself.

"All I know is he's out of town for a couple weeks." I figured I'd give her that much so that in his absence, I wouldn't have to deal with her popping in again.

"Fine," she grumbled, jamming her keys into her purse. She righted the strap on her shoulder just as the elevator door opened and jetted passed me. I watched the doors close behind her as my cell vibrated in my hand.

I smiled when I read Joseph's text.

No matter what she says to make U feel inadequate, remember U have the key that works.

I read his text twice before unlocking my own apartment door, his encouraging words hugging me the way he would—with warmth and compassion. I held my cell as I hung up my coat, wondering what I should text back to him. I reckoned he was worried about our little encounter and was dying to know what went down.

I walked to the kitchen and pulled a half-pint of Graeter's ice cream from the freezer. As the door closed, I caught sight of our photo booth pictures clinging to the front. I plucked the strip from the magnet holding them and gazed at the shots. For the first time since we'd taken them, I regarded each one carefully, recoiling at my goofy poses and facial expressions. But as I studied Joseph's, my heart melted. The camera had captured the blatant admiration in his eyes. If I didn't' know any better, he looked like a man in love.

Staring at the pictures, I snagged a spoon from the drawer and traipsed into the bedroom. Consumed with staring at the two of us as a couple, I absently got ready for bed. My PJs were on, my spoon was primed in the container, and Joseph's apartment key lay reverently on my nightstand. All nestled under the covers, I picked up my cell and texted him at last.

I survived unscathed. Rest assured, what little emotional stress I endured this evening, can be remedied with ice cream therapy.

Within minutes a new text came through.

I'm so sorry U had to deal with this. I will B taking care of it immediately, if not sooner.

Part of me felt sorry for Caroline. Maybe it was the creamy, chocolaty goodness sliding down my throat that eased the burn in my stomach and made me sympathize with her just a little. Giving up Joseph, would have to be the hardest thing she's ever had to do. I'm certain if the roles were reversed, I wouldn't go down without a fight either.

I sucked another heaping mound of ice cream off my spoon and texted a thoughtful reply.

Go easy on her. I'm betting underneath all that scaly skin and fangs lies a heart.

Anxiously awaiting his response, I scraped out the last remaining dollop of ice cream and tossed the spoon into the empty container. Setting the cup on my nightstand, my cell vibrated once more.

This is why I adore U. Leaving UR grandmother's now. Talk to U tomorrow. Gnite

I texted back my farewell, clicked off the light, and snuggled deep beneath my quilt. I laid on my side, gazing at the strip of photos leaning against my lamp and the key propping it up. I hated that I couldn't see the real Joseph or kiss his warm, soft lips goodnight. But I closed my eyes feeling quite content that the man in the sepia photos had strong feelings for me. He may not have admitted his love for me exactly, but his testimony of "I adore you" was good enough.

Chapter Nineteen

In the following days, I kept myself busy working extra shifts. I decided to be a generous employer and give all my college employees some much needed R&R after they came off a grueling, hard-core week of finals. Donna was certainly happy about it, going so far as to bear hug me the day she stopped in to pick up her check.

I even visited my folks a couple nights after work to help them pack and wrap Christmas presents. Grandma, who'd been staying with them while Joseph made the repairs, was extra happy to see me. Of course, when Mom stepped out of the kitchen to yell at my father for golfing in the living room again, she thanked me for convincing my mother to ship her bedroom suite to Florida. Seeing the tears of joy in her eyes was worth every bit of strife my mother had given me. I'd do anything for my grandmother.

Two days before Joseph was due home, I came to the conclusion that it was time for me to quit playing the Good Samaritan for everyone else and grant myself a well-deserved occasion of selfishness. I took a nap right after work, showered, and made a pot of coffee. In the quiet hours of the evening, the recurring thought of Joseph stepping out of his sister's shower clung to my brain. I finally figured out the perfect Christmas gift for Joseph that didn't require the spending of money, like he and I'd agreed upon.

I selected a clean white towel from my bathroom closet

and dug into my mess of embroidery thread and needles from a container beneath the bed, choosing a color that matched his Montana blue-sky eyes. Sitting at the table, with the city skyline lighting up the view through the tall windows, I sat down and began stitching. Like my grandmother had taught me, I outlined the letters J, A, and S as a starting point. I monogramed his initials on the towel with the S in the middle much larger than the two beside it. It took me well into the early hours to finish it, but I didn't care. I'd taken the next day off so I could get ready for Christmas Eve at my apartment.

That morning, I enveloped his special towel in matching blue tissue paper and laid it reverently in a long white box. I wrapped the box in blue and silver snowflake paper, topping it off with a large UK blue bow.

Once that was finished, I made another pot of coffee, wrapped the rest of my family's gifts, and began the daunting task of cooking and baking. I wasn't the best chef in the world, but with Grandma's recipes, I could fake it.

Determined to make a dent in the food preparations, I tied on my apron and readied my utensils. I peeled and diced apples for two pies; measured, dumped and mixed all the ingredients for three dozen chocolate chip cookies; and smothered a whole ham in butter, brown sugar, cloves, and beer. I'd made a total mess of the kitchen in just a few hours. Clumps of batter littered the counters, assorted dirty bowls and measuring cups filled the sink, and white, powdery flour dusted every available surface, including my face and clothes. Despite the extra work I'd made for myself pulling cleanup duty, I was pleased I hadn't burned anything to a crisp.

As I untied my filthy apron, a knock came at my door. I

dusted my hands off and abandoned the kitchen left in ruins, eagerly hoping it was Joseph.

I peeked out the peephole and saw him standing in the hallway, his trusty toolbox at his feet. My heart leapt like a gymnast on the pole vault. I ripped open the door and threw my arms around his neck. He staggered back, unprepared for my enthusiastic greeting, and wrapped his arms around me for security.

"Whoa, whoa. Hey there."

I relished the feel of his strong arms around me and savored the smell of his skin. I burrowed my nose along his throat and had no qualms about staying there for the rest of the day.

"I take it you missed me?" The even tone in his voice caught me off guard. His embrace weakened and I slid down his body, a little embarrassed with myself.

I cupped his face and took a long hard look at him. His hair looked like he'd just rolled out of bed. His eyes were heavy and blood shot. And his smile appeared forced and hesitant.

"I'm sorry I practically tackled you. I don't know what came over me."

"Don't be sorry. It was nice to be welcomed home like that for a change." He reached up and dusted the flour from my cheek. "Don't you look cute."

"Yeah, I've been baking all day," I said, brushing some residual flour from his neck.

He sniffed the air. "I can smell it. Apple pie?"

"And cookies," I concluded, rocking back on my heels.

"If it's anything like your lasagna, I know they'll be delicious."

I smiled at his compliment and took his hand. "Come

on in and—"

"Actually," he said, picking up his toolbox. "I'd really like to get some sleep. I'm beat."

"Right," I nodded, forgetting about the long hours he spent day after day working on my grandmother's house. "I take it everything's in working order now?"

He ran his hand through his hair, yawning. "Yep. All fixed and up to code. The movers came today too…for your grandmother's bedroom furniture. I helped them load it so they wouldn't scratch it."

"Thank you." I appreciated that more than he'd ever know. I wanted to hug him again, but resisted. For whatever reason, the thought of Caroline popped into my brain and I spoke before I knew what I was saying. "Did you get a chance to talk to Caroline?"

His brows furrowed. "No. I didn't have time. To be honest, I didn't have the energy to deal with her. With everything's that going on, my sister's move, your grandmother's house, Christmas, I put it on the back burner for right now. Sorry, I know that's not what you wanted to hear, but—"

"No, I understand. You've got a lot on your mind."

"Yeah, I do." He started to back away and I panicked. I didn't want him going to sleep thinking I was overbearing. He had always liked the fact that I was independent and didn't throw myself at him.

But I just did.

I felt like I had suddenly made the biggest mistake in our budding relationship and this was Joseph kindly withdrawing from it. I shouldn't have been surprised. I do it all the time. I'm not a serial, ruined-relationship survivor, but a relationship ruiner. Perhaps it was force of habit.

The air around me thinned. The walls closed in and the temperature spiked. Inwardly, I kicked myself, feeling my throat constrict as I drew in calming breaths. I swallowed and played it cool, backpedaling into my apartment. "You get some sleep, and I'll see you tomorrow."

He nodded lethargically and yawned again. "Right. Tomorrow."

With his toolbox dangling from his fingertips, he dragged his boots across the floor and unlocked his door. Without a second glance in my direction, he entered his apartment and shut the door.

I shut mine and collapsed against it. *What was I thinking coming on so strong?* These two weeks of being without him made it easy for me to forget what our relationship was like beforehand. I'd almost forgotten that Joseph and I interacted more like close friends than lovers. We were casual and spontaneous and hardly got hung up on relationship etiquette. We were content to take things as they came and, most importantly, have fun in the process.

So what did I do? I smothered him with affection the minute I saw him. I might as well have cinched a ball and chain around his ankle, for goodness sakes.

Squeezing my eyes shut and feeling a serious headache coming on, I pushed from the door and headed into the kitchen. Nothing helped settle nerves like good old fashion housework. From the looks of the mess in front of me, I should be cool as a cucumber by the time I finished.

As I scrubbed the dishes, I worried I'd overstepped my bounds with Joseph. As I dried them, I fretted over how clingy and pathetic I looked leaping into his arms. As I put them all in the cabinet, I dreaded the thought of him waking up and having second thoughts. I wiped the counter clean and wished I could go back in time and tidy up this mess with one swipe.

For starters, I'd open the door like a normal person and kiss his cheek with a cordial 'hello,' instead of bounding into his personal space the way a WWE wrestler would clothes line his opponent off the ropes. Then, I'd suggest he get some much needed rest. Men loved their sleep and women who insisted they indulge whenever possible. And lastly, I'd have kept my mouth shut about Caroline. Who in their right mind brings up the subject of The Ex, when it was better for both parties to forget she even existed?

As I tried to make sense of my rambling thoughts and suspicions, I came to realize one thing. He didn't forget about her. He basically swept her under the rug. A convenient ploy, it seemed, if he still had feelings for her.

I drummed my fingers on the sanitized counter and ruminated over this revelation. If I had to think about it, Joseph seemed to do this often where Caroline was concerned. Which would explain why she kept creeping back into his life. Whether she was too self-absorbed to recognize she was fighting a losing battle or he felt something for her deep inside, I deserved to know the truth. It wasn't fair for me to be strung along until one of them figured it out.

Straightening my spine, I marched towards the door. He would tell me how he felt about me. I wasn't taking no for an answer either, sleep or no sleep. I yanked open my door and took one step across the threshold. The elevator dinged and the telltale click of what only could be Caroline's Prada heels sounded on the hallway floor.

Chapter Twenty

I shut the door quickly while holding the handle turned, a technique I seemed to have perfected in the past weeks. I held the knob in a tight grip and left the door cracked a little so Caroline wouldn't notice as she walked by. Through the narrow opening, I saw the short black mini dress sashaying at her thighs, most likely a designer label that cost more than my yearly salary. Her expensive French perfume left a trail behind her, assaulting my nose. Her hair cascaded down her back in golden waves and the muscles in her calves flexed with each determined step. This was a woman on a mission.

I swallowed hard and waited as she knocked on his door. Like so many times before, I hated the thought of eavesdropping, but I felt I was left with no alternative. With Caroline making her last stand, it was crucial to my poor heart that I find out just how Joseph felt and how he was going to handle this unexpected situation.

She knocked a second time with more force and I swore I heard her sigh. I laid my ear alongside the crack so I wouldn't miss a single word. My heart thumped in my chest. Joseph's door opened and I held my breath.

"What are you doing here?"

There was little emotion in his voice. Given the flat tone of his greeting, I couldn't tell if he was just groggy from his interrupted nap or perturbed about her wakening him up. I hoped he was glaring at her.

"I wanted to talk," Caroline said sweetly. I should have known the woman was capable of sugaring her voice to that of a delightful person.

"We have nothing to talk about, Caroline. I told you, it's over."

A good start so far. They were through and she couldn't grasp it. I could live with that scenario.

"Joseph, you don't believe that."

"I do."

"You say that now because you're confused."

"Confused?"

I thought the same thing as Joseph. What's to be confused about?

"You don't know what your heart wants," she continued. "And that's not your fault. It's mine. I blamed you for not being there for me, when all along you were. It was I who wasn't there for you. Between my modeling career and traveling to Milan and Paris, I just didn't have the time to devote to you. But now…" I heard her voice escalate, emphasizing the grand finale of her monologue. I imagined her swaying closer to him, batting her lashes, and brushing her long pretty nails down his chest. "Now I do, and I know what it takes to be committed. I'm willing to give you my all, Joseph."

She paused momentarily and brought out all her seductive powers when she ended her speech with one soft, dulcet word. "Everything."

I had to give her credit. She knew what she was doing. She knew exactly what to say to bring a grown man to his knees. I knew what "everything" meant. I could only imagine how often that one little word helped her gain everything she ever wanted.

"Are you finished?" I heard him mumble. My brows rose in curiosity. He didn't sound the least bit interested in her offer.

"Yes, I'm finished. Talking, that is. So, why don't you invite me in and let me—"

"I don't think so," he commanded sternly.

Yes! Thata boy. Tell the conniving wench no. Goodness knows she's never heard that before.

"Caroline, I'm tired—"

"Ah, baby, I can see that," she cooed—with so much pity it was sickening. "You look exhausted."

"No, I'm tired of *this*," he corrected. "I'm tired of your advances. I'm tired of your head games. The way you talk to Jamie...."

"Jamie?"

"Yes, Caroline. You continually cut her down, and she hasn't done anything to you. I don't like it."

I couldn't stop the smile that inched upward on my lips. I loved that my southern gentleman found his backbone and stuck up for me. This was really getting good.

"Fine, baby. I'll apologize to her, if that's what you want."

"Geez, Caroline," he sighed. "You're not listening to me."

I had no idea what he was doing at this moment, but I could just imagine him threading angry hands through his hair. I'd never encountered this side of Joseph, but I had to admit, it was exciting to witness. Especially when I was not on the receiving end of his aggravation.

"I don't want you to apologize to Jamie. In fact, I don't want you to talk to her *at all!* Ever again. Do you understand?"

"I hear you, Joseph," she tried to soothe. I imagined Caroline was getting pretty squirmy. She was losing this game and she knew it. I waited for her to pull out the big guns. "I get it. She's a good friend of yours, and if you and I are to make this work, I have to play nice. I can do that. Whatever it takes."

Holy crap. She was desperate now.

"Joseph, I love you. I always have."

There it was. The love card. She threw it on the table and I held my breath waiting for Joseph to fold. I brought my fingers to my lips and tore the top off a nail. If he didn't soon get rid of her, I'd have the ugliest hands in Cincinnati for Christmas.

"I know you love me."

Was he going to cave? *No! You can't give in to her. Joseph, no! Please don't. Please don't break my heart...*

"And you know I've never been able to reciprocate."

"And that's okay, Joseph. I know you have a difficult time letting your guard down and allowing your heart to feel. But I can wait. I know I said I couldn't, but that was before I really knew what I risked in losing you. I—"

"Caroline." The harsh, unyielding tone of his voice returned. My heart skipped. "I *can't* love you."

"You can if you—"

"I can't. I can't love you because..." His words trailed off and my breath caught. "Because I'm in love with someone else. There I said it. I'm in love."

My mouth dropped wide open. Did I hear him right?

"In love?" Caroline asked. "With who?"

I heard Joseph sigh, but he didn't say a word. Instead, Caroline broke in, exposing her claws.

"Jamie? Next door? That little mousy thing?"

"Lower your voice, Caroline," I heard him scold. "You may think she's mousy, but I think she's the most beautiful woman who ever walked the face of this earth."

Caroline was in as much shock as I was. "Jamie? The Jamie in Loft B, right here." I imagined her pointing her manicured finger down the hall.

"Yes."

My heart soared and every muscle in my body wanted to leap for joy. Trembling with elation, I continued to listen. This was very best day of my life.

"You're sleeping with her, aren't you?"

I wanted to laugh. Caroline couldn't have been more furious with her accusation.

"Actually, no. We haven't even gone there. And I'm fine with that."

I thought back to my college psychology classes. Caroline had one more defense mechanism to go through. She'd already been through the Denial stage and then the Anger stage. All that was left was the Bargaining stage.

"Joseph, sweetie, she can't give you what you need. You're a man and you need a woman who knows exactly how to pleasure the wild animal in you. We both know that's not so easy to do."

She uttered a fake, cutesy giggle. I wanted to vomit.

"Caroline, how do I say this so you'll understand?" I heard him draw in a huge breath. "I don't love you. I never will. We are finished, and there is no hope for us ever getting back together. Ever. I love Jamie and I won't have you ruining the best thing that has ever happened to me. I've tried to be nice about this. I've tried for years to make you understand that I can't fall in love with you. I've changed my locks, for God's sake, and you still can't get it through your thick skull that we're done. Finished. I didn't want to end it this way, Caroline, but you leave me no choice. I want you to walk your little Prada pumps down to that elevator and never come back. If I so much as see your face or even find out you stepped one foot in this apartment complex, I'll call the police."

"You can't be serious, Joseph."

"I've never been more serious in all my life. Goodbye, Caroline." His door closed.

"Mark my words, Joseph, you'll be sorry you ever said goodbye to me."

I don't think so. The only one sorry was Caroline.

I heard her harrumph and stomp down the hall. My heart swelled so much I thought it might burst. Hearing the ding of the elevator was like striking my own exclamation point at the end of *Don't let the door hit you where the good Lord split you!*

I closed my door quietly. In silence, I fist pumped repeatedly and mouthed the words YES! over and over.

He loves me!

Joseph Alexander Scarbrough loved me and told Caroline to kiss his sweet little ass goodbye in the most profound, indisputable way. I twirled and jumped, shimmied and cha-chaed around the room. *I won!* I won the most perfect man in the world and I didn't have to plead, beg, borrow, or steal to get him. He was mine, fair and square. Was this for real?

I panted from the exertion of my spontaneous victory dance and slumped onto my couch and closed my eyes. I sat there giving myself time to let this all sink in.

I was the most beautiful woman to walk the face of this earth.

I was the best thing that had ever happened to him.

He can't love Caroline because he's in love with me. Me!

Me, me, me, me, me!

I wanted to run next door and tackle him with the biggest hug imaginable. I wanted to thank him for kicking Caroline to the curb, once and for all. I wanted to tell him how much I appreciated him. For everything. For being my neighbor. For welcoming me to the building in nothing but a towel. For making me laugh and squishing cupcakes in my face. For risking life and death just to hang Christmas lights in a tree. For helping my grandmother and taking his vacation time to do it. And best of all, for loving me the way no man had ever loved me.

I bolted upright and scavenged my apartment for my cell. I punched in 411 and gave the teleprompter the name Miranda Cromwell, Lexington, Kentucky. I connected to the number specified and paced the floor.

"Hello?"

"Miranda?" My heart was in my throat. "This is Jamie. Joseph's friend—neighbor."

"Oh, yeah. Hi, Jamie. How are you doing? Joseph told me you're coming to my parent's place for Christmas. He's really excited for you to meet everyone."

"I'm excited too. And that's kind of why I'm calling. I want to give Joseph something really special. And you know him better than anyone. So, is there something he's wanting? Maybe something big for the farm? A tractor? I don't know. I was just thinking I could get him something he could use when he buys the farm back from you."

"Well, that's really thoughtful of you, but…"

"But what?"

"Yeah," she said, hesitating. "Joseph broke the news to me the other day that he's not interested in buying the farm back."

"He's not? Why?" I couldn't begin to fathom why. That family farm meant so much to him.

"I don't know. He said it just wasn't in his plans right now."

I stood stunned. For the life of me, I couldn't understand why he'd let this once in a lifetime opportunity slip through his grasp. The last I talked to him, he seemed excited to buy back what Caroline had convinced him to sell.

"Jamie?" she said after a time of silence.

"Yeah. I'm here," I stammered. "I just can't believe this."

"None of us can. We are all so very disappointed."

At that moment, I knew what I had to do. For Joseph. For the man who meant the world to me. I'd give him the one thing that meant the world to him. Our deal of not spending any money on each other's gift be damned. "Miranda," I stated firmly. "Is the farm still up for sale?"

"Kind of. My uncle agreed to buy it as a last resort. He's like my father. He doesn't want the property to go to outside the family."

"Okay, good. Then I want to buy it. For Joseph."

"Jamie…"

I knew she'd try to talk me out of my plan. If our roles were reversed, I'd probably do the same myself.

I straightened my back and dug in. "Just hear me out."

Chapter Twenty-one

It took a long time to convince Miranda that me buying the farm for Joseph was a sensible idea. From the minute she balked, I knew I'd have my work cut out for me, but I pled my case the way an proficient, well-versed defense lawyer would—a regular female Johnnie Cochran. After a grueling debate about what was best for my bank account, the hefty down payment at closing, my insistence that only Joseph's name should appear on the deed, and the fact that he might still refuse to sign despite my generous offer, I had her on board. With the closing date being the day after Valentine's Day, I had my work cut out for me to keep this a secret.

The next morning, though I'd barely got any sleep reeling over my grand scheme, I awoke with a huge smile on my face. Excited to see Joseph's handsome face, I showered and got all dolled up in a shimmery green dress I'd bought from Kohls while he was out of town. Complete with spaghetti straps and a low cut back, I couldn't wait to see the look on his face. I applied a subtle amount of makeup and glittery body cream and finalized my glamorous look with a swipe of Pucker Me Pink lip gloss.

I strapped on a pair of dazzling silver sling-backs and entered the kitchen to begin the day's preparation. With my parents and Grandma coming over around four o'clock, I had some time before I needed to put the ham in the oven. Joseph's whimsical knock resounded upon my door just as

I sorted cookies on a tray.

Practically skipping across the room, I ran to open it. I brushed my hands down my dress and gave myself one final check. I bubbled with anticipation and crazy exhilaration and threw open the door.

Joseph stood leaning against the frame in his customary casual stance. He wore a sleek black suit, white shirt, a holly-green tie, and silver cuff links. His unruly lock of hair lay tamed and off his forehead. His face was cleanly shaven, showing off the sharp, strong edges of his jaw and cheekbones. With one hand in the front pocket of his pants, he held a box wrapped in red and green paper, a shiny silver bow topping a cluster of cascading ribbons. To say the least, he looked absolutely dashing and oh so debonair.

His eyes fell over me in the same surprised manner. He drank me in from head to toe, one sparkling fragment at a time.

"Wow," he muttered, shaking his head. "You look..." He swallowed and pushed himself from the door, squaring his shoulders. "...gorgeous," he breathed. "Like Christmas morning."

He reached out and brushed my hair off my shoulders, getting a better look at my outfit. I spun for him, revealing the open back. I heard him groan and his arm snaked around my waist, pulling me against his chest. I felt his warm breath on the back of my neck as he nuzzled my hair.

"You smell just as good as you look."

I giggled when I felt his mouth brush the bare skin on my shoulder. I reached for his face and cupped his smooth cheek. "Merry Christmas, Joseph."

He twirled me back around so I faced him and kissed

me softly. "Merry Christmas to you too, Sutherland." He handed me the present and bowed slightly. "And this is for you. But," he added holding it away from me. "I think we should wait until later. When everyone leaves."

The hint of something devilish to come oozed from his statement. I grasped his tie and pulled him back into my arms. "I think that's a great idea." My arms automatically wound around his neck and he tossed the box on the couch to reciprocate the gesture. His grin, absent the dark shadow of scruff that usually accented his lips, knocked me for a loop. I wasn't used to seeing the polished, clean-cut look of my next-door neighbor, slash superintendent, slash boyfriend. He had to be the sexiest man in the universe, and I was the luckiest girl to have all three to myself.

Like the gentleman he was, he stripped off his suit coat and helped me put the seven-pound ham into the oven. We peeled and chopped potatoes, talked about his adventures with helping the moving men load grandma's sleigh bed, laughed like idiots when he didn't notice that the top came off the pepper shaker and dumped a mound of black in the pan, and sneezed the rest of the time scooping it all out.

As we finished preparing the rest of the side items, my family finally showed up. Joseph slipped back into his suit coat before answering the door and, of course, was the crowd-pleaser. Grandma gushed all over again, remarking how he should never hide his handsome face behind all that scruff. Mom gushed too when he complimented her on the scarf she wore, claiming it brought out the youthfulness of her timeless beauty. No surprise that Dad enjoyed Joseph's company, as he finally had someone to talk sports with. Joseph knew as much, if not more than my father, discussing the up and coming talent of the Bengals defense and how the offensive line would be Super Bowl worthy if they had a better quarterback.

The day went off without a hitch, including dinner. Everything turned out edible, as long as you didn't count the unusual spicy flavor of the mashed potatoes. Not much was left of the ham or the rolls, and the apple pie was devoured once I brought out a pot of coffee.

With our stomachs full, we ended the night exchanging gifts. Conversations, laughter, and more stories flew at every turn as each person opened their present. I was especially pleased when Joseph opened his from Grandma. She'd crocheted him a new blue hat, one that rivaled his Montana blue-sky eyes, and when he put it on, she smiled the biggest smile I'd ever seen. My dad was thrilled with his new putter and mom couldn't stop talking about the new laptop Joseph and I picked out. With them moving to Florida, we thought she'd enjoy posting all their beach pictures on Facebook and Skypeing all her close friends back home.

By ten o'clock that night, Dad ushered everyone out the door so they could get an early start on tomorrow's drive to Destin. I hated to see them leave, especially my grandmother, as I had no idea how long it would be before I saw her again. I promised to come down for a visit as soon as spring rolled around, and hugged her tight. Joseph escorted her to the elevator, which again was the highlight of her evening, and reminded my father to call once they made it safely to the Sunshine State. I hugged my family again as the elevator door announced its impatience with repetitive attempts to close and subsequent dings. Eventually, I said my final goodbyes.

The elevator door closed and Joseph turned to me in

the hall, snagging my hand.

"That went well," he said, walking me back to my apartment.

"Yes, it did." I looked at him with admiration. That awesome chunk of hair had fallen out of its place. A five o'clock shadow had already started to darken his jaw. The top two buttons of his white dress shirt gaped open and his tie hung loose around his neck. Only Joseph could make unkempt look sexy. I reached up and pulled the knot free, liberating him from the manacles of refinement. "You were a huge hit today."

He pulled me close. "I was, wasn't I?" He kissed my nose. "I think your folks liked me...not as much as your grandmother though."

"There's only one person who likes you more than my grandmother."

He played dumb. "Oh, yeah? Who's that?"

I snuggled into his chest and wrapped my arms around his waist. "Me." I relished the warmth and smell of his skin radiating through his dress shirt. "I adore you, Joseph."

He lifted my chin with his knuckle and gazed into my eyes. The struggle he had for admitting his true feelings was written all over his face, but I didn't mind. I already knew how he felt. Besides, why ruin a good thing with a worn-out phrase?

I stood on my tiptoes and kissed his lips. "You think too much," I quoted him from a few weeks ago. His laughter wrapped around me like a warm snuggly blanket. I didn't think I'd ever tire of it. "Shall we open our presents now?"

He draped his arm over my shoulder and ushered me to the couch. "Good segue."

I sat down beside him and put my gift in his lap. "You're looking at the queen of segues. And sentiment," I added.

"Let's open them at the same time. One two three."

We gave each other curious looks and then dove in. The sound of popping ribbons and shredding paper filled the quiet apartment. At the same time, we both dug into the shroud of tissue paper and held up our gifts. Mine was his UK jersey I'd worn the night of our first official date. Our eyes met and we laughed together, knowing without explanation the sentimentality of that article of clothing.

"I can't believe you gave me your favorite shirt."

"My lucky shirt," he amended. "Besides, it looks much better on you anyway."

"Thank you. And I'm so wearing this to bed tonight." I held it up over my chest and remembered the morning I awoke in his bed wearing nothing but it and a pair of panties.

"You're blushing, Sutherland."

"Am I?"

"Yes, you are." He regarded the terrycloth towel in his lap and ran his fingers across the matching blue stitching. "You put a lot of time in this. Thank you."

"Does that mean I did okay when it came to...how did you put it? Ingenuity?"

He laughed and his eyes sparkled like tinsel on a Christmas tree. "You did just fine. I'm impressed. And grateful." He leaned over and cupped my cheek. "Merry Christmas."

He kissed my lips ever so sweetly and I was lost in the moment. I couldn't believe I had a man as wonderful as this guy. He was selfless, considerate, and so attentive to the things I needed in life without having to be asked. He kept me on my toes with his wit and continually made me laugh. And oh, holy hell could the man rock a suit and tie. How did I ever get so lucky?

When the kiss ended, I melted into him, snuggling into the warmth of his body. He leaned back into the couch and drew me with him. The feel of his sturdy physique offered me the support and comfort I craved after a long day of entertaining. The smell of his skin permeated through his dress shirt and soothed my senses like an effervescent analgesic. I didn't want to let him go.

I heard him sigh and his head drop back against the cushion. "What a day."

I smiled, listening to his even breathing and the rhythmic thump of his heartbeat. He was like a veritable hypnotic audio sleep aid. In this position, I knew I could fall within a few minutes. Somehow I found the will to speak. "This has been the best Christmas ever."

"It ain't over yet, Sutherland. We still have tomorrow."

My smile faded. I was reminded of that old saying: *Every good thing must come to an end.* The last thing I wanted to do was say goodnight to him. My arms automatically tightened around him, holding him captive. I had all I wanted right now in my hands and I didn't want to give it up. It had been the first Christmas where I wasn't alone.

Joseph?"

"Mm-hm?" His chest rumbled like a drowsy bear.

"I don't want you to leave." I said it quickly before I could talk myself out of saying it.

He stirred and brought his arms around me. "I've no intentions of leaving you. I plan on sticking around for a long time. Get used to it."

I smiled. As sweet as it was for him to ease my mind about our future, he didn't understand what I meant. I angled my head to look at him and he peeked at me from beneath closed lids. I touched his face, my heart kicking up speed for what I was about to say. "I mean, I don't want you to leave...tonight." I fidgeted, not knowing how to explain myself without sounding too needy. Too dependent. "I know this sounds stupid, but I don't want to sleep alone, Joseph."

His smile returned and his brow kicked up. "I don't think you should. From experience, if you recall, it gets rather drafty in nothing but a jersey. Assuming you *are* wearing my lucky shirt to bed, I'd be a pretty lame boyfriend to let you freeze to death on Christmas Eve."

I giggled timidly, appreciating his casual, offhandedness. He had such a way of putting my troubled mind at ease without trivializing my concerns.

"Now you go change into that jersey and I'll clean up our mess."

I stood, clutching his shirt against my chest. An image of him whistling at the sight of my bare legs flashed in my insecure brain. "Don't be surprised if I'm under the covers by the time you come in."

"Whatever makes you feel more comfortable." He didn't budge from the couch, but his eyes followed me as I walked toward the bedroom.

Like a skittish colt, I dashed into my bedroom. Heat blazed through my whole body knowing I'd be laying against taut, warm male skin soon. As wonderful as that sounded, I was at such a disadvantage knowing Joseph looked like a Greek god and I, a peasant girl.

I think she's the most beautiful woman who ever walked the face of this earth.

His compliment echoed in my head and I tried to believe it. Trembling, I slipped out of my dress and into his jersey. I could hardly believe what he said about me or that I wasn't going to be sleeping alone at Christmas.

I ran to the bed and yanked the covers down, slipping beneath them. I pulled them up to my chin and nestled down into the crisp, cool sheets. Waiting. Anticipating. Wondering what *he'd* wear to bed. Would he sleep in his dress slacks? *No, too uncomfortable.* Boxer briefs? I could only hope.

It seemed like forever before I heard him moving in the living room. By the sound, I determined he was balling up the tissue and wrapping paper and throwing them in the trash. I heard his footsteps throughout my living space and then dead silence. What was he doing now?

With a casual grace that only Joseph could pull off, he stepped into my room donning nothing but his monogrammed towel. He stood like a tall glass of ice water on a blistering hot day in the dessert. From the first time we'd met, it was like déjà vu all over again. Only this time I wasn't hiding the fact that I stared at him in a towel. I gawked at him like there was no tomorrow.

The man was blessed with long legs, giving him that manly six foot three height. His upper body was hard and lean, the kind of hard a man gets from swinging a hammer and tossing hay bales; not from hours lifting at the gym. His hair was tousled, and the mild shadow of dark, day-old scruff added a hint of bad-boy to his boy-next-door appeal.

"How's it look?" he asked, padding over to my side of the bed as if he were parading down a catwalk. "Does it make my butt look big?"

I laughed aloud at the customary female conundrum he used as a joke. I watched him turn for me and wiggle his cute little tush in the process. "Your butt is perfect. Now, get in here and warm me up. I'm cold."

He held my gaze as he slipped beneath the covers and reclined atop me, his weight pushing me down into the mattress. Unable to breathe, I drowned in those eyes.

Tenderly, he brushed his straight nose along mine and stared back. I could feel our hearts pounding as time stood still for us. So quiet, so close, so…did I dare think it…so in love?

Ever so gradually, he lowered his mouth to mine. The wait was torture, but worth it. I closed my eyes and savored this moment. Our tongues twisted in a slow, erotic dance, and I felt the sensation burn low in my stomach. He tasted of cinnamon and coffee and Joseph, my three favorite things. If we kept this up, I was pretty sure something else would land on my favorites list.

He smiled and rolled to his back, pulling me with him. I looked at Joseph lying on my pillow, a smug little smile adorning his lips. "How can you do that?"

He tucked one hand behind his head, his bicep bulging. "Do what?"

"Just stop and smile like you're happy…and not be…"

"Sexually frustrated?" he finished for me.

I laughed at his ability to put it so frankly. "Yeah. Aren't you the least bit upset that you're lying in my bed and—"

"Jamie," he said, cutting me off. "I'm not upset. I'm not anything. And I sure as heck ain't anything like your asshole boyfriends who made you think sex is the only way for a relationship to work. It's obvious you're not ready or you would've initiated it." He caressed my cheek with the back of his hand. "I'm not going anywhere, Sutherland. Even if it takes weeks, months—years. I'm still going to be here. You're living proof that good things come to those who wait, and I've got all the time in the world for you. We've taken baby steps to get where we are, and I'm totally fine with that. When you're ready, I'll be here."

"You're amazing."

"Yeah, yeah," he said, putting me in a headlock. "Close your eyes and get some sleep."

I laid my head on the smooth, hot skin of his chest and snuggled into his arms. I laid there with the biggest smile on my face. "Joseph?"

"Hmm?"

I circled his nipple with my finger. "Remember when we spent the night at your sister's and I woke up in your bed?"

"Yeah."

The deep sound of his one word reply rumbled in his chest. "Were you sexually frustrated then too?"

His laughter shook my whole head. "Shut up and go to sleep, Sutherland."

Chapter Twenty-two

I opened my eyes the next morning to the sight of Joseph sleeping next to me. I had to blink several times before I realized I wasn't dreaming. He lay there, so innocent, so peaceful. I hadn't the heart to wake him.

This was a dream come true for me. Sure, I'd done this once before with him, but the last time I was so distraught over the fact that I found him in my arms that I couldn't appreciate the moment.

This morning was way better. We'd planned it. No surprises. And I felt like a woman who had nothing to fear. My life was perfect with him in it.

I stared at him, taking advantage of the opportunity to admire him at such close quarters. He had long lashes for a guy, dark ones that curled up slightly on the tips. He had tiny pores and a clear complexion, probably the result of regimented washing and good facial products passed down from his sisters. His lips were an attractive shade of rose, but not too pink, kissable even as he slept. Everything about his face was absolutely perfect. Even the tiny scar above his left brow couldn't mar his looks. If anything, the blemish gave him character, a flaw that proved he was human after all.

I reached up and caressed the rough whiskers on his face. He stirred and I stopped, waiting for him to settle back into his dreams. I hoped they were of me.

Slipping from beneath the heavy weight of his arm, I

sneaked out of bed and tiptoed to the bathroom to shower. I wanted to make a good impression on his parents. I already had the advantage of not being Caroline in my favor, but I also wanted Joseph to be proud of the woman he was falling in love with.

The incredible thought buzzed in my head. Joseph…falling in love. With me.

I could turn a cartwheel right now.

In the span of an hour, I showered and brushed my teeth, dressed in another fancy outfit that would match the heels Joseph seemed so fond of, and curled my hair. After applying a little makeup, I padded back into the bedroom and stopped dead in my tracks.

Joseph, with his back to me, was climbing out of bed, his glorious naked backside as visible as a winter moon on a clear midnight sky. He stretched and the muscles in his back and tush flexed in the most alluring way. He turned to retrieve the towel that had come off amid the tangle of sheets, and saw me.

"So sorry." I turned my head and rotated like a top. I could feel my face burning. "I didn't realize you were awake."

He laughed in his cute, casual way. "Sorry, I thought you were still getting ready."

I didn't dare peek over my shoulder. "I can get your pants for you."

"I'm good. Just had to find the towel and put it back on. Must have come off in the night."

I wish I'd have known that when I woke up.

He came up behind me and whirled me around, pulling me into his arms. He kissed me on the forehead and ran his hand down my hair. "Good morning, Sutherland. Don't you look nice?" I watched him step in front of the bathroom mirror and run his fingers through his hair. He looked himself over, checking the shadow of scruff on his face. "Should I shave?"

"Who you looking to impress by shaving? Candace?"

"Right." He rubbed a hand over his whiskers. "I'd rather impress you."

"Then leave it."

He smiled wickedly at me. "Scruff it is, then. Do you mind if I take a shower here?"

"Knock yourself out. I'll even run next door and get a change of clothes for you, if you want."

"Thanks. Just jeans and a dress shirt, though. Bottom drawer."

I crossed my arms. "You going commando?"

His laughter echoed against my bathroom walls. "Hardly. Second drawer from the top. And a toothbrush, if you don't mind."

"Okay. I'm on it." I snagged his key from the bedside table and left him to get ready. I started the coffee pot, and then skipped next door to his apartment. It was the first time I used key since he gave it to me. I felt empowered.

Flipping on the lights, I closed the door behind me and gazed around his home. The natural scent of Joseph surrounded me. How happy it made me to breathe it in and let my senses indulge.

As I walked to his bedroom, THE photo album caught my eye. Like the last time I was in here, it sat on his coffee table, begging me to take a peek. I bit my lip. What would it hurt?

I walked over and picked it up. *Just a quick look.* I braced myself to see Caroline's Barbie Doll face. Not exactly the way I'd choose to start my day but such are the wages of sin. I flipped the cover open. But it wasn't Caroline I saw on the first page. It was a woman I'd never seen before. A young twenty-something with Joseph's Montana blue-sky eyes and his straight as an arrow nose. Her arm draped around Joseph's shoulder and they both looked so happy in this picture. I guessed that I was looking at Lindsey.

I flipped the next page. Lindsey again. This time on the back of a horse.

Next page. Lindsey on the beach, buried in the sand with a nice pair of sand-mound breasts someone had shaped for her. I laughed and turned the next page. Lindsey with a pair of thick-lensed glasses, her eyes the size of saucers. There was a caption below that read, "Look! You can hear me blink!"

I cracked up as I could actually hear the blink-blink sound effect of a cartoon character blinking. I loved this woman. I couldn't stop. I flipped through the next pages.

Lindsey and Joseph swinging from the tree house rope out into the lake.

Lindsey, Miranda, and Candace, and what I believed to be a six-year old version of Evelyn, Miranda's daughter, holding paint brushes and wearing handkerchiefs on their head. Paint splatters and swatches in pink and yellow randomly covered their faces, as if they'd spent more time painting each other than the walls.

Next page: Lindsey, wearing an elegant long red dress, in the arms of a handsome fellow, whom I assumed to be her high school prom date. The next page displayed yet another prom date picture, this time in a sparkly blue dress, with a more dramatic pose than the first.

I studied each picture, my heart melting with every

single one. The fact that Joseph had a collection of photos, documenting the memories of his sister, had me admiring him that much more.

I turned over the last page of the album. There were the photo booth pictures from our Kenwood Mall shopping extravaganza. My breath caught and my knees went weak. I had to sit. I wasn't strong enough to take this standing up. I felt so special to have been added to his book of treasured memories.

I closed the album, hot tears burning my eyes. I had suspected Caroline occupied these pages, when all along it was his family. The people he loved and cherished. And I was in there.

I placed the book back where it belonged and walked to his bedroom. As I retrieved his jeans, shirt, and boxer briefs from the chest of drawers, I pondered my impulsive decision to buy the farm back for Joseph. If I had any doubts, they were totally gone now.

Joseph's heart was the size of Texas, and I'd be damned if I'd give him any less. He deserved to know what unselfish love was. To know it's possible to be loved unconditionally without expecting a thing in return. Love was not about finding that perfect someone who makes you happy—but rather it was getting lost in the pursuit of that person's happiness with no regard for your own.

Joseph taught me that. He made me realize love wasn't a destination, but a journey. A voyage of baby steps and the commitment of cherishing the now along the way. At any moment, that precious 'now' could be ripped from our hands. I only had to look at the pictures of Lindsey to know how quickly life can change.

I loved Joseph. I knew that now with every breath I

took, but words were inadequate and most times useless. Joseph and I both had grown to detest those three, little, threadbare words, because of the pathetic people in our past. And although I might not be able to voice my love for him now, come February—if I could hold out that long—I'd give my heart to him the way Joseph was sure to understand.

* * * *

Christmas at his folk's place was like nothing I could've ever imagined. It was loud the minute Joseph and I walked through their door, the whole place full of excitement, laughter and conversation. Candace waved from the living room, the impersonal greeting I half expected from her, and went back to yelling at the basketball game on TV. Evelyn sat next to her, her nose in an iPhone, texting, until the second she saw Joseph. Her eyes lit up and she came rushing toward him, throwing her arms around his waist. I saw the love on his face as he hugged her back. Kissing the top of her head, he introduced her as his favorite niece.

"I'm your only niece, Uncle Joseph," she quipped back.

Out of nowhere, Miranda's twin boys ran around my legs. Spencer, their father, said a quick 'hello' and chased after them while Joseph embraced his sister.

"I thought you said you wouldn't be here for Christmas, Randi."

"I thought so too, but Spencer insisted we fly back for the holiday." She watched her husband headlock one son and tickle the other. "Guys, seriously. Settle down."

"Oh, they're fine," Joseph's mother said, coming around the corner. "And you must be Jamie." I balanced the apple pie I'd brought in one hand and held out my other to shake hers. She dismissed it and pulled me into a tight hug. "Shaking hands is for stuffy old men."

Joseph's mother was taller than me by a few inches. She carried herself with poise and grace without being too rigid. Her perfume was subtle and not outdated like so many woman wore at her age. She was probably the most beautiful sixty-year-old woman I'd ever seen. I imagined she was a blonde bombshell in her younger years.

She accepted my dessert and smiled warmly. "Aren't you just a pretty little thing? I love that dress, Jamie. And those heels. You have remarkable taste, my dear."

"Thank you, Mrs. Scarbrough." Like Joseph, his mother was easy to warm up to, unlike Candace, who obviously didn't take after the maternal side of the family. I could tell Mom and I would get along just fine.

"Joseph." I could hear the love in Mrs. Scarbrough's voice as she hugged him. "Merry Christmas, darling."

"Merry Christmas, Mom. Where's Dad?"

"In here!" Mr. Scarbrough called from the kitchen. "Your mother's got me slicing this damn ham. I'm missing the game!"

Mrs. Scarbrough rolled her eyes. "Joseph, why don't you help him before he drops it on the floor."

Joseph called his two nephews, and told them if they hauled all the presents in from his truck, they'd get to open theirs first. Spencer followed the rambunctious boys outside to make sure they didn't drop or break any and Miranda took my coat. In no time, I was inducted into the Scarbrough house of chaos.

While Joseph and his father tended the roast, Miranda and I assisted Mrs. Scarbrough in setting the table. Amid the clatter and clinks of the china, Christmas music played in the background, and shouts of disgust erupted at intermittent times from the televised NBA game. It was a holiday get together unlike anything I'd ever witnessed. With sports actually allowed in the house, my father would feel right at home here.

I couldn't help but take in all the pandemonium; the boisterous chatter, the hearty laughter, and the way everyone in this family spoke over each other. Aside from Mrs. Scarbrough—and Evelyn, whose whole world lay in the palm of her hand (literally)—their voices carried from room to room. It amazed me how anyone could concentrate with so many conversations going on at one time.

By the end of dinner, I'd gotten used to the racket, and I no longer flinched at sudden loud noises. Having everyone jammed into one room, around one long table, cured that mighty quick. Not long after we ate, I began collecting dirty dishes and washed them by hand. Miranda joined in, while Candace and her father, still absorbed with the Knicks game, made their way back into the living room.

Though I knew Joseph would've liked to watch the game, he commandeered Henry and Hunter, giving Spencer a break. He chucked them over his shoulder and marched around for effect. I heard giggles and growls resounding as he played something akin to Conan the Barbarian, body-slamming them on the couch beside Candace. I stifled a laugh as she socked him in the arm.

Miranda reached across me for one of the dishes I'd rinsed and toweled it dry. "You doing all right?" she asked, ignoring the pile up session her twins had initiated upon Joseph's back.

"Yeah, I'm great." Joseph shouted a fake cry for help from all fours as the boys clung to him like rabid spider monkeys. "You're kids are sure—"

"A pain in the ass, I know," Miranda said, shaking her head.

"I was going to say having fun," I corrected politely, taking notice of Joseph's hearty laughter as the twins rode him like a horse. "But I think someone else is enjoying himself more."

Miranda smiled. "Yeah, Joseph's great with the boys. Always has been. He'll make a great father one day."

Miranda's statement hung in the air and I wasn't certain how to respond. I'd not given thought to Joseph having kids, or actually to me having *his* kids, especially this soon in our relationship. But the thought now tingled in my brain.

For the first time in my life, I could actually see myself wanting kids, wanting to do more than just nurture a coffee shop from a one-bedroom apartment in the city. And if Joseph were the father, I'd be even more interested. *Baby steps, Sutherland*, I could hear him say.

"So," Miranda finally said. "What did you finally decide to get for Joseph for Christmas?"

I laughed nervously. "Well, we made a deal not to spend money on each other. Our gifts were supposed to be something we already owned and wanted the other to have."

"Oh yeah? That sounds like Joseph. Very noncommittal."

"Actually, I liked the idea," I said without going into much detail. "It relieved a lot of unnecessary pressure, you know."

"Sure. So, what was the present of choice?"

I think I blushed a little. "I gave him a towel. With his initials embroidered on it." She looked at me oddly and I suddenly felt the need to elaborate a little. "That's how we met. He was wearing nothing but a towel."

"Really?" she asked, drying another dish. "But I thought you guys met in the hallway of your apartment?"

"We did. But…"

"I don't think I want to know the rest," she said cringing. "And he gave you?"

"His UK jersey."

Her mouth dropped a little and her eyes widened. "His jersey? The one with the number thirty-three on it?"

"Yeah. Why?"

A curious smile quirked up on her lips. "You do know the importance of that number, don't you?"

I bit my lip. "No."

She came closer to me and spoke low. "That's Lindsey's number."

"Oh." The word came out as a muffled realization, for words utterly failed me.

"See, Lindsey used to play fast-pitched softball in high school and she won all kinds of awards. Broke lots of records. I think some of her records still stand for the state of Kentucky. Anyway…" She looked over her shoulder to make sure Joseph couldn't hear. "The school retired her number and held a huge ceremony. It was a big deal for all of us. Not long after that, Joseph was at a UK game and bought a jersey with her number on it. He wore it all the time."

I stood stunned. I had no idea that the sentiment of that jersey went beyond being a UK fan. I glanced down at the soap bubbles, pondering all the new facets of Joseph's character. This was a man who wasn't in the least one dimensional. There were so many sides to him, as unpredictable as they were fascinating, and each time I discovered a new one, I fell that much harder for him.

Miranda nonchalantly bumped my elbow to gain my attention. "I know it's not exactly as profound as an engagement ring, but that's a big leap for Joseph."

"Right. Right," I uttered, overwhelmed by this news.

"Hey," she said, touching my arm. "This is a good thing. For you, especially." She squeezed my forearm and smiled. "Joseph would never part with that jersey unless…"

I hung on her last words, waiting for her finish, but Evelyn came rushing up beside us, her phone in her hand.

"Mom, Samantha said I could spend the night at her house tonight. Can I? Please?"

Miranda struggled to composed herself, blindsided by the interruption of her daughter's question. She stammered as she gazed at me.

"Please, Mom…she's my best friend. One last time before we have to leave for Denver tomorrow?"

She smiled and gave in. "Sure, honey. Tell her we'll drop you off in a little while. After presents though."

Evelyn kissed her mom on the cheek. "Thanks, Mom. You're the best!" She skipped out of the kitchen, texting as she plopped on the couch next to Candace.

"I'm sorry," Miranda apologized. "Where were we?"

I looked at Joseph, who taunted Candace with a piece of mistletoe he'd just pulled from his pocket, and laughed. I didn't feel the need to delve back into the conversation. I understood the significance of his gift without Miranda having to spell it out for me. I hugged her and whispered in her ear. "I treasure everything your brother has given me, the best being his heart. I won't break it. I promise."

She hugged me back and I could feel her body trembling a little when she did so. I'm sure a lot of it was due to the loss of her sister. Holidays always made the loss of someone we love so much more poignant. I couldn't imagine the void Lindsey's passing left in this family's world. But also knowing Miranda was a mother hen in every sense of the word meant she wanted the best for her little brother, especially since he'd been hurt before.

She pulled away and wiped her tears before they could be seen. "I didn't mean to push all that on you, Jamie," she whispered. "I just wanted you to know how Joseph feels…in case you were having second thoughts about buying the farm for him and all."

"No," I insisted, taking hold of her hand. "I'm not having second thoughts. In fact, I feel you should know that I want nothing but the very best for Joseph. I'd give him the whole world, if I could."

She glanced over at Joseph. "I haven't seen him smile this much in years. I think you already have, Jamie."

Chapter Twenty-three

A month and a half later

February 14th. A Tuesday. A world-renowned feast day. A Hallmark holiday for some. But for me, it was a dedicated, heart-doodled square on my desk calendar, depicting a date for which I'd been waiting so long. I Xed out the space and smiled. Today was Valentine's Day and the night I would give Joseph the world. Well, at least twenty acres of it.

We'd planned to go to dinner after I closed the coffee shop, where—I had no idea because he said it was a surprise—and then we'd head to some charming bed and breakfast place he found near Lexington. It went without saying how excited I was, but for multiple reasons.

One: To see the look on his face when I presented him with the check that would make his dreams come true.

And two: To spend some quality time with him after so many weeks of being without him. Once Christmas and New Year's passed, we hardly saw each other except on weekends. Our work schedules had conflicted, and when he wasn't working long hours on some tenant's clogged drain or retiling a floor, he was often traveling to his family's farm to help Candace with the horses.

Any other woman might suspect a lover on the side. I knew better, however. Joseph was a lot of things, but not a liar or a cheat. I no longer suspected the worst or drew up cynical scenarios of how his feelings for me would eventually fizzle. I'd known from past experience how exhausting those thoughts could be. The strain of suspicion alone had ended many of my otherwise healthy relationships. Because of Joseph, I was over that way of thinking. Totally liberated.

At six-forty-five, I poked my head out of my office and caught Melissa's smile as she rang up a group of customers. "Get ready, Jamie. I got this."

I loved that Melissa shared my excitement. It seemed we both lived vicariously through each other.

I closed my office door and kicked off my shoes. I untied my apron and hung it on the back of the door. Digging into my duffle bag, I pulled out a change of clothes. Joseph and I made a deal not to get all dressed up, so I pulled on a pair of jeans and a pretty blue and white sweater. I released my hair from its ponytail holder, shook it out and gathered the majority of it back into a relaxed bun, letting a few loose strands frame my face. I freshened up my makeup and slipped into my favorite pair of knee-high, leather boots. After swiping some gloss across my lips, I was ready for my date.

With a few minutes to spare, I slid behind my desk again and made some last minute scheduling changes. Hearing the door chimes and Melissa bidding the last patron farewell, I prepared for her to slide into my office like Cosmo Kramer in an old Seinfeld episode.

Like I predicted, her entrance was anything but subtle. The door swung open, hitting the wall with a thud. Melissa's hand was still attached to the doorknob though so she smacked into the door too. She grinned at me. "What time is Joseph coming to pick you up?"

I checked the clock on the wall. "Any minute now."

She sauntered up to my desk and sat on its edge. "Is tonight *the* night?" She wagged her eyebrows, indicating there was more to our date than just a good meal.

I bit my lip. "Maybe."

She whipped a dishrag at me. "Oh, come on! Don't you think it's time already? Geez Jamie, how long are you going to make the poor man wait? You've been dating for over three months. If that hunk of manhood was mine, I'd have jumped his bones the first chance I got."

"It's not something you plan."

"Hello!" she sang out. "Yes, it is!"

I tapped my pen on the table. "I don't know. I prefer spontaneity."

She scoffed. "Even spontaneity requires a little planning, Jamett Penelope Sutherland. Tell me you at least shaved your legs."

I laughed. "Yes, I shaved my legs."

"Thata girl." She jumped to her feet and danced around my office, singing her words as if they were from an actual song. "Oh my gosh, I've waited so long for this...I can't wait to hear how things go tonight...It's going to be amazing..." She stopped in her tracks. "You better call me first thing in the morning."

I thought about the extensive preparations I'd made for this night, despite denying so with Melissa. I'd bought two cupcakes from the bakery that Joseph liked so much and placed them in a box with red ribbons and hearts. Beneath my jeans and sweater, I wore the sexiest, laciest, reddest lingerie ensemble I could find at Victoria Secret. I hoped he'd take so much great pleasure in unwrapping both gifts that it took all night.

"How about first thing in the *afternoon*?" I bartered.

She growled a wicked laugh. "Oooo, you naughty girl. Even better." She gasped and looked toward the café. "He's here!" If it wasn't for Melissa's supersonic hearing, I wouldn't have known Joseph had showed up. "Hurry, Jamie!" she called, ushering me out of the office with my coat, purse, and gift.

I could see Joseph through the tall, plate glass windows. My heart skipped. He wore his Carhartt coat, a pair of jeans, boots, and a white button-up shirt. His face was full of scruff, his bright smile meeting his eyes. I melted.

I unlocked the door and let him in. The cold winter wind rushed in behind him. His hands reached for my elbows and he kissed me gently, avoiding the gift box in my grasp. "Hi there, Sunshine."

"Hi." A squeal escaped me. I didn't mean to sound so giddy, but I was. So was Melissa as she uttered an empathetic "awwww."

We both smiled at her and stood in front of each other in awkward silence.

"So," he finally said. "You ready to go?"

My stomach somersaulted. "Yes." I looked toward Melissa. "Are you okay locking up?"

"I'm fine. Now, you two kids run along and have fun," she said, pushing us both out the door. "And don't forget to call me, Jamie."

She and Joseph exchanged peculiar looks. Something was definitely up between them, but the moment Joseph's hand touched the small of my back as he opened the door to his truck for me, I became incapable of coherent thought. Even through the thickness of my coat, I could feel the sweet intimacy of his touch. How would I feel later when we didn't have the separation of clothing between us? The blush that started on my cheeks traveled all the way to my toes.

From the passenger seat, I watched him shut my door and circle the vehicle. He climbed inside next to me, and I couldn't help but notice the look of anticipation on his face. He smiled as he turned the key, the engine roaring to life.

"You look beautiful, Sutherland."

"Thank you."

He checked his side-view mirror for oncoming cars and pulled out. We left Cincinnati behind and drove south to Lexington, talking about our hectic work week. That was one thing I loved about our relationship. We never seemed to run out of things to talk about and when I spoke, he listened as if everything I had to say was of the utmost importance.

As we neared Lexington, I noticed Joseph got strangely quiet as I rambled about Grandma and all the fun she was having in Florida with my parents.

"Sorry I'm talking so much. I'm just thrilled she's enjoying the sunshine and the beach. Mom's even got her wading in the ocean, which is huge, because Grandma doesn't swim."

"We should schedule a surprise visit soon. Don't you think?"

"We?" I asked, liking the sound of us taking a vacation together.

"Sure, why not? I bet your grandmother would love to see you."

"She'd probably enjoy seeing you more." I imagined Joseph in his swim trunks, his tan bare chest glistening in the hot sun, and I knew Grandma wouldn't be the only person enjoying his visit.

"We're almost there," he said turning off the freeway at the Georgetown exit. I racked my brain for what fancy restaurant he was taking me to. He reached behind the seat and pulled out a blindfold. "Here, put this on."

I looked at the satiny red material in his hand. "What's this for, Mr. Christian Grey?"

He chuckled. "Don't worry, there's no Red Room of Pain where we're going. Just put it on and savor the anticipation."

I did as he asked, my head spinning. Did he intend for me to be blindfolded for most of the evening? I bit my lip. I'd never done anything like this before. Was he the kind of guy who liked to spice things up on a regular basis? With Joseph, I wouldn't be opposed to a little kink.

"You can't see anything, can you?"

His deep voice sounded so erotic from behind the blindfold that I felt it everywhere. I finally understood why blindfolds were so popular among couples. "Not a thing."

I felt his hand take hold of mine, and I relished the warmth and strength of his grasp as he spoke to me. "I hope you don't mind, but I decided instead of going to dinner at a crowded restaurant, we're going to order take-out from the bed and breakfast. Does that sound good to you?"

The thought of being totally alone with Joseph sounded more than good. Blindfolded and alone with Joseph sounded even better. "I'm game for whatever you have in mind."

I heard Joseph clear his throat, the kind of sound that defined exactly what he was thinking. Not too much longer now and I'd know for sure.

As I sat in total darkness during the rest of the drive to the B&B, my other senses kicked in and I could smell him now more than ever. I couldn't wait to get there and bury my nose in his neck. I imagined slow dancing with him and breathing in the scent of his warm skin and cologne as we waited for dinner to be delivered.

I heard him downshift and felt the truck veer to the right. In a short distance, we turned again and I could tell we were climbing a small hill. He slowed the vehicle to a halt and killed the engine.

"Keep that blindfold on, you hear? I'm serious, Jamie. Don't peek or you'll ruin my surprise."

What kind of surprise? I couldn't imagine what he had planned and the last thing I wanted to do was ruin it. "I won't. Scouts honor."

"Good. Sit tight for a second." I heard his truck door open and shut, and felt the rocking of the vehicle as he slid to the ground. His boots sounded along the paved ground, growing more distant with each step he took. I listened closely. Where in heck could we be?

Again I heard his boots, this time coming back toward the truck. The shuffle of heavy fabric surrounded me in the cab and the truck rocked momentarily again. What was he doing now?

Finally, the driver's side door opened and I felt him slip back inside. I jumped as he slammed it shut, the smell of my handsome, mysterious Joseph tingling my senses.

"Okay, you can take off the blindfold now." I felt his hand on my leg. A jolt of warmth raced through me like an electric current. I almost didn't want to rid myself of the blindfold.

I reached up and pulled it off anyway. The cab of the

truck was pitch black. I realized he'd blanketed the vehicle with a canvas cover.

He clicked on an LED lantern and placed it on the floorboard. He sat facing me, a small rectangular gift box in his hand. "Let's play truth or dare. Here's the truth."

I took the box from him, my eyes glued to the pair of pink and purple bows topping it. "We're going to open our gifts in here? In the truck?" I thought about my gift and how I intended to give it to him in a more romantic setting.

"*You* are," he said complacently.

"But why in here? And what's with the cover?"

"Will you quit asking so many questions and just open your gift."

I bit my lip again, enjoying his little game. "Fine. I'll open it." I lifted the lid of the dainty present and inside lay a fortune cookie (should've expected that) and a skeleton key with a purple satin ribbon tied to it. A tiny memory from my childhood filtered in when I'd imagined inserting this very skeleton key into a lock below the crystal knob on my grandmother's bedroom door. At the tender age of four, I'd pretended I was a beautiful princess living in a grand Victorian mansion where Grandma and I would have tea and crumpets like the English aristocracy.

"Do you know what that is?" he asked.

I picked it up and admired the nostalgic Colonial design of the vintage pewter key. "This is a key to my grandmother's bedroom. Does she know you have this? And why are you giving it to me?"

"The truth is in the fortune cookie."

I looked at the key again. I had no idea what Joseph was up to. And whatever it was, what did this key have to do with it? I cracked open the cookie and unfolded the little slip of paper inside. I read the words to myself and I smiled like I'd been given a five carat diamond ring. It read:

I LOVE YOU A LATTE

Seeing his heart and soul spelled out on a cookie fortune almost meant more to me than hearing it from his lips. Almost.

I flipped it over and read the back. I froze. I read it again, then looked at him. "Why is my grandmother's address written on this fortune?"

"Because it's yours now."

I didn't think I heard him right. "I don't understand, Joseph."

He opened his truck door and squeezed out, jerking the car cover off the cab. Lit up before me was my grandmother's house. I recognized it instantly, but it wasn't the same. The color of the siding was no longer pale blue, but a light mocha. The tin roof was a deep chocolate brown, swirling like Hershey's syrup around the single dormer window above the porch. Crisp white bargeboard trimmed the gable roofs and fancy, white-washed spindles and railings sectioned off a charming sitting area filled with white wicker furniture with brown and pink paisley cushions. Above that, hung a huge sign that read *I LOVE YOU A LATTE Bed & Breakfast and Coffee Shop*.

I felt a painfully-sweet tightness in my chest as I stared through his windshield at the magnificent view before me. My eyes burned with tears. I brought my hand up to my mouth to keep my chin from shaking.

Joseph opened my door and bowed like a gentleman, holding out his hand for me. "M'lady."

I laid my hand in his. I bit my lip to control its trembling. I could hardly speak, much less move. "Is this…?"

"It's all yours, Sutherland. I bought it from your grandmother before she left for Florida."

I gawked at him, unable to process this staggering revelation.

He reached in, lifted me from the truck seat, and carried me toward the house. I couldn't stop staring at it as I held on to him.

"You bought my grandmother's house?"

"And renovated it to be a Bed & Breakfast slash coffee shop. What do you think?"

Tears ran down my cheeks and my chin quivered. I was so overwhelmed with emotion I could barely think at all. Joseph Scarbrough had bought my grandmother's house for me and turned it into the most beautiful Victorian Bed & Breakfast I'd ever seen. But how? How did he do all this without me knowing? "When did you…"

He carried me up the porch steps and sat me on one of the chairs, taking a seat beside me. The sharp smell of paint and brand new patio cushions wafted around me.

He took my hand. "Do you remember when I took two weeks of vacation to help your grandmother fix a few things?"

"Yes…"

"And lately, when I said I was helping my sister with the horses? Well, I wasn't. I was here, renovating, painting, knocking down walls and opening up rooms. Sanding hardwood floors and building cabinets. I didn't think I was going to get it finished for Valentine's Day, but I did." He paused and inched his bottom off the edge of the seat, his face serious. "I wanted to surprise you, Jamie, especially after it broke your heart that she was selling. And, of course, once I told your grandmother what my intentions were, she practically moved heaven and earth to get the paperwork going. I hope you can forgive me for lying to you."

A laugh escaped me despite the tears pouring from my eyes. "Forgive you? Forgiving you is easy, Joseph. It's making sure you understand my deepest appreciation that's going to be impossible. I have no words to tell you how grateful I am that you did this for me. That you thought enough of me to spend all your hard-earned—"

I stopped midsentence, suddenly realizing why he passed up the opportunity to buy his farm back. All his funds had gone to purchasing and renovating my grandmother's house. "But what about your farm, Joseph? You—"

"That farm will have to wait. This was more important. You..." he paused a moment, "...are more important." He reached up and caressed my wet cheek with his thumb. "Making you smile...that's what means the world to me, Jamie. Besides, my uncle is buying the farm tomorrow, and he said if I ever decided I was ready, I could buy it back from him. So all's not lost."

I wasn't sure what was more profound. The fact that Joseph bought my grandmother's house for me as a surprise or that I was about to buy his farm for him. "Joseph, I need to tell you something."

He stood and pulled me to my feet with him. "It'll have to wait. Right now, I want to show you the inside. Come on."

His childlike eagerness was adorable. He unlocked the front door and held it open for me. "Welcome to *I LOVE YOU A LATTE Bed & Breakfast and Coffee Shop.*"

I stepped inside, my gaze taking in everything brand new that mingled with the old and familiar. The walls looked revitalized and clean with a fresh coat of paint, while my grandmother's accent pictures still remained where they had always hung. I was glad to see he kept the old woodwork, but what was once dark and dreary, now trimmed each room with bright white modern appeal. Grandma's furniture and antique collections sat proudly in the renovated spaces, maintaining their lovely vintage charm on the refinished hardwood floor.

I stood in awe of Joseph's hard work and craftsmanship. "I can't believe what you've done to this place."

"I tried my best to liven up the house without removing the things that gave it its warmth and nostalgia." He turned me around to face the stairs and helped me out of my coat, hanging it on Grandma's coat rack beside the door. "For instance, your grandmother's phone table. I kept it and the stained-glass lamp, she said you loved so much, against the stair wall. It's behind the new counter I built where your customers will check in and order their coffee, but at least, it's there for you to use at your discretion."

I remembered as a child thinking what an elegant little nook my grandmother had set up against the wall beneath the stairs. I thought I was hot stuff the first time I sat in that chair as a child and made a phone call to my parents while they were on vacation. With everyone converting to cordless phones, I thought it was the neatest thing to be forced to sit in one place and have a conversation. Who knew I'd be using this phone table as an adult? I grabbed his hand and gave it a squeeze, words failing me.

"And upstairs," he said pulling me along, "I left your childhood room as is, save for a new paint job." I peeked in and smiled. My old room looked much larger with the lighter color of paint brightening the walls.

"And the other room up here," he said, leading me down the short hall. "I had to make a few minor adjustments to accommodate the addition of another room. I built a new wall here, and moved the original door down. Now there are two doors and two separate rooms, but…" he added, stepping in and opening yet another door. "The rooms can be contiguous, if the customers prefer adjoining rooms. Good?"

I couldn't stop smiling. "It's fabulous, Joseph."

"I still have a little more to do in the kitchen," he said, leading me back downstairs. "Everything's been rewired to code for the coffee shop, but I figured I'd let you pick out the machines you wanted since you're more educated in that field." Pointing to various things, he continued. "I left your grandmother's table and hutch, and since she had so many assorted coffee cups and saucers, I thought perhaps you might actually use them instead of those Styrofoam cups you have now. Unless of course the customers want their coffee to go, then you might want to have both. Your call. Sound good so far?"

I hardly had time to respond before he led me down the back hall to the bathroom. "Again, here, I repainted, fixed the leaky toilet, and tore out the floor. The old one had some water damage, so I laid a new subfloor and tiled it. I wasn't sure on the color though."

His choice of tile and the matching grout looked perfect. *Everything* was perfect, as far as I was concerned. I couldn't believe the amount of work Joseph had done in such a short amount of time. "Joseph, you did an amazing —"

"Wait, you haven't seen the best part yet. The grand finale!" He led me to my grandmother's bedroom door and gestured toward the crystal knob. "I believe you'll need that key."

I almost forgot I still had it. I stepped toward the door and inserted the skeleton key, the blunt edges of the beautiful crystal knob pressing into my palm. I opened the door and sucked in a huge breath at the beautiful transformation of the room.

An enormous, intricately carved, Victorian sleigh bed with a rich chestnut finish sat in the center of the room. A matching armoire and chest of drawers stood on either side of the bed and one of my grandmother's handmade quilts draped over the king-sized mattress. Coordinating pillows of black velvet and white satin perched at the headboard, while two stained-glass lamps embellished a pair of bedside tables. Victorian-style drapes with tiebacks and tassels hung on the windows. It was the most remarkable replication of French-inspired elegance.

"What do you think?"

I could hear the uncertainty in his voice, but I couldn't speak. Nothing I could possibly say would ever express my true feelings for the hard work and careful consideration Joseph had put into this project. I turned and threw my arms around his neck and sobbed. "Oh, Joseph."

"Hey, there" I heard him say, his hand cupping the back of my head as I wept. "Are you okay? Did I do something wrong?"

"My goodness, no," I cried. "You did everything right. You are the most amazing man I have ever met." Tears poured from my eyes. The front of his shirt was soaked. "You can't begin to understand my happiness right now. No one has ever done anything like this for me. Ever. Oh my goodness, I have to sit down."

Joseph held me tight and walked me to the edge of bed. I sank into the mattress, closing my eyes. He knelt in front of me and held my hands in his own.

"The hard part's over, Jamie. We just have to get people to come here and we're set."

My gaze flew to his. How could I run two coffee shops? How could I choose between the business I started on my own and the one that Joseph generously built with his own sweat, blood, and money? I couldn't fathom closing down the one in Cincinnati. "How are we going to do this? Please don't think I'm being selfish, but I don't want to close the coffee shop I already own."

"You won't have to. I've already taken care of it. You know that friend I was setting Melissa up with? Well, that was my way of getting her cell number, so I could run it by her. And she's agreed to manage the Cinci shop, so you can live here."

"What about you?" I clutched his hands and panicked at the thought of living two hours away from where Joseph lived and worked. "I can't live here without you."

"We'll make it work. Don't worry, I'll be here every weekend."

Weekends weren't enough. I needed to be with him every day. Then it occurred to me. Of course, he would be close by. I reached into my back pocket and pulled out the envelope. His name decorated the front in bold calligraphy.

"What's this?" he asked.

"It's my Valentine's gift to you. Think of it as a way to keep you from commuting from Cinci to Lexington."

He narrowed his eyes as he pulled out the check. I watched his face furrow for a second and then draw backward. His brows lifted in surprise and disbelief. "Am I looking at this right?"

I smiled. "Seems you're not the only with a plan, Joseph. Your uncle's not buying the farm tomorrow. I am. You just have to be there to sign your name on the deed."

"Jamie, I can't afford two mortgages on my salary. I just took out a loan to buy your grandma's house. The bank won't give me any more money."

"You won't need anymore. I'm buying it."

"Does Miranda know about this?"

I knew it was hard for him to think she'd agree to sell to someone outside the family. "Of course, she did. How else could I do this? My name won't be on the deed, because I want it to be yours, free and clear. I'm just the bank."

"Jamie, this is too much. You can't—"

"I can and I already have. Trust me, it's not going to break me. I'm making money hand over fist with the coffee shop in Cinci. And this bed and breakfast will surely pull in more revenue. The first year is always the hardest," I admitted. "But, I bet I could draw people in by hiring…oh, I don't know…a hot superintendent slash grounds keeper slash bellman who lives right down the road from here."

He laughed at my idea, but I think I had him sold— especially the part about living right down the road. He ran his hand through his hair as he stared at the numbers on the check.

"Joseph?" He looked at me and I could see the emotion swirling in his Montana blue-sky eyes. I pulled him closer to me, my knees on either side of his ribs. He pulled me closer to him, as I wound my hands around his neck, playing with the hair at his nape. "Say you'll sign it."

He started to shake his head, seemingly undecided, but I cupped his face and redirected his attention. "Look at me, Joseph. I want this for you. I want to give you back the land you should've never parted with. If I didn't need your signature on the deed, I would've already bought it for you and we wouldn't be having this discussion. But given real estate law, I can't purchase it without your John Hancock."

"Are you asking me to quit my job in Cinci and move here with you?"

"Yes," I said matter-of-factly. "Quit your job, move here, and work for me."

"Is it really that simple?" he asked.

"It's only difficult if we let it be." And I truly believed that. Finding the man of my dreams had been the most daunting task of my life. But building a life with that man, knowing he loved me enough to forsake his own dreams, would be a piece of cake. As far as I could see, there was nothing ahead of us but blue skies.

"Truth or dare, Jamie?" His question came out of nowhere.

"What?"

"Answer me. Truth or dare. And then I'll agree to sign."

I looked at him sideways, unable to predict where he was going with this. We'd already played 'truth' by coming clean on the selfless gifts we'd schemed behind each other's backs. Maybe he wanted something a bit more intimate than just confessing truths. Looking at the handsome man kneeling before me, I was ready for something that required a bit more action. "Okay, let's go dare this time."

His mouth kicked up in a devious smile as he yanked his shirt from his body and tossed it aside. My mouth went dry gazing at his beautiful muscled chest and shoulders.

"I dare you..." He placed his hands on my upper arms and urged me backward until I was totally reclined on the bed. He climbed over my body until we were eye to eye. "I dare you, Jamett Penelope Sutherland..."

My eyes widened as I heard my hideous birth name. I was going to kick Melissa's ass for that slip. I just knew it was her who told Joseph my real name.

His hot mouth dove to mine. Every thought scattered as he smothered them all with his kiss. I thought of nothing but his warm, velvety tongue sliding along mine and the solid, muscled body pressing me into the pillow top mattress.

His hand gripped my shirt and pulled it over my head. Breathlessly, he whispered, "I dare you to..." His eyes opened in surprise as he took notice of the lacy red bra I wore. He groaned and dove back to kissing me. His mouth trailed to my neck, and I was helpless to fend him off, even if I had wanted to. The feel of his warm lips, wet tongue, and rough prickly beard had me begging for more.

With the merest of brain function left, I was dying to know what he wanted of me. "You dare me to what, Joseph?"

I moved beneath him, feeling his hot skin against mine. He pulled away and his eyes darkened. A great, tumultuous storm raged in them. "Marry me, Sutherland."

Silence slammed into the room. Only the ticking of Grandma's grandfather clock in the hallway disturbed the hush of this moment for I swear my heart stopped. Was I dreaming? Was this man—the man who had me at "Welcome to the building, Jamie;" the man who gave his whole heart to me; the man who'd already made my wildest dreams come true—asking me to marry him?

"Did you hear me?"

"Yes."

"Yes, as in yes, you heard me? Or yes, you'll marry me?"

I stared into his beautiful eyes and felt my heart pitter patter against my ribs. I smiled as he lay upon me, his breath held, his body tense. I'd never seen Joseph Alexander Scarbrough so nervous.

"Yes, I'll marry you," I whispered, caressing his gorgeous face.

I felt his body relax and he sighed, his lips pressing against mine. His arms snaked around me and pulled me against his chest. I felt his mouth at my ear, his heated breath bathing my skin.

"I love you, Joseph," I whispered, my body quivering beneath his touch.

A mischievous chuckle shook his body. "I dare you to prove it."

His hand blazed a path down my side and caught the waistband of my jeans. He tugged on the zipper and my breath caught. I heard his boots hit the floor in the same moment his knuckles grazed my tummy. I shuddered at his intimate touch. I knew it was going to be one seriously long, wholly satisfying, blazing hot night with a man who knew exactly what he was doing.

There was only one thing Joseph needed to learn. And that was never to call me by my real name.

No worries though. I had two icing-heaped cupcakes still sitting in a box to help me get that point across.

THE END

Author's Note

The names of my fun-loving protagonists, Jamett and Joseph, came from the reminiscence of my imaginary friends when I was a little girl. While I no longer indulge in invisible camaraderie, their names have stayed with me into adulthood.

With this in mind, I wanted to take my childhood friends and recreate them into something more profound than a distant memory of my tender youth. I wanted to build a believable world where two unlikely people grew to be steadfast friends and eventually fell in love despite the odds.

I thank you for reading the *Jamett and Joseph* series, and I hope that you'll take a moment to leave an honest review.

I also want to let you know that I'm in the process of writing more books in this series. The best way to find out when they'll be releasing is to join my newsletter list. My subscribers are ALWAYS the first to know.

Again thank you for choosing to read my books. I cannot say it enough.

Best wishes,
Renee

If you enjoyed this book by Renee Vincent, please consider leaving an honest review at your favorite vendor. Reviews not only give credibility to an author's work, they also help other readers find quality books worth reading.

About Renee Vincent

RENEE VINCENT is a *USA Today* bestselling author of romance and women's fiction. Her books have earned numerous accolades, including a #1 Bestseller for Viking Romance.

She lives on a secluded hundred-acre horse farm in the rolling hills of Kentucky with her husband, two beautiful daughters, a pair of nocturnal dogs, and a cat who thinks he's the master of the house.

www.ReneeVincent.com

Books By Series

Vikings of Honor Series
Sunset Fire, Book 1
Emerald Glory, Book 2
Souls Reborn, Book 3
Tempered Steel, Book 4

Mavericks of Meeteetse Series
Longing for Langston, Brody & Liv, Book 1
Made for McKinley, Jonas & Ava, Book 2
Falling For Forester, Cole & Crys, Book 3
Wild for Wallace, Sawyer & Charlotte, Book 4

Jamett & Joseph Series
The Start of Something Good, Book 1
The Road to Something Better, Book 2
The Gift of Something Grand, Book 3

Stand Alone Novel
Silent Partner

Mailing List

Sign up for Renee Vincent's author newsletter and reap the benefits of being one of her loyal subscribers! One lucky winner is drawn each month. What's more, you get a FREE BOOK just for joining.

Go to ReneeVincent.com, then click on "Newsletter" to sign up and start reading!

ReneeVincent.com